Acclaim for
SMOKE RI

"A searing, lyrical story about the racial tension that lies just millimeters beneath the surface of Canadian society. . . . Foss's strength lies in the beauty of her writing, her ability to capture the nuances of both band council and small-town politics, and her vivid characters. . . . A glorious read."   – *Toronto Star*

"A stunning novel, epic in scope and tragic in vision. With a voice as clear as it is relentless, Krista Foss shows how a blockade raised by First Nations women against a development on Mohawk land can be a metaphor for the barriers that separate us all."
     – Wayne Grady, author of *Emancipation Day*

"*Smoke River* packs some stunningly hard punches – here is racial tension rendered with penetrating insight, raw feeling, turbulent violence and profound compassion. . . . A morally complex, magnificently vivid novel full of characters who live and breathe. This is a dazzling debut."
     – Lisa Moore, author of *Caught*

"By allowing her vivid ensemble of characters to grab hold of the wheel, Foss manages to steer the novel away from an object lesson in Native–white relations to focus on the personal quandaries that arise from the characters' complex, overlapping allegiances. . . . She probes their doubts and uncertainties in subtle, interesting ways."
     – *Globe and Mail*

"The poignant tale of two families experiencing a crisis and the unravelling of a long-forgotten history and slew of secrets. . . . Foss's flowing prose and attention to detail will quickly cement her voice as one of great importance in Canadian literature."
     – S *Style & Fashion Magazine*

SMOKE RIVER

KRISTA FOSS

EMBLEM

McClelland & Stewart

Emblem is an imprint of McClelland & Stewart, a division of Random
House of Canada Limited, a Penguin Random House Company

Emblem and colophon are registered trademarks of McClelland & Stewart,
a division of Random House of Canada Limited,
a Penguin Random House Company

Library and Archives Canada Cataloguing in Publication
is available upon request

ISBN: 978- 0-7710-3614-9
ebook ISBN: 978-0-7710-3613-2

Typeset in Dante by M&S, Toronto
Cover photograph: © Crystal Marks
(smoke): © Nikolay Dimitrov / Dreamstime.com
Printed and bound in the United States of America

McClelland & Stewart,
a division of Random House of Canada Limited,
a Penguin Random House Company
www.penguinrandomhouse.ca

1 2 3 4 5   19 18 17 16 15

For my sister, Katrine

PROLOGUE

Shayna has always liked May, its warm afternoons and cool evenings promising all sorts of rebirth. She stands at the edge of a freshly planted tobacco field. Some new shoots list precariously into the space between the rows, risking root shock. She kicks off her flip-flops, as she did when she was a girl who abandoned footwear every year from mid-May until the end of August. By then she could sprint across gravel without a grimace, the soles of her feet indifferent to thistle, tough as jerky. Now the bottoms of her feet complain upon meeting the cat-tongue soil, sandy and wet. *Stop being so middle-aged*, she wills herself. Her big toe cramps.

She's in no hurry. The sky is dark and clear. Under a moon of dull zinc, the seedlings cast small shadows, easy to miss. Shayna scans for fallen plants and, spotting one, kneels down, pushes soil against its base, presses until the shoot straightens and aligns with the rest. Just as generation after generation of jack-planters – men with bourbon or rum in their accents – did before her. And before them all, Attawandaron women, who buried the cold slime of fish scraps in the earth to fertilize the new shoots.

Her fingers drum along the plastic buttons of the shirt she wears – his shirt – and she slips the buttons open, one, two, three, until just one cinches the fabric closed at the base of her sternum. If the plants are just in, he'll have been up since five a.m., his belly mean as a barn cat by the time the hired college students left for the day, his muscles sore and satisfied, his skin dry and radiating, the sun in his core. Shayna pictures him stopping at the door before he goes inside to wait for her. He'll have a smoke, admire how the tobacco shoots warm the furrows with a greenish glow. He'll want the cooler nights and warm days to toughen the roots, make them deeper and more resilient. She imagines worries gathering around him like whispers, repeating rumours of all the things waiting to rob him of the field's bright possibility in the ten weeks ahead – late frost, nematodes, cutworms, wireworms, budworms, hail, drought, mould. A withholding sun. And finally price. Only the elders consider tobacco a sacrament; everyone else treats it as another word for money.

The porch light is on. Barefoot, she is silent on the back step. Shayna places her forehead against the screen door and hesitates, wondering what the hell she is doing. Veins like hungry taproots spreading from her fingers, her jaw, deep into the country of her body. She is neither young nor old. Her grandmothers' spirits exhale lake breath across the tobacco plants behind her, stooping them with dew, raising a shiver along Shayna's back. She turns the handle, steps into the unlit kitchen. Now that she has crossed his threshold a first time, she will do it again. He is there, still and shirtless, a metre away. He steps forward and stops. She picks up a whiff of peaty smoke from him, the copper sharpness of his tumbler of Scotch. He has been waiting for her with a certainty he doesn't have about his crop; he must have known she'd come to him eventually.

It was his neck – not the fair hair, not the patrician blue of his eyes – that gave her pause the first time they met. Despite the fineness of his European features, his precise, over-educated talk, that work-leathered neck betrayed something essential; he was built from sun, sky, clay. She'd sensed a kindred restlessness too, the same tangled aches inside him.

Shayna, he says, because she hasn't given him permission to shorten it. He doesn't reach for her. Instead, he stands so near she feels his pulse, smells the long, hard workday on him before he takes a draw of steadying breath, dips his thumb into the tumbler of Scotch, brings it to her bottom lip and rubs softly. She leans into his steadiness, his smell. For that moment, she stops wanting to be some other, better woman.

CHAPTER 1

Coulson studies Shayna's sleeping face and asks himself when it will all go to hell. Last week, two tanagers landed on the branch by his bedroom window. He'd watched the male place food down the open beak of its mate, their necks a tango of scarlet and tawny green feathers, their cries at once delighted and anguished. You can't predict a moment like that. And now this woman – the same kind of waiting surprise.

In another life he drank espresso in the morning and Cabernet at night, picked up smooth shirts from the dry cleaner, pressed his slippers into antique Persian rugs, made love to a woman who was as cool and perfumed as new linen. He'd had a decade of her geography: beautiful but unsurprising. Marie had the prettiest smile, the smallest hands, of any woman he's known.

Shayna's hands are strong. Even the whitish spittle in the creases of her pink-brown lips – this is something he can love.

How different she is from Marie, who delivered her stings under cover of honey, her voice trembling with sweetness, leaving him unsure exactly when or why he'd been hurt.

He has the urge to pull the sheet from Shayna, to see her nakedness pimple in the morning air's tang, the pale light. But there is coffee to make. Eggs and bacon. He wants to baby her – hand-feed her like an abandoned pup, rub the knots from her muscles, brush her hair. He edges quietly out of bed and leans over Shayna for a half-second to confirm that her eyes are still closed, pulls on his jeans, and quits the house barefoot to have a smoke. The sandy soil squishes between his toes. He walks among the tobacco, sturdy after a month of good sun, stretches his arms towards the expanding light, and inhales all the hopeful-ness of the Interlake morning.

I can't sleep here with that smell, Marie said the weekend they arrived to get the farmhouse ready to sell. Both of his parents had wanted to die on the farm, and they got their wish: a year after a stroke felled his father, his mother's heart failed as she was peeling freshly picked turnips. Marie had crunched up her nose at the kitchen's archaeology of odours – decades of frying bacon, sausage, and minute steak, of scrubbing dirt-stained bodies with carbolic soap – as she wiped the surfaces with pine-scented cleaner. He'd kicked off his three-hundred-dollar shoes, walked among the abandoned tobacco fields, tangled with wild carrot and amaranth, and reacquainted his naked soles with the salve of dirt. Then he stripped to the waist and weeded and turned the soil of the large kitchen garden, occasionally catch-ing a glimpse of Marie through the window, her face salted with distaste, her straightened hair dishevelling in the humidity of scrubbing and bleaching.

Oh, I can still smell it, she'd said again, lying on her back in his parents' bed that night, her eyes widened to the moonlit ceiling. Coulson was crisped by sun. He'd had too much to drink at dinner, had ignored Marie's hurt looks and fallen into the cool, worn sheets with a kind of satisfaction, a pleasure he'd forgotten. Beside him, she smelled as exact as air freshener. He knew then that he wasn't going to leave these walls of dolomite and limestone. And she was.

Shayna may give him an hour of her waking life or just fifteen minutes. Back in the kitchen, he rifles the pockets of her jeans, abandoned on the floor and damp with morning, finds a cellphone, which he leaves on the enamel table, and shoves her pants into the oven, turning the dial to two hundred degrees. The coffee is percolating, eggs cracked, bacon sliding in the pan. Shayna's cellphone bleats. Those infernal phones. Will it bring her to the bottom of the stairs, wearing his robe and a face that's already halfway out the door? *Potatoes would be trying too hard*, he decides. The cellphone starts up again, jittery as a marsh bird, then goes silent after three rings. Coulson wonders if he should wake and alert her to the insistent caller. Instead he covers the cooked bacon, puts it in the oven to stay warm by the jeans. The eggs sizzle in the frying pan. He carafes the freshly made coffee. *Toast*, he thinks. The cellphone rings anew. He recognizes the persistence of a telemarketer who hasn't checked the time zone, ignores it out of spite. He pours two glasses of orange juice, fishes out a tray from the back of the pantry, wipes it with a damp cloth, then lays out Shayna's breakfast. As he pulls her jeans from the oven, the phone starts up a fourth time. That's the one. He feels her hands slide across his lower back like a sweep of cards that ends his luck.

She's already moving across the room, a small, naked woman the colour of milky tea, leaning against his kitchen table, cupping the phone to her ear. With her face wan, the bed-sheet creases on her cheeks, she is even more desirable.

"Now? What? Okay. Okay."

She clicks the phone shut and turns to him, her eyes falling on the warm folded jeans in his arms.

"I'll need a fresh shirt," she says.

"What's going on?"

"Oh, I'm about to reclaim some stolen property."

He is silent.

"I should have mentioned it earlier," she says.

"Can you eat? I made eggs." He hates the plaintive tone in his voice.

She moves forward, bends to lay her cheek against his bare belly, and lightly kisses his rib cage.

"I need to go."

"I'll drive you."

She looks up at him, her face tender and amused. "You won't have to. Just going across the road. I'll cut through your field."

She tugs the jeans from his grip and presses her nose into them. "Mmm. Bacon."

In the crack of morning light peeking through the bedroom's custom-made blind, Ella Bain notices a small figure quit the Stercyx farmhouse. Who but a lover leaves at such an hour? She sits on the edge of the bed and tries to focus, but there is no more detail to squeeze from the bright morning. It is none of her business. Plenty of lovers must have come and gone in all the years Stercyx has lived alone at the farmhouse, but this is the first she's witnessed. She wishes she could see what kind of woman he would take to his bed. Certainly there was plenty of speculation around Doreville when he first moved back. She listens to her husband's contented breathing behind her, leans closer to the windowpane, just for a second. Then she pulls herself away. If she rushed into her running gear, took her normal route in reverse, she might get a look at the mystery woman. But that was a lot of effort. What would it be like to sleep in? Better still, what if she slipped her hands under the drawstring of Mitch's pyjamas and started the day sticky with saliva and semen, her stale mouth ransacked by his stale tongue. She imagines Coulson's salt still on the skin, the lips of the woman leaving his farmhouse. Would a small change in routine redraw her life? She turns to look at her husband, curled into a cetaceous hump on the other side of the bed, and wonders if she has a duty to risk it. And then why it feels like a risk. Or a duty.

Just recently, after a second glass of wine, Marguerite from her book club confessed she makes love with her husband every morning. *Doesn't it become routine?* Ella asked. Marguerite – who pronounces her name with a tarty French accent, though she can't speak a word of the language – curled up in her chair and smiled like some sort of feral cat. *No, darling. I don't think I could start the day without it now.*

If only she could see his face within the swaddling of bed-sheets, she might press her cheek against his neck, probe his ear with her tongue, discover if they still have the imagination for unscheduled pleasure. But Mitch shifts jerkily, nests more bedding around him, and settles into a phlegmatic, gape-mouthed morning snore. Ella turns again to the blinds; the sunlight pokes around their edges, sulphur-bright, slightly hectoring. The figure that left Stercyx's door has disappeared. Ella heads to the washroom.

Twenty-five minutes after her feet hit the pavement, she leaves behind the figure eights of houses with their backyard gazebos and pergolas, their saltwater swimming pools and engineered waterfalls, routes around downtown Doreville, and arrives back on Highway 3, near where it cleaves the Stercyx farm from the strafed two hundred acres of the development. Her project. The western and southern edges have been calved from the reserve by a winding creek that empties into the river; the northern boundary is marked by a county road leading into the reserve.

Mitch doesn't want her haunting the new development. But she is unsettled by the woman leaving Stercyx's farmhouse, by Mitch's snoring, the way he dodges her questions about the development like a welterweight. And the new billboard is up. She's curious to see it.

The sun turns the asphalt into crushed crystals, and Ella, who dreads more fine lines pleating her eyes, wishes she'd worn sunglasses. She turns away from the brightness and notices Stercyx's handiwork – the neatly tilled furrows, the tender green of immature tobacco plants – keeping pace with her on her right. Tobacco. Mitch wanted it in the name of the new development, but Ella balked. Her immigrant parents had picked, stitched, and graded the crop. During its harvest, her father's skin was freckled with the leaves' tar and her mother's ankles swelled. Tobacco juice stained their fingertips yellow-brown despite the rigours of nightly scrubbing. At night they dragged their humiliation and grit across their rented bungalow's threshold. And Ella left out the back door.

Tobacco Valley Estates, Mitch said. *It's the history of the place.* She shook her head, crossed her arms. *They're using it in all the new men's colognes.* He wasn't going to let it drop. *And besides, smoking's cool again. It's got a whole retro masculine appeal.* That was going too far. *I'll take every cent of my money out of the development,* she told him. His cheeks had gone flaccid. *Geez, Ella, lighten up. You can't go making ultimatums every time you don't get your way.*

Two weeks later, the development was christened Jarvis Ridge Country Club Estates. She'd found history they could both live with: the surname of an early colonial administrator; a nod to the glacial silt and sand that had forged the interlake delta, made it decent enough for agriculture, ideal for a small golf course and a man-made lake. *You* can *change the history of a place,* Ella thinks, *with the right packaging.*

The billboard is within view, but Ella doesn't raise her eyes until she is close enough to take it all in. She slows her pace, looks up, and the images come into focus. *Let them do their job,* Mitch had insisted. But Ella had ideas. And now she wishes she'd been more forceful. The gigantic sign depicts a slim, athletic, vaguely thirty-something couple. *Too big,* Ella thinks. The woman a bland, over-plucked yoga mummy. The man with a motivational speaker's klieg-light smile, pomaded hair. Each holds a flute of sparkling wine. *We're not selling houses,* Mitch insisted. *We're selling people a vision of themselves.* But as she comes to a stop underneath it, Ella wonders whether people don't have more originality and better taste. The billboard couple hover over a monoculture of dirt welted with tire tracks. An 80% PRE-SOLD! banner hangs over a corner of the sign. Mitch has assured her that, while not quite true in the purest sense, it meets industry standards.

Realizing anew how much of her carefully hoarded, smartly invested money buoys the mortgage on the land makes her breath suddenly shallow. She's supplied the regular cash flow by doing the thankless missionary work of the Doreville and District Tobacco Diversification Office for the past two decades. She saved 10 per cent of her yearly earnings even as successive governments tired of the office's mandate, clawed back funding, first for educational conferences, then publications, then secretaries, and finally leases, leaving Ella as a one-woman operation with an Execushare cubicle above the strip mall's EB Games emporium. And when one day Mitch pointed to a new listing for the property across from Stercyx's farm, raised his eyebrows, and said, *Whaddya think?* she'd surprised herself as much as him when she said yes. Yes for a project that would make Doreville an estimable, desirable place to live. Yes to making money faster than her more conservative investments could. Yes to being part of something constructive, forward-looking, tangible. *Now, take a deep breath. Trust that I'll take care of this,* Mitch had said. *Because*

I'm the one who knows real estate. In the first several months she'd said yes to that too, she really had. But now her money has become an acreage of mud, a smarmy billboard, a bunch of unanswered questions cooling their shared bed.

Ella adjusts her eyes to the glare coming off the paved highway, unhitches the water bottle from her belt, and takes a long draw. And there it is, another thing that's amiss. A dump truck has turned into the Jarvis Ridge development's entrance but has not advanced beyond the first few metres of dirt road. The driver and his passenger have clambered out. Ella hears alarmed voices. She moves closer, but there is the problem of how close she should get, how involved. Already she can hear Mitch's reproach, as if she were breaking a trust.

Two women are standing with their arms linked and their legs apart, blocking the development's entrance. Ella's mouth dries. She leans forward, brings her head to her knees, calms her laboured breath. Sweat slides from her forehead and chin.

And what comes into her head, as it hangs in the morning heat, is not a strategy for this unexpected situation but a vision of a room in her home, corridor-shaped and banked with windows, set off from the rest of the house like a design hiccup and used for overflow during all those years she and Mitch spent making the rest of their home a showpiece. It had never occurred to Ella that she had plans for the room, that she'd integrated it into some imagined future self who'd make things, add beauty to the world. Not until Mitch bought an awkward antique railway partners desk, plopped it in the middle of the space, and winked when he found her standing in the doorway with her arms crossed. *Squatter's rights*, he said. *I need a new office.* Ella has told herself that Mitch's use of the back room is temporary, until the development gets into full swing and he rents something in town, as she does. Except "full swing" is taking a while.

At this very moment Mitch will be slipping on his khakis, dusting his clubs, rehearsing his pitch to the hesitant city couple he is to meet at a sister development, the Northbrook Golf and Lifestyle Community, to sell them on their future happiness in Jarvis Ridge. He needs the model home finished by its planned completion date. He needs the lots cleared and staked. They both need this success.

"Ladies, I'm going to give you one more minute to get the fuck out of our way," says the truck driver, a ruddy young man in a T-shirt. "Then I'm getting back into my truck and I'm driving through."

"This is disputed land. You won't be getting through today. Or tomorrow. Not unless the dispute is settled."

Ella recognizes that the older woman who answers him is Helen Fallingbrook. For the past three years Ella has bought a ticket for the annual powwow from Helen. True, she never intended to go. But surely this was evidence of her overall friendliness towards the natives, some diplomatic immunity she can leverage.

The other man, bowlegged and beer-bellied, pulls off his cap and throws it to the dirt at their feet, raising a rainbow of dust. "You have to be fucking kidding! What is with you people? Didn't win enough at bingo?"

Disputed, Ella thinks. *Disputed*. Surely not. Mitch assured her that every clause, every rider, every possible contingency or claim has been scrutinized, plugged. *Airtight*, he said.

His cap abandoned in the dirt, his face red, the older man climbs back into the dump truck, this time on the driver's side, and pumps the gas so that it whinnies like an upset mare. His younger co-worker scrambles into the passenger's seat. The truck edges towards the women. They pull their joined arms taut and thrust their faces forward. The woman who holds Helen's hand looks around Ella's age. She is radiant in the loose man's shirt she wears, the weathered blue jeans, her beauty free and unmannered. For a second, something hard and sore suspends itself in Ella's chest. *It's her*, she thinks. *That's Stercyx's woman.* The idea feels like a vice, makes it impossible to think. This other woman laughs once, brief and throaty. *No, surely not*, Ella decides, and she's surprised to feel so relieved. Stercyx loves his land with a kind of chivalric fidelity; he would not keep company with someone so blatantly disrespectful of property rights. *And this is baldly unjust*, Ella thinks.

She's one of the tolerant ones. She smiles at Bobby Horse even when he is staggering drunk in the middle of town. If her neighbours express discomfort with the natives, Ella reminds them how they all buy their cheap smokes up on Highway 3. She forces herself to read the tidbits of history tucked into news coverage: treaty rights that date back to the 1780s, stalling by government lawyers. Migod, she even turns her dial to the aboriginal station now and again. She loves Susie Stonechild! – she can sing a few bars of her new single!

The dump truck inches forward. Helen and the younger woman are both silent now, but Ella's pulse yammers. Something unsavoury is about to take place, the kind of incident that could taint the project, make it seem unsteady or leaky. Suddenly she is very much interfering, in a way that Mitch wouldn't sanction, in a way that puts her whole body between a moving truck and two hand-holding native women.

"Stop! Stop!"

Ella's right hand slaps the hood of the truck and she looks through the windshield to catch the driver's eyes. She sees what a surprise she is – the trim redhead in jogging gear suddenly leaping in front of his custom grillwork. When he turns off the engine, she turns around to face the two women.

"Helen, we know each other. This is vandalism. It's illegal. And I want it to stop."

She regrets using the word *vandalism*. She tries to calm herself, keep her manner open and receptive. Helen Fallingbrook is a small woman, corded with hard work and decency.

"What's legal and illegal is a bit tricky, eh, Mrs. Bain," she says.

"Helen! This is private property. It belongs to my husband and me. We're *good* people who have a lot of money invested in it!" Worms of panic begin twitching under her eyelids.

"It belongs to us," says the other woman.

Ella looks towards the unfamiliar voice. "Do I know you?"

Ella holds out her hand, but it hangs unmet in the air. The woman looks Ella up and down, makes her wish she'd worn older gear. Her Lycra tank, the coral running shorts are so new, so obnoxiously bright and pricy.

She turns back to the older woman. "Helen?"

"I think you should go, Mrs. Bain. I think you are out of your depth."

Ella feels the flush on her face. What to do, what to do?

She'd tried not to be rankled when the back room became crowded with a scanner, a printer, some lumbering bookshelves, and the smell of stale cigars. Then it was painted, a horrible shade of brown. Just like that – Mitch Brown – without a moment of consultation. *Havana Gold,* he called it. And before she could let out a squeak of protest, he raised his hands and said, Terra nullius, *Ella. This room has been empty for years.* Still it isn't until right now, her sweat puddling in the small of her back and the humiliation of being asked to leave yet another place soaked with her money, that she feels the measure of what has been stolen from her, and how hard it will be to reclaim.

She wipes her eyes on her forearm and focuses. *Get angry,* she tells herself. *Don't be so clouded by liberal pieties that you won't name it, won't do something about it.*

She wheels around to the dump-truck driver, whose face, pink with frustrated violence, hangs out the open window.

"Do you have a cellphone?"

He nods.

"Call the police. Get them over here. *Now.*"

Ella hears how ferocious she sounds. She is going to make things right. Justice will brighten her day.

∽

As they wait for the cops to arrive, Shayna lets go of Helen's hand and stares into the middle distance. The two men stay in the truck, listen to the radio, drink from a Thermos, and glare. The runner paces alongside the road. *That's a type of woman,* Shayna thinks. Burnished like copper gold. Lean and hipless as a teenaged boy. There was a time when that kind of woman would walk into a room and Shayna would feel low, crawl into herself, pucker with contempt.

The police come and it unfolds the way Helen, whispering, assured her it would. The men are told to go home. They will need an injunction before the women can be arrested and work resume.

"In the case of treaty disputes—"

The jogger's body spasms with disbelief. "It's private property!" she insists.

The officer repeats with a flat drone that in cases involving land disputes with natives – a word he lowers his voice to use – all municipal detachments must consult with the region's Policing the Aboriginal Community Team. "The officers from PACT have been informed and will be monitoring the barricade. If a resolution is not reached through negotiations or court orders, PACT officers will arrive to design a policing solution within a week." He doesn't make eye contact with any of them.

"A week. A week?" The jogger flaps her hands. Her voice thins. "That's utter bullshit!" And then she turns on her heel and runs off down the road. The brightness of the day burns the colour from her.

When the figure disappears and the truck barrels down the highway, Shayna's shoulders drop. She walks into the development and surveys. The land is plucked, deboned, dried. She closes her eyes to see past the insults and breathes it in. At first there is nothing but the smell of overworked dirt, arid and ungiving. She concentrates, slows her breathing, waits. Finally it arrives, the slightest mutiny of scent: sweet clover seeds germinating in the backhoed earth, an insurrection of moisture beneath the drained and filled pond, an invasion of pollens breezing in off the river. Everywhere the nerve endings, the memory of life, of what has been. She smells him too: her boy, Pete-Pete. The way a child's skin, flush with spring air, the excitement of catching frogs at the pond's edge, was a universe of smells, the land and sky, the nitrogen, hydrogen, and carbon of creation. Her people called the place simply *o'tá:ra*, their word for clay as well as clan, for everything that was land and family and how who you were and where you lived were indivisible.

With her eyes closed she sees the scrubby trees, brush, and sedge meadow that contained their summers and autumns of hiding-and-seeking; Pete-Pete somersaulting in the milk vetch and sweet pea, curling himself into a hummock of earth, imagining himself a fawn, scentless and hidden in plain sight. The first summer they played, he was three. She'd finish counting, open her eyes, and spot him almost instantly, his little denim bum poking up from behind a tree stump or his lime Ninja Turtle hoodie bright among the tangle of wildflowers. By the next summer he had improved. She resorted to instinct: thinking like a child, exhausting those spots first. By the third summer she had to look in earnest; sometimes an hour would go by but she didn't want to give up. He expected her to try. Her tactic became to cover the territory as quickly as possible, her quick breaths drying her tongue, hurting her throat. She started making rules – not beyond that tree or past the ditch by the road, or anywhere near the creek's edge – fencing him in where there were no fences.

One October afternoon when he was five, she couldn't find him after two hours of looking. She vowed that the game-playing would stop; he was too good. She began to call out. There was no answer. She broke into a trot, inspecting every tree trunk; she grabbed a stick and dragged it gently through the thickness of oat grass and goldenrod, hoping it would snag him. Then she was full-out running through the russets and dried seed heads, the wet mulch of fallen leaves and naked bramble. The sky became a gutted mackerel: grey-silver, lurid red. *Pete-Pete, Pete-Pete, I give up*. The wind threw back her voice. *Come out. It's over. The game is over*. She jumped over stumps. Her knees hurt. It started to rain. *Where are you? Answer me. Answer me!*

The worst was happening in her head; she began to run scattershot, back and forth over the same spots, wherever the compass of her panic directed her. She couldn't see him, hear him, smell him. The clouds split open and she felt close to doing the same. Finally she stopped, bent over for a breath, and chided herself to calm down, pay attention. When she straightened, it was the flashing brightness of his eyes, his little grin that caught her notice. A hundred metres ahead of her was a patch of gooseberry bushes in the middle of the field, tough old things with sharp, unforgiving thorns and unpicked berries, overripe and burgundy brown. She'd run past it several times without looking, stared into it without seeing. He was there, still as a small animal, tucked in under the branches so as not to get scratched. There hadn't been a moment when he was in trouble.

She ran to the patch, fell to her knees, pulled him into the cinch of motherhood. The rain wet his face so he was shiny as a newborn. *Tomorrow. Can we play again tomorrow?* He was laughing – a sound that was joyful, at ease in its world. Each time she stepped on the land, she heard it again.

∞

The first to arrive are teenaged boys, curious. They skid their BMX bikes to a halt on the gravel shoulder, let them fall to the ground. Al Miller, a traditional council chief, and his sons drive up in a pickup loaded with old mattresses and discarded lumber. They proceed to drag them across the site's dirt-road entrance.

"Gotta make this barricade look serious, huh, Helen?" He winks at her.

"Minnie's on the way with a cooler, sandwiches."

Shayna scrolls through her cellphone address book, rhymes off names.

"No, not him. He supports band council," says Helen.

"Jenny Hill?"

"Wish-washy."

"What about the Porter twins? Their ma?"

"Good people. Longhouse. They'll help out."

Shayna clears her throat. "What about Ruby?"

Helen imagines the sheen of effort that forms under Ruby's lower lip around this time of day, the first hour or so after opening the Three Sisters snack shack on Eighth Line, which the two have co-owned for a decade. (*Three sisters?* white folk always ask. *So where's the third one?*) The last thing she said to Ruby: "Sure a little resistance might not be good for you?"

Her sister had smiled, looked wistful. She held up her coffee in a little salute. "We're Mohawk, Helen. Resistance is a scouting party for a fight, nah?" Then Ruby turned back to the fry basket, gave it a wiggle. Bright beads of oil scattered in the sunshine as the door of the shack closed with a bang.

Helen shakes her head. "No, not Ruby. Not now. But what about those Johnson boys – they back from university?"

After the mattresses and lumber are heaped in front of the entrance to the Jarvis Ridge development and Minnie has distributed egg salad sandwiches and plastic cups of watery lemonade, Ryan Isaacs delivers two empty oil drums for fires at night. Al creates blocks of shade by stringing tarpaulins between lengths of pipe and setting out borrowed lawn chairs underneath; the half-dozen adults get out of the sun and settle into silence.

The teenagers tear through the obstacle course of surveyor stakes on their bikes, until one wheels towards the adults on the lawn chairs and shouts. "So, whatta we doing now?"

"We're doing it," says Helen.

The boy's face is bright with impatience. "But you're not doing anything!"

The adults laugh.

"We're doing what we're good at," says Al. "We're waiting."

Helen watches the teenager jump back on his bike and make circles around the barricade. She smiles and wonders when it will all go to hell.

CHAPTER 2

From her vantage on a bench outside, Cherisse has yet to see a single customer walk through the doors of Curiosities 'n' Collectibles and set off its teeth-grating chimes. Yup, that's weird, even for the overpriced junk shop. And inside, the woman behind the counter has opened her cash drawer a half-dozen times, bumping it closed with her hip as if the contents were tea leaves she was trying to shake into a different reading.

Cherisse looks around. There are three unclaimed parking spots outside the Main Street shop fronts, on a Saturday morning. That never happens. Another oddity: there's an entire stack of fresh ciabatta loaves remaining in the window of Paulsen's Bakery and it's past eleven a.m. For a couple of years now she has watched the pale-faced big-city refugees who buy the large homes on Doreville's outskirts go batty for fresh-baked bread – as long as it's called anything but bread. *Migod, there's ciabatta in this little town! Pain ancien! Baguette! Focaccia!* Not today. People are avoiding the town. It hasn't been a full week since her crazy aunties got their barricade up in everybody's face, but there's no denying Main Street is already a whisper less welcoming for a girl like her.

She gets up and moves towards the junk shop. Within sight is the treasure she has been stalking this past month: an atomizer made from crystal, cubed like a chunk of river ice, the blue white of winter light caught within it above a shadow of smoky topaz. Cherisse stops and leans against the Curiosities 'n' Collectibles window, studying the atomizer displayed there – its engraved Steuben crystal orb, its threaded puffer, its swan-necked plated pumper. *Nothing special there,* she thinks. But the crystal, the contradictions of its colours, they make her breath catch. So, how to get it for the money stuffed in her pockets?

She opens the shop door and her shadow elongates in the banner of sunlight that precedes her. The owner looks up; her hands crab across the counter, seize upon her eyeglasses. And Cherisse is waiting for this, the moment when her black hair, brown skin, cut of jaw register and the woman's shoulders slump with disappointment. Ah, there it is. *Let the games begin,* Cherisse thinks.

Because now the owner has a dilemma: how not to appear overtly suspicious while at the same time not letting the native girl out of her sight. Just in case. So many things – the vintage Stratton cigarette case with the creamy enamelled front, the Baccarat hand-cut crystal powder dish with the Bakelite lid – could be slipped into a pocket or a purse. Cherisse gravitates to those things just to make the woman flutter about like an injured bat.

"Can I help you?"

The owner has moved in close, and she blinks as if startled by the abruptness of her own voice. Cherisse loosens her grip on the cranberry goblet she's holding. In a flash, the woman's hands have taken it from her, placed it back on the crewel-edged runner with the rest of the set.

"If there's something in particular you're looking for, I can tell you right away whether or not I have it. Might even know somewhere else you could find it."

When Cherisse asks to see the atomizer in the window, the shop-owner's face tightens; she draws her shoulders up like a scarecrow, and in that half-second Cherisse can tell the woman might resist selling it – to *her*. But the woman exhales a lungful of stale breath, shuffles over to the window display. Instead of handing the atomizer to Cherisse to examine, she walks past her to plunk it on the counter by her cash register.

"It's delicate," she says.

Cherisse comes over and stares down at it, runs her finger along the glass, squats by the counter so she is eye-level with it. When she depresses the pumper, she sees the shop-owner flinch.

"Can I lift it up to the light?"

"Why?" says the shop-owner.

"The crystal – I want to see its quality, its colour."

The woman sighs, flips her wrist, and Cherisse takes the atomizer into her hands. It's cool and sharp against her skin, like ice. And for a moment she remembers a little white dog that nuzzled its way into her life several years earlier and stayed for a winter, the prettiest thing she'd ever possessed.

There is no price on the atomizer. Cherisse can't help but wonder if it was removed in transit from the window to the counter.

"How much?" she asks.

Now the woman picks it up, lifts it to the light, wrinkles her brow. Her eyes flit from Cherisse to the atomizer and back, as if she is estimating both the object and its buyer. Finally she clears her throat. "Ninety-five dollars."

The price sounds like a dare. Cherisse inhales, hangs her head for a second. Might as well make a production of it. She pats all her pockets in succession, yanks five- and ten-dollar bills from her jeans, and finally two twenties from the breast pocket of her jean jacket. She squints back at the shop-owner, in the way you do when you know someone is taking advantage of you. *What was its price an hour ago?* she wants to ask. Instead she lays her money on the counter like a magic trick and points at each bill with her finger.

"Five fives is twenty-five, plus two twenties is sixty-five, plus three tens. Ninety-five. There."

The shop-owner slides the bills into her palm and counts them again. Cherisse picks up the atomizer, and when she feels the cool throb of the glass, the sting of its price recedes.

"I can wrap it," the shop-owner says. Cherisse just shakes her head.

They stare at each other for a last long second – Cherisse holding a hunk of smoked ice crystal, the shop-owner sucking on the end of her eyeglasses – and though the summer air is hot and dry outside, she feels a shiver. *I'm her only customer today*, Cherisse thinks, willing it to be true, and the woman's eyes flicker as if divining this. Neither of them say goodbye, thank you.

～

Joe usually takes the long route back to the reserve, along the banks of the river. Today he tells Cherisse he wants to hustle, open up the smoke shack a little earlier than he usually does, so they'll cross the McKelvey Street bridge and boot along the highway through the suburbs and tobacco farms as if they were townies. Cherisse nods. But even as he feels enlarged by this ambition, he also knows the thinness of it, how just about anything will prick and deflate it. If he rushes back home, if he throws the grocery bags inside the trailer to empty later, if he just keeps moving, then it's possible he could have the smoke shack open by noon and enjoy at least five hours of business. But he knows other operators are already open – solid women who'll have the breakfast dishes done, fresh coffee in a Thermos and a ribbon dress hemmed and still have time to open their smoke shacks before ten a.m., or middle-aged dads who've shorn their lawns like a golf-course fairway before the sun got high, then roared up to their shacks on the back of an ATV. Smoky Joe's, at the very end of the row, as the locals call Ninth Line, is always the last to open. Anyway, who would be buying smokes on a Saturday morning already heavy with heat? Still, the sense of missing out dogs him like his bad tooth.

Joe eases the truck over the McKelvey Street bridge, listening to the rattle of steel under his treads. He turns his head to see the panorama of the Smoke River breaking into foamy moustaches over the fast-moving shallows in the distance before slowing and pooling into sluggish greenish depths by the bridge.

"No . . . you gotta be kidding . . . no . . . Jesus."

He slams his palm against the steering wheel. He can feel himself already adrift, already moving away from today's target, because once he is over the bridge he is turning the car left, pulling it up to the river embankment, indignity making him gulp air like a drowning man.

"I thought we were going straight home," Cherisse says. She's turning something over and over in her hands, something he doesn't recognize. When she does things like this, odd things, it is easier to see her as an extension of himself, as he did when she was an awkward preteen, with bones too long and heavy for her meagre flesh, green eyes so big and bright they startled people. He'd wanted her to stay that way. And maybe, just maybe, it's because of her, and all those ways in which she is increasingly like her mother – long gone but for the desperate phone calls asking for money – that he wants to be the hero of this situation.

He stares out the truck window. "Unbelievable," he says under his breath. "Un-fucking-believable."

Cherisse looks up when he opens the door of the truck, still cursing. Her hand grabs his forearm. "Whaddya doin' there, Joe?"

But she must know; she must recognize that the man wearing waders and standing in the middle of the warmed murk, casting flies as bright as jungle flowers in defiance of both community-mindedness and seasonal licensing, is Elijah Barton. It's one thing for Barton to thumb his nose at people like himself – the man is richer than the whole alley of smoke-shack operators put together – but it's quite another thing to be deliberately trying to piss off the townies, already made skittish by this barricade business at the development.

Joe doesn't care that it's going to embarrass his daughter; he has to say something to the guy. He has to let him know that it isn't okay. That there are regular guys like Joe who need the townies for business, need them to feel comfortable driving out to the reserve. His boots hit the soil before Cherisse can catch at his shirt. He slams the door to her plaintive "Don't" and then he's standing on the bank, fists jammed in his jeans pockets, clearing his throat.

"What you catchin', 'Lijah?"

The man submerged to his knees in the river is shorter, his face pockmarked from teenage acne, his eyes small and hard. When he turns his head, his smile is the smile of someone with means, the smile of a man who doesn't give a shit and has the money to ensure he doesn't have to. Cherisse's mother, Rita, had a thing for him once. Joe could see how Barton's fuck-you attitude must have been attractive to a wild thing such as her, a woman who could never outpace her demons. Elijah raises his arm, pulls the rod over his shoulder, then flings it forward with enough wrist that the showy fly flirts with the surface of the water, skipping beside sunken logs, a tangle of submerged bracken.

Nervy fucker, thinks Joe. *He's stalking a largemouth.*

"Fish," he hollers back to Joe Montagne. "I'm catching fish."

Elijah shakes his head. *That man,* he thinks. While shrewder smoke-traders have built expansive homes with hot tubs and satellite dishes, Joe still lives in a trailer and drives a rusty GMC, its missing hubcaps and gnarled front fender broadcasting his money woes as surely as his bad teeth. Yet Joe gets some things right. The guy wouldn't irritate him so damn much if he didn't.

"You know the season hasn't begun yet. You gotta licence?" Joe yells from the bank.

Elijah ignores the question. He knows the river's differences and divides, its seasons and its tempers, with an intimacy he's never shared with a lover or a friend. Wherever he is on it, it's familiar, it's home.

There's a tug on his line that has some heft to it, some girding for a fight. Elijah feels the tension and begins the tango of tightening and releasing to prevent a snap. The fish is ill-tempered and scrappy; it expected to be left alone in this stagnant bath, where it can ambush frogs and sunfish and exploit its terminal unpopularity to survive – qualities Elijah understands too well.

Thinking like a largemouthed bass brought him to this spot, kept him patient, helped him choose just the right fly. Now his fly is hooked into the fish's flat lower jaw and a fourteen-pound line connects the animal to Elijah where he grips reel and rod; it turns them into a single entity, a hybrid of man and fish, at war with itself. Joe will have to wait.

You need to know who you are, his mother once told Elijah. She must have had enough of relatives and former friends from the reserve passing her on Doreville's streets as if she were a stranger, some whispering *witch* under their breath. As the young boy holding her hand, Elijah felt the tremor of hurt run through her arm into the squeeze of her fingers against his palm. The year he turned twelve, she announced they were leaving his white father and the gabled Queen Street house with its balustrades and velvet wallpaper, its languid two-storey views of the Smoke River, to return to their people. But she'd lost more than her official status by then; she was unwanted, as if by marrying a white man she'd bartered away her own skin. So they squatted on the edge of the reserve in a rundown cabin on the piece of land now being fought over. She died a lonely woman, with few comforts and fewer friends. And except for the river, Elijah grew up belonging to no one and nowhere.

"Did ya hear me there, Barton? You making a statement, fishing this close to town?"

And there it is: the hiccup in his attention. Elijah loses the tension. The fish dives deep, dragging the line to where it risks being entangled in sunken debris. Elijah jerks hard. Hard enough or too hard, he can't tell. The fish rockets out of the water, a ballistic of spines and bulldog jowls. It's a beauty – four, maybe five pounds – and while he takes its measure, the fish slams its tail against the air, jerks its head, and the line snaps. A gleam of muscle noses into the water, disappears back into the murk, taking the exquisite fly Elijah tied himself into the depths.

He lets his arm drop so the rod is half submerged, hangs his head for a second. The sun is too high for Elijah to start again; that largemouth will sulk somewhere unreachable. He shrugs his shoulders. At least he knows where that bastard fish hunts – the river has only so many hideouts with water quiet enough for a largemouth. *Another day*, Elijah thinks. He gathers his line, wades out of the river, and climbs up the bank. Joe holds out a hand to yank him up, and Elijah takes it.

"Don't need a licence, 'cuz I'm native. Remember, Joe? Territorial rights. If you don't use 'em, you lose 'em, eh?"

"Yeah, but man, you could fish anywhere. Do you have to do it right in town? In a spot where everybody can see you? Especially now, with the barricade."

Elijah unfastens his waders, lets them fall to the ground and steps out of them. "Yes, I do," he says to Joe. He smiles and claps the other man on the shoulder. "Yes, I do."

He makes for his own truck – bright red and meticulously shiny – already thinking about that first yank of a cold beer, the sizzle of grilled steak, succour for the lost fish, when he looks up for half a second and sees her, Joe's daughter, sunk low in the cab of that godforsaken wreck of a vehicle, her eyes to her lap. He can tell that she wants to be anywhere but here. This is the part of Joe that trumps him – the fact of his daughter, the ties to others who buried Montagne's prospects under the weight of responsibility. Elijah doesn't wave at the girl, or even nod.

For years he's caught glimpses of her haunting the places he haunted as a young boy, combing the river as if it were a constantly refreshed treasure hunt, first as a barely-there slip of a child, later a gangly girl with an awkward gait, then a teenager with a runaway's eyes. In his head the sightings of her are fluid, intermingled with the first time he saw her mother, Rita, and learned how a wild, impulsive unhappiness makes some women even more beautiful. *You have more nerve than any man I know, Elijah,* she said to him on a hazy afternoon when they were lying half dressed on the riverbank, his hand lost in the silk of her hair. *But I'm not sure you have the heart for the likes of me.* So much truth in her laughing voice. And it's because he had too much need for self-preservation, too little imagination, to take her on, to really love such a woman, that Elijah can't feel superior to the man who did.

∞

"You know, I don't get him. Don't get him," says Joe. "Guy runs his business like a white man. Bottom line all the way. Lays people off so he can automate. Then sponsors lacrosse teams and scholarships like he's the friggin' bank. Won't even live on the reserve – too good for that. But he has no problem letting his factory runoff stink up the creek. Now in town he's all native, all Warrior. Territorial rights! Fucking with 'em all the time. Don't respect it. I don't."

Cherisse is not listening. She knows Joe. He's only getting started; he'll barely take a breath before they're home. She imagines jumping out of the truck, running in the opposite direction, never looking back; all the while her father would still be talking to her, talking at her, his mouth a squeeze-box of outrage. If she snapped, *At least Barton has money!* that would shut him up. But there isn't much point hurting his feelings; he'd only get all hangdog and drive her more crazy.

And now, on this summer day working itself into a remorse-less heat, Cherisse has the cool weight of the atomizer to pin her in place, to get her through the hours in the smoke shack while she rings in the purchases and her father makes awkward chit-chat with the customers that makes them leave sooner, buy less. It's the inevitability of those hours ahead of her that sinks her lower in the truck. Some white person will want to know if there is Kentucky tobacco in the rollies – Jeezus, does she know, or care? – because Kentucky tobacco is too sharp for them or makes their head ache. And Cherisse might fake it, hold the Ziplocked bag up to the light and pretend that it's all in the colour, muttering something about curing that she makes up but the customer might accept because she's native and such knowl-edge is apparently inborn. But it's just as likely the customer will persist, because even though they're going to save $250 on their cartons, it's not enough for them: *Would it be okay if I just light one up? I can tell right away.*

Cherisse will nod. And a person who would never smoke inside their own home won't think twice about filling up the little plywood shack with the rollie's acrid stink, because the sun is beatin' overhead outside – *hotter 'n hell, eh?* – and that will make him or her sweat. All she will have to keep her head cool is the atomizer, a piece of ice that never melts, a memory of what is gone.

Several years earlier, she'd been leaning against a tree across the street from one of the beautiful painted verandahs of Doreville's grand homes that lined the riverbanks. It was November and Daddy Joe was late picking her up, when she felt something soft brush up against her shin and looked down to find a low-lying cloud of white fluff, a tail that was no more than a furry rudder. The little dog had come to her unbidden, so unlike the reserve's strays with their hungry grins, worrying abandoned takeout containers in the strip-mall parking lot. She reached down and gently plunged her hand into the animal's fur, half afraid that it would be as soft as it was. The dog turned up eyes of shining agate and licked her hand with a tongue warm and wet as an infant's. And Cherisse was already telling herself how the animal would prefer its new life and its new home, that where the river wended through town, the rich folks had removed trees so they wouldn't obstruct their view. They'd tamed the river's banks with cement boat launches and retaining walls, and plucked reeds and dodder from its shores. It couldn't be much fun for a dog, or a child. But on the reserve, the river's edges were like the wind or summer sunsets, belonging to no one and everyone. There the Smoke's banks were thick with a tangle of old pines and dogwoods, reeds and stooping willows, their hips half immersed in the water like grandmothers leaning over to rinse their hair.

By the time her father rolled up in the rusted truck, Cherisse had convinced herself the dog had asked to be taken, even begged a little. *It followed me, honest. It has no collar, Pa*, she said, holding the dog in her arms. She ignored his stiffness, his shaking head as she clambered into the rusty truck's cab.

No baby, no baby. That dog belongs to someone. Look how clean it is. And well fed. We're gonna catch shit for even looking at it sideways, much less having it in the truck.

He sat there and waited. Even though Cherisse was then only thirteen, she understood there were greater fears working the twitch in Daddy Joe's jaw. They both knew there wasn't much he could do for her outside of frying a venison steak or reaching things in the top cupboard of the trailer kitchen, with its split vinyl benches and stained Formica counter. She held on to the dog and stared forward too, repeating, *It has no collar.* Minutes passed. She studied the dog's fur, the changing scenery of its whiteness – bright and dull, like ice and snow.

Joe kept his eyes straight ahead, started the engine, and said, *Put it at your feet till we're out of town.*

The truck turns onto the paved road that leads to Smoke Shack Row, and her father is still ranting and Cherisse is turning the atomizer over and over in her palms, letting herself fall into the cubes of light and shade. He doesn't ask about it. He won't. It's as if he feels safer not knowing too much.

Her father wheels the truck in a wide, ragged arc up to the trailer behind Smoky Joe's. It will be one p.m. before they get open. Joe rests his head on the steering wheel; he pants in the heat like a tired burro. Cherisse cups the atomizer in one palm and, with her free hand, lightly rubs his shoulder.

"It's okay, Joe," she says. "It's okay."

CHAPTER 3

At Mitch's behest, Ella jogs around the barricaded development all week, a detour that adds three kilometres to her route and has left her with a threatening twinge in her right ankle. Today she is too jazzed to run, too afraid of missing his phone call bringing news of the injunction. She finds herself in the kitchen instead, with unspent energy.

Waffles. She imagines lightly browned, buttered rafts delivering mounds of fresh raspberries, sour cream, strips of bacon to two incredulous teenagers. The prospect makes her smile. When Las settles into university life in the fall – after he recovers from the initial euphoria of freedom, female adulation, perpetual parties – he will certainly ache for all those special things only she can do. Lately she has been seized with short, sharp stabs of panic: Will he eat anything fresh? Keep track of all his assignments? Sprinkle antifungal talc on his shower shoes?

It is almost too much responsibility for a young man, especially one with the distractions of good looks and athletic gifts. Ella can barely believe that his three-year-old arms once clutched her neck so that his torso and legs coiled tensely against her ribs. *Mommy. Mommy.* Mitch had scolded her for breastfeeding Las after age two, but she couldn't stop herself. Las was her first child. She wanted her little boy to take what he could get, to have the best of her, to be greedy in their earliest intimacy, and in doing so forge something between them that was unbreakable.

Her chest tightens. Arrhythmia? Perhaps she has been too lucky with her health, with her kids. She calms herself by visualizing. Las slicing through water, chasing a personal best. Las, dripping wet, a medallion hanging from his neck, waving to the crowd. Las graduating with honours.

Ella keeps an eye on the frying bacon, whisks the waffle batter. She raises her brows when Stephanie, groggy and pyjama-clad, slouches into the kitchen.

"Hmm, number-one-son breakfast. Smells good."

"Still ten minutes away. You have time to dress, Steph."

"Can't. Golden Boy's doing his ablutions."

"Don't call him that." Ella looks up. "You could make an effort with that hair."

Ella tries not to fret, but her worries build like a funky smell. The credit union manager called two days after the barricade went up. Two days, and already that woman was making mewling elliptical references to their future ability to pay the mortgage. Ella was reassuring, asked the manager about her kids as if there were nothing else on her mind, and ended the conversation with a throaty giggle about middle-aged husbands. Yet every day that passes without the injunction edges her nearer to thinking there is a *problem*. She plunges the whisk into the waffle batter for a final beat, clangs it against the edge of the metal bowl.

She is not a woman who cowers from the first prickle of trouble. Mitch is the one who teeters under pressure and suffers poor impulse control. He's likely to swear *Damn natives!* in front of the soap-scented urbanites who are prospects for Lot 22 or 34, pound his steering wheel so that flecks of saliva hit the dashboard and the fragrant couple in the back seat exchange cringing glances. *Faith is such a tender thing*, Ella thinks. People have to look at mud and a billboard and somehow imagine their three-thousand-square-foot brick-veneer dream home with street hockey games out front, community corn roasts in the backyard. What is absent is supposed to be obvious and alluring – they'll leave behind the whine of streetcars and expressways, the chafe of humanity and gritty air, the vulnerability to strife. She dribbles batter into her beloved Norwegian waffle maker and stares as if the spun yellow were a riddle. Surely Mitch understands the thin, easily bruised skin of his clients' resolve. Surely he won't fuck it up.

"You worried about the barricade?"

Ella looks up from the waffle maker, a bit startled, having forgotten that her daughter is there. Steph's soft shape is spread over the banquette like a pile of laundry. *That hair*, thinks Ella. Its nihilistic shade. Inexplicable girl.

"No, not really. Just thinking. Lots on the go!" She flashes her daughter a smile, mimicking the steeliness of those TV correspondents reporting from war zones with smooth hair and flawless lipstick. "What is your brother doing in there?"

"Do you want me to get him?"

Ella closes the waffle maker's lid; she has two minutes before they crisp perfectly. "No, I'll do it, darling. Though seriously, Steph, you could come to breakfast a bit more put together. Are you watching the time?"

The smell of butter and bacon drifts up the stairway and creeps under the second-floor bathroom door, collects in the sweat on the walls, crowds the bathroom. Las sits, showered and naked, on the closed toilet seat, his head between his knees, listening to his mother in the kitchen. He imagines her slicing fresh fruit, juice bleeding into the crooks of her fingers, along her palms. He sees the bright vinyl sunflower placemat, the folded linen napkin, the glass of milk she has laid out. All for him. Sometimes he hates how much she loves him; it presses against his temples. If he stood up right now he could sprint downstairs, past her through the open patio doors, leap over the backyard fence, and listen to her pitchy humming turn desperate and warbly. *Las! Las!* Her beautiful boy, her star athlete. *Come back! You've got nothing on!*

Las wipes away the steam on the bathroom mirror, stares at himself. Gordo got him drunk again last night. His mouth is gummy, his gut is tight, his head thrums. There's a weird gash on the inside of his right calf. And man, if he could just puke up the whole mess of it, all the stupid asshole moves of his life, all the dullness of this shithole town, he would, even if it meant puking up part of his spleen, a kidney. Hell, he'd give up a lung. If anyone could get by on one lung it was him. Only he'd have to forfeit his swimming scholarship – don't think he wouldn't – his easy ticket to university.

And there's his mother's face again. How does she do that? Get into his head all the time. All those expectations, all those hours of trucking him to and from practices and meets – it's a belt she's looped around his throat. *Study economics*, she said, when all he could do was shrug his shoulders at the sight of the university application. *Don't be like me*, she told him, *with a community college diploma but smarter than everyone else with their graduate degrees. And still people don't listen to you. They want those letters after your name.* He doesn't want the letters. He wants money. He wants freedom. He said as much. She'd pulled the ballpoint out of his hand, wrote in the statement of intent herself. *Oh, Las.* He could see the little furrow in her forehead, like a dented spoke, her lips flat and bloodless, the grey eyes moist with fresh disappointment. And all his power gone, *phssst.* One day he won't need her approval, won't need her at all. But when. When?

There's a *tap, tap, tap* on the door. "Las, your breakfast is ready, dear."

He clenches his fists, stands and leans his head against the door. "Yeah, yeah. I'm coming."

The shadows of her feet split the crack of light coming from the hallway. She stays by the door silently for another half-minute. He doesn't move. Finally he hears the soft exasperation of her socks along the hardwood.

Las turns, flips up the toilet seat, jams his finger way down his throat and lets go.

Stephanie watches her mother return to the stove and lift half a dozen expertly crisped heart-shaped waffles from the steaming pewter and dig a scoop into the butter. *Here we go*, Stephanie thinks. One generous soft sphere for the edge of Las's plate, and now – *whoa, didn't see this coming!* – a smaller one for Stephanie's. She must know I'm watching her lowball both my appetite and butter-worthiness. *So freakishly predictable*, Stephanie thinks. *Because I have hips. Like a normal fucking female!*

But she doesn't say anything. Her mother must have held back the guts gene from Steph's DNA. Las slides onto the banquette opposite her with a belch. Stephanie surveys the outline of her brother's deltoids under his tight T-shirt, the sunbleached tips of his uncombed hair, his overall irreproachable hot-guyness. *Stupid as shit, though.*

How easy it would be to shock her mom, her dad, Las, if only she had the nerve. She'd announce her intentions to see a drag queen show, chew qat with the high school's two Somali kids, wear a headscarf in solidarity with the quietly courageous Nala Nahid, or hold hands with a girl and walk the length of downtown Dorkville. Yup, there'd be some jaws hanging open.

"Hungry?" Her mom's laser-whitened smile beams at her brother.

He nods. Her mom slides a heaped plate in front of Las, who doesn't acknowledge it.

"Ma, what's going on with the barricade?" he says. "Fucking natives make us look like wimps."

"Dad and I are working on it. Something's close."

"What's the holdup? You own the property, they're blocking it. It's against the law. Drag the assholes off there. Christ, I'll do it."

Stephanie stares at the three small heart-shaped waffles on her plate, the half-dozen raspberries, teaspoon of sour cream, half scoop of butter, and two strips of bacon, cooked the way Las likes, a molecule this side of carbon. She feels the hunger that will outlast this breakfast and the humiliation of already wanting more before she begins.

"Whose law?" says Stephanie.

"Wha?"

"You said it was against the law. So I asked you whose law."

Las chews a mouthful of waffle. As he pushes his food down, his face folds into a simian squint. "Our law, you idiot. The law of the land!"

"Steph, let your brother finish his breakfast."

The glare she aims at her mother, who's eating a bowl of muesli doused with vanilla soymilk and wiping the counter between bites, goes unanswered.

Stephanie feels wobbly in her conviction. Daryl Inksetter followed her around like a puppy dog all grade nine, and she had rushed to keep her distance from him, not because he wasn't cool – Stephanie herself never made a team in Dorkville's blood sport of cool – but because his hair was cut in a mullet and he wore a buckskin and bead choker that was, well, too native. In grade ten there was Nate Bastine. She'd caught him taking all of her in, up and down, in what her photography teacher, Mr. Ward, would surely call the "appraising gaze" or the look of the "surveyor." At the beginning of grade ten it so flummoxed Stephanie that she thought she would burst into tears. But he was native, and she was already scrambling for friends. So she unthinkingly abided by the unspoken rule that you didn't hang around with the native kids, that they roamed apart in no-entry-allowed packs, at the back of the classroom or on the periphery of the cafeteria or at the far end of the soccer field.

And if occasionally there was a kid like Phil LaForme, who as a fullback on the football team penetrated the inner circle of Dorkville popularity, it was largely because he cut his hair like all the other football players and preferred American Eagle shirts and jeans to the low-riding Iroquois gangsta vibe. Most of all Phil was appreciated because he did not make them uncomfortable, he did not remind them. Even when there was a protest or a blockade or it was National Aboriginal Day, Phil didn't force people to recognize that he was native.

"It's an important point, Mom. Since when are the Mohawks subject to our laws? Are they a conquered people? Did they sign a treaty giving away their sovereignty?"

Las stops eating, holds his fork in the air.

"What the fuck, Steph? When did you turn red? This is about your family, about our private property." A spray of maple syrup and sour cream speckles the table in front of him.

Her mom clunks her bowl down on the counter. "Steph, really. Why do you have to be so provocative? It's stressful enough, what we're going through. Everybody has to obey the law."

Stephanie feels her face burn. "You guys don't get it. Most of the Mohawks were British allies. They never agreed to be subject to our laws. In fact, the British signed treaties *protecting* them from some of our laws. I can't help it if I'm the only one in the family who knows something about *history*."

Las stands up abruptly; his plate rattles away from the edge of the table. He glares at Stephanie. "You know what? You're making me sick!"

"Las!"

Stephanie wishes her mother's protest sounded stronger, wasn't so easily ignored.

Her brother points his long arm at his mother. "And you and Dad are a fucking embarrassment!"

Her mother reels back. The beckoning cheep of a cell-phone frees her; she runs to locate it, her face drained of colour.

Stephanie turns to the abandoned syrup-soaked waffle hanging over the edge of her brother's plate. With a queasy mix of vengeance and self-loathing, she spears it. She doesn't feel as if she's scored any points. She is as much a hypocrite as they are. Perhaps worse.

Her mother returns to the kitchen, fist-pumping the air and yelling, "We got it! Las, Steph, we got it! We got the injunction!" Steph looks up with a weak smile, then shoves the last piece of waffle in her mouth.

CHAPTER 4

Mayor Peg Redhill sits in her plum-coloured suv with the windows closed to keep the air conditioning in and the public out. The barricade is just temporary, she tells herself. A minor blip. Cooler heads will prevail. She takes a big gulp of coffee that scalds her throat, makes her eyes water. When she thumbs through the messages on her smartphone, everything blurs except a succession of capitalized texts from municipal budget chief Reid Wellings.

WAIT! Lawyers on phone NOW. Do NOT talk to press about injunction YET.

She fumbles in her purse. Damn, no reading glasses. It takes her a moment to focus on the words between WAIT, NOW, NOT, and YET. Even in his texts Wellings has a talent for sweaty condescension. She looks up at the Jarvis Ridge billboard. The giant legless couple with impossible good looks appear to be falling out of the photograph while gripping beaded glasses of

Chablis. Across the road from it is a green flat-line of tobacco. *Such a mixture of intransigence and hope in this place*, she thinks. The barricade – its milling natives, scattered reporters, awkward sentry of cops – looks like an accident scene, jarring but temporary. Surely it can't stand in the way of all Doreville's recent good energy.

The sun presses its pink-umber belly into the horizon. She stops idling the car, afraid it is sending a message that she's ready to bolt, though without air conditioning she will look as greasy as an Easter ham on camera. Interlake special constable Reggie Holland, newly arrived, walks into view with his nice, if tired, eyes. Peg Redhill feels better instantly. There is a handsomeness to his kind of burly, settled man that she is always ready to appreciate. She detects the oppression of middle age in him: a marriage that's fleshy but reliable, two kids under the age of ten, a golden retriever that sits on command, and a debt load that wakes him up at three a.m. with panting existential panic. His blonde-helmeted wife with the Slavic jaw had better rub that man's strong back. She cranks open her window, dabs at her forehead with a tissue, notices that her nail polish is chipped. Peg tucks a hand under her arm, checking for dampness on her favourite salmon-coloured silk-blend blouse. But Constable Holland is looking baked by the sun too. They're all overheated, anxious.

"Mayor Redhill," he says, and his large hand folds over the edge of the open window.

"Constable Holland, good to see you."

Reg leans in. "Thought you should know there's a special team from outside of Doreville they've put in charge of policing."

"Yup, yup. Knew that." She smiles, lets her eyes wander to his shoulders, the small scar under his chin.

"They will stick-handle the response to the injunction, but I expect it's all going to be straightforward – getting the barricade down, peaceful dispersal of the crowd – you know the drill. Not too complex, even for these regional desk jockeys." He winks. Peg wonders if he's making an extra effort to seem assured, light-hearted.

"Okey-dokey, sounds good. Let's get this done. I have no appetite for this, Reg. Every one of these little disturbances costs the town money, lots of it."

"So, you talking to the press soon?"

"Just waiting for the go-ahead."

As if on cue, Peg's phone vibrates. Constable Holland ambles away. She wants to call him back, make a quip that will light up his smile.

Reid Wellings sounds as if he isn't inhaling enough air. "We can't support the injunction, Peg."

"Oh Christ. You can't be serious."

"The lawyers say that because we have not assumed responsibility for the roads through the development, it's not our issue. Can't risk the liability."

"Omigod. Do you realize the position I'm in? We're going to look spineless."

"Better not to say anything, Peg. Just leave."

"Are you kidding? I've been here for an hour; they all know I'm here. I'm not scurrying away like some nervous ostrich."

"Peg, I'm telling you—"

She clicks the phone shut, shouts, "Asshole!" into the emptiness of the car, and turns to see a petite brunette in khakis, a snug lavender blouse and a fresh application of lipstick moving towards the truck with an officious gait. Just as Peg reaches for the button to close her window, a manicured set of fingers grabs on to the glass.

"Mayor Redhill. We're hoping to get you on camera before the injunction is served so we can catch all the action and meet our deadline."

Peg wonders how she got so old that everyone looks younger than her own kid.

"Otherwise we're going to have to say you were unavailable for comment and run a B-roll of you sitting in your truck."

Where do they come from, these women? Girls, really. Playing dress-up, icing their eyes and lips in birthday-cake colours, asking serious questions that they themselves don't fully understand. A college diploma, a microphone, and skinny, Stairmaster-hardened calves. And do they really expect her to speak plainly? If she could raise the money to move the reserve to the other side of the country, she'd personally pay business-class fares for every one of these Mohawk troublemakers. That would make the girl's pretty little mouth pucker with surprise.

Peg takes a deep breath and musters her high-wattage maternal warmth. "Your deadline, of course. I'm so sorry to keep you waiting. I'll be right with you."

Peg pinches her waist. She hates the thought of being on the late news looking bloated, overfed, hypertensive. Then she presses on the door handle and unfolds herself from the car, freighted with all the ways Doreville's potential could be looted if she doesn't do the right thing.

∾

The first rule of remaining unnoticed in a town like Doreville is not to drive up in a limited-edition Mercedes the colour of a newly birthed fawn. That's a car people look twice at, often stooping to the window to remark *Nice ride*, or *I'll be getting myself one of these little babies after the Dodge Caravan kicks it*. It's a car people remember. But today Elijah Barton wants to be another forgettable schlep rubbernecking the little drama at the new development: curious, but not curious enough to quit the inside of his vehicle, with its tinted windows and anonymity. As the mayor shambles into the fray, Elijah pulls his red pickup into an inconspicuous vantage point thirty metres behind her SUV. He looks around and sees at least a half-dozen other Dorevillians just like him, sunk low in their car seats and truck cabs as if they were at a drive-in movie.

Even he can see that the policing situation is a mess. Holland must have been stuck with the thankless task of negotiating how the chain of command would work between the local cops and this infestation of out-of-district forces. By the way Holland keeps looking to the sky and then letting his shoulders slump, Elijah guesses the hapless guy had his sights on an afternoon golf game, now downgraded to a bucket of balls at the driving range. Soon he'll have to give up that too, and even the Sunday night barbecue, coming home instead to grilled food shrunken and cold in its foil wrappings.

Just beyond the mayor's car somebody has set up lawn chairs and a hibachi. Beers are being tossed from open coolers. *Townies are treating it like a freakin' tailgate party*, Elijah thinks.

Ten metres ahead of him, a box-jawed sergeant leans into a young local cop, yelling. "Let him go. Right now!"

Holland moves towards them. The young cop, his face rude and red as a baboon's arse, is holding on to the scruff of a native kid, Marty Horse, Bobby's son. Never misses an opportunity to cause some shit. The young cop looks like a recent college graduate with a short fuse and too much to prove. Elijah likes that he won't let go of Marty, that he challenges the out-of-district sergeant, who must have a criminology degree and probably wears aftershave to work, and somehow manages to outrank not just the kid cop but Holland, who has to be a decade older than him. Elijah rolls down his window to hear better, pulls his truck in closer.

"I caught this kid in the midst of a *criminal* act. Breaking into the parked cars of local residents. Two windows were broken."

"Let him go. You were ordered not to use force. You are under my command."

"Were we ordered to ignore criminal acts? Auto theft is *not* peaceful protest. Sir."

Constable Holland steps into the melee a bit tentatively. It must be unclear to him just how much authority he has at the moment. But he simply leans over and lays his hand on the young cop's shoulder.

The sergeant, smelling his advantage, ups the ante. "One last time, let him *go*. And I'm taking your badge number."

Holland nods at the younger officer, who releases Marty. *Mistake*, thinks Elijah. And sure enough, Marty scrambles away a few metres, turns, flips up his middle finger, and laughs wildly. The other local cops hang back silently, their faces flat with disbelief.

"I think you're understood. No need to press it much further." Holland smiles at the sergeant, offers his hand to shake. The sergeant simply moves a few yards away and pulls out his phone. Holland turns, reaches out to pat the rookie's shoulder, but the young cop keeps his eyes down, remains stiff with anger. Elijah rolls up his window.

∽

Helen Fallingbrook paces the margins of the media pack. Reporters irritate her, the way they jostle like crows over a bit of foil. Still, Shayna insisted they participate in the press conference, claiming it will be a good opportunity to present their side of the story, no matter how far down the columns of type it appears. And no doubt Shayna is right. The reporters will respect her niece – her cool command of the facts, the barely used law degree inflecting her talk with authority.

Minutes earlier, Bobby Horse pulled Helen aside to loudly insist Shayna couldn't represent the Great Law if she were seeing a white man, especially one who lived across from the development. "She's an apple," he said. "Only red on the outside."

Helen was not going to let a hothead like Bobby dictate spokespeople. She fired back with uncharacteristic irritation, "Great Law? Whose version can you recite? Gimme a break, Bobby. Don't you just show up to burn things?"

There were chuckles from those who overheard her, but it left Helen with an anthill of worries. Is it a problem, this tie between her niece and the farmer? Certainly even the slightest suggestion of Shayna's being compromised is troubling, now that people are showing up at the barricade whom Helen doesn't trust, whose reserve politics neither woman share.

She tries to see beyond the crowd to what they are reclaiming. Townspeople and outsiders see a discrete, strangely shaped piece of territory, a passing patch of scrub or an inconsequential shape on the map. Helen imagines its sedimentary layers of memory and reinvention: Attawandarons coaxing tobacco from the glacial silt; Europeans plundering basswood, ironwood, oak, maple, and tulip trees, then ultimately the softwoods; expropriations, swindles, reworded treaties pawing away at the rectangles of forested river frontage awarded to the tribes who'd stood with the British in all their wars. The hunting gone. The unrooted sandy soil blowing everywhere. *Dunes that showed up in a matter of hours, blocking roads,* her mother, Lena, telling her. *Blow pits in the middle of fields.*

The government's grim-faced economists designating the interlake delta as wasteland, unsuitable for growing. And then an American soil chemist arriving with an appetite for cheap land and a vision of a tobacco plantation system north of Virginia. Poor Kentucky sharecroppers following. Belgians turning up next. And tobacco growing everywhere – except here. Somehow the kidney-shaped *o'tá:ra* remained uncultivated, ignored or left alone, assumed to be among the reserve's diminished holdings, a challenge to their collective forgetting.

When Helen was a baby, Lena had taken blows from an old Belgian who'd set up a sawmill among the *o'tá:ra* pines. She got a few of her own in too. He left a swath of savaged stumps; Lena was charged with assault. And the land was assumed again by her people; they didn't care whose name was on its official title. They knew to whom it belonged.

The mayor steps into the fray, and Helen stops her pacing to listen. Poor Peg Redhill always looks as marbled as bacon in the glare of the TV cameras. The city television station is here, and so are reporters from the county weekly, the big local daily, and the all-news radio station. They lob all the expected questions.

What will the mayor's office do?

"It's out of my jurisdiction. My hands are tied."

How is the town dealing with it?

"The people of Doreville are very patient and resourceful. That's why we are the fastest-growing community in the inter-lake basin."

Does the town support the developer's injunction against the barricade?

The mayor pauses. "Well, that's a bit tricky. In spirit, Doreville is behind any development that brings new money and growth to the community. But because we haven't assumed the roads on this particular development – it's just too early – we can't technically support the injunction."

Peg Redhill beads up in the glare of the cameras and her cheeks splatter with purple. She appears trapped. *Where is Shayna?* Helen wonders.

A lavender-sheathed television reporter moves forward. Her voice is loud, triumphant. "Mayor Redhill, if the Town of Doreville will not come out in support of the injunction, how can people not interpret that as support for the barricade?"

The crowd of reporters moves in tighter around the mayor,

shoving tape recorders and microphones closer to her mouth. Helen cringes at the disrespect.

"The Town of Doreville does not support the barricade." The mayor sounds newly unsteady.

A voice Helen recognizes asks the next question. "Mayor Redhill, if the town has allowed this development to go forward – approved the land purchase, the zoning – for all intents and purposes it supports the development. You can't have it both ways, can you?"

The cameras swing around to find the questioner, and Helen sees in the parting crowd the small, sure stature of her niece.

"We don't support the barricade. We support the development."

Stick with the short answers, Mayor, Helen thinks. *We'll all do okay then.*

"But isn't it true that, at every stage of this development, our people have filed considerations against it? And isn't it true that, if you were to support the injunction, you would be financially liable to the developers if it turns out – as we think it will – that we have a legitimate claim to this land? Isn't that what you're really trying to avoid?"

There is a collective inhale among the crowd around the mayor. *It's the "gotcha" moment,* thinks Helen. She suspects that most of the reporters, including the young woman from the television station, haven't done their homework. But even if they don't fully understand their own good luck, they have the predatory sense to keep their microphones in position, their tape rolling, until the meaning of what's happening becomes clear.

Peg Redhill looks as if she has been struck. Her mouth opens like a hungry goldfish's.

"Mayor Redhill, isn't it incumbent upon someone in your position, an elected official in paid office, to understand the protracted legal battles that lead to barricades? And isn't part of your job to protect the town from financial liability, just in case we're right?"

Helen wiggles into the group, reaches for Shayna's arm. The slender bicep is hard, tensed for battle, familiar. Helen pictures her mother's jaw, as sharp as a Dutch hoe, her eyes tight and unsmiling. "Is this the direction we want to take?" she whispers into her niece's ear. "Won't embarrassing the mayor hurt us later?" But Helen can feel them – the dead grandmothers – huddling around Shay, giving her little room to move.

It's too late for Helen's cautions. The mayor's eyes are bright with the same combatant's spark as her niece's. "It is pretty clear what we support. We support growth," she says. "We support good, hard-working people." She clears her throat. "Some of us are busy earning our way. We don't have the luxury of sitting around, blocking progress."

Helen draws in a breath of disappointment. Flashes of light stripe the mayor's face. Now all the reporters are yelling, asking her follow-up questions, hungry for more remarks they suddenly recognize will make their editors smile.

Peg's face darkens with realization. She waves them away. "I've said enough. That's it."

The reporters circle Shayna. In the aureole of camera lights, her proud face and dark hair are arresting. Helen notices that Shayna is wearing earrings, little winks of silver in the lights, and her eyebrows are freshly plucked into questioning arches.

Behind them, Peg Redhill hobbles towards her truck with a rounded back. Helen feels an unexpected urge to comfort the woman. *Perhaps I am too old-fashioned for this game*, she thinks. In her mother's generation, the skilled hunters left the lame to coyotes and other predators.

∽

The injunction arrives after eight p.m., when the sky looks like carbon-flecked amber. The man who brings it steps out of a black town car. Las, who is standing with Gordo on the other side of the street, recognizes the profile of his father pressing himself into the back seat of his lawyer's vehicle, watching. They have lined up with the twenty-odd Doreville residents who have come to see things made right. *Get out of the car, old man*, Las thinks. *Take charge.*

But no, it is this other man, wearing dress pants and a sports jacket, who holds the manila envelope, the gleam of his good shoes catching the last rays of sun as he walks towards the barricade. The natives huddle together in front of it, like an undisciplined football squad. Off to one side there is still a sparse collection of reporters and a TV crew. More police begin to move into formation across from them. Las recognizes the deep blue uniforms of riot cops, but he can't see any shields, helmets, guns.

"They're goin' in soft," says Gordo under his breath.

They lean side by side on Gordo's red truck, drinking the last beers from a six-pack, denting the cans with veiny grips. The man in the dress pants stops. He extends his arm and the manila envelope hangs in the air between him and the Mohawks, who stand in an unmoving row three metres away.

An old woman moves forward and takes the envelope.

"Showtime," Las says.

She opens it up, pulls out the legal-sized sheet, and reads it. Las and Gordo chuck their empty tins into the back of the pickup and follow the other onlookers across the pavement to get a better view.

The woman takes the sheet and folds it, then calls out. Another woman approaches. She is smaller, younger, her hair loose, falling over the shoulders of an untucked man's shirt. The new woman reads the document. The watching crowd is a shuffle of feet, impatient whispers.

The document is handed back to the older woman, who steps forward and rips it into dozens of small pieces. The younger woman crouches, scoops the shreds together in a pile, pulls out a lighter, and sets it on fire. An ululating cry breaks out among the Mohawks.

Las feels wild with rage. *The law*, he tells himself. *No respect for the fucking law*.

The paper burns fast, leaves a ragged twining of smoke. The women walk back to their people at the barricade and begin to talk and laugh.

Nothing else happens.

"What the hell?" somebody from the crowd of townspeople yells at the cops. "Do something!"

Then they are moving forward, two dozen law-abiding Doreville citizens who have come to see justice served, and all of them are yelling, screaming at the cops and then at the natives, who begin to taunt them back. Somebody picks up a rock and tosses it towards the barricade. It is answered by a dozen rocks, all of them rookie pitches, none drawing blood.

The man in the dress pants turns on his heel and does a half lope to the black car, which accelerates away once he clambers in. Las's father pivots in the back seat, and for an instant their eyes meet. Las holds his gaze, but the old man looks down quickly.

"No, don't run away!" Las shouts. But the car is an onyx blur.

The police fan out to separate the townspeople from the natives. Somebody yells, "They have their backs to the law-breakers. They're protecting them!"

They all start yelling after that. They yell in disbelief and outrage. "Get off our land," the natives yell back. The police remain in a stiff-necked line and say nothing, do nothing. And then, after forty minutes, the voices become raw and they fade out slowly, like all the songs Las hates. Close by, two men start talking about a motocross race in the next town, and whether they can reach the beer store before it closes, and the futility of staying here in the dark, wasting this good summer evening, when they could be watching the prospect of a decent crash. The crowd drifts away until there is a just a single pickup, the same colour as Gordo's, at a remove from where the action had been. Finally, it too leaves.

Las's voice is ragged from the strain of yelling. His fists are curled and he does not want to go home, cannot go home, where the lawyer's gleaming black car sits in the driveway.

"I need to hurt something," he says.

Gordo snickers.

When the reporters have scattered, Shayna feels a caffeine flush, triumphant. She turns to look for Helen, to see her good work reflected in the older woman's eyes. But her aunt is nowhere in sight. The barricade supporters have wandered over to behind the development entrance, where a new urn of coffee has arrived and blankets are being handed out to those staying the night. Her elation loses its ballast. She was expecting pats on the back, some parsing of the scrum's to-and-fro, even being ribbed for having tidied up for the cameras. She's been looking forward to it.

Now only one figure waits for her in the dusky light, his thumbs tucked into his belt. Coulson's shirt looks fresh, even new. For her? She feels a flash of irritation. There is only so much of her to go around. And this stuff between a man and a woman requires some effort, initially at least. She is out of practice. If she leans against him, surely he will bend and kiss the part in her hair, tell her she has done well. But those smiling eyes of his are bright, a measure too intense. She feels the urge to turn and run.

It's only a year since she got a first impression of him, literally – a large bootprint in the mud among the *o'tá:ra*'s prolific black raspberry bushes. She didn't presume the berries were only hers to pick, but they were small and seedy, not as popular as summer's later arrivals: raspberries, blackberries, gooseberries, elderberries. She could usually assume that it was just her picking, and perhaps a few grannies who understood the sweet magic of black raspberries lightly stewed with mulberries or tossed with a teaspoon of sugar and the season's first strawberries. But the bootprint maker had been sloppy, stripping some vines bare and crushing others, still hung with unready fruit. It was greedy, expedient behaviour.

Shayna preferred going to the patch in the coolness of dusk, but the prints had dried by then, having been made in early morning's dew-soft ground. The next morning she was up early, arriving at the bushes with a Thermos of tea just after the emerald flash of sunrise. He was already retreating. It surprised and somewhat delighted her to see the back of a tall, broad-shouldered figure holding a dainty basket, when she'd expected an old man with a coffee tin or a teenaged boy with a grocery bag and more energy than sense.

"Hey," she said, and the man turned. His whiteness gave her a small shock. Even if the *o'tá:ra* wasn't technically on the reserve, everyone knew that her people made use of it without interference.

"Hello," he said. "How can I help you?" This interloper's face would have been boyish had it not been cut by the blunt axe of hard work and hours outdoors.

Shayna hadn't really thought out what she was going to say. If he were one of her own people, her authority as a berry picker, a keeper of the patch, would have done most of the work. But this man, whom she recognized now as the tobacco farmer from across the road, would want something like an explanation. She hesitated.

"I like these berries," he said, holding up the basket. "Put them on my breakfast cereal just like my ma used to. This is her basket."

"Yeah, but you're . . . um . . . kind of like a rutting moose the way you stomp all over the bushes. Lots being wasted because of you."

His face flushed, but the laughter that followed was only vaguely apologetic. "Well," he said, "that won't do. Forgive me. This was going to be my last basket anyhow."

He nodded his head and turned to walk across the road, then stopped, put his basket on the ground, and returned. "Excuse my manners. My name's Coulson," he said, sticking out his hand. "Coulson Stercyx."

His big palm, cooled by the dew of raspberry leaves, swallowed hers entirely. She felt calluses press into her knuckles.

"Shayna," she said.

"Just Shayna?"

"Shayna Watters," she said, using her former married name. He let her hand go, and she noticed that the tips of his fingers were berry stained, just like hers.

∞

As the only white person on this side of the barricade, Coulson is starting to feel damn awkward. *So much quiet fury for a woman,* he thinks as he looks at Shayna's unmoving figure. Still, he can't go home without her. Two weeks have passed since they last woke up together. How unexpected it is to be middle-aged and filled with toppling desire.

"Shayna." He steps forward, reaches for her hand. "You look like you could use a shower, a good meal. A firm bed."

He wants to quit this scene, have a drink, get out of this stiff new shirt, feel the slide of her skin against his. But she shakes her head, slips out of his grasp.

"We have to make some strategy decisions. I have to stay," she says.

"It sort of looks like your strategy's decided."

There's heat in her face and her eyes. He's not used to chasing women; he's unused to asking.

Are you coming home with me? Marie had petitioned him in the end, it must have been a dozen times. He lying silent in his parents' bed as she packed, tears streaming down her face. *Are you coming home, Coulson?*

"The meeting's important. I'll stay," Shayna says. "You can go."

Her dismissal rankles. He can't face his empty bed. "C'mon,'" he says. "They're not going to miss you for one night."

Marie was holding her suitcase. Wet drips, sooty with mascara, slid from her chin onto her white blouse. She'd wiped her nose with her sleeve. He'd never seen her do such a thing, not in nearly a decade of marriage. She asked one more time, her voice cracking like fine porcelain. *Are you coming home with me?*

Shayna looks at him as if he's an alien, beyond comprehension. He feels impatient. The barricade seems a kind of hijinks to him, injunction-burning a rash tactic to gain attention. The real work would happen in somebody's office, the sorting through of titles and surveys. He is about to say as much but thinks better of it.

"Well, after you're done with strategy, you can just slip through the fields. The kitchen door is always open. The light will be on." He hates the entreaty in his voice. He wants Shayna to choose him. Women always have. Why, all of a sudden, do things have to be different?

He's risked embarrassment for her already. A month after that first encounter with Shayna, he baked a crumble, using the last of the frozen black raspberries and a recipe smeared with buttery thumbprints, handwritten by his mother. He covered the crumble with a red-striped tea towel and delivered it, still warm and smelling of brown sugar and oats and musky cobbled fruit, to the archives department of the reserve's cultural centre, where she worked. His note said: *Enjoy. – Coulson Stercyx.*

He'd thought that was recklessly romantic. There was no reply. He started taking more trips to the new grocery store outside town, where everyone from the reserve shopped, hoping to bump into her.

Helen Fallingbrook, who worked in his kitchen from late August into September to feed his harvest crews, must have known, must have smelled the yearning on him.

"My niece borrowed my truck earlier. She's going to drop it off here so I can pack up my stuff," Helen said on the last day of last year's harvest. "Hot day out there. You might offer her a cold beer."

So she came to him after all, on a beautiful September afternoon, and sat at his picnic table with curious eyes and a beer in her hands while Helen packed up her big steel cauldrons, muffin tins, twenty-cup percolator. Then he made them both dinner: grilled steak, potato salad, homemade beet slaw, more beer. He poked fun at Helen, got her niece laughing.

Still, it would be months – including all of a cold winter – before Shayna would come to his bed. It was never a certainty. But after he'd studied her inscrutable face in the waning autumn sun, he'd known he wouldn't stop trying. He couldn't help himself.

"Good night, Coulson," says Shayna. She raises her arm and gives him a wave. She walks towards Helen, who has emerged from among the coffee drinkers behind the entrance.

He looks around to see who has witnessed this rebuff. There's just the indifference of sky and highway. He kicks the dirt and smacks the back of his fist against his forehead. Already she infuriates him in a way no other woman has.

Coulson checks his watch to calculate the hours before closing time. *No point wasting a new shirt*, he thinks.

CHAPTER 5

M itch Bain drives to the liquor store. It is a Wednesday, before lunch, and he feels sheepish. He sits in his car and inspects the parking lot for familiar vehicles.

There are two things he wants to avoid. He does not want to be questioned about the barricade. *Hey, what's your next move? Will it delay construction?* He does not want to listen to a tirade about the police's failure to protect a respectable, hard-working, law-abiding citizen like himself, a businessman who just wants to make Doreville a better place. *Can you believe the cops, those friggers in government?* People's outrage on his behalf has worn him out.

And now, four days after the injunction was set aflame, his bottom lip is numb from hours spent on the phone with lawyers and political aides, none of whom can agree on whose jurisdiction the barricade falls under. He has barely left his office since, excusing himself from family meals, sneaking about like some furtive, light-shunning rodent for snacks and bathroom visits. But it's not just the calls that keep him there. The prospect of encountering Las alone, seeing again his son's look of contempt and disappointment, fills him with parental dread.

Today he awoke with a thirst – a thirst for Scotch that couldn't be exorcised by deep breathing or by shoving handfuls of smoked almonds into his mouth. He wants a drink. And he wants to be able to purchase a very nice single malt without being seen by a neighbour or friend who will force bonhomie with a wink and a nudge at his brown bag. *Betcha been needin' a lot of that lately.*

Thirty minutes earlier he hiked himself up on the kitchen counter and, balancing on his knees, reached into the very top cupboard, where Ella kept herbed vinegar, Thai fish sauce, pickled mango – a variety of gifts and impulse purchases exiled for being frighteningly exotic, a little too outside their palates. This was where he hid a bottle of twelve-year-old Scotch, a showy thank-you from a grateful client. It was the one place that had eluded Las and his ne'er-do-well friends, who consistently ransacked the house's other booze supplies. He ran his fingers along the glass shapes on the shelf, searching for the squatter, rounder prize, and managing to ignore that his knees were wet from a spill left on the counter – Las's handiwork, no doubt.

Mitch felt keenly then how different he is from his son, whose limbs are long and flexible. It took an unaccustomed thrust of his shoulder to get his short arm to extend upward to the cool neck of his quarry. When he gripped the bottle, there was a sudden, jabbing pain. In reflex, Mitch yanked back his arm. The bottle of Scotch flew downwards and bounced off the counter to the tile floor. If there's a sound that can break a man's heart, it is the simultaneous *thunk* and *crack* of an unopened bottle of pricy Scotch hitting unforgiving slate. His centre of gravity shifted, the spill on the counter added glide, and seconds later, Mitch bounced off the counter too, following the bottle with a bruising thud of his own.

The sight of the Scotch's amber puddle roused him like an electric shock. He uncrumpled himself, stood up, grabbed a roasting pan from the oven drawer, scooped up the leaking bottle, and placed it in the pan, where it opened like a boiled clam, releasing a gush of peaty liquid. Tipping the roasting pan as if salvaging turkey juice for gravy, he poured the liquid through a fine-mesh strainer into a tumbler. He swirled it with anticipation, took a long, loving sniff, and brought it to his lips. He would have drunk it too, were it not for the thought that a little shard could make its way past his tongue, begin a hidden insurrection in his pulpy depths, a rent in his throat or stomach, that would widen, infect, ultimately fell him in the prime of his life. And what kind of legacy was that to leave for his wife, his kids?

Already one investor was making noises about the development acquiring the tarnish of a troubled project. To compound matters, the representative of a numbered company approached his lawyer two days earlier with an offer to buy Jarvis Ridge at just below the original price, reasoning that the barricade had greatly devalued the property. Mitch dismissed the idea without hesitation; he was certain that the law and his good name would prevail. And there was not just a fat profit to be made but enough to ensure that a future community centre would be named in his honour. There had been so many other calls, but he never pressed for details.

No, he wasn't going to make it easy for everyone with a premature death caused by a reckless chug of compromised liquid. Mitch emptied the glass into the sink, tidied the kitchen, and, realizing he was still thirsty as hell, drove to the store to get a virgin bottle before he gave up on the whole enterprise.

He gets out of the car, turns his head in a 180-degree survey, peers through the display windows as he walks towards the entrance. Not seeing anybody he recognizes, inside or out, he lets his chest deflate and walks into the liquor store.

❦

When Elijah Barton spies the unmistakable soft and inoffensive profile of Mitch Bain stooped by the shelf of single malts, reading bottle labels, he can't resist the tug of his own history. In the 1980s, before Doreville could justify its own high school, most adolescents in the interlake basin were shipped to Central Pemcoe Secondary. It was a sprawling school filled with the sons and daughters of farmers, bankers, and merchants, all of whom made their money, one way or another, from tobacco. On the outer edge of the basin, the reserve had its own high school, a temporary building made of siding that was always in violation of the fire code or without sufficient teaching staff.

Elijah Barton was one of the region's three dozen non-status native kids forced to attend Central Pemcoe. He was neither tall nor short; he wore his hair cropped above the ears, long in the back, with a thin single braid that reached farther down his spine and was tied with an osprey feather he'd found in his backyard. Years later, former students would remember the boy with the thin braid, the pocked cheeks and flint-coloured eyes, but they would never connect this memory to who Barton became: a wealthy man with a collection of limited-edition Sedona watches and bespoke shirts, the man who ran the reserve's most profitable business and was its only legal manufacturer of cigarettes.

For Elijah, his two years at Central Pemcoe meant inhabiting all the spaces the squat, gregarious Mitch didn't have to – under the stairwell, in the back of the cafeteria, and hours and hours in the smokers' pit. Even here in the liquor store, three decades later, what Elijah sees is the sixteen-year-old Mitch, his chin a scrub of hair tufts and angry pimples, turning in his seat and accusing Elijah of copying answers from his grade ten general-level math exam. *Go ahead and cheat, fuckhole. You're not even going to graduate. You're going to be a loser all your life.*

It turned out that the first part of what Mitch had predicted was true. Elijah did give up on high school before that semester ended. But he tucked Mitch Bain's taunt like a shiv into his sock; he wasn't going to let a milk-breathed, dough-faced boy predict his future. Especially one who was only taking general-level math himself.

Elijah takes a route around New World Wines and approaches Mitch from the imported beer aisle. As adults they encounter each other at the biannual Chamber of Commerce general meetings. He had a meal – a memorably awful one – at the man's house just this past September. Their respective business ventures make it into the pages of the *Interlake Post*. Elijah has yet to see a flicker that suggests the man remembers his own words from all those years earlier, or has the humility to take them back.

He clears his throat. "Looking for a good Scotch? Can I make a recommendation?"

Mitch turns, offers a quick grunt and weak smile. "Oh, hey, Elijah. Yeah, yeah, sure . . ."

∞

Mitch straightens and silently curses himself for not having done a more thorough reconnaissance. Elijah is going to be smug about the barricade; he won't be able to stand it. He'll have to divert him with another topic and keep him on it.

"Can't choose between the Dalwhinnie and Laphroaig."

"Laphroaig. No question."

That sureness, it feels almost arrogant, thinks Mitch. But wasn't it the same smirk, slightly wry, that drew him to Barton when they met at the Caledon Club a year ago? Mitch was taken aback that a native man could afford the fees. It soon became clear that Barton had more money than most of the members, certainly many times more than the Bains. He racked his brains when Elijah said he'd attended Central Pemcoe, that they'd even been in classes together. He couldn't remember him, nor any native kids for that matter. Still, Mitch thought it shrewd to cultivate such a business ally. He invited him to dinner.

Barton stares at him. *He expects me to start talking about the barricade*, thinks Mitch, *and I won't. I just won't.*

"You know, I'm leaning towards the Dalwhinnie," he says instead. He can hear the waver in his voice, the tentativeness it betrays.

The dinner started with ceviche for an appetizer, followed by seafood risotto with braised fiddleheads and a salad of bitter greens. The menu was Mitch's idea. *I think he's probably like most men and would prefer a steak and some roasted potatoes*, Ella had said. (*Dessert?* she'd asked, and he shook his head. *Bad idea with all that diabetes in their community.* She'd made a snarky remark about why, then, they'd purchased enough wine for a wedding party.)

When Ella came out in a lovely grey peau de soie blouse, worn with trim dress pants and shiny flats, Mitch stood back and shook his head. *Would you consider that black cocktail dress I bought you last Christmas?*

He didn't want Barton to judge him on their centre-hall-plan home alone. Ella was the showpiece, the proof of his prowess as a man. Twenty years into their marriage and there's still a bit of the not quite tall, not quite handsome, not quite affluent son of a grocer left in him. Not quite worthy of coppery, lithe Ella Nagy, swishing past the grocery store windows in an eyelet skirt that lifted ever so demurely in the breeze to reveal a pale flash of thigh. A year older. A star athlete. A conscientious student. There are still days when he asks himself where he got the balls to pursue her with such a gentle, unrelenting sureness. And even now, despite the internecine pettiness of a long marriage, he's still not sure he deserves her. Let other men think he does:

there always comes an ineffable spike in regard after he introduces Ella as his wife.

The cocktail dress was a tight shift with a daringly exposed back – too formal for a dinner at home. And when, five minutes before their guest was expected, Ella swanned into the kitchen accessorized with teetering pumps, sheer hose, and a dainty diamond tennis bracelet, he regretted his request. There was something geisha-like about her in that outfit as she carried in hot dishes, tossed the salad, and cleared the plates; it irked Mitch, tempting him to whisper that she tone it down.

All that effort, and for what? When Mitch offered a chilled Viognier he described as unoaked and fruit-forward, Barton asked for beer. It hadn't occurred to Mitch to see if Las had left any. The Arborio rice was undercooked. Ella fished through the risotto to retrieve its morsels of salmon and shrimp as if she were beach-combing, but Barton ate his serving with gusto. Did that mean he was undiscerning or just polite? Mitch couldn't tell.

"The fifteen-year-old Dalwhinnie has too much ethanol on the palate, weird finish – probably too much attack for a man like you. The ten-year-old Speyburn is probably more your speed," says Elijah.

Mitch feels warmth spread out from his sternum, creep up his neck. He had welcomed Barton into his home and the man thanked him by letting his eyes stray along the curve of Ella's hips, down the backs of her legs as she filled his glass with Perrier or poured him a cup of coffee. When she admired the rose gold of his watch, its corona of tiny diamonds, he held it out towards her. *The band is farm-raised Louisiana gator,* he said. *Give it a stroke.* She reached out and ran her fingertip along the shiny strap. Mitch watched her face brighten like a tulip.

Now here's Elijah in jeans and a black golf shirt, standing with one foot propped on the lowest shelf of liquor, revealing a flash of caiman-skin boots. Mitch tries to imagine himself in such footwear but can't. He won't be talked out of the Dalwhinnie, dammit. And *attack* is exactly what he is after. But "I dunno" is all he can muster.

"You see, the Laphroaig – and I'm talking the Quarter Cask here – is more of a peat monster. It risks being a bit offensive, all that iodine and sea salt in it. Tarty as hell . . . the way I like my women." Elijah throws his head back and laughs at his own joke.

Mitch gets a buzz in his jaw that he hasn't felt since high school gym class, when the football players fell to their knees and waddled after him in the locker room, as if he wasn't already painfully aware of his short legs. He doesn't laugh or smile, but the other man is undeterred.

"Lots of smoke, lots of history in that Scotch. Probably not for you, though. Speyburn is much more vanilla, more palatable." Elijah winks.

There's a smarting sensation behind Mitch's eyes. Alertness pulls his shoulders tighter. "Yeah, but look at the difference in price," Mitch says, reading the shelf labels. "With the Dalwhinnie I can get a fifteen-year-old Scotch for the same bucks as the ten-year-old Laphroaig."

Elijah moves his foot, claps his hands together. "Ah, but waiting longer does not necessarily improve the payoff. That's the trick."

"With Scotch?" Mitch asks, suddenly unsure whether they're talking about the same thing.

Elijah stays silent. Mitch grabs the Dalwhinnie bottle by its neck and nods. As he is about to pass, Elijah sticks out his hand; it feels more like a challenge than a gesture of amity. Mitch grasps it, imagines that Elijah's boots feel much like his palm, cool and slippery smooth. But then the grip tightens. There is a grin on Elijah's face again, and it somehow feels like four knuckles have been rammed square into Mitch's solar plexus. By the time he gets back to the car with his bottle of Scotch, he is shaking. His thirst for a drink has disappeared. He feels its absence like a spiritual void.

∽

Elijah watches Mitch Bain hustle out of the liquor store, fondling his piss-water Scotch as if it were his pretty wife's ass. He chuckles, grabs a bottle of Laphroaig for himself, and then, on a whim, a bottle of Dalwhinnie.

Around the same time that Elijah forsook mainstream education, a simple poster, the masterwork of some zealous public health bureaucrat, was whittling away at the fortunes of Doreville's white folks. On it were two photos: the first was of a healthy lung, wetly pink and blue-veined; beside it, a shot of the blackened, necrotic lung of a smoker. All across the country, the poster was being hauled out near the end of phys. ed. class and hoisted for the benefit of squeamish preteens, sitting on the gym floor, still recovering from laps and jumping jacks. It was posted in the waiting rooms of doctors' offices and Planned Parenthood centres. A few renegade public health nurses tacked it up in the bathrooms of local bars. Damn poster was everywhere. Lots of people kept smoking, for sure, even if the poster was burned into memory. Nobody wanted to be associated with that ugly ulcerating lung on the right. Politicians – who for decades had regularly invited Doreville's biggest tobacco growers on trade junkets to Europe and Asia – stopped visiting the region for photo opportunities. Subsidies dwindled. Cigarette taxes climbed. Doreville, and its hallmark crop, had become a political liability.

At seventeen, Elijah had made two important discoveries: it was surprisingly simple to make cigarettes, and there was a surplus of tobacco to make them with. He borrowed money to buy a small rolling machine that fit in the back of a friend's truck. A pocketful of cash bought him tipping and rolling paper, filters. Stung by the depressed prices the big cigarette producers were offering, and shut out of owning a crop quota by the clubby marketing board, the local independent tobacco growers were willing to drive a load into his laneway, just outside the reserve, at night in exchange for thick envelopes. In his first month of business, Elijah sold out all of his product – harsh, unsophisticated rollies in freezer bags of fifty or a hundred that were 50 per cent cheaper than the highly taxed name brands. He didn't spend all this new flush of money on himself; instead, he expanded.

To his fellow Mohawks, making and selling untaxed cigarettes represented economic sovereignty. Everyone else, even those who piled into minivans and pickups to buy their discounted smokes on the reserve, considered it illegal. The more money Elijah made, the more he craved respect outside the reserve and beyond the town's tight fists and small minds. So he decided to make nice with the feds. He started to pay taxes. He built a gleaming new cigarette plant on the reserve's main road, using a nice dollop of federal business grant money. Suddenly he was the reserve's largest employer, even though the entire native population was pissed at him for selling out to the oppressors. He started exporting his cigarettes to Europe and Asia as well as supplying the smoke shacks. He joined the Rotary Club and sponsored softball teams, on and off the reserve. He began construction of a ten-thousand-square-foot ranch house on prime river frontage. Within a year he was a "force for change," according to the *Interlake Post*. His move into legitimacy, its speed and deftness, conferred upon him a trickster's duality: everyone respects him; nobody trusts him. It is a contradiction Elijah is happy to abide.

Ten minutes after his encounter with Mitch Bain, he is driving down Tenth Line, listing the different home styles like hockey cards. Trailer. Trailer. Shabby bungalow. Modest side-split. Trailer. Ah, there's a keeper: a brand-new four-bedroom Cape Cod–style home with an SUV parked in the circular drive. Smoke shack? Smuggling? Or one of those back-to-the-rez liberals with a fat-paycheque job in the city? He makes a game of guessing. Several thousand reserve residents without drinkable water, their cisterns and wells polluted by upriver agricultural runoff and industrial wastes, but this guy's got a Jacuzzi and home theatre. "And why not? Why the fuck not?" he says aloud. He passes two other similarly new and jarringly luxe homes before he reaches Industrial Line, where the gleaming headquarters of Flint 'n' Feather Tobacco Incorporated is located.

On days like these, he just wants to smell the future. The plant is divided into two factories; Elijah walks into the primary processing facility, where a load of flue-cured Brazilian is being puffed and sweetened like breakfast cereal. There is a good amount of reclaimed tobacco from spoiled cigarettes and enough stems and factory-floor offal for reconstitution. His great-grandfather trapped beaver, hunted deer using the same principle: nothing goes to waste. He's the real deal now; a recent investment means the actual amount of tobacco he throws out has decreased. Just like the big boys. Except he won't add diammonium phosphate to the mother liquor. He won't strengthen people's addictions with ammonium hydroxide either. A clean, chemical-free smoke at a sixth of the price.

He sinks his hands into the tobacco rag that comes off the cutter, ready to be turned into cigarettes. There is a slight newness to its odour, but when he breathes in more deeply he can smell the ameliorants – a little bit of glycerol, a hint of butterfat – that will make his higher-end Warrior brand of cigarettes taste smooth, a bit grassy and sweet. Just like a good Scotch. Or at the very least, better than a rollie. Business is good, and if it stays that way, if his export markets build, soon he will have to build another plant. That requires land, and there's not much available. *You can fret about these things*, thinks Elijah, *or you can just wait.*

CHAPTER 6

In late June's heat wave, Herman's Dairy Bar reeks of souring cream and artificial caramel. Parents, their crabby children in tow, roll in from the hot and breezeless outdoors to be greeted by a whiteboard scrawl of sold-out favourites. The sight of each new customer after four o'clock on a Sunday makes Stephanie swear under her breath. Her apron is gaudy with Gumball Surprise and Rainbow Sherbet smears. She feels yeasty and sticky. And now there's a line snaking along the counter, while her relief, Brittany, a jock-tacular girl with a terminal grin, has yet to show up, though it's fifteen minutes past the start of her shift.

Half submerged in a bucket of Naughty Monkey, rooting around for remnants still frozen enough to hold the shape of the scoop, Stephanie hears the front door's *whoosh* signal more customers. "Christ almighty!" she seethes, and for a horrible, unexpected moment, the shop becomes quieter. Half her body is still bent inside the ice cream freezer, but she could swear she heard somebody hiss, with the fleeting sibilance of a punctured hose. *So many Jesus Crispies in this frickin' town*, she thinks. So quick to take offence.

Brittany finally arrives at the back entrance with a series of bumps and crashes, ploughing her mountain bike through the narrow, tub-stacked hallway before stowing it in the tiny lunch-room, where it obstructs the staff washroom. Stephanie, eyes down, keeps working, though she has already loosened the ties on her apron, ready to quit the fetid sweetness the second the other girl's volleyball-champion legs appear behind the cash.

The line along the counter crushes inwards, leaving a gulf between it and the most recent customers. Stephanie, who won't admit her nearsightedness, has to focus to make out Nate Bastine, his hands on the shoulders of a young boy who may be eight, standing adrift at the back of the shop. The singlet he's wearing shows off his good shoulders; he is darkened by the sun and his hair is longer. She can't tell if Nate is looking at her with recognition or to avoid the glare of the sneering father she has just served. She smiles. He smiles back, and everything that was already sticky on her is stickier still.

The young father, his face soft and florid, whispers under his breath and shoves his three-foot charge, gooey with melting Naughty Monkey rivulets, towards the cash register. Stephanie drops her gaze and rings them in. Brittany emerges, ablaze with Friesland genetics and a clean apron cinched tight at her small waist, her white-gold tresses pulled into a ponytail. Nate moves forward so the little boy's chin is level with the end of the counter.

The young father, now exiting, turns and addresses their backs. "Fucking nerve."

The words land like overturned tables; everyone stares into empty space. Stephanie waits for another adult to censure the man. But all have cast down their eyes, except for Brittany, who glares at Nate.

He doesn't flinch. He doesn't look in the direction of the man. His eyes continue to scan the menu board, even when the shop door slams with an insulting suck. Brittany's eyes gleam. She scrutinizes Stephanie's dishevelled hair, the butchery of cartoon colours on her apron, and grins. "You can count out your tips," she says. "I'll serve them."

And at that Brittany lines herself up with Nate's shoulder. "So, what do you want there?"

Nate reaches for the young boy, pulls him closer to his hip.

"What's it going to be? I've got lots of good citizens to get to."

Nate leans and the boy whispers. He points. "The orange one."

Brittany doesn't ask what size or type of cone. She opens the ice cream freezer as if she were mad at it and assaults a bucket of sherbet with her scoop.

Stephanie wants to move but can't. Ahead of Nate, the other customers clear their throats, shift their feet impatiently. A few seconds later, Brittany holds out a cone to Nate's young charge that is half the size of their smallest order. The scoop is lopsided, mushy, with trails of electric orange running down the cone.

The boy hesitates. Nate's face darkens. Brittany pushes it farther in his direction, her pelvis flattening against the ice cream fridge, her bum in the air, and the sherbet dripping onto the boy's sneakers.

Stephanie takes a big suck of air, grabs Brittany's shoulder hard, and wrenches the girl's arm back over the counter. The melting cone welts the varsity athlete's face with a bright orange swipe before hitting the wall behind the counter and slithering to the floor.

Now Brittany and Stephanie face off behind the counter, Brittany looking ferocious with her sherbet-gashed cheek, ready fists, and Christian predestination, while Stephanie, with her loose, filthy apron, waxy bangs, and non-belief, is less so. The whole of Herman's Dairy Bar is hushed but for the beleaguered chug of the air-conditioning fan.

Stephanie senses the other girl's calm heat, all the twitch fibres of her muscular legs tensed and ready to spring. The shakes move up from her ankles and threaten to topple her at the knees. The sharp tang of adrenaline is on her tongue. When she manages to speak, her voice is high and uncertain. "Just quit it, okay?"

Brittany's lips curl like some sort of roused serpent. Her body relaxes. *What the fuck*, she mouths.

"I'm taking these customers, Brit. Then I'm leaving," Stephanie says with more authority. She breathes again, recognizing that somehow, miraculously, control has shifted back to her, and it will take a while for Brittany to figure out that she has not, for once, come out ahead.

Stephanie won't look at Nate because her eyes are watering and she's trying to control her trembling hands. She remakes the younger boy's ice cream with an extra scoop and hands it to him. Their fingers brush on the waffle cone, and she has to resist the urge to grab those little hands and beg for forgiveness. Not just for her failure to do the right thing sooner but for everyone else's, the whole mess.

"It's on the house," she says. She's not allowed to comp, but she does it anyway because she won't risk sending them to the cash register, where Brittany has planted herself. Now she just wants them to leave, for their sake and hers.

But when Nate holds open the door for the young boy and exits without looking back, Stephanie feels a constriction in her chest. She throws off the apron, grabs a napkin, and scrawls her cellphone number in large print across it. Underneath she writes, *Call me – Stephanie*, in script. Let Brittany take her tips for all it matters. She hustles out the back of the shop and around it, just as Nate is putting the truck he's driving in gear.

Stephanie shouts, "Hey!" and hurries to his open window, her eyes wide, manic in her new fearlessness.

His jaw softens as he reads the napkin, but all he does is nod quietly before engaging the clutch. Stephanie's eyes linger on his bare shoulder, the long, muscled slope of his arm, the wisps of his dark hair, and she feels uncharacteristically indifferent to her own overheated, unshowered wretchedness.

At the back door Brittany awaits, the cash register abandoned. Her arms are crossed, her eyebrows bullying her hairline. "Like, don't your parents own the land they're having their little circus on? I mean, what's your fuckin' problem? You want them to break the law? Can't find another way to rebel?" Her mouth hangs open in a sinkhole of disbelief.

Determined to enjoy this singular moment of her own invincibility, Stephanie brushes past as if all the Brittanys of the world have been wiped from the planet.

Nate Bastine had upset all of Stephanie's expectations about native kids, ones she didn't know she had. Sure, he had an eagle feather tattooed on his neck, wore a black jacket emblazoned with "Native Pride," walked with a swagger. But he did not sit in the back of the class, plunk himself down at a peripheral cafeteria table for lunch, or drift beyond the soccer field before or after the bell rang. He took his sketch pad to every subject in grade ten, and it was the first thing he opened when he sat down, regardless of whether the subject was Math or Chemistry or Civics and Society.

It wasn't so remarkable that Nate knew many of the answers when teachers made a point of interrupting his doodling to ask him about cosine law, chemical nomenclature, or MLA citation style. What made Stephanie uncomfortable was how surprised she herself was that Nate knew the answers. In North American history he actually put up his hand and corrected the teacher, firmly but persistently, not caring that the whole class had gone silent as Mr. Bigelow stammered something about "evolving interpretations." It was the only subject Nate put his hand up in, the only time Stephanie noticed a native kid offering an answer. And Nate Bastine looked everybody directly in the eyes. He did not avert his gaze, ever.

In second-semester biology class, Nate moved into the seat behind her, and all period she listened to the soft sanding of his charcoal pencil working the paper. The sound lightly tickled the exposed skin on the back of her neck; her cheeks flamed and she found it hard to concentrate. It frustrated her. Being one of the smartest kids in all her classes was one way Stephanie separated herself from the rampant assholism of high school, and especially her brother, Las, who'd scored a windfall of looks and natural athleticism at birth and had coasted on it ever since. She was more frustrated still when it became harder to choose what to wear to school in the morning, now that the back of her outfits seemed to matter as much as the front. She caught herself fancying a beautiful shoulder tattoo peeking out from under her bra strap and winding like ivy up the base of her neck.

For the last few weeks Nate was in school, several times during biology he'd sing her name – *Stephhhaneeee* – in a gentle, beckoning near-whisper. A little sweat would break out on her feet and between her thighs and under her arms, and she would feel thrilled and alarmed at the same time. Only once – she was wearing a light blue cotton scoop-backed T-shirt and she feared being ridiculed for her expanding armpit stains – did she risk turning around to deliver a scolding *Shhh!* But Nate just smiled at her, with a smile that was all eyes and teeth and made her sweat all the more, the wetness spreading in an oblong between her legs. Horrified, Stephanie had to skip photography, her favourite class, in order to slink home so no one could witness the mess he'd made of her.

The last time she'd seen Nate, she passed him leaning against a locker, sitting and sketching. He lifted his head to say simply and clearly, *I like you.* Two girls standing across from him snickered. Stephanie kept moving down the hall, because flirting with – much less dating – a native guy who wasn't Phil LaForme was a kind of social suicide, and it was hard enough being curvy and smart. So she just kept on walking, though her chest hurt, her head swam, and her tummy was already cramping with the sourness of regret.

Nate never returned to school after that. The rumour was that he got drunk, stole a pearl-coloured Hyundai, and resisted arrest when he was stopped in downtown Doreville. When Stephanie first heard the rumour, she sat in a carrel in the school library for an entire day, missing all her classes and feeling angry at natives for doing those things to themselves, for making it so impossible to reach across the divide and be their friends and, maybe, even more.

After spending six months in the courts and juvenile detention, Nate must have figured there was little point in finishing high school. Last fall Stephanie returned to school and everything was the same for her, except she didn't sweat and she didn't worry about the backs of her outfits and she didn't look forward to biology.

Halfway into her walk home, Stephanie's feeling of triumph quickly tailspins into dread. Herman, a bulb-nosed Dutchman, is too in thrall to Brittany's tight shorts to ever take Stephanie's word over the bronzy glamazon's, even if it is Stephanie he calls into the small office beyond the lunchroom for lectures on how Indonesian palm oil is killing the Canadian dairy business, all the while eyeing her boobs proprietorially.

The toe of her shoe catches on a ridge of sidewalk. She stumbles, and as she straightens, a telltale *ping* sounds from her pocket. Stephanie fumbles for her cellphone.

Nate has texted her. THX FOR EARLIER. U AROUND TONITE?

Her heart lifts. Instantly – too instantly – she replies. SURE, WHEN?

By the time she reaches the long drive of her house, she feels covered with a protective coating, as tough and light as Teflon, that Brittany and Herman cannot scratch.

Because of the barricade, Stephanie's mother has lost her energy for the happy-family artifice. She eats looking out the window, ignoring her husband's sullen face, her son's catatonia, and the cellphone on Stephanie's lap – a brazen disregard of dinnertime rules. An hour has passed since she replied to Nate's THX text; there have been none since.

The panic Stephanie hopes to hold off until after dinner threatens to mutiny. She wipes her lips with her napkin and peers down at the darkened phone. On impulse she thumbs in OK. WHEN? WHERE? hits Send, and immediately feels desperate. Only a loser texts twice in a row looking for a reply.

Stephanie steals a look at Las, hunched over his food like a bored zoo inmate. What kind of cosmic overlord made things come so easily to a guy like him? When she was an already well-endowed fourteen-year-old, her brother looked at her one day and said, *You're no beauty but you've got big tits. That's the only way you're going to get a guy, Steph. Might as well get used to it.*

She'd adored Las before that, bought the fiction of older brothers, reached adolescence still hoping he'd deliver. Then he started hanging out with creeps. She didn't know what she'd done to deserve his cruelty, only that it began after Gordo found her asleep in front of the basement TV one night when Las was upstairs raiding her parents' booze stash.

She awoke with a frightening pressure against her body and a hand across her mouth, her lips stinging from potato chip shrapnel and salt. Gordo reeked of uric acid, cheap cigarettes, and stolen liquor. She thought she was going to suffocate, screaming into his rough skin. She pushed her hands into Gordo's chest, but there was no give against his weight. His unwashed face was crushed into the crook of her neck, his fingers pincer-like at her breasts. Stephanie closed her teeth against the callused hand he shoved against her mouth; it tasted of solvents and burger grease. His other fingers were pulling at her waistband. He bit into the tender flesh above a nipple. Gordo's hips were shoved against hers; she could feel his erection against the thin material of her pyjamas.

The door at the top of the steps opened. When Las came down to the basement, Gordo jumped up, brushed his pants. Stephanie gasped for breath and started to whimper. Las looked at both of them. Tears were running down her face. There was a moment of silence between the two friends. She waited for her brother to be her big brother.

Then Las spoke. *Found whisky. Let's get out of here, shithead.* They turned and left her alone in the basement, damp with tears, greasy with intrusions. Something no tougher than a new blister crackled and broke inside her.

She remembers all of this while watching her brother's blond tendrils move as he eats, hiding, then revealing a strong brown neck, an unbreakable clavicle. Stephanie wills herself not to look at the phone.

"Are you losing weight, Las?" she asks, feigning a hint of alarm, her voice loud enough to startle her parents out of their thoughts, make them look up from their plates. *Bingo.*

Her mother pushes out her chair, leans over the table, and brushes aside her son's hair. She grabs his chin. "Whoa, honey, you *are* looking thin. What's going on?"

Las swats her hand away with an "I'm eating, Ma!"

But it's too late. Stephanie knows the idea will be like a burr to her mother; she'll scratch at it until its excised. Parasites! Anemia! A convergence of unseen threats worming their way through the young prince's bloodstream.

"You've barely touched anything on your plate." Her mother shoves the tray of grilled sausages, a bowl of macaroni salad towards him. "Are you taking your supplements?"

He glowers. Her mother reels out of the kitchen towards the first-floor bathroom, yelling, "Where are the multivitamins?"

Her father shakes his head, refills his glass of wine, and leaves the table with it, muttering something about policing at the barricade. Las decamps as quickly, brushing roughly against his sister, muttering, "Nice fuckin' going, Steph." And Stephanie can't help herself; she smiles, delighted at the distraction.

When her mother returns, holding a supplement bottle, Stephanie is clearing the plates. "He took off, Mom."

"Oh dear. Do you think . . ."

"I'm guessing he lives."

Her mother heads to the hallway. Stephanie hears her knock on his bedroom door. "Las . . . Las."

Now the phone is on the counter beside the sink. She picks it up and checks the charge, then places it down. As she rinses and stacks each plate, her eyes flit back to the phone to see if it is winking at her, offering to save her from a loveless adolescence and an evening stuck in the oppression of her home. At seven-thirty the dishes are stacked, the table wiped, the floor swept. She thumbs in WE STILL DOIN SUMTHIN? to Nate, hits Send, and vows not to check the phone for a whole half-hour. After which she checks every ten minutes, sitting on one of the kitchen stools, leaning into the black granite island, slumping over the phone, lifting it up and placing it face down, lifting it up again. Could she text Nate a fourth time without it being cyberstalking?

When her father comes in, she makes no attempt to hide her compulsion. She feels him watching her.

"Thanks for cleaning up, hon."

Stephanie nods, her eyes still on the phone. *Please go*, she thinks.

Mitch pours himself a generous measure from the bottle of red wine he opened at dinner and then takes out another glass, fills it halfway, and slides it towards her. "It's summer. Enjoy yourself."

Stephanie looks at the glass, looks at her father, and wishes he didn't understand her as much as the offer suggests. Her eyeballs burn. He squeezes her shoulder, which means he wants to leave before tears fall. And after he does, she drains the wine in two swallows, reaches for the bottle, admires the label with its vaguely Latin name, its promised tastes of cassis and smoke, and pours the remainder into her glass. *Why not?* she thinks, carrying her newly full glass into the living room, turning off all the lights, and falling into her Nan's puce wingback chair. She lifts and lowers her phone for the next ninety minutes, twice getting up to assure herself that the time on her cellphone is the same as on the kitchen clock. *Letting somebody hope is a cruel sport,* she thinks.

When she has finished the wine, she returns to the kitchen, finds a three-quarters-full bottle of Gewürztraminer tucked into the refrigerator's side door. After the sourness of the red, the white tastes so cool and sweet it makes her cry.

∽

Ella feels like a ghost haunting what was once an enviable family life, a busy, productive contentment. The frustration of the barricade has made them subject to public sympathy, private isolation. Behind the door of what was to be her dream room is her husband, Mitch, hiding away, yelling, begging, cajoling into the phone at all hours. Las is lost to his headphones, too upset by everything to allow her to minister to his hurts, and losing weight. In the face of their helplessness, they've all gone mute with embarrassment. And now, after ten p.m., Ella wanders in and out of the darkened rooms of her house, not up to the energy of bright lamps, their suggestion of activity, of occupancy.

She leans into the living room, wondering if she should fire the housekeeper, return to vacuuming and dusting, when she notices a shadow awkwardly sprawled across the ugly pink-brown wingback Mitch insisted on bringing home, giving a place of honour in the living room, after he moved his mother to a retirement home. There is a small aureole of electric light from an open cellphone, casting in silhouette her daughter's small nose, her bottom lip protruding in a quiet exhale.

"Stephanie?"

The cellphone clicks off. Ella cranks the dimmer switch and the room brightens with clarified-butter light. Her sixteen-year-old daughter's dark head, streaked with fluorescent pink, is bent over the phone in her lap as if in prayer. Ella has only to close her eyes to see the child Stephanie once was, a toddler blameless and soft as catkins, with black hair and lashes auguring future charms. How not to feel constantly disappointed? It was so easy to love the girl then.

"What are you doing here in the dark?"

Stephanie lifts reddened eyes to her mother, umbrae of dissolved mascara beneath them.

Ella wishes her cramp of maternal protectiveness had lasted longer. But Stephanie's perpetually wounded glance, the soft distension of those lips, only reminds her of the girl's truancy from soccer camps and swim lessons, the pockets stuffed with Caramilk wrappers and emptied Frito-Lay bags. It makes her wonder where she went wrong. With Stephanie she'd started off cajoling, progressed to helpful suggestions, and ended up threatening, forcing protein shakes on her, withholding her allowance, and, on one horrible spring afternoon when Stephanie was twelve and not yet immune to her mother's disapproval, demanding she jog. Stephanie's flesh had shuddered, her chest had heaved with sobs and protests, until Ella was so rattled, so embarrassed, that she yelled, *You have nobody to blame but yourself, young lady,* before she ran ahead and out of sight; she could no longer be implicated in this thing her daughter was, so different, so far from her. When she returned alone, Mitch took the car to fetch Stephanie and found her on a side road, bawling. He refused to speak to Ella until she apologized to the child, who was by then buried under Hello Kitty pillows on her four-poster bed and wouldn't acknowledge her mother's forced contrition.

Ella's eyes alight on a wineglass on the end table beside the wing chair. "Stephie, what is this?" She grabs the glass, tips its floral liquid towards her chin, and sniffs. "Are you stealing our wine?"

"Dad let me. He said I could have some. He even poured it."

Ella feels unsteady. The inadvisability of Mitch offering his depressive, overweight, underage daughter a glass of wine when she is alone at night catches in her throat like a fishbone. When it comes to Stephanie, her husband always takes the easy way out.

Steph stares up at her. Is it a beseeching look? Ella wants to reach out to the girl, be the balm to her troubles, but the effort makes her rigid. Daughters are so eager to repel their mothers.

"This" – she points at the glass – "is the last thing somebody like you should be indulging in."

With shaking hands, Ella quits the room. She doesn't acknowledge the punctured sound her daughter makes.

⁓

Stephanie, collapsed deeper in the chair, hears her phone finally *ping*.

F'D UP. SORRY 4 NO REPLY. @ CRNR CLEARVIEW & WILDWOOD 15 MINS?

She stands up and looks at herself in the reproduction baroque mirror over the mantle. Even with puffy eyes and a glaze of sweat, her face is quite pretty. At certain angles she could even be compared to her mother – a darker-haired, more voluptuous version.

Stephanie hears the muffled voices of the television in the basement; her mother has uncharacteristically retreated there. Her father never leaves his office anymore. She goes to her bedroom, puts on a fresh T-shirt, reapplies her makeup, and leaves the house quietly, through the garage.

Nate is waiting for her. He reaches out a hand. She hasn't expected this, how easily he offers a gentle touch, how it thrills the words right out of her. They walk in silence for a few minutes.

"That was one nice ice cream cone," he says finally. They laugh and go quiet.

Stephanie thinks hard about what to say, then croaks out, "Brittany's a piece of work."

She's grateful when he laughs again. But more silence follows, and she is conscious now of the lines etching his palm, the warmth of its centre, the pads of his fingers pressing her thumb inwards like a broken wing. So much of just one hand to know and understand.

"I could have been a bit smoother. You know, not just blurt out something in the hallway," he says.

She wants to cry with relief. "No, no. I was such a bitch about it." He doesn't say anything.

She takes a risk. "You know that whole term of biology? I chose what I wore because of you."

He stops walking and turns towards her. They're far from her house. He draws a finger along her jawbone. He touches her hair. "I kinda knew that's what you were doing," he says.

He wraps his arms around her shoulders and pulls her inwards. She is enclosed, dizzy with sensation. He nuzzles her neck, and for the next fifteen minutes he breathes ever so quietly into her skin, holding on to her as if he's been waiting, waiting most of his life, just for her. And Stephanie thinks, *Ah, this is what it is to feel alive.*

CHAPTER 7

June is coming to a close with a sticky slap; purslane and sorrel spring from the over-chewed mud of the development, thriving in the heat. Even pummelled into hardpack, the *o'tá:ra* is beautiful. Helen reaches into her satchel and pulls out a twist of dried tobacco, kneels in the dust, and lets the flame from her lighter lick the leaf edges before inhaling deeply. From inside her chest she pulls forth gratitude, sends it skyward.

When she was a child, her mother told her their religion began with an illness. The sickness transformed a not-so-great man into a great one, because it brought him a vision. Helen imagined that the man suffered from a cough that blistered his lungs, woke him with chills and vivid, feverish dreams. Her own childish dreams were sharply coloured, but none of her dreams brought messengers drenched in supernatural light, speaking a message that would untether her people from the pale saviour of the priests and ministers who raised their churches, set up missions. Among them Helen ached for such dreams, such messages. There were so many things her young mind failed to understand: neighbours' children dressed like white kids, taken to the churches built by men who didn't live among them, the painted exteriors like bleached bones.

And sometimes those same neighbour children showing up on the back porch, cupping an aching ear or holding a sore stomach until her mother crumpled dried tobacco leaves in a small clay bowl, dropped in a woodstove ember, and blew smoke into the child's ear or exhaled it over a glass of water for them to drink. *Hard not to stumble*, Lena whispered after them, *with a foot in two worlds*. But even she couldn't protect her own children from this two-worldedness forever.

Across the road, the commercial tobacco plants in Coulson's fields are, to her eye, precociously tall and green, more than a week ahead of schedule. Even now, despite earning money from the crop herself, it bothers Helen how a living thing nurtured by resources shared by all – sun, soil, water, air – can confer its blessings on just a few. It's like storing all the food and gifts at one end of a canoe, and in so doing making the journey perilous for everyone.

As a youngster she smoked wild tobacco – Indian tobacco – that made her head spin, her lungs sore. She learned moderation that way, how strong medicine can heal you or hurt you. *Get sick only once*, her mother told her. *Otherwise you don't respect it*. The wild plants grew along the edges of Emerson's Creek, just beyond the shade of the few remaining large maples at the east end of the *o'tá:ra*. It was a rogue crop from centuries earlier, before her ancestors' tobacco was replaced by the variety favoured by Europeans, a plant that had bent the backs of black slaves and made white Virginia plantation owners rich – and so too the Interlake farmers.

Wild tobacco was cultivated through conscious neglect, the ability to leave something alone. Its blooms were left untopped, and by July the trumpet-shaped petunias would bend in the breeze, a flutter of yellow prayers lifted to the heavens on two-foot stalks. In the fall the leaves would wither on the stalks and dry, cured by the winter's freezes and thaws. Her mother would send her out in springtime to pick the black leaves, lay them on the rocky embankments in the sun. Then the older women would smash open the seed pods, sow the wild tobacco anew so the cycle would repeat. Before anyone dared to fill a clay pipe or take their bundles home, leaves were crushed and tossed into the creek, flung into the air, tucked into rocky crannies, and finally burned, acknowledging all the spirits who'd contributed to their good fortune.

This plant marked the seasons for her and she thought it would always be so. Lena kept her daughters – Helen, Ruby, and Bertie – hidden from the Indian Superintendent's agents without desperate measures; other women gave up their status, married non-natives, in order to keep their children out of the government-mandated residential schools. Helen's mother would have done that too if it hadn't seemed like capitulation, another way for the white man to win. Instead she used stealth and imagination to protect her daughters. But Helen was the oldest girl, the surest on her own; she became restless, harder to hide. And one day, just like that, her summers of berry picking, tobacco smoking, and fishing were over. She was grabbed as she turned down the dirt road to her home with an armful of kindling, her pockets stuffed with chestnuts. Her mother was outside, hanging up the wash. Lena looked up to spot the grey government van, and she must have known. From the back window of the retreating vehicle, Helen watched Lena give chase, eyes bulging, open mouth rubbery with panic.

Later she understood how much her mother had given her. In every grade they put her in, Helen was the oldest student – a difference the nuns and priests interpreted as the intransigence of her ignorance, ungodliness. But she had language the other children didn't, words for all the ways a river is not just a river but a whole lexicon of different animations – rain-stirred, pollen-clouded, ice-covered, meltwater fresh. She had had eight summers of wild tobacco, whose taste she would conjure to heal her swollen cheeks, beaten with a ruler by the frocked instructors every time she spoke her Mohawk words.

Ruby and Bertie arrived together eighteen months later, with fewer years of Lena's wisdom and ferocity to hard-coat them, fewer Mohawk words, and no such taste of tobacco to conjure as a salve against the hurts. It was because of this, Helen believes, that Bertie could not resist the nuns' ideas about salvation, her uncleanliness in the eyes of a punitive god. She came out of that school and kept her crucifix, her prayer book, her rejection of Shonkwaya'tihson, the Creator. When Lena was out of earshot, she announced that she was a Catholic. What Ruby and Helen saw was a casualty.

By the time they all returned to the reserve, their mother had been bent and silenced by too much forfeiture. The stand of maples and the little creek had been expropriated by the government for a four-lane highway that cut a convenient diagonal from the big cities in the northwest to the shoreside cottage district in the south, bisecting the *o'tá:ra*, making it smaller still. One day, as car after car whizzed past, Helen walked among the ditches that diverted the creek under the asphalt, and she searched until she found one plant with a lemony blossom. The next spring she came back, crushed the blackened pod against the rim of a galvanized steel drainage pipe, and sowed wild tobacco seeds all along the culvert, keeping just a few for her mother's garden. In this way she made change and its inevitability something circular; in this way she reminded herself that not everything of the past can be swept away, that choice and intention are palpable forces of resistance.

The memories lighten the heaviness of the June afternoon

and the niggling worry about the unfamiliar faces at the barricade, the ones that make her chew the inside of her mouth. It's a large reserve; she doesn't know everybody. But so many of these new faces belong to men, burly ones. Until now, theirs has been an action of women – small, determined mothers and aunties like herself, supported by a handful of teenaged boys, some grandfathers, and middle-aged men with arthritic knees. And Shayna, who has abandoned an expensive education, the certainty of financial reward, for the pull of history and her own nature. These other men seem like interloping weeds to her, unruly in ways over which she has no control.

Helen finds her niece sitting on a toppled oil barrel, fussing with her phone, staring at a number as if daring herself to call it.

"Shayna. We have visitors, no?"

The late June light feels stiff as starched bedsheets. Helen squints and points to the outer rim of the property. A half-dozen beefy figures, two in camouflage cargo pants, gesture like prospectors over the expanse of graded dirt.

"What do you think?"

Her niece stands and shades her eyes with her palms.

"Advisers."

"Advisers from where?"

Divisions stripe their people like plaid. There are those who belong to the other tribes of the Iroquois Confederacy – Cayuga, Oneida, Seneca, Onondaga, Tuscarora – among them some who resent the Mohawks' pre-eminence, their persistent activism, their nationalism. There are those who follow the old longhouse religion and buy their groceries and play bingo beside all variety of Catholics, Protestants, Pentecostals, evangelicals, and atheists. Within their own faith are those who believe an oral version of the Great Law that prohibits war and violence, and those who follow a written version, which interprets resistance as using whatever means necessary.

"*Rotiskenrahkete*," says Shayna.

Helen takes a small step back, closes her eyes for a moment. The appearance of these men, from the Warrior societies on the shores of the great river in the east, suggests a shift. She thinks about how, even with a clear sky, the subtlest cooling of the air makes any kind of weather possible. "Who sent for them?"

Shayna shrugs. Helen need not have asked. Land has a way of stirring up competing agendas. It doesn't matter; they are here. Everything is already different.

Helen looks into the sun, feels the heat on her cheeks, and forces herself to accept. There is nimbleness in certain kinds of acceptance. She has spent a lifetime mastering this nimbleness.

༄

Across the field from the barricade, the big man squats. With less agility, the five men around him fall to their haunches too.

Shayna wanders over. She won't confront them and they will pretend she is not here, a compromise they both can live with. For now.

"It's a bitch that they cut down all the trees," the big man says.

They nod. She watches them survey the lack of cover and lookouts with worried brows.

"One flyover and they'd nail all our positions. Our numbers."

Shayna looks up. Ex-military men who understand the way land is defended do not frighten her the way they frighten Helen. When her older sister, Rita, was four, Bertie, her mother, moved them away from the Smoke to live beside Big River, whose rapids swallowed a yearly sacrifice of unskilled canoeists and rafters. Shayna was born there, the daughter of a Warrior named Rick, a thickset man of few words who did his best to treat both girls as his own. But Shayna was so clearly made from the same clay as him, so clearly his. She followed him everywhere. She just assumed she'd be an activist like him; he never gave her reason to think otherwise, for all the times Bertie snorted at the suggestion.

The big man lights up a cigarette. The next man to speak has a scar on his mouth: his upper lip looks like a beheaded worm. "Whaddya think there, Louis? Foxholes? A berm or two?"

Everything is in plain sight. Shayna wishes the developer's backhoes had left at least a hillock. The trick is always to make them believe you have more men, more firepower and technology than you do. When she was ten there was an action at the rapids. Against Bertie's wishes, Rick let Shayna follow him around as he instructed her Mohawk aunts and uncles to leave dummies sitting in their pickups. They ran past the soldiers, put on different jackets, ran past again – the press reported there were twice as many of them. They painted shoeboxes black, mounted them high on posts so they looked like cameras or strapped them to their backs like claymore mines. The women sewed bags in the shape of semi-automatic cases, filled them with sand. At night they unloaded them from the backs of trucks where the soldiers could see. It bought them time. *Those French cops get buck fever,* Rick told her. *They'll shoot at anything that moves. And shooting first is a great weakness, the thing to be avoided.*

"Nah. This place is too flat, too naked. I think we have to switch it up maybe."

The man named Louis once more surveys the land around the barricade. She wonders if it disappoints him that there will be no army for such a territory. Calling in the military didn't work out so well for the politicians last time. And when the cops shot a native protestor at an Ojibwe reserve five years earlier, there was an inquiry. Still, these men would prefer facing down an army than a patchwork of cops.

Shayna remembers her father as she watches Louis. *The military has more discipline. We understand each other; there is even some respect,* Rick had said. *Cops are always confused about who is running the show. The army at least tries to weed out the bigots. The cops promote them.*

But this is so small-time, she thinks, *there isn't going to be much of an adrenaline rush.* And men like them need their highs. That's what Bertie said anyway. She said Rick had a temper, spent her money on drink and drugs, though Shayna never saw the evidence. After a decade with Rick, a decade when Shayna felt watched over, Bertie moved her two daughters back to the Smoke without him. Rita dropped out of school at fourteen, and Shayna swore she would not speak to her mother ever again. For a year she mostly made good on her threat.

Louis sucks on his cigarette, and Shayna notices a faint shake in his wrist that he's trying to ignore. He pats his pockets, fishes out a caramel, sticks it in his mouth, and sucks. Out of the corner of her eye, Shayna sees Cherisse parking Ruby's truck by the small bridge spanning the creek between the reserve and the new development. A new worry. Cherisse shimmies out of the passenger side of the truck and jumps so that she lands like a video-game heroine, raising dust whorls from the dirt. Two bags of takeout food, blotched with grease, are clutched in her hands.

She barrels over the bridge and through the thicket that separates her from the flat acres of baked mud. She is quickly snared in brambles that catch her forearm, dragging thorns along her skin. Shayna watches her niece lick her arm clean like a kitten. Even from the distance the bushes shimmer with the shiny dark eyes of ripened berries.

The summer that cancer felled Bertie, their Aunt Ruby dragged Shayna and Rita to all the reserve's best patches, made them pick until their fingers were the colour of midnight and their arms looked as if they'd been attacked by horny tomcats. A berry for every tear they cried, or couldn't cry. But Cherisse is oblivious to the berries, as she is to the history that sweetens them – makes them bitter too. The food delivery is a chore, some payment to Ruby for all the free snacks Cherisse charms from her. It's obvious, even from a distance, that she wants to get it over with without being seen by townies, or anyone who will assume she's in league with her aunties; otherwise she'd have driven up to the barricade from the highway.

When Cherisse is ten metres away, two of the Warriors stand. The girl straightens from ankles to chin in the heat of their appraisal.

That one has no idea who she is, Shayna thinks.

"Hey, it's Hot Red Riding Hood. You takin' food to Gramma, baby?" They chuckle, a low roll of thunder.

Cherisse has rules for escaping the rez. The cardinal one she's told Shayna more than once: *Don't get involved with native men unless they have swag like Elijah Barton and live somewhere where there's high-speed internet and no boil-water advisories.*

"You better watch out, because we're all Big Bad Wolf clan." More laughter.

"Hey, what's your name? Come and have a beer. What's your name, sweetheart? Don't leave. Don't leave."

Shayna had wanted to ask Louis if he's met Rick, but she realizes he is no older than her. And the only father she's ever known died in a work accident a year after Bertie left him, an event she broke her silence for, if only to assure her mother that she didn't blame her. She walks towards her niece, puts a protective arm around Cherisse, and steers her towards the barricade. The men pull back into their group.

The first time Cherisse ran away, she left Joe Montagne's trailer in daylight and ended up at Shayna's door just before two a.m. She was eleven years old, barefoot, wearing a thin nightie, the big toe of her right foot mashed and blackened with blood, her shins covered in mud. Through the door's thick screen, her bright green eyes atomized like shattered gems.

Where have you been? Shayna said, adjusting her sight to the darkness.

I went for a swim! The girl laughed. Shayna raised a finger to her lips, pointed to the room where Pete-Pete slept curled against her husband, Clarence.

Cherisse pushed the screen door wide, opened the refrigerator, and drank strawberry juice straight from the jug, damp hair ends staining the cotton down her back. For the next two years Cherisse would call Shayna's house her home, yet disappear from it at all hours of the day and night.

Mix of coyote and bobcat that one. Can't do much to contain her, a resigned Joe said when he dropped off a garbage bag of clothes that summer. *Nocturnal as shit, just like her mother. She'll come back when she's hungry.*

Where is her mother? Shayna asked. *Where is Rita?*

Dunno. Joe shrugged his shoulders. *Dunno this time.* And because of the heaviness of his eyes, Shayna didn't press.

When Cherisse slipped away for her night rambles, Shayna couldn't sleep for the imagined dangers of the unlit roads, the forest, the river currents, men stumbling out of the Legion. The social workers who were always around, making notes. But Cherisse always found her way back, even when at sixteen she ran away again. That time she left the reserve entirely, unmooring the demons of bad dreams into Shayna's sleep: Cherry's face and body bloated and bruised, her hair shorn away, those beautiful eyes sinking away from the world. But Cherisse came back, thinner, even more reckless. It was this ability to return – or her inability to stay away for long – that made her different from her mother.

There's a hardness to Cherisse's glance, a twitch of disappointment in the corner of her smile that reminds Shayna of Rita.

Just last week Joe told her that Cherry had quit her correspondence courses again, determined to become a recording artist. *Hey, she got the voice, Shay. She's anytime as pretty as that Crystal Shawanda.* Shayna had rolled her eyes when he wasn't looking.

Cherisse drops the bags of food at Shayna's feet, gives her a cool peck on the cheek. "Yo, Auntie. Food from Ruby."

A group of teenagers race around in the dirt on their tricked-out bikes. A tall, slim boy emerges from the barricade crowd and approaches them on foot. The bikes drop into the dust and the group gathers around the new kid. Shayna watches. When she worries that she will become one of those shrewish older women, perpetually disappointed by the young, this guy – this Nate Bastine – is tonic to her. If only he were a few years older, he'd be perfect for Cherisse. He came out of the detention centre a different boy, one with a straight back, jaw thrust out towards the horizon, and eyes hardened with purpose. That wasn't the usual outcome. *Some kids gotta have a taste of where they don't want to be to know where they do*, Rick told her once.

She clasps her niece's arm, tries to turn her head towards Nate. But it's like clutching a butterfly by its swallowtail. And now the boy is sauntering over to the huddled Warriors.

"Come, let's find a place to sit and eat some of this food. You look thin," Shayna says. Maybe Nate will turn around, wander back towards them. If she could just get the two to talk. Perhaps two years isn't such a big difference.

"No time there, mama. Lots to do tonight. Gotta fly. Just here 'cuz Ruby asked."

Cherisse yanks free from Shayna's grip, gives her a quick squeeze, and turns back the way she came. Shayna watches her niece hurry back across the mud field, kicking up catcalls again from the group of men. She feels the urge to chase after her, to protect her from herself.

"I'm your auntie. I'm your friend," she says aloud. But Cherisse has more understanding than she lets on.

Helen comes up behind her. Shayna can feel the older woman's warmth, the brush of her arm, the glance that follows her own, watching Cherisse's skinny jeans and teetering heels disappear into the berry patch.

"Leave some of the worrying about that one to me," Helen says. Shayna reaches for her hand, leans her head like a child on the older woman's shoulder.

"Truck's in the driveway." Helen turns her niece around, points to Coulson's farmhouse across the highway.

Shayna shakes her head. "I need a shower."

But it's more than that. Shayna aches to see light cut through her own back windows. She wants to open and shut her kitchen cupboards, shake out the pillows on the wicker rocker, walk from room to room, lean against the door jambs with folded arms and imagine a chair she will reupholster, a wall she will paint.

"Go," Helen says with a gentle push. "But don't leave him waiting too long. Never let a fire go out if you expect to be warm another time."

Thirty minutes later Shayna pulls past ditches overgrown with cattails into a hidden gravel drive that leads to a low-slung house, pushing up from the cheek of earth like a winking eye. She opens the door, half expecting trouble – marauding raccoon kits or meal moths. But there is only quiet and dust, reminders of her uneasy contentment with solitude.

She kicks off her shoes, sinks her bare feet in her granny's braided rag rug. Its faded coils release a sharp, old scent. Shayna fills her lungs.

Her mother gave their childhood home to Rita, who let it rot away during her serial abandonments. But the land itself was left for Shayna. She had no need of it until her marriage ended. Suddenly the house she had with Clarence felt too much like his ally: the gleaming modernity of its taps and surfaces, the walls that had witnessed her worst tempers. She moved out. Clarence moved away. And a cousin named Mark, along with his round-bellied wife, backed a packed GMC into the driveway and unloaded their much happier lives into the compact three bedrooms and unfinished basement.

It had rained every day of the four weeks it took Old Man Johnson to build Shayna a new home. She insisted that it rise up across from where the carcass of the original house had been long interred. They used century-old blueprints she'd found in the archives, and reworked them to include bigger windows, entrances at both ends like a longhouse, plus a third opening out to a patio, from the kitchen at the centre of the house. Helen helped scrounge timber from all over the reserve and raised a crew of men paid with Ruby's cooking and twists of her garden tobacco.

She moved in on a crisp May weekend when the rainclouds had wandered west. It was not a perfect structure. The lintels tilted ever so slightly. The front room's slant necessitated cedar wedges under the tables and shelves to keep them plumb. On a humid day she smelled again the rainy month when the house rose up from the earth. Still, it was comfortable, solid as the women of her clan, and like them, it held memory older than its bones.

That very first weekend, Ruby arrived with Lena's rug. How could she refuse?

It's old, Ruby said, handing it over, rolled up in newspaper. *Still, don't get precious about it, Shay. That old woman would have preferred it disintegrating. Long as it was touching the treads of her clan. You gotta step all over this thing. Make your granny smile.*

When Ruby left, Shayna unfolded the rug over the kitchen table. She traced her finger along the tightly braided coil at the centre as it wound outwards, following one strip of printed cotton as it disappeared into the next and imagining the frocks her aunts had worn as youngsters, tired bedsheets, summer pyjamas, Lena's old housedresses, curtains. All their florals and checks faded by sunlight and repeated washings, memorialized into a soft blur of pinks, yellows, blues, and browns. Shayna tested the stitches that held the coils together in a large oval. There was little give. Still, she laid the rug by the kitchen door, where it would be trampled by fewer visitors. She wanted it to last forever.

The next morning she dragged a garage-sale iron table from the back shed and set it under a large yew tree just outside the kitchen. She propped the door open and, with the sun on her shins, she made herself a plate of eggs and toast with jam, her appetite growing apace with the brightness. The food was placed on the iron table and Shayna went back to grab a full pot of freshly brewed coffee and a chair to sit on. Just as she stepped onto the rug at the kitchen door, a large crow swept under the yew, grabbed her toast soaked with runny yolk.

No! Shayna thrust forward, but the foot of the chair grabbed the rug, causing her to tip and release the carafe. It bounced at the threshold and spilled its entire contents on the old rug. The crow alighted with a series of scoffing cries. The best of her breakfast was squished in its beak like a bright yellow grin.

She fell to her knees. The rug had absorbed every drop of the black liquid; its delicate pastels were swollen and brackish. She grabbed a handful of clean dishtowels, pressed them hard into the old coils, one after the other. Despairing, she emptied a can of soda water, and then another, over the oval to lift out more of the offensive colour.

By the time Ruby arrived for a mid-morning cup of tea, the rug was drying in the sun, all of it stained brownish yellow, the colour of nicotine. *Well, Lena did enjoy her smokes*, she said.

But Shayna was contrite. *Should I machine-wash it?*

Not sure it's worth risking that half-century-old hand stitching. Ruby rolled her hand along the rug and chuckled. *You know, your granny was silly for runny eggs on toast.*

Before she left, her auntie added, *I think you should put that rug where everybody's sure to step on it. Lena'd want as much – a little reminder that history's underfoot. That coffee stain? Just another story it has to tell.*

It has lain by the eastern door ever since. It raises up a perfume of burnt sugar and old leather with every foot it encounters, filling her front hall with an odour people don't forget. There are other smells that greet Shayna as she wanders through her rooms – thyme and sage drying in the kitchen, maple ash gone cold in the woodstove, summer pollens drifting in the unscreened bedroom – but that rug is the smell of home.

She flops on her bed and is overcome with lethargy, the seductive pull of the familiar. The rest of the evening could sort itself around a cup of tea, a book, the eleven-o'clock news, and the quiet breezes. She wants to build a warming fire in the outdoor pit – the night is cool enough – wrap herself up in a blanket, plug in her headphones to late-night radio, and lie in the hammock strung between the yew and the spruce. But Helen's words come back to her and Shayna shivers. Always another fire needs tending. She sighs, gets up and showers.

An hour later she parks again at the barricade and crosses the highway on foot. Once she enters Coulson's fields she finds herself rushing. The tobacco plants slap at her playfully. She sees his kitchen porch light on, and the idea of its vigil, its constancy, reassures her. She has missed him.

And then he is there, a dark silhouette coming out of the kitchen, the aluminum door slamming shut behind him. He lights a cigarette and its ember moves like a distracted firefly from his hip to his mouth and back again. Shayna hurries. She wants a taste of that cigarette still damp from his lips. He takes two extra-long drags, drops it, and crushes it under his boot. She is about to emerge from the plants, to call out, when he turns. She expects him to go back inside.

Instead Coulson makes a diagonal away from her. In five big strides he is in his truck and the engine growls into the cool night. Where is he going? She changes her direction too, makes a hard left through the tobacco to his gravel lane. Now she is running, roughly shoving away the leaves; a few snap brightly, dismembered from their tender stalks. She launches onto the gravel, straightening herself with her arms up, landing in the crossfire of his truck headlights. The truck tires skid and then the vehicle is still, its engine idling.

Shayna stands like scared game, dazzled by the high beams' brightness, wondering why the rules of engagement are so unclear with this man. He nearly begged her to come to him a week ago; now he doesn't get out of the truck. Shayna shakes her head, walks alongside the Ford, and opens its passenger door, blinking to adjust her sight.

"That's a dangerous way to get a guy's attention," he says. She feels a slipstream of coolness chasing his usual friendliness.

"Where are you headed?"

"Beer's all gone and I'm thirsty. Thought I'd have a few at the pub in town."

There is a moment of quiet between them. Shayna climbs into the truck. She feels out of breath and a bit foolish. But she's resolute; she's forfeited the quiet of her home, even blow-dried her hair for him. The scent of crushed peonies is dabbed on her wrists and temples.

"I could use a cold beer," she says, and she slams the passenger door shut as if that decides the matter. His eyes are on her in the dark. She wants him to reach out and touch her. But he puts the truck in gear and they drive onto an emptied highway, an indigo-drenched night. Fresh air from the open window fattens Shayna's lungs. The horizon simplifies into dark saturations: earth, trees, sky. She smells the berms, sprung with wildflowers, and the spruce, their great, sap-thickened throats respiring heavily into the dark. She is so happy – to be moving; to be away from the barricade; to be doing something other than chairing meetings and talking and worrying about Porta-Potties and bottled water, high-heeled nieces and men with cloudy intentions; to be sitting next to this man with his palpable desire; to entertain the inevitability of sex – that it doesn't really register, until the truck slows and pulls into a parking lot, that they haven't said a word to each other during the twenty-minute drive.

She uncurls herself in the seat a bit drowsily, stretches her arms, and looks through the truck's front window to see that they have come to the back of the pub, its alleyway entrance. When she reaches for her door handle, Coulson's palm is on her left shoulder, pressing gently. "We can't go in there," he says.

She looks at him blankly. Already humiliation, like an ill-behaved child, is taunting her. "I don't understand."

Coulson turns in his seat, grabs her hands. She lets them go limp.

"Shayna, your picture was on the cover of the local paper. Burning an injunction, a legal document, part of a process that most of the folks in that pub right now believe in. And they're two or three hours into their cups already. How is that going to be comfortable for you? For us?"

Shayna takes a deep breath and swallows a mix of comprehension and disappointment. "So, comfortable is something we care about?" She smiles to make it easy for him, for all the toughness he projects.

He drops his head in thought. "I have an idea." He holds up a finger, jumps out of the truck, and runs into the pub, emerging a few minutes later clutching two bottles of beer in each hand and wearing a big smile. "Barmaid's a friend of mine," he says with a wink, handing her the beers to cradle.

They drive to the river, slump back into their seats, and drink in silence. The beer tastes cold and delicious and she feels unburdened, not of desire for him but of something more confining: the hope, the expectation that he'd be a better, bigger person than she is.

Back at the farmhouse she bites his shoulder, yanks at his clothes. She can tell he's surprised, aroused by the sting of her fingernails in his flanks, her push and pull, not understanding how it will end: with her slipping out into his fields when she has exhausted him, letting him wake alone, braided in sheets, with no one to claim, while she sleeps alone in her own space under the shadows of yew and spruce. With her going back to the barricade, washed with dawn, her head held high, her face sheepish and thankful as a returning runaway's.

CHAPTER 6

Peg Redhill's own mother had demons – long afternoons spent alone in a room with the shades drawn, warm chamomile and rosemary compresses over her eyes, her body shaking with an epilepsy of sobs. Yet every morning the woman had breakfast ready, the radio turned to a morning show, a pot of coffee brewed for her husband. Peg remembers this, remembers how her mother said, *Always get up. You can't know if it's going to be a good one or a bad one, but the odds are better that it will be a good one if you're out of bed.*

Still, Peg can't pull herself from under her comforter. She knows that out there in a bright puddle of daylight wait two newspapers, a local and a national, both referring to her as "Doreville's controversial mayor." There are land disputes all over the country. Ho-hum. But she'd opened her big mouth, said something that in private company wouldn't rate a snort but in public was considered scandalous and newsworthy.

At five-forty-five a.m. Reid Wellings rang with a tipoff. An emergency meeting has been called for this afternoon; there is a motion to sanction Peg, prohibit her from speaking to the press for the duration of the protest. Reid assured her someone will vote against the motion, but Peg knows it will be like throwing a pebble at a bulldozer. The council is populated by the wholly spineless and the mealy-mouthed. She'll leave the papers unread.

But now, damn it, her eyes are open and she can't go back to sleep. Not like this, with her flesh sponging up dread like an ugly spill. She doesn't have the energy to guess which ferret-like councillor brought forth the motion against her. But there isn't one among the half-dozen on whom she can count for fealty or a principled defence.

She rolls over, pulls open the drawer of her nightstand, and scoots her hand through its contents, hoping for the thin plastic oblivion of a pill bottle. Her mobile whirrs on the table like a sparrow in a birdbath, and by habit it's in her hand before she's thinking clearly.

"Peg Redhill?"

The voice is young.

"Mm-hmm."

"My name is Trudy LaVette and I'm a producer with CJYT's *Big Bob's Tell It Like It Is Hour*. We're national. And well, Big Bob himself loved your comments in the papers and wants you on a call-in segment. We're calling it 'Why don't natives have to obey the law?' His show starts at two p.m. We'd call you about one-fifty p.m. and the segment would run from five after until the news break at the half-hour. Are you available?"

Peg looks at her clock. It isn't yet seven a.m. Her first reaction is that it's a joke, and she can't afford another misstep with the media. She affects a considered tone. "I have a very busy day today, Miss, uh . . . Perhaps you'd prefer to speak to one of the other councillors or the federal spokesperson who's handling the barricade communications."

"No, no, Big Bob has asked for you specifically, Mayor Redhill. Over the past few weeks dozens of callers have left your name on the Who's Telling It Like It Is Today Hotline. That's how we pick our guests."

"Big Bob asked for me?"

With the phone pressed to her ear, Peg pulls herself up in bed until she can see reflected in the dresser mirror her own furry head, its skin a grid of bedsheet creases and wrinkles. A post-menopausal Muppet. *Now there's a woman who looks like she tells it like it is.*

"Okay," she says, realizing that her council will be voting to sanction her while she's doing a radio interview. "Why not? You can reach me at this number."

And with that she swings her feet to the floor, takes a deep, solidifying breath, searches for a missing slipper, hobbles to the bathroom, and splashes water on her face. It would be nice to have a close friend to call up, to commiserate about her misstep at the press conference and ask, *Whaddya think?* about the radio show. Ella Bain, for instance, who has a genius for understanding what looks good to others.

They were friends once, she and Ella. Shared bottles of wine and recipes for low-fat brownies and summer salads. They had long conversations, sometimes on the phone with sobbing (Peg's) or over coffee in one of their kitchens (Ella's, most often). They'd meet in the park behind the United Church, both of them chasing after young boys who walked early, those first steps morphing instantly into running, climbing, and throwing rocks, toys, their bodies at the world and each other. Ella, pale and pretty and already pregnant with Stephanie, never seemed to break a sweat. Peg had smarted at their differences – her new friend's fine bones, orderly modern home, enterprising husband. Peg felt she was all flesh, disorganized, suddenly conscious of the abandoned cars on their property outside of town. Brad was still around then, hollering at her late into the night.

Husbands. The dull anguish of marriage. Little boys who couldn't distinguish *d* from *b*. The cost of leaking roofs, and the neighbour's hot-tub shenanigans. They talked about everything. But mostly, really, she talked while Ella had nodded like a social worker, sometimes using lines such as *How did that make you feel?* – which made Peg suspect, if only for a fleeting second, that Ella's sincerity was an act.

It was success that spoiled things between them. Brad died, and instead of crumpling, Peg blossomed. She found herself a businesswoman and then a city councillor. There was less to cry about to her friend and more to laugh at. But even though Peg's calendar was busting with new responsibilities, it was Ella who became impossible to pin down for lunch or a cup of coffee. Too busy with Las's swim meets. Renovating the kitchen. Big tobacco diversification project. By the time Peg was first elected mayor, her friend's retreat was complete. Ella would wave to her in passing, then, a few years later, barely wave at all.

∽

By seven-fifteen a.m., Las is underwater. All the voices in his head – his mother's, the new coach's, the old coach's, people cheering from the stands. *Don't let yourself get out of shape over the summer.* He'd thought the scholarship would eat up pressures, make him feel free. Instead the university swim team sent a program of recommended summer workouts: swimming, running, weightlifting, stretching, more swimming. There is a website to track personal bests.

He prefers the outdoor community pool to the Olympic-sized indoor one. There, at least, he knows it's summer. His mother had tsk-tsked. *You can't work on your times if you're not using a regulation-sized pool,* she said as he brushed by her in the kitchen. Even in the early morning there is no shade on the pool's surface. The reflected light makes his eyes squint. The water is tepid, sliding off him like oil. His arms windmill, his legs kick, and he can't get far enough fast enough. The drills are memorized, but on each lap he argues with himself about the math. This pool is fifteen metres shy of Olympic length. It is easier to calculate in his head if he rounds the difference down to ten.

Water is supposed to be the place where he can't be reached. The way his body slides is a kind of flying, getting him above and beyond the things he can't say aloud: how he has no hunger for any of the things his parents, his teachers, the other kids at school expect – a good job in a big city, car, condo, girlfriend, investment portfolio. The wetness tricks his body, cools him as he works, distances him from his own exertion, allows him to go farther than he should. Submerging his head in the pool's bell-jar protection, its muffled noises, its Bimini blue, its softened light, he can outpace them all.

But something has shifted. His rhythm is off, and when his head dips below the surface, all the noises are still there, his new worries slipping under the water's surface with him, edging past, reaching the wall before him. He isn't halfway through the drills when he stops adding in the extra laps to compensate for the shorter pool. *Just today,* he tells himself. *Tomorrow I will start doing the entire thing.* When he pulls himself from the water at eight a.m., slinks into the dressing room, he's already a cheat, wringing concessions from the next day's workout.

His hair still wet, Las arrives at the back of the Redhill house from the alley, locks his bike, presses his nose against the basement window, and taps lightly. "What the fuck, Gordo. Wake up, man."

During the last week of classes the humidity crawled inside the school walls and everything clung – shirts to skin, girls to boys, girls to girls, all of them to the chairs, the walls they've spent the past four years despising. And the chatter about grad dates, summer jobs, moving into residence, and buying shelves from IKEA elongated horribly into student loans, career tracks, making real money. It made Las itchy. He couldn't pretend he was happy or excited about anything other than getting away from his parents. And now he wants only to get fucked up.

Las straightens and walks around the house to the carport Gordo built himself to keep the bird shit off his truck. *Think my ma the mayor could swing a place in the burbs with a garage? No, we gotta live in a gingerbread house with nowhere to fuckin' protect my ride.* But the carport is empty. Two bundled newspapers lie on the step, from a throw that fell shy of the porch. Las picks them up to slip inside the screen door. NATIVES DEFIANT: MAYOR FACES SANCTION reads one headline through its plastic wrapper. His thumb presses down, creases the page. *Defiant* was a word for fast cars, marines, raunchy rock.

Where the fuck is Gordo?

There weren't many places to hide out in this town. Las hoofs it from the Redhills' to Doreville's small civic square, at the end of its downtown strip. The early heat is like steel wool against his lungs. He dips into the alleys, works the rears of buildings until he comes to the back lot of the library. Sure enough, he spots his friend's distinctive red truck with its gleaming chrome grill and the oversized tires with custom rims that seem goofy to Las, though he'd never say as much. Metres away, Gordo leans against the yellow Tyndall-stone building, smoking a joint to its nub. Las watches him for a moment, the picture of a small-town loser, before walking into the deserted parking lot.

"Where you been, shithead?"

Gordo grins, takes a last, long drag of his butt until it is just an ember between the hard skin of his thumb and forefinger. He puts it out with his tongue. "Here and there. You?"

"Looking for you."

"No shit."

Gordo slides down the wall into a squat and Las joins him.

"Oh man, my head feels like it's going to explode. My mom's on my case constantly. Everyday there's another email from the university. Register for this, pay for that. I can't get a—"

"I'm not your therapist, faggot."

Once, while they were sitting together drinking beers at the Legion, Gordo hit Las hard, right on the temple, knocked him out for no reason at all. Las missed a major swim meet while in the hospital waiting for test results to rule out a concussion. The lie he told never fully satisfied his mother, who thereafter stepped up her campaign for him to find better friends.

"What you got going on today, Gordo?"

"I'm doing it, dumb-ass. Shouldn't you be in training, varsity-arse?"

"Done for the day."

Las grabs a stick and starts skewering ants with it. He can't imagine ever hitting Gordo first or even returning a punch. One counterstrike from him would be just the invitation his friend needed to go apeshit. And Gordo was a guy just one push away from apeshit. *That boy has no impulse control,* his mother said once. *He'll go too far one day.* And Las remembers thinking she'd finally got something right.

Gordo saunters back to his truck. Las takes a deep breath, tries to stop the spinning in his head. He should leave. He should tell Gordo to go fuck himself. But, as always, there is some place his friend can take him that he can't get to on his own.

∽

Cherisse is pacing in the woods behind the smoke shack with her earbuds in. For the tenth time she focuses on the way Susie

Stonechild's voice breaks, lingering on the phrase "her pain that no one knows" before her voice sails upward, floats into the refrain, "gravel dust 'tween painted toes." It's the cracked quality, the slight imperfection in Stonechild's delivery that's the heart of the song. Cherisse turns down the volume, replays it, and hears herself match the singer's voice right up to "knows." But what follows is not the same, nowhere near. She has the note right but not the ability to breach the note, to deliver its heartbreaking hitch. The song ends one more time and she punches the air in frustration.

She pulls out her earbuds and hears the door of the trailer slam shut. Joe Montagne shuffles from the trailer to the smoke shack, holding his aching jaw where there's a molar he's not dealing with, scratching his stubble with the other hand, and he doesn't see her. "Cherisse. Cherisse, where are you? I can't find the cash box."

Cherisse pops in her earbuds and listens to the song again. She could get away with singing the note straight, but then what good would that be? All it would mean is that Susie Stonechild is an artist and she is a weak imitation, a pageant singer. Her father's head bobs up like a prairie dog in front of her. The toothache must be getting to him; there are bluish pouches under his eyes, his lower lip droops. She'll have to get a cup of coffee, a few Aspirins into him if he's going to make it through the day.

"Cherisse, you drop-ass princess, get over here. It's past nine. Where'd you stow the cash box? Day's a wasting." He turns and shuffles over to the smoke shack. She hears him discover the cash box, locked, on the third shelf. His head pops out. "Stupid, stupid! Cherisse, if Bobby Horse was sniffing around, he'd have this nicked for sure. Damn shack door is so flimsy."

"Yeah, yeah." She didn't lock up properly the night before. She never does. All the cigarettes – cartons and boxes of them – are still neatly stacked on the shack's counters. It's a pain dragging them back and forth to the trailer.

"For fuck's sake, nobody wants to buy damp smokes. They have to overnight in the trailer, Cherry."

Joe comes out of the shack carrying the cash box, plunks it on the picnic table outside.

Cherisse laughs. "Even you can't smoke that throat-scalding shit. Aren't those du Mauriers tucked in your back pocket?"

Cherisse makes to reach for them. Her father slaps her hand away. He opens the tin box stuffed with yesterday's so-so sales, curses her again for leaving it in the shack all night, then counts the money, compares it to the piece of paper with his inventory list and does the math – twice. Cherisse considers simply telling him outright that she helped herself to a little something, but she hates to waste the possibility that he won't figure it out.

His eyes narrow, his lips curl. "Thieving sow!"

She hoots. He taps his foot, lights up a smoke, appears to direct all his energy into sucking it ferociously. Already trucks are chewing up the highway; as they whiz by, she knows he is suffering a tremor of panic because she's not waiting for them behind the smoke-shack counter, her long hair brushed out against her bare shoulders, a breakfast cigarette curling smoke between her shower-wet lips, her green eyes flashing, her bright teeth catching customers' glances. She brings in business. She knows it. He knows it.

"Jesus Christ, Cherisse, you're robbing me blind. What for this time?"

Cherisse smiles, leans down, and pulls up her pant leg, revealing a knee-high patent leather boot with a gold-tipped stiletto heel. "Makes me look like a rock star, huh?"

"How much?"

"You don't want to know."

She throws her head back with a taunting laugh, and then he's yelling at her as if he's stepped on a rusty nail. Cherisse slips inside the smoke shack and starts singing the Susie Stonechild line over and over again as she sets up for a day of charming money out of strangers.

"You're bolder 'n shit," Joe Montagne says, following her. "Like a pine marten. But scrawnier."

"But with a pretty voice, nah?"

Say it, she wills him. *Tell me I can turn a green peach gold with my voice. Tickle the dollars out of an old man's fist. Get the fuck out of Dodge on the strength of my talent.*

"Your voice is a beauty, Cherry."

She laughs, fills a jug with water – "I'll make you coffee, Grumpy" – and she sees him smile despite the ache in his jaw.

∽

Gordo pulls his truck alongside a ditch near a massive pin oak at the edge of Stercyx's tobacco fields. He jumps out, reaches into the back for a grimy cooler, nods at Las to take a handle, and they climb down the small earth slope, carrying the beer-filled box to a spot that's within spying distance of the barricade. That's the plan so far: watch the natives, get shit-faced and even more pissed off.

"Here."

They plant the cooler. Gordo lifts its lid, pulls out two beers, throws one at Las, then worms up the slope on his belly and digs his elbows into the dirt. "Can see the fuckers perfectly from here."

Las steals a moment to press the coolness of the can into his forehead. Lately he feels anger in new places: the back of his head, crammed under his scapulas, tightening his hip flexors, his jaw. It's a cramping, lactic acid kind of anger, numbing and queerly alive. He imagines kicking the neighbour's yappy Westie, pissing all over the banded cigars in the bottom drawer of his father's desk, jumping that wannabe white boy Phil LaForme and hearing the satisfying crack of a nose, a wrist. He closes his eyes and guzzles the beer quickly for its analgesic effects.

The second and third, the same. It's just past noon. The beer runs through him and he is up, fumbling among the young tobacco plants for a place to take a piss. He's working a nice buzz, his neck already browned in the sun, his mouth clammy with alcohol.

Down at the end of the row of plants he sees a figure, bending and rising, stretching out a length of arm, drawing it back in sharply. Las steadies himself, focuses, and realizes he is looking at the back of Coulson Stercyx, planing a rectangle of wood steadied on two sawhorses.

His mother calls Stercyx a cautionary tale: someone who had promise once because he went to university, left Doreville at eighteen, landed a big city job and a classy wife, and vowed never to come back. *Drove a sports car,* his mother would say. *Wore beautiful suits. All on a swimming scholarship,* she'd add and arch her eyebrows. *Could have made a fortune if he sold that land. Now he's stuck here. Wife left him, and he's growing tobacco. What a waste. Can you imagine?*

She always repeated that last question with high-pitched disbelief, as if Las couldn't be counted on to judge the man harshly enough. And even through the haze of beer and from a distance, he sees she was right – he won't judge him. Stercyx is all muscle and sinew, lean as a mule. What he notices now is how the man moves around the wood. Las wonders what it would feel like to build something. He imagines being Stercyx, standing on his front stoop at the end of a workday, surveying the measurable impact that his hands, his sweat have made on his environment.

Las holds his own strong arms out in front of him. After he finishes a swim practice or a race, he can only stare at the blank, unblinking pool, its water calm and unchanged by him. *What is the point?* he wonders. *What the fuck is the point?* His father is a wet-eyed man who spends his life making phone calls, faxing contracts, scribbling numbers on the margins of newspapers while his body turns flaccid, his breath sour. Other men feel the give of wood under their saws, their hammers. Other men build. Las looks at his palms. He wants to be Stercyx. He wants to work with wood in the high heat of the day. He wants to be a person who makes things, not the one who hires him and runs away at the first whiff of trouble.

He returns to the ditch, flops down beside his friend, stares at the barricade. He finishes another beer and then the sun flattens him like roadkill. An hour later, Gordo's rough palms chafe against his sun-beaten skin.

"Wake up, asshole! I'm outta smokes."

∽

Cherisse fools with the radio's dial. It has been a slow day, so slow Joe hightailed it after lunch. It's a bit of a waste too that she feels better about herself than usual, her hair shiny and full, her face rested, and her new boots paired with her skinniest jeans. When she feels pretty like this, her regulars almost never ask for change back from a twenty. She twists the dial for music and catches a familiar word from a faint signal.

"Welcome back to CJYT and *Big Bob's Tell It Like It Is Hour.* We've got a switchboard full of callers wanting to congratulate Dotville mayor Peg Redhill for telling it like it is when some natives put a barricade in front of a new development."

"Doreville."

"Uh, sorry, Mayor Redhill?"

"Doreville. The name of my town is Doreville."

Cherisse turns up the volume. All these strangers who clearly don't live in Doreville want to speak to the mayor. She claps her hands together. Dowdy Peg Redhill, a woman who wears pocketless jeans with elasticized waistbands, is getting attention from a big city radio station for saying some dumb-ass things. Surely that means anything is possible – and many more things are possible for a green-eyed beauty who sings like a cross between Emmylou Harris and Shania Twain.

"You rock," one caller salutes the mayor. The next practically begs, "Please run for mayor in our town." Cherisse smiles at the mayor's embarrassed thank-yous, her exaggerated folksy twang. So when an angry-sounding man tells the mayor, "It's time natives face up to the fact they gotta live under our rules," Cherisse fist-pumps the air and says, "Holla!" to no one in particular. She isn't about to piss off the white folk – farmers, cottagers, Doreville locals – whose dollars financed her first guitar, the distressed leather jacket, the sexy boots, and soon her first professional demo CD.

Before the show ends, a sleek buff-coloured sports coupe pulls up to the smoke shack. Cherisse feels her shoulders stiffen and she turns off the radio. Elijah Barton steps out of his car, opens the shack door with an authoritative shove, and barely looks at Cherisse. He comes only if her father is not there – the rusted truck an easy tell – and he doesn't say much at all before buying a carton of Warrior cigarettes. Usually she says nothing much back. Maybe it's the mayor being on the radio, maybe it's her growing confidence about her voice, but today she feels bold.

"Don't you have a factory full of these smokes five minutes from here?" she asks.

Elijah's head snaps up in surprise, as if she's broken an unspoken rule. They both know he's not here for the smokes. "I like the way you display them," he says.

"You mean stacked up and shoved against the wall." She snorts. "Yeah, I'm a genius with that."

He looks at her for a moment, and she doesn't like the way he searches her eyes. It's as if he's looking for something that belongs to him, as if one of the diamonds from his watch has popped out and landed in them.

"Those ones over there in the plastic bags are cheaper." Cherisse points to the Super Sack of rollies. She has nothing to lose.

"The quality is better in these, thanks." He holds up his factory-made cigarettes. Then he pays, as he always does, with two twenties; after she gives him change, he leaves another twenty on the counter before walking away. The first time he did this she followed him out, holding the money towards him. He shook his head. And she saw that he was a man who got his way, that refusing the tip would be uncomfortable for both of them.

Now every twenty of his he keeps only adds to her urgency. *One day*, Cherisse thinks as she watches the sports coupe drive off, *I will do better than this guy who leaves money as if he owes me.*

When Elijah's car is a fading moan, Cherisse turns the radio dial again in search of music. She finds a Top Forty station, pulls out her compact, wets her lips, and steps out of the shack to practise her choreography. Susie Stonechild may be a great artist, but too few people hear her music. Cherisse won't make the mistake of getting stuck in the aboriginal artist rut, consigned to rotation on specialty stations with small audiences, playing healing centres and bingo halls. Nope, you have to have the whole package in today's market. And so she will do it all – sing, play an instrument, write her own music, dance, and look super-effin'-hot. That's how you bust out of the reserve, the small town, your own skin.

A red truck with flashy custom work approaches. Cherisse is in mid-swivel, her arms folding in and out from her chest. She stops, her hair lands on her shoulders and slides down her back, and she turns her face towards the vehicle with its specialty grille and fender vents. *Uh-huh*, she thinks, sizing up the two passengers. Grade-eight faces pasted on men's bodies. One ugly and one cute. Ugly is familiar; he's been here before. But Cute is new, and she likes the look of him. Surfer-blond hair, lips stretched over perfect teeth. A baby with a bruiser's bulk.

Ugly jumps out of the truck, holding a beer. "Hey, Pocahontas. How's it be?"

"The name's Cherisse," she says, then laughs too wildly, hearing her name sound as tart as the best kind of trouble. "I wouldn't mind a beer, if you've got extra."

"Las, get this fine young lady a beer, will ya."

Cute throws a beer to Ugly and opens one for himself.

"So, what's your clan, princess?" Ugly asks. "Are you Wild Potatoes, baby? Pigeon Hawk? Opposite Side of the Hand? Painted Turtle?"

Oh, this one is an asshole, Cherisse thinks. He holds out the beer and lets her tug so that her hand slips, touches his, before the can is released.

"Those aren't Mohawk clans." Cherisse steps back inside the shack, moves quickly behind her counter. "You buying smokes?"

"Get over here, Las. We got a real businesswoman on our hands."

∽

Las shuffles over, dizzy now from heat, lack of food, dehydration. His head thrums as they climb the steps into the smoke shack. He has never been here before. He's made a practice of avoiding the reserve, and coming now feels reckless. Still, up close this girl is startling: long legs in skinny jeans and high boots, pretty hips, and onyx hair that swings out like a gleaming thrill ride when she tosses her head. A face that's high-boned and brown, with eyes shining like bright jade. He's never seen such an oddly beautiful native girl before.

Gordo buys a plastic bag of fifty cigarettes, stows them in the truck, and returns with three more beers.

"Hey, princess," he says. "You're not going to keep those sexy boots stuck out here in Nowheresville on a fine summer afternoon, are ya?"

He slides a beer across the counter towards the girl. Las pops open the one shoved towards him. His friend knocks the lip of his can against it with a nod of his head and an exaggerated wink. "*Salut!*"

The girl takes a thirsty pull. Las studies her raised chin, the way she arches her elegant neck towards the sun. His fist tightens around his beer can and he crushes it.

Gordo lifts his arm for another toast. "Here's to pain and pleasure in equal measure."

Las wishes he were back in bed, able to redo this day from the start. He bends over and tries to get more oxygen into his lungs, his blood, his brain. He'll be leaving in a few months. And what will happen when Las comes home to visit? Surely he and Gordo will be embarrassed to be seen with each other, Gordo with his small-town loser's puffiness and Las all prepped out and lean from a season of meets. He can imagine the awkward half nod from across the street and the comment Gordo will sneer under his breath. He'll have a new friend by then, perhaps another high school senior with a promising athletic career who'll be a magnet for the girls Gordo can't quite seem to attract, despite his bad-boy status.

"Can't do it," Las says.

"Can't do what?"

"Whatever we're doing here."

"Are you shitting me?" Gordo hisses and windmills his arms, but Las dodges.

Sensing the change in mood, the girl tosses her beer can into a pail and hooks her fingers into the waistband of her jeans. Las notices where the fabric of her shirt has lifted, revealing a slender brown hip bone. "Yeah, you two better shove. I've got things to do," she says.

"A fuckin' waste. I fucking wasted my day, my beer with you, man," Gordo says. "You're walking home, asshole."

There it is, thinks Las. He feels a worrying flame of hate inside of him. It's burning up his biceps, fists, groin, shins. Las turns around, quits the shack. It will take him at least an hour to get back to the suburbs and he'll have to cut through Stercyx's farm in order to avoid the barricaded development. The whole day feels like an insult now. He doesn't wait to see if Gordo leaves.

Las crosses the road and marches down Ninth Line in his flip-flops. A minute later the hard consonants of the girl's anger cut through the late-afternoon heat. He hears Gordo's truck tear out of the smoke shack's gravel drive. Las thinks his friend will surely pick him up after all.

The engine slows and then it's beside him, Gordo leaning towards the open passenger window and leering in that way of his that doubles for an apology. Las pivots. He is reaching for the passenger-door handle when a gob of spit lands on his cheek. The truck's tires churn and it screeches away, trailing the sound of Gordo's taunting glee. Las shakes the dust from his eyes. The globule of phlegm crawls towards his jaw and he brushes it off with his knuckles, then wipes them on his shorts. He looks back and sees the girl from the smoke shack standing at the side of the road, watching. From this distance she seems small and breakable. He can't remember her name.

CHAPTER 9

A moat of electric blue surrounds the barricade's single Porta-Potty. There's an odour of sewage tented over it, heating up in the sun. Shayna listens to the rings at the rental company that won't answer her. They've taken her cash deposit and dropped off the toilet, but now she can't make them do the promised maintenance. The rings switch to voicemail and Shayna clicks off, dials again. She wants to speak to a human.

A teenaged boy rides his bike through the blue water, splashing the grey sides of the plastic structure, flecking it with soiled tissue and a shaming yellow-blue stain. Prepubescent bystanders cheer. Another contender mounts his bike to do the same. With her phone still pressed to her ear, Shayna marches over to them, one arm waving for them to stop. The next boy pedals wildly, a peacock tail of effluent churning behind him. She recoils to avoid the spray. The kids shriek in delight.

Shayna pulls the phone away from her ear and starts yelling.

"Stop it! Right now! You're making a mess!" She pushes the watching kids back from the growing mess and grabs in the air for the cyclist.

There's a faint "Hello, hello" coming from the cellphone clutched in her hand. Shayna slaps the phone back against her ear, holding a small boy's collar in her free hand, his bicycle balancing against her hip. "Yes, hello. Are you still there?"

There is just dial tone. She screeches in frustration, lets go of her young captive. He tears away, turns so she can see him laughing at her. She has stepped into the moat up to her ankle. "Fuckin' hell!" she yells at the top of her lungs, and this delights the little gang of spectators even more. Disgusted, she winds up and pitches the cellphone, watches it skid into the dust by Helen's approaching feet. The older woman bends to pick it up.

Shayna can't look Helen in the eye as she offers an arm, pulls Shayna from the moat, gets her to shake her foot free of clinging detritus. *You and Rita are three mamas worth of work,* her aunt had said the one time Shayna asked why she and Ruby weren't married, didn't have kids of their own. *Bertie needs all the help she can get.*

"I'm getting Jim Maracle to drop a load of fill on this mess. He'll empty and move the washroom this afternoon," Helen says.

"But we've paid the company for that service. They're ripping us off."

"Well, their service's a load of crap." Helen grins.

"We shouldn't just take it."

"At least this way it gets done," Helen says. "That's better, isn't it?"

Shayna's jaw tightens. The year her mother moved them back to the Smoke, an upstream chemical company spilled malathion into the river. Dead fish floated on the water's surface for weeks. And within a month, all the well water coming into the Eighth Line homes lining the Smoke's banks began to smell of charred toast and pine-scented disinfectant. The company issued a statement claiming the spill was insignificant, that "remediation had been swift and effective, but as a temporary precautionary principle, homeowners may want bring in their drinking water." Bertie read aloud the statement in the paper and soon after began buying gallons of bottled water for her daughters to drink, continuing to make her tea from the well water right up until she got sick. Everybody just carried on, just accepted the river's befouling, the poisoning of their own aquifer, as if the water on that part of the reserve had always been undrinkable. The temporary situation became permanent. *One good thing,* Bertie said again and again with a light chuckle, *there's a lot fewer skeeters around, haven't you noticed?* But Shayna knew what was missing; she remembered scooping handfuls of well water into her mouth on a hot summer afternoon, its lightly mineral taste cooler and sweeter than any she'd drink again.

Helen leads Shayna to a large plastic cistern, tips it so she can rinse her foot, grab a drink. "Joe Montagne's around. Jumpy as a terrier. Says the council chief wants to have a chat with you."

"The chief?" Shayna raises an eyebrow. "What's that about?"

"Don't know. Can't hurt to check it out. It's quiet here."

"Yeah, but it's tense," says Shayna. "Don't you feel it? As if everyone's waiting for something to happen, someone to make a move. And those Warriors – here all day and then gone. Someone's putting them up at night. But who? Where?"

Helen shrugs. "Well, my guess is there'll be nothing much happening in the next few hours. Might as well find out what the chief is after. Strikes me as the smart thing to do. Though you might consider fresh socks first."

"Smart," Shayna repeats. "Smart is good."

Helen and Ruby were visiting Big River the summer Bertie announced she was sending Rita to a Catholic school that fall, in the small French suburb outside the Seaway reserve. The aunties howled. Shayna'd never heard either raise her voice. An argument raged into the night, the indignant slap of their palms making the china tea caddy on the kitchen table jingle like wind chimes.

At one point Bertie stood up, her face slick with tears, her cheeks splotchy. She reached into her ample cleavage, pulled up a silver crucifix, and kissed it. *I've always believed. I've always been a good Catholic. I married a Catholic.* She pointed to Rick's chair, the one he'd vacated when the yelling first began. *And I will have my girls raised in the faith and get a decent education.*

If Lena were alive it would kill her, Ruby said quietly.

Shayna, tucked inconspicuously into the space between the ash pail and the woodstove, worried that her mother was risking unsettling a sleeping ancestor, bringing bad luck upon all of them.

A month after her eleventh birthday, Rita left for Sainte-Thérèse-de-Lisieux's Holy Martyrs Catholic Elementary School in the suburb of Île d'Or, wearing a crisp white shirt and a blue and yellow plaid kilt, her hair pinned back with plastic barrettes, pink as cupcake icing. *You look beautiful,* Shayna whispered to her. *You'll be the prettiest girl there.* Secretly she was jealous that Rita was being sent to the white kids' school, a place that required such an important-looking get-up, while she'd be stuck in the funky-smelling portable on the reserve in hand-me-down jeans and sneakers. Rita left the house singing that first day, and Shayna watched her as if she were a luna moth or a gazelle – some creature that was beautiful and unknowable and didn't belong to the same world she did. The feeling persisted even when Rita returned from school sullen. Her sullenness grew over the next months, the way the great river flooded, sweeping away what was pretty and familiar.

One day Shayna waited for the bus to drop off her sister at the edge of the reserve. Rita tripped off the last steps. As the bus pulled away, gap-toothed boys and pigtailed girls threw apple cores and balled-up chip bags from open windows, their mouths stretched grotesquely around words Shayna didn't understand. *Maudits sauvages! Maudits sauvages!*

Rita grabbed Shayna to shield her and they sprang into the ditch.

What happened? What are they yelling? Why are they throwing things?

Rita straightened. Her eyes were wet with shame. *They think I'm a stupid savage.*

Why Rita? Why? Shayna asked again and again. But her sister didn't answer. Rita's face became grey and hard as she hustled home.

It confused Shayna. Her older sister spoke three different languages – French, English, the Mohawk Helen had taught them. There wasn't a birdsong she couldn't mimic. She had a genius for scouting out foxholes, warm with squirming pups in spring, and nests of baby snakes. Second only to Rick, Rita was the smartest person Shayna knew.

That night she crept closer when Rita declared to Bertie, *I won't go back.*

You have to go back. I paid for that uniform.

Rita pulled out a Hilroy notebook, folded to a page where there was a great big X in red ink in the margin. *We're studying saints. I wrote in my daily reflection that Saint Francis was a Mohawk.* She pointed to the Île d'Or Holy Sepulchre Catholic Church calendar picture of the rope-waisted friar tacked to the kitchen wall. *Mom, you told me he must be Mohawk. You said it again and again. "Saint Francis is just like us. He calls the sun his brother, the water his sister. He makes a sermon to the birds. Mohawks are the true Catholics!" How many times have you said that? So I wrote that in my reflection. The teacher, she grabbed me. She dragged me to the front of the class and made me read it aloud. Then they all laughed at me. She laughed, and all the kids laughed with her. There are no Mohawk saints, the teacher said, and there never will be. And they laughed more. Stupid girl, they called me at recess. Stupid, stupid, maudit sauvage.*

∽

Joe opens the truck door for Shayna. He knows he should ask her a question first, he should let her speak, that there's something uneven in the way he leans on her level temper and good sense. He drums the fingers of his left hand on the steering wheel, chews on his right thumbnail until it is shredded and gristly against his tongue.

She lifts herself into the seat, a smaller, shorter woman than her older sister. Hers is a different kind of beauty, Joe has long observed, concentrated like a fuse, while Rita was a brush-fire, someone you noticed from a distance, couldn't safely get too close to.

"Since when do you do the grunt work for band council, Joe?" she asks.

"Chief's brother's a dentist," Joe says, cupping his jaw and winking to suggest that he's shrewder than expected. "I want him to owe me a favour or two."

She looks out the window and he feels it coming – the thing she always asks, the only thing that matters, as if she's checking up on him. "So, how's Cherry?"

Because money is a weathervane with his kid, Joe's made a point of knowing where Cherisse hides her cash: an empty club-sized tampon box shoved at the back of the bathroom vanity, on the side where the cupboard door hangs off its hinge. She must have figured he'd scrounge for money in her private spaces, rifling through her bedroom drawers, all the containers atop her dresser, every pocket, purse, and boot. Too easy. But a space they shared? That was a fuck-you hiding place. And it would have worked, it would have outwitted him, had he not already lived with her mother, had he not come to anticipate the hoarding that preceded her tendency to bolt. And the wiliness too – there was plenty of that. So when he found Cherisse's cash months earlier, he left it alone, knowing she would check it daily. He took to checking it too. The day he finds it empty, he'll know she's going. Maybe he'll get a chance to talk her out of it, or at least to say goodbye, remind her he loves her – a moment her mother never allowed. He checked for her cash this very morning. It was there, and there was a lot of it. That was money for a different kind of leaving: the permanent sort.

"Well, to be honest, I got a bad feeling. Think she might be getting ready to go again, you know. But a big kind of going this time."

Shayna straightens. He thinks of Lena, then of Helen, and of all the stiff-spined ferocity that runs through their clan's women the way some families are riddled with diabetes or double-jointedness.

"Why, Joe? What's she saying? What's she doing?"

He feels the accusation in her voice. *Are you watching over her? Are you doing a good job?* There's a tremor of guilt, of sadness, unsteadying her uprightness. Like him, Shayna has got some things wrong in her life, failed to read the signs. It joins them, this fear of fucking up again.

"Dunno, dunno." He swats at her questions as if they're gnats. "Just want you to keep an eye out, ear to the ground kinda thing."

"I'm at the barricade, Joe. She won't come near it."

He pulls in at the council offices, a boxy building of glass and dolomite. The trip is over, and he's uncertain if he's accomplished anything. He wishes he felt better. Rita would sit up in bed, her tongue clicking, her arms windmilling against the walls that held her, beyond the reach of the moon and its calming shadows. *This place, this place,* she'd cry. *I'm penned in. Can't breathe.* Joe would use his firm voice: *You stay. You stay, baby. We belong here.* But she'd shake her head so hard she'd stripe him with snot and tears. *No, we belong there. And there. And there.* She'd lance each direction beyond them with her finger. *We belong on all of it.*

Shayna places her small fingers on his forearm. "I'll do what I can, Joe. In the meantime, sit her down, talk to her. Just ask her what's going on. Take charge."

He nods his head. She jumps out of the truck. "You coming in?"

"No," he says. "Chief wants to speak to you alone."

Her forehead wrinkles. Then she straightens again, and walks into the building with the bearing of a much taller woman.

∞

When Elijah Barton's mother realized she could not get land on the reserve, she moved with her son into an abandoned vinyl-sided cottage on the edge of the *o'tá:ra*. It had an arabesque of carbon on the wall behind the kitchen's wood-fired cookstove. She nailed sheets of plywood to rebuild the floor's sag; she sewed curtains from frayed bedsheets; she knit long tubes and stuffed them with newspapers to shove against winter's drafty door jambs. They turned a toolshed into their outhouse, snuck water from the wells on nearby properties or boiled creek water. His mother believed she was returning to a life she remembered from her childhood, where a large kitchen garden, generosity, and the dexterity of her skills – the ability to sew, bead, weave, cook, can, cure, grow, gather, barter – were enough for a good existence. But her people were gone, others were mistrustful of a woman who'd lived so long in town, lying next to a white man, and what she knew how to do could not cushion her against their new privations. Still, she never wavered; she bore the hardships as if they were a change in the weather.

But Elijah felt trammelled. For the first six months he'd go to bed, turn his face to the thin wall, and sob without making a sound. Then one day, from the stoop outside his mother's shack, he heard a distant singing: a female voice for sure, but an alto with a soprano's soar. He wandered across the creek and into the forested southern tongue of the reserve in search of its source, imagining a broad girl with a large chest and a throat like a hollowed tree stump, enough body to cradle such big notes. What he found, at the edge of the Smoke River, was Rita, thin-limbed and lanky in her cut-off jean shorts and bathing suit top, shiny hair reaching to her hips, lungs holding up the sky. She had pulled together long willow vines and was braiding them into a swing while she sang.

He stepped back, watched her, until she swung around in mid-refrain and pointed in his direction. *You! If you're gonna stare, you might as well help me.* She continued to sing, and though he hovered closer, Elijah was unsure what to do. Finally Rita drew the braided vines to the river's edge, threaded her leg through the loop, grabbed up high, and kicked off with her free leg, then cinched it tightly against the other one. She swooped down, pendulum fast, as the vines strained to their full length over the water, where she let go, her foot slipping free of the willow noose like a princess casting off a slipper, her whole body outstretched towards the sun. He opened his mouth to call out as she fell into the water and held his breath until she broke the surface, throwing her head back so her wet hair slapped her shoulders. Her laugh was full-throated and reckless, huge, like her singing.

Elijah wasn't one for big words. But later in his life, whenever he heard someone say they had been enchanted, he remembered that first encounter with Rita, and thought, *Yeah, I know what that's all about.*

Driving home early from the cigarette factory, Elijah notices Joe Montagne pull into the council office driveway. He slows down, cranes his neck just as a woman walks away from Joe's shambolic truck. Something about her is familiar. On an impulse, Elijah pulls his red pickup into the same driveway, tucks it between two suvs so he faces away from Joe. His hand shakes as he adjusts the rear-view mirror. *Rita,* he whispers. Could it be?

At the door, the woman turns and waves in Joe's direction. Facing outwards, her pretty face is lined with worry, every ligament of her petite frame clenched, determined. Elijah slumps. Never before has he mistaken Shayna for her older sister.

Joe backs up his truck, tears away from the council building. Feeling sheepish, a bit foolish, Elijah is about to do the same, when he hesitates. *There's a reason for everything,* his mother would assure him when he was a miserable young man. She refused to leave the old cottage on the *o'tá:ra,* even as its bones sank into the ground. She died before he turned twenty. To the outside world, she was poor and friendless when her work-weary heart misfired and her soft body crumpled into the folded faded linens under the clothesline. By then Elijah was making enough money to ensure that she was never cold, never hungry, and that there were plenty of beads and broadcloth for her clever hands, seeds for her garden, and just enough ease that she could sprinkle suet on the kitchen window ledge to coax the crossbills and vireos from their branches on a crisp October evening. She was as happy as she could be for a woman who understood happiness as a kind of frill, an invention foisted upon her quietude by an unquiet world. Or so she led him to believe. *Possibility is more interesting to me than happiness, Elijah,* she said once.

Shayna leaving the barricade for a late-afternoon visit to the council offices presents all sorts of interesting possibilities. He has nothing to lose by hanging around for a bit.

Chief Jonah White may have convinced other folks that his ability to break even running a Stop 'n' Go is tantamount to business acumen, that his adeptness at retelling a joke or funny story is the same as negotiating moxie, but Shayna has little patience for men like him. Her people believed in the traditional council – the one where women such as her grandmother were enfranchised and powerful – and resisted the federally imposed idea of governance, its trickle-down of undeserved payoffs and goodies accruing to opportunists such as White and his cronies. Still, she is nervous. As a point of honour, she has rarely ventured into the new band council building since its cost overruns became a heated controversy. The automatic door's pneumatic *whoosh*, the lobby's bright, antiseptic gleam unnerves her. From behind a polished marble barricade, a receptionist's head bobs up.

"Can I help you?" She eyes Shayna's grime-stained jeans.

"My name is Shayna Fallingbrook. The chief asked to see me."

"Oh." The girl drags a polished red fingernail along her computer screen and then taps the keyboard. She throws a clipboard on the counter.

"Conference room 22B. First right, then left, then left, then right. Can't miss it. Please sign in, and don't forget to initial when you leave. They're waiting for you."

"They?" Shayna says, and scratches her name on the sheet.

The girl shrugs and offers a conciliatory smile. "Yup. Looks like you're a popular gal."

Shayna slips into the closest washroom and fumbles for the cellphone in her purse, only to find it uncharged. She scrubs her hands, rinses her face, runs her fingers through her hair. The bottom of her pant cuff has a weird blue stain and a crust of dirt. The last two buttons of her shirt are missing. "Shit!" she says. Helen would counsel her to stay cool, stay strong. *Even if it is an ambush,* she'd say, *what have you got worth stealing?*

The conference room's shades are drawn and it smells of new carpet. As her eyes adjust to the low light, Shayna makes out the silhouettes of four figures, all large-shouldered, facing her from one side of an immense round conference table.

"Come in, come in," says Chief White, and he draws himself up out of his seat, holding out his hand. "We have coffee, tea."

Shayna sits opposite the men so the table obscures her pant leg, the scruffy half of her shirt. She puts her palms out flat, places the dead phone beside them to suggest a time limit, looks up. The first set of eyes she meets are those of her ex-husband.

Clarence is smiling at her. "Hello, Shay," he says, and it is the voice she remembers, the voice of a man who never yelled but who expressed his belligerence with greasy fingerprints on the remote, the noises he made eating an orange, the always empty gas tank.

"We asked Clarence to join this meeting because he's got some expertise, you know, on the legal stuff regarding land."

Shayna nods her head slowly. She met Clarence at law school. He was a Mohawk from Big River, his father a sometimes friend of Rick's. She was the better student. She got multiple offers after passing her bar examinations; he got one. But it was Clarence who thrived among the city towers, the press of people in the subways, the traffic that drowned birdsong and breezes. She walked out of her office tower one day, late for a lunch appointment, saw her passing reflection with her expensive leather boots and tight skirt, clutching a mobile phone, looking as if she'd mow down anyone who delayed her, and suddenly she couldn't reconcile her reflection with the women who'd come before her, or the woman she wanted to become.

"Sooo," says Chief White, "we wanted to talk to you about this barricade business. Perhaps you could fill us in on your strategy."

Shayna takes a long breath. "I'm a little confused about how this concerns you at all. Hasn't the band council formally distanced itself from the barricade?"

"Well, that situation is . . . you know, fluid," says the chief. He folds and unfolds his hands, then his eyes dart to Clarence.

"Shayna, the thing is, at this point you really need a focused message," Clarence begins. She's irritated by his tone, the effort he is taking to explain things to her. "When you're dealing with the media," he continues, clearing his throat for emphasis, "and especially the government."

Chief White nods eagerly, as if Clarence's words were edged in gold leaf.

"We have a message: the land doesn't belong to them. It belongs to us," she says. "And we filed claims and considerations and followed the rules and somehow that didn't work. So now we are being a bit more, y'know, proactive, as they say."

"Yeah, but . . ." Clarence says, and she remembers that *but*. He said it exactly the same way every time she muttered about more and more blonde baby mamas showing up on the reserve pushing strollers with blue-eyed natives, hanging dream catchers in their bedroom windows, sporting Turtle Island tattoos. *But we're all hybrids, Shay*, he'd say.

If everybody is native, no one is native, she'd spit back, *and surely that must be the plan. First missionaries and churches, then residential schools. And now legislation that defines a race by giving it no definition worth having. Hand out the funds and rights. Water down the cultural and blood ties. Keep everybody just poor enough. It's the politest genocide on the planet.* This was the kind of stuff she'd offer for every *but* he supplied. Finally he'd wonder aloud if she were paranoid. Shay'd call him a sheep. *Baa, siksik, baa.*

"But you need to be precise, Shayna." And what she hears is an old exasperation, his implying that she's given to fuzzy theories and overreaction. "For instance, you should have a figure in mind."

"A figure?"

"For compensation. Surely you've reviewed the title history on this property," he says. "You'll have to argue that the band was improperly compensated for the land, rather than trying to prove it was taken from them in a series of complicated boondoggles. The evidentiary through-line is so much clearer."

Shayna gives a little laugh, shakes her head. Farmers are selling their acreages and new houses are rising up from graded mud flats. Her people – his people too – are being surrounded by Walmarts and Japanese maples, Montessori schools and discarded Frappuccino cups. Meanwhile their treaty claims cram banker's boxes, gather dust in the offices of lawyers and overpaid consultants. The reserve population is growing, the land base shrinking. And what does the band council do? Burns sweetgrass for every visiting politician. Hires show-me-the-money Mohawks such as Clarence who say *evidentiary* and – always – *easier*.

"So, let me guess. The band council has a figure in mind. And you're offering to distribute this compensation."

The chief shifts uncomfortably, whispers to the two men on either side of him.

"Shay, you have to be realistic," Clarence says. It hurts her to smile. "Elected council has a good track record with the right people in government. You and your troop have no credibility. The feds' negotiators will run circles around you."

A funny way to exact revenge, she thinks, *but effective*. Perhaps she has it coming. In the last six months of their marriage, Clarence would push her off him at night, saying, *Stop!* She would grope at him with her fingertips, with her tongue, her teeth. Nothing registered – not the salt of his sweat, the tang of his ear, not the stubble of his chin, the soft flesh of his ass. She'd begin to scratch, scratch, scratch at him as if she were trapped in a box of his flesh. He'd pin her to the bedsheets. *Stop!* When he moved into Pete-Pete's old room, she'd slip into the house's dark hush to destroy something he loved, ripping each page of the first book his mother had bought him, running a nail across the ridges of his mint-condition Hank Williams seventy-eight. She mined a talent for hurting him. And every time he came back to her, wearing long sleeves and pants to hide what she'd inflicted upon him, she only wanted to do something worse.

"We want the land, not compensation. The land itself," she says finally. "The tiniest fraction of what was originally promised to our people."

Chief White's shoulders drop.

A long, disapproving *phssst* comes out of Clarence's mouth. "You're not serious," he says. "You can't be serious, Shay. You're going to argue the original treaty? That will take forever. *Forever.* They will tie you up in discovery so long you'll run out of money before you see the inside of a courtroom. That plays right into their hands. It's idiocy – criminally stupid."

"Sorry, I didn't catch that last word," she says. She's halfway out of her seat.

Clarence shakes his head.

After all these years she still can't tell if he is angry or truly surprised. *Our kid is going to preschool in the Legion?* he asked when she announced that Pete-Pete would learn the Mohawk language before he mastered English. She had to clear away beer bottles and ashtrays in the morning, wash the tables with baking soda and vinegar, open the doors to fresh air before the elders showed up.

Konkwehon:we, Pete-Pete said one day, pointing to his chest, looking up at his parents. His smile used every part of his face.

Yes, baby, real people. You are one of the real people, Shayna whispered. Her chest rattled. Her eyes watered. After that, nothing but her child could sate her hunger, ever really fill her up. Clarence knew it.

She pushes back her chair. Her ex-husband will suffer for that unkind word; she needn't draw more attention to it. Still, she can't muster the grace for shaking their hands. She leaves wordlessly.

Outside the council offices, Shayna is marshalling her resolve to walk back to the barricade when a voice from a parked truck stops her. "Can I offer you a ride?"

She starts. Elijah Barton is hanging out the window of his red pickup. *There are more reasons to be wary of this man than to trust him,* Shayna thinks. But she is tired and the distance she has to walk daunting. She climbs in.

Inside, the truck gleams with newness. Shayna sinks back. He will ask her what she is doing here, and she hasn't the energy to lie. Perhaps Clarence better understands the nature of the compromises required when being strategic, when making alliances, she thinks. But she's smart enough to recognize everything that a man like Elijah can lend to their cause. For now, that feels smart enough.

CHAPTER 10

When her father, Vilja, died – his body jaundiced, thin as a stewpot chicken – Ella started to run. It was the winter she was in grade ten. The high school track and field stars were the high-cheeked children of landowners and tobacco farmers, realtors and bank managers. Her father had picked tobacco in the summer, cleaned toilets in the winter. Accents clung like gristle to his and her mother's English, and the air in their rented house was oiled with cooking and nicotine. Tryouts were in April. She tied on the North Star runners her mother had fished from the discount bin on her twice-yearly bus trip to the Pemcoe Zeller's and told herself, *I will make that team.* The December air was chafing, the roads polished with new ice. Damp and salt loosened her shoes' leather stripes, which flapped as she ran.

The echo of her father's deep voice, his singing, followed her through the wintry monochrome. *There are things I cannot be and others I can,* he told her once, and she wondered then if he were making excuses for the drafty house, the fact that he was not the popular musician he'd been in Budapest. When he was gone, the words took a different shape. Surely he was telling her to focus on what was possible. So she ran.

Every day she returned from school, did the dishes left by her mother, thawed a portion of venison left over from her father's hunting trips or a package of beef kidney bought on sale from the IGA, checked her parents' darkened bedroom to whisper, *Édesanya?* and listened for a soft murmur of *Édesem* from her mother's lumpen grief. Then she layered her clothes and tied on the North Stars, stiff from sitting by the radiator. Her toes were angered by chilblains and her legs protested with shin splints, but she grew stronger and faster. And as she did, she imagined her lungs being scrubbed of her father's endless cigarettes, whose smoke still hung in the curtains, clung to the threadbare settee, and permeated the synthetic down of her winter jacket.

By the time she was in grade eleven, Ella was a regional 1,500- and 5,000-metre champion. But in the district competition that year, her first, she choked. She'd never been on an overnight excursion outside Doreville, had never seen a university campus, never connected running to a future, an escape. *You're holding back, Ella,* her coach said. *You have more doggedness, more potential than anyone I've ever seen. But it's as if when it really means something, you don't know how to turn on your win switch.*

Her coach bought her new shoes. He slid the box across his desk towards her without a word. Shame bled warmth into her cheeks. *Next year,* he said, *you will win the district. These will help.* She took them. They were part of the either/or dilemma he presented her with. She couldn't leave this place, couldn't do better than her parents, without finding her win switch. There were six weeks left of grade eleven when she began to run trails along the banks of the Smoke River, jumping over logs, landing in brackish puddles, letting the sumac switches flagellate her, all the while repeating in her head, *Turn on your win switch.* After a month, her forearms and calves were striated with bramble scratches, her feet blistered from the ungiving new shoes. She felt no nearer to understanding what the coach wanted from her when she stumbled over a large rock and yanked an ankle ligament.

Cross-train, said her coach when she hobbled through his door. *Go work out with the swim team until the end of the school year. They haven't competed yet, so they're hungry. It'll be good for you while your ankle heals.*

In the spring of that year, an Olympic-size swimming pool had been added to Pemcoe Secondary. Derek dePonde, who supplied curing kilns to every big tobacco grower in the region, made a donation that got his picture in the local paper and his name on the beet-coloured brick. The bronze letters were a foot high: DEREK DEPONDE POOL. Everyone referred to it as *da pond* at first. After the elementary school kids started busing across town to take swimming lessons, it became the *DDPee.*

The pool change rooms still had the smell of new paint. Ella was issued a standard one-piece racer-back red Speedo that clashed with her hair, flattened her breasts like a gymnast's, and pinched her uncomfortably at the inner thighs. The other swimmers were broad-shouldered girls with big voices who shook their legs and slapped water over their bellies like playful seals.

There was a nervous ferocity to the way the girls torpedoed down the fifty-metre lanes, slicing up the two million litres of water. Ella struggled to keep up in the outside lane, pulling herself out of the pool at the end of practice. Spent, she sat on the tiled edge, her head down, her shoulders slack, her legs dangling in the water.

In the half-hour between the end of girls' swim team practice and the beginning of the boys', when the pool was deserted, Ella would linger in the water, waiting for the terminally boisterous girls to vacate the change room. She dreaded that one of the nicer ones would try to start a conversation with her. *You're doing so well! How is your ankle healing?* She wanted to be alone with the shower's inexhaustible water pressure, its perpetual heat. She didn't want new friends she could never invite back to her smelly home.

One day she was on her back in the water, her legs kicking aimlessly, when she heard a splash and felt a surge that pushed her sideways. Surprised, Ella let go of the flutter board under her head and stopped kicking. For a moment she was entirely submerged and looking at a long, tanned figure parting the water as if it were soft butter.

She made her way to the ladder and turned. The swimmer had already pushed off from the opposite end of the pool and was rocketing back towards her – a goggled head, a gleaming set of arms vectoring outwards with a fringe of water unravelling behind. Mr. Ellis, one of the history teachers, appeared at the end of pool with a whistle around his neck. *Stercyx! Stercyx! Save something for practice.*

As Coulson Stercyx pulled himself to standing at the pool edge, rinsed out his goggles, and bowed his torso in a luxurious stretch, Ella recognized a force both big enough and graceful enough for all the pool's newness, its upstart ambitions. That's what the win switch looked like – she knew it. It was a thing to behold. She never shook off that first impression of him.

Ella glances out the window at her back gate and the meadow beyond it and feels the cramp in the small of her back relax. She is wearing a fresh cotton blouse, slim-fit black jeans, new open-toed sandals with a saucy wedge. Under her arm she has tucked a fresh copy of *Tobacco Diversification Strategy: New Challenges and Opportunities for Interlake Farmers*.

"Where you off to?" Mitch asks as she applies melon lipstick in the hallway mirror and fluffs her hair.

Thirty days into the barricade and her husband is like a dented boat; formerly purposeful and energized, he lists towards being hangdog and needy. Ella has overheard him trying to move things forward. His voice resonates through the office doors. If it is loud and exhorting, tinged with desperation, she knows he is talking to lawyers or politicians. *Do something. Get the cops to raid.* A softer voice, on the verge of wheedling, means he is assuring skittish creditors and presold unit holders. *Hang on. It'll blow over. The properties will go up in value.*

Twice now, after talking late into the night, a tumbler of Scotch at his wrist, Mitch has fallen asleep at his desk. A case of Dalwhinnie arrived midweek, delivered by cab from the liquor store. *When did we start getting home deliveries of booze?* Ella barked from the foyer. He answered by pushing his door shut.

"I have an appointment with Coulson Stercyx. You know how slippery he is. This is the best time to meet with him."

All morning she's searched for a focus, something that will help her to feel well-groomed, unafraid, purposeful. Her office is clean. Her calendar is organized. That leaves only one unfinished item on her to-do list: her yearly discussion with Coulson Stercyx. He vexes her more than any of the region's other remaining tobacco growers – a motley tribe of grizzled Belgians, paprika-stained Hungarians, garlicky Poles, and their ill-mannered, entitled, agricultural-college-graduate sons. She is wearing down the others in stages; Coulson is the only one she can't reach. As the clock inched towards noon and she couldn't conjure a more appealing task, she picked out a freshly dry-cleaned outfit, hopped in the shower, brought a heartfelt brio to her toilette.

"Do you have to look so damn good to see a farmer?"

Ella swings her head around and notices the slackness of her husband's face, the puffiness under his eyes. "Mitch, it wouldn't hurt to tidy yourself up, get yourself out of the house.

You'll feel better." And then she sails past him, out the patio doors and through the back gate.

∽

It occurred to Mitch at a young age that he would never have his wished-for growth spurt. His stocky frame held fast to a boy's softness; it resisted muscle no matter how many pull-ups he did, sneaking out to the monkey bars at a nearby primary school. His face, the thinness of his hair, the seriousness of his expression seemed to have slid towards middle age by the end of adolescence. He learned quickly to offset his deficits with good manners and strategy. At seventeen he was the point man and bookie for the drag races that made Doreville summer nights hum with distant engine song.

The tobacco growers' kids had Trans Ams, shovel-nosed Firebirds, and Ford pickups, even Buick Regals. The native kids had Dusters, juiced-up GMCs, and no fear. And Mitch, who'd found late in his high school career a branch of mathematics that appealed to him – odds – developed something he'd never had before: a reputation. He wasn't known as a pothead or a rebel or a rich kid, but everyone knew Mitch had a taste for a gamble, and that he could be trusted with others' money. The protocol was simple: a challenger pulled his muscle car into Mitch's father's grocery store parking lot, found Mitch in the store behind the deli counter, and asked him if the store stocked *Road & Track* magazine. *We only stock* Car and Driver. *It's better,* Mitch would answer. And then they would wander over to the sundries aisle, which was usually deserted, and arrange the race, the preliminary wager. Over the next few days, prospective bettors had to buy a pack of gum or cigarettes from his father's store if they wanted to get in on the action. It was good business, and if the old man suspected anything, he never said so.

In 1981 the best place to drag race was along the dirt and gravel road that passed the outer boundary of the reserve and divided two large tobacco farms, one of which belonged to the Stercyx family and the other to a Frenchman named Flavelle. Mitch and his friends called the road Tobacco Ridge. It sat at a slight elevation from the fields it bisected, a narrow drumlin that made driving at high speeds in the wrong direction all the more thrilling for the steep bailout required should an oblivious driver come cresting over the ridge going the right way.

The man who was killed in the last drag race Mitch organized was named Barrett David Williams Junior. He was a six-foot-three God-fearing Jamaican with a low laugh, and a fierce work ethic. On the Stercyx farm, where he started as a primer, then rose to become the harvest foreman, his name had gone through a series of truncations. B. David Jr. turned into Big Davy Jr. and finally just Big Junior. Rumour had it that old man Stercyx paid all his primers a premium to stop them from being poached by other growers, and Big Junior got double that. One large-framed red Raleigh three-speed bicycle was kept just for him. Other growers never said it to Stercyx's face, but Big Junior's special treatment made them grumble in private, *All the primers will expect it.*

When Greg Sawicki rolled up to the grocery store in a new Chevrolet Camaro Z-28 that day, Mitch felt smug. He thought the new car's tangerine colour was deeply uncool. And he figured Sawicki for the kind of guy who would forfeit a manual transmission for the extra ten horsepower that came with the three-speed automatic – which was going to make it too easy. Mitch bet on Stu Green, a huge kid from the reserve who put out his cigarettes on his biceps and drove a mustard-coloured Pontiac GTO he'd restored in shop class.

Mitch didn't go to the race, but he remembers the phone call that night and the way he watched a mosquito sink its proboscis into the damp flesh of his forearm as his throat tightened.

Who won?

He could hear Sawicki take a deep breath on the other end of the line. *We didn't finish.*

Whaddya mean? You mean you lost and Stu won. Ha!

It was a scratch, man. Something got hit. Everybody took off.

Mitch imagined the tires' egg-beater chew against the asphalt, the car underbellies pinging with pebbles. *Could you see what it was? A deer? A dog?*

I don't know, said Sawicki. His voice sounded high, helium-thin. *It was big. A deer maybe.*

Well, did you hit it or Stu?

Both.

They went quiet.

Did you go looking for it?

Everybody took off pretty fast. I could hear something moan. But it was dark out there, man. It was thrown way down the embankment, into the field.

They stopped talking.

Dented my hood.

Standing there in the dark of his parents' kitchen, Mitch wanted to scratch the flesh from his arm, if only to relieve the bad feelings in his gut. He hung up the phone and stood still, not knowing what to do.

Two days later, his father lowered the newspaper at the breakfast table, took off his glasses, and squinted at his son. *Stercyx's foreman was killed on the ridge. Car that hit him was travelling so fast his body and his bike were thrown fifty metres into the fields. Cops figure it was drag racers. Damn awful way to die.*

Mitch shovelled spoonfuls of cereal into his mouth to avoid his father's eyes.

The man had four children back home. What he was doing out on a bike at that hour, God knows. Stupid. Stupid people.

That afternoon Coulson, home for the summer from his

first year of university, showed up at the grocery store. Two years older and nearly a foot taller than Mitch, his bare arms muscled and tight. He had an angry line for a mouth. For a half an hour he did nothing but follow Mitch. He stood at the end of every aisle Mitch was stocking and stared, clutched fists hanging at his sides. By the time his father summoned him to the back room, Mitch was shaking.

What's that guy want?

I dunno.

Well, go ask him!

When Mitch approached, his voice quavered. Coulson reached out, grabbed the straps of Mitch's apron, and tightened them like a noose at his neck. *Don't suppose you stock* Road & Track?

Mitch shook his head. Coulson let go with a shove. Mitch thudded against a shelf, sending a jar of raspberry jam crashing to his feet. Coulson turned and went, leaving Mitch with a spray of jellied viscera speckling his shins.

In a small town there is no hesitation between tragedy and gossip. There were lurid rumours about where Big Junior was returning from that evening; a pox of speculation outpaced any police investigation. No witnesses came forward; no good citizens pressed for answers, indulging instead in a general indifference to the fate of migrant workers, unless they stole money or messed around with local women. A week after the hit-and-run, Greg Sawicki's new Z-28 was found at the bottom of a quarry pond. Mitch's betting days were over. Thereafter he avoided Coulson Stercyx if he saw him on the street.

Three decades later, it's a habit he can't break. And now the idea of his sleekly groomed wife cutting through Stercyx's fields in her snug jeans for an unscheduled rendezvous with the brutish farmer leaves Mitch ransacking the pantry in search of the undrunk bottles of Scotch he has hidden from his son.

Coulson is on a ladder fixing a rack in his kiln when he sees a woman cut through his north field of tobacco plants, rib-high and shiny green. In less than two months the plants will be felled, their broad, papery leaves cured yellow. He can already see how the earth holding them now will be chafed and bristled.

The tobacco quakes and leans, arms raised in a green hallelujah to the sun, coyly flashing him glimpses of the woman's long neck, her torso, and a roll of denim-clad hip. He wipes his brow, fires up the cordless drill, feels the wood give to the bite of a screw.

Even in the eye-smarting brightness he can discern it is not Shayna. How he wants to imagine it is her, leaving the barricade, calling him away from his own work despite the hours of good light left in the day and all the tasks piling up like arguments against pleasure. He imagines taking a swallow of dark beer, sliding his malty tongue around her ankles, up the inside of her legs. He can already taste the syrup of Shayna's skin, feel her fingers bounce like thrips along his back. He's losing patience with this barricade business of hers, how it has emptied his bed, complicated every trip into town.

Ella spots Coulson on a ladder. Even from this distance she is struck by the romance of the man – the sureness of his feet on the rungs, his strong arms raised above his head, a muscle twitching in the thick of his neck like a beating wing. Still glistening.

The sight of him focuses her on how to phrase her approach so his face doesn't bunch up, so he doesn't immediately shut her down. Isn't it just about finding the words that will paint the future like a landscape, a place he'd like to inhabit, a place that will pull him forward into redemption from tobacco's dirty, soulless profits?

Ginseng is all about sex, Ella said to Martin Wirkus a year earlier. *And that's why it's a good investment. Sex is inevitable. Smoking, not so much anymore.* It had taken years to wear down Martin, one of the region's largest tobacco growers, and she credits the sex talk for ultimately making him relent. A sentry row of narrow, flat-topped tents covers his fields now. Under each black polypropylene tarp are raised mounds covered in straw mulch. This summer, nothing green will peek out from them. The soybeans and feed corn Martin planted on his remaining acres will help pay his bills for the next five years before he gets to harvest his first crop of ginseng. But if he protects the tender roots from winter frosts, a litany of vengeful fungi, and excess moisture dripping off the shade cloth, and if those roots grew into shapes that vaguely resemble a human trunk with skinny limbs, his Asian buyers will reward him generously. But until then he'll need a lot of hand-holding.

Ella visits weekly. They'll both need some patience. *It's not natural,* he repeated for the tenth time last week, his hands hanging like drought-sickened leaves. *You work the fields all your life and you think sun, sun, sun. Will there be enough hours of it? Even when you want rain, you still want the sun the very next day. And now I grow a crop I have to hide from the sun; I spend money keeping the sun out. Cables, poles, connectors. Diggers. Yeesh.*

She can see he is resisting the vast scale of the changes ahead. Should she have elaborated on them more? But he's a man of the land, an old, block-headed Pole, the kind who won't let women explain farming to them. Still, ginseng is for nomads. A second crop can never be harvested on the land used to grow a first crop under artificial shade – the buildup of soil pathogens is too great. After he finally gets his first harvest, he'll have to pull up the poles, cables, connectors, and tarps and move them to land where the root has never been cultivated. Poachers could be a problem too. Once the mature plants produce their pretty red berries, people other than Martin will be keeping tabs on his crop. There's a price to be paid for every kind of success.

∞

Coulson tests his handiwork, swings himself down from the ladder, squints into the light, and turns towards the trim figure now stepping out to where he has set up easels for the priming tables.

"Good afternoon, Mr. Stercyx."

It's stinking hot. He takes off his cap, mashes it into his eyes to wipe the sweat from them. "Ella, how long have we known each other?"

"Oh, I don't know, about thirty years. Forever." Her laugh is anxious.

She's a metre away from him now, but with the sun still in his eyes he can't focus, can't locate her freckled cheeks, the country-club nose, the mouth that twists nervously in his presence and makes him want to either kiss her or say something mean – he can never decide which.

"When are you going to start using my first name?"

"Well, it's just that I'm here on business."

He snorts and turns. "What business do you and I have?"

She holds the report in front of her. Coulson notices the fine bones of her hands, the glint of her wedding ring.

"You won't come to my office," Ella says with a feminine vibrato that reminds Coulson of his ex-wife. He wonders for a second what Ella looks like naked, what she sounds like laughing wildly, what's the dirtiest thing she has ever done.

He's dripping with heat, so he strips to his cotton singlet and uses his balled-up shirt to wipe dry his face and underarms before waving at Ella to follow him to the farmhouse. If she didn't fit so nicely into her jeans or there wasn't something sweetly vulnerable in her constant lip-sucking, he would have stopped giving her the time of day years ago.

Ella thunks down her folder on the kitchen table. Coulson watches her wrinkle her nose and he becomes aware of the farmhouse's intractable must, faintly acrid, collected from his parents' hard work, harder worrying. And it comes back to him again: his enchantment with Marie, the way she slid through her world like a tall ship, an elegant anachronism. And all the nights after he realized he'd driven her away, how he tossed and turned in the farmhouse bed, tormented by the desire to lay his rough hands on the talc of her skin just one more time.

Coulson turns to the refrigerator. "Beer?"

Ella waves her hand, wipes crumbs from the vinyl padding of a kitchen chair, and sits primly on its edge. "It's a bit early for me." She worries the grit from her sandals, brushes her shins, and smooths her folder on her lap.

He pulls two bottles from the refrigerator. "Well, then, I'll have to drink both."

Just as he hopes, she purses her mouth into a little dried apple as her gaze surveys the modest kitchen, finds his shirtless torso and then retreats. "You realize I'm here professionally."

Coulson harrumphs. "You cut through my fields . . . Mrs. Bain."

"I don't like driving past the barricade. It's awkward." She coughs.

They look at each other. He takes his first sip of beer, and out of a habit from adolescence, swishes it in his mouth until wet glimmers on his lips.

"Coulson, there's a new program I want to talk to you about."

He puts the second beer on the table in front of Ella, leans against the kitchen sink, and rests his own beer on the lip of his belt buckle. "Guess the barricade's not so great for the real estate business."

She flinches slightly. *Ah, there's the fighter,* he thinks.

Ella pulls her glance upwards from his knees until she meets his eyes. Then she reaches for the beer in front of her, holds it in the air in a toast, and takes a swig. "Truth is, it's a real drag for us," she says, breaking into a wary smile.

"So this program," he says. "Lemme guess. Next spring the government wants to buy out my quota, and you've got it figured out that even with my investment in the kilns, the price is right and this would be an ideal time to move out of tobacco and into something else. So what is it now? Hemp? Asparagus?"

Ella straightens, clears her throat, opens her folder. She begins talking about Brazil's cheap labour and better growing season and the folly of trying to compete with South American tobacco. She stops and stares at him with an expectant tilt to her head.

He says nothing, keeps her hanging there, her chin tipped sideways. Let her worry over whether he's contemplating his glorious future growing cut flowers and sweet potatoes for bio-diesel or simply considering the freckles at the base of her neck. She might believe this shit, but he's unconvinced. For now anyway. Finally he lets her off the hook. "Sorry, did I hear you say 'baby vegetables'?"

"Mini cabbages. Broccolini. Rainbow silverbeet. The market research coming out of Australia is encouraging."

"You want me to grow mini cabbages?"

"Coulson, after next spring, most of the other large growers who've held out will take this buyout. And the government won't keep coming back with these offers. They've already completely shut down the eastern growers." She hesitates, then adds, "You know, your property has huge agritourism potential too, being right across from a new golf course."

Agritourism. Golf course. Adults in short pants pushing little white balls over a bent grass monoculture. It catches like a splinter. Coulson puts on a fresh T-shirt that he grabs from a hamper sitting on the stovetop. Now the beer has worked his tongue loose, and he feels impatient with the game he plays with this woman.

"There'll always be tobacco grown in the Interlake. The land's made for it, Ella. And me, I'm not good for anything else either. Certainly not corn mazes and fuckin' pony rides!" He wishes she could fathom the cruelty of a rogue frost, or how a spot of blue mould can crater a grower with worry. When you survive these things over and over with a crop, there's a relationship, a level of trust and inborn knowledge that you don't throw away the minute a pretty suburban wife wags a cheque at you.

He doesn't have the energy to apologize. She's already on her feet, her face screwed tightly with offence. "Tobacco really is over this time, Coulson," she says quietly. "Call me if you have any questions."

Then she slips out, leaving the report on his table. Coulson watches her through the kitchen window. At first she teeters through his fields in her high-heeled shoes, then she reaches down and slips them off.

And in that movement he sees again his ex-wife's similar slim-hipped polish, and he remembers how much pleasure he derived from simply watching her, sitting in a small café on a Saturday afternoon. He remembers white linen napkins, the gleam of polished cutlery, his fingers looped around a tulip glass of Duvel, a book on his lap – often his well-thumbed copy of Marcus Aurelius's *Meditations*. Two hours of quiet, surrounded by assurances that he'd done well for himself: the cool pressure of a fine watch on his wrist, the wild tobacco and bergamot drift of his cologne, the waiter bending to refill his water glass. And finally Marie, arriving with shopping bags, dropping into her chair with a slight flush on her cheeks, sweeping back her auburn hair with hands moving excitedly at her throat like startled doves, telling him about misadventures in the market and the wine store. Her laugh as pale and delicate as the rest of her. Every moment of those afternoons was such a relief to him for its distance from a childhood scoured of leisure and good taste.

The thought of Ella's primrose-polished fingers denting the folder she clutched reminds him of the things he left with Marie: his mother's porcelain dishes, passed down by generations in her family; the antique set of leather-bound Shakespeare works bought on his first trip to London; his swimming trophies; a closet full of Savile Row suits. When a year passed without hearing from him, Marie had taken all his things and given them to Goodwill. *I had to do it in order to move on,* she said over the phone a month later. *Sorry.* It was this act of disposal that stung him most. He hung up, laid his head on the kitchen table. He'd always assumed she'd keep something of him – a neatly packed carton stowed away – the way he held on to the scent of her hair, the cream of her skin, the dry effervescence of her voice.

Coulson looks again towards the departing woman. With her sandals wound about her fingers, Ella starts to trot through the tobacco before breaking out in a full run, her bright hair flapping against the back of her neck. He picks up the report she left behind and reads every word.

CHAPTER 11

"The cops are coming tonight," Gordo says. He's made a habit of listening in on his mother's phone calls, scanning her emails. "A riot squad from the big city and tactical units from three different counties. They're gathering at the river. A tidy little massacre – should be fun."

They work up an agenda for the evening: get drunk in Gordo's basement, stay up until the sleepy lawbreakers at the barricade hit their pillows, head out to mess things up just as the cops arrive. Las goes looking for gear in his parents' garage and stumbles upon three forty-ouncers of Dalwhinnie tucked among a subterfuge of caulking tubes and bottled mineral spirits. The idea of his old man hoarding liquor like some amnesiac squirrel cheers him. He swipes the bottles and shows up at Gordo's basement door for six, holding out the Scotch as appeasement for all the ways their friendship has been weird of late.

Gordo's eyes widen greedily. "Let the games begin!" he says.

They make their way through a whole bottle, then start the second one, mixing it with water, then Coke, and, as they get more drunk, chocolate milk.

There's a pile of hockey sticks stacked in a corner of the room. Gordo was serious once but didn't make the cut. Las knows not to bring up the subject. Still, the Scotch makes him feel strangely loose, incautious. Suddenly he's up, grabbing a stick, pushing the old coffee table away with his shins. "Basement shinny! Let's do it!'

"You giggle like a girl," Gordo says, but he's up too, moving chairs and boxes against the basement walls, picking his own stick. There's no puck to be found, so Las grabs his friend's plastic deodorant container from the bureau, drops it, and thwacks it with his stick so it sings across the laminate floorboards and hits Gordo's socked feet.

The sight of his friend hunched over, coddling the deodorant with his stick, looking so small and serious, makes Las laugh. Gordo launches towards him, elbows first, pushing him back against the wall as the deodorant flies past his ankles.

"Goal!" Gordo shouts. He raises his arms in the air.

"All right, Fleury, I'm on it!" Las kicks off his flip-flops, gathers the makeshift puck, and charges for the old refrigerator on the other side of the room, holding the stick in front of him inexpertly. He senses that the purchase of his bare feet on the laminate is an advantage. He's still laughing, but the mood in the room has changed.

Las is moving forward, but just as Gordo lunges at him, he dekes sideways. Gordo's feet slide out from under him. He lands hard on his right hip. Las pushes the puck around the coffee table and takes a long, sloppy shot that makes the deodorant slide past the refrigerator nonetheless.

Las hoots. "One-one!" He turns and offers a hand to Gordo, who is still laid out like a beached sea lion. Then he fetches the deodorant, holds it out to his friend. "Face-off at the crease."

Gordo grabs the deodorant. "It's cracked, you asshole. You've fuckin' wrecked it."

Las shrugs. "It's not like you buy the good stuff." He's thirsty again. He drops his stick, falls onto the couch, and twists to reach his drink, resting on a milk crate.

"So, Las, my friend, you still keen on hurting something?"

Las has one hand around the plastic cup while the other pours a generous refill from the second Scotch bottle. He chuckles. That's more like it. He feels lighter.

Then Gordo swoops towards him, holding his stick high and swinging it hard against Las's side at kidney height. "Theo Fleury? I'm goddamn Marty McSorley, asshole."

"Jesus fuck!" Las lets go of the Scotch bottle. It splashes, urine-bright, against the wall behind the lamp. He reaches his hands behind him, discovers the patch of hot, tender skin on his lower back, and groans.

Gordo laughs. "Stop being such a girl." He pulls Las erect by his hair, looks into his face. "It's easier to hurt something if you're hurtin' first."

Fifteen minutes later, Gordo's truck careers wildly up the lonely county road that avoids the barricade, heads north along the reserve's western boundary, and turns east on Ninth Line. The last bottle of Scotch is clenched between Las's knees. He lifts his shirt slightly to press the coolness of the vinyl seat into the long welt on the small of his back. There's a sting, followed by an amplified beat of pain. He closes his eyes. *C'mon, man, it's not that bad.* The worst of it is being suckered by Gordo, never seeing it coming.

When they approach the smoke shack, Las glances through the passenger window at the long, flat land south of Ninth Line. In the distance, the barricade is lit up like a bush party. He makes out the shredded carcass of the model home in silhouette. Smoke hovers on the southern horizon like a swarm of dark gnats. "Fuckers," he says under his breath, imagining the model home's studs and subfloor fuelling the barrel fires. Las twists open the Scotch bottle, takes a large swig.

The truck slows and turns into the driveway of the last smoke shack. "Leave some of that for me," Gordo snaps.

Ahead of them is the slight figure of the green-eyed girl, a cash box tucked against the lovely curve of her hip, as she cuts across from the shack to a nearby trailer. Las laughs at the sight of her. He doesn't know why.

"Hey, girlie!" Gordo shouts. He hops out of the car, leaving the keys in the ignition, to cajole the girl into selling him cigarettes. Las follows.

She looks at them warily. "Kinda late to come here for smokes."

"It's okay," Las says with the hunk-with-a-heart-of-gold voice he uses to offset his friend's whiff of felony. Las points to Gordo behind his back, mimes guzzling a drink. "He gets like that."

This seems to relax her. She smiles. "Whaddya smoking?" she asks Gordo and he holds up his empty package. When she turns back to the shack to open it, Gordo punches Las hard on the shoulder. But Las doesn't care. He's already moving past his friend towards the shimmer of perfect hair on a girl whose name he can't remember.

Gordo pays for his smokes and slips behind the shack to take a piss. Las grabs the girl's wrist lightly, leans into her with his best varsity athlete smile, the flash of his suburban teeth, and says, "Let's play a joke on that asshole."

And just like that they are wheeling down Ninth Line, Las behind the wheel and she shyly pressed against the passenger door, watching through the rear-view mirror as Gordo runs out to the road, one hand hitching up his fly and the other wagging a fist. It's a joy ride. Pure and simple.

Shayna thinks of crows and the way they wait. She thinks of tree branches filled with birds like thick black leaves, silent on a breezeless night. How the quiet of their trespass belies the calamity of their flight. The hoarse irritability, the heft of wing. Sometimes she wants to be such a bird, to wear the wedge of onyx tail feathers, raise the fused wing bones, take her sustenance through a curved beak. Blink with the eyes of a thief. Helen once said that Shayna was like a crow, the blue-purple gloss of her hair, the intelligence of her eyes, how she'd become a messenger for their people. She'd groaned. *And aren't they also tricky and unreliable?* They both laughed, dropped the subject.

But black birds are perching in the station between rest and waking. She feels them watching her. They know she aches to lean into the warm breast of sleep. Yet the cool, sunless air can't be stamped out of her clothes, her skin, her sleeping bag's thin layer of down.

She senses these dark birds gathering around her, waiting for the barricade fires to burn down; for the young boys to slump forward; for the older men and women to lean back with their eyes closed and mouths open; for the Warriors who have hung around the margins for two weeks but now moved in with their serious tents, their nylon revolution, to go quiet too. The crows are silent on the subject of whom to trust.

Forty minutes later, Las abandons Gordo's truck midway between the highway and the development entrance. There is still time to keep the plan in play. Gordo will be pissed, but not enough to bail entirely. It's an easy hike on foot from where Las left him on Ninth Line.

A hundred metres in the distance there are dying fires, figures bending, sitting, curling up, everyone fighting sleep except Las, who feels awake, more awake with his growing sense of outrage. His parents' property . . . his property. He crawls through the dark, drops low to his haunches, and tries to locate Gordo among the shadows.

Is he imagining movement, a brief, glinting conspiracy, within the low, dark cloud south of the development? He feels a thrill but can't trust his night vision, so he unfolds himself, stands, and refocuses his eyes. Suddenly there's a tightness around his calf, a sharp thumb pressing into his skin, and then something hitting the back of his other knee, making him topple sideways over the shoulders of a crouched, sweaty body. Gordo. The vaguely unwashed reek of cigarettes and kerosene gives him away.

Las lands heavily on his elbow, and his chin bounces off the hard dirt. "Fuck!"

"No standing up, remember?" Gordo punches into the darkness, but excitement has sharpened Las's intuition and reflexes. He rolls easily out of his friend's swinging range.

"That was a shithead move, taking my truck," Gordo says, lighting a cigarette. "Leaving me with my pants down. You parked it like a girl, by the way. Hope you got what you wanted, fuckface."

Las chuckles. He feels as cruel as, even crueller than his friend. He wonders if Gordo smells it the way an animal does, this recalibration of fearlessness. "So, is that it in the distance? A line of cop cars, vans?" he asks.

"Yeah, they're waiting," says Gordo. He takes a long drag. "I have it on good authority that by now some politician has been pulled out in his jammies. Once the cops get the legal green light, *bam!* Let the good times roll."

"So what're we doing, man? Moving in closer to watch the show?"

"No, you thickhead," Gordo says, as if Las's transgression earlier in the evening is forgotten, as if the plan was never threatened. "Once the cops pounce, there'll be a dozen empty squad cars. We're just going to trot past the raid to that parking lot down there. Think how much fun we could have in one of those babies! And who do you think is going to catch shit for it?"

He pulls out two camouflage kerchiefs, shoves one towards his friend, then wraps the other around his nose and mouth.

"Shit," says Las. He ties on his kerchief and raises a closed fist into the night.

Gordo hands him a black baseball cap emblazoned with a gold sun, inside of which is the profile of an Iroquois Warrior. "Now cover up that blond hair, asshole."

Helen wears her tiredness like a heavy coat. She cannot sleep, so she walks around the makeshift camp, collecting empty coffee cups and tossing them into the barrel fire, its cooling embers purring back at her with each offering. Suddenly the porch lights of houses beyond the river go off, then come on, go off again, like fireflies. *Ga'hai*, she thinks at first, witch lights. At the edge of the barricade encampment she focuses her old eyes to see what witching is before her, and it is then that she hears the soft crunch of feet dropping in unison on dry earth.

When there are a few metres between her and the line of advancing dark-clothed bodies, she catches the dull glint of eyes, the cream of young skin washed in the pink of excitement and fear. Shoulders moving in front of the distant lights and out of the way again. Out of the shadows come dozens and dozens of cops, marching close together. They reach the edge of firelight, and the line breaks up. Helen sees another wave of them following behind.

"Wake up! Wake up! Raid!" Helen's old voice wobbles and pitches into the dark.

∽

Las and Gordo watch the south horizon and it begins to move forward, a long, deep blur hurrying towards the barricade, silent as spilling ink. A single thin cry sounds from near the protest site. And just then the blur pixelates over the barricade, churning up a panic of wails and shrieks. Las wants to move closer, to see it in all its ruthless glory. Dark figures, their many shadows crossing the barrel-fire's light, fall sharply on the sleeping protestors like obsidian chess pieces.

"There's gotta be two hundred of them," he says. A rock pings him on the cheek and he looks over.

Gordo is standing, his body pointed in the direction the police marched from. "Now," he says and he sprints past the protest and its cries of betrayal.

Las follows, his eyes focusing on what's taking shape in the murk: neat rows of squad cars parked on the riverbank at the southern end of the development. "This is fucking crazy," he whispers under his breath. But fucking crazy helps him forget what he is becoming.

∽

When they descend, a great cloud of shadows and movement, Shayna is surprised at how real they feel. For a moment she hopes she will be taken into flight. Something comes sharp at her side and she is awake, her heart quickening, her sleeping bag ripped so the night's cool air alerts the surface of her skin. Then comes a superhuman pull. "Get up!"

Not a bird. A man. Shayna struggles to stand but her bare feet slip on the sleeping bag's lining, so she can't get purchase. She is wrenched upwards again. Her shoulder pops. She smells the heat of this man, hears his animal grunting and tastes the ozone burn of his urgency. She scissors her legs wildly, kicks them free; her toes grab the earth, but he pushes and she slides. His strength seems huge as he pulls her away from safety, into the darkness. Shayna hollers. She bends her knees, tucks her legs under to slow him down. He stops. The grip on her shoulders loosens, and with her one strong arm she elbows behind her, hitting the plush of his groin. There is a groan, a hissed "Fuck," and the offending arm is dropped. Shayna scrambles to a standing position, turns around, and becomes a twister of one-armed scratches and punches. She kicks his shins. Then he catches her free hand again, with a clasp that crunches her wrist, and she starts screaming with the high notes of a bird whose nest is being pillaged.

She expects her cries to cut through the dark, but they don't, because all around her there is yelling. All her people are screaming, clawing, flailing. Before she takes her knees to her ribs to make herself curl, Shayna peers back at the man who has immobilized her arms. He is dressed entirely in black, the leather of his gun holster and boots gleaming like feathers, his face as pale as new corn.

᭕

Helen will not stumble in front of them. She stops. "Move to the road," the cop chants over and over. "This is private property. Stand on the highway. Comply willingly and you won't get hurt." Let them shove an old lady. *Thump* come the boots. A chest pushes up against her back, propels her forward. She keeps her feet steady, walks ahead with her head held high. And then she is among a dozen or more protestors, half stooped with grogginess, standing out in the middle of road in the tawny rose of sunrise. Six others, handcuffed with their hands behind their backs, are face down in the dirt of the ditch, an officer kneeling into each back as if over a felled buck.

Helen turns to see Nate Bastine jump on the back of a flushed officer with massive arms who has pinned a small figure, spread-eagled under his weight. "Get off her! She's a woman! She's our leader."

Two other officers come running. One grabs Nate's arms, the other kicks his knees hard, so that he lurches forward.

Helen moves over to them, pushes herself between Nate and the officer now winding up to boot him in the stomach. "That's not a good idea," she says, and she points to the half-dozen protesters who have pulled out cellphones, aiming them at the officers. "Let them go. He's right, she's our leader. And she's pregnant."

The officer subduing Shayna looks up at Helen, and she sees alarm register in his face. "She didn't comply peacefully," he says. His voice is unsure.

"Did you hear me? She's pregnant."

The cop lifts his knee from Shayna's back, but she remains lying on the ground, like a swatted bug. Nate is freed with a shove that leaves him sprawling in the dirt; he springs to his feet, his face inflamed. Helen raises her hand. "Thank you for your courage," she whispers to him, and he brushes the dirt from his chin, his thighs, and backs away.

She turns to the officer who's pinned her niece. "I hope you didn't hurt this woman. You better get those handcuffs off."

Helen squats by Shayna, sees the dirt that rims her niece's mouth and wipes it with her sleeve. The officer looks sheepish and unlocks the cuffs. Helen helps her to stand, brushes the dust and grit from her clothes.

Shayna grabs Helen's neck and leans in, her eyes round as suns. "I am?" she asks shakily. "Am I?"

Helen doesn't answer. Instead she draws Shayna back towards her people, who have gathered in a protective oval on the asphalt, blocked from moving back into the development. To a one they have all fished in their pockets for cellphones. They thumb in the numbers over and over. "They've cut the mobile service," somebody yells out.

Suddenly two teenagers bolt. They run across the empty mud, past the development with its fires gone cold, its ragged sentry of police, towards the creek. An officer swears under her breath, but none make chase.

Fifteen minutes later, Helen sees what the police officers didn't anticipate. Already far, far in the distance beyond the highway, on the outer reaches of the reserve, are pinholes of light from a convoy of cars, trucks, motorcycles headed in their direction. It grows in length. Within minutes of running away, the teenaged girls had reached the reserve and the nearest house with a phone. And that phone call fell like the first of a domino run.

∽

Elijah parks himself by the side of the road across from the barricade. What he sees is a failure of pragmatism. At the entrance of the development is a riot squad formation of police: blank faces, no shields or helmets. He imagines the plan being hatched in the cop shop and subsequently molested by several layers of hand-wringing bureaucrats. *There's only two dozen protesters. We'll send two hundred cops.* Somebody there signed off on that, believing numbers would do the work of actual strategy.

The cars and trucks are rolling in now. *This is where it gets interesting.* He jumps out of his pickup and marches into the crowd. He yells, and they yell too. "Who's in charge? Who the fuck is in charge here?"

More vehicles arrive. Whole families from the reserve are running, running towards the line of cops, who push them towards the road, farther from the development. Moms, kids, teenagers, and men, some already kerchiefed. The traffic spilling out of the reserve doesn't let up. Elijah sees that some of those front-line cops look pretty worried now, wondering what their superiors have set them up for. The numbers have been reversed; now there are easily four times more natives than cops. It's as if the top of an anthill has been sheared off: the whole reserve could empty onto this patch of land in a few hours. And the TV cameras have arrived.

"This is an illegal raid! These cops have assaulted women, old ladies!"

There is a hiss of outrage. *Any second now,* Elijah thinks. And sure enough, he sees a rock arc towards the line of cops. More vehicles arrive. More rocks are scooped from the ditch, hurled into the sky. The morning showers bruises.

Elijah turns. He won't be immortalized in a photo with rocks flying overhead. He slips back to his truck and drives away.

∽

Las wants to piss himself laughing. They just walk right up to it, slip into the seats, touch the radio and computer. And there is the big yellow plastic key ring hanging from the ignition. Seconds later they are gunning that baby through the main streets and around the burbs, then cutting up the county roads like they're in a chase scene, flinging gravel, the windows open, leaving a war paint of tire rubber on the asphalt.

"Neeed for speeeed," Gordo yells.

Las laughs. It's all funny. In a matter of hours he has done the worst things of his life so far. There's no going back. Yet it doesn't feel so terrible – it's fuckin' hilarious.

Gordo presses his foot onto the brake, the car doughnuts, and the gravel makes a glockenspiel of the car doors. They slide into the ditch by fallow fields of rye grass and alfalfa.

"Time to burn, baby."

Along with flares, folding pylons, and a locked shotgun box, there's a can of gas in the trunk. Las hungers to keep the sensation stoked. "Let's sniff the shit first."

"Why the fuck not?" Gordo says. "We're native, aren't we?"

They both laugh, pull their kerchiefs off their chins, stick their noses in the gas can, laugh again. Gordo giggles like a girl as he splashes gas on the car seats and in the trunk and tosses the match in with no warning.

Las falls into the sweet-smelling tangle as the blast of flame muscles him backwards. He is floating, floating on the alfalfa, which is green and runny and as cool as menthol. It's all funny and pain-free, and even when he actually starts to feel kind of wet, he is dry-heaving with giggles. His focus pushes through the blue. Gordo stands above him, pouring gas from the can into the palm of his hand and then flicking it at Las as if he's a farmer sowing seeds, except what's sown dissolves into damp stains on Las's shorts and T-shirt. And even in his elation, Las recognizes the game his friend is about to play.

Sure enough, Gordo has one last sniff and tosses the empty can. Then, with his best slasher-film laugh, he takes out a matchbook and lights one match after another, tossing them so they fall at Las's feet, then by his arm. And because it is such an asshole move, this too is for Las the funniest thing, the idea that Gordo thinks he's going to light up his buddy like a Victoria Day bonfire.

Shit, Gordo never stops. Man, is he ever a prick. Las quits laughing. He comes up on his elbows, lifts his hips for leverage, and kicks out one leg so that his heel mashes Gordo's nuts. A second hard kick nails his doubled-over friend on the side of the face, so that he falls. Then Las jumps up, panting. He wants to boot

Gordo in the head hard enough to hear his skull bones crack, feel a piss of cranial fluid on his toes. But Las is wearing flip-flops, so the worst he can do is take a heel and pound it into Gordo's ribs.

Then he is flip-flopping through the field. Its plants are soft and light as a girl's hands against his thighs and ankles. And he is laughing, laughing into the magenta sunrise.

∽

Joe pulls up in his truck just as the police decamp and the sun makes a rosy crest on the horizon. He imagines what was said to bring about this retreat: *We're dangerously outnumbered. The situation is* not *under control.* He feels badly for the guy who had to make that call. A line of black backs moves away from the development, just quickly enough to outpace the jeers that follow. Only a few protestors make chase; the rest swarm the development once again, while others refuse to leave the highway where they've been corralled for hours.

Joe watches a hydro tower fall onto rain-softened earth, attached by jerry-rigged cables to two pickups. Seven storeys of galvanized steel are dragged through the ribboned mud of a not-yet-finished hydro cut intended to bring electricity to the sprawl of new homes, out onto the highway. Against the asphalt, the steel makes one long complaint. And then it is left to rest. An abandoned trailer home, delivered from the reserve by another truck, is unhooked behind the tower. Gravel, lumber, garbage become a tangled bricolage behind, around, and under the tower and trailer.

Joe scans all the people he sees, the insides of moving vehicles as well, for the daughter who hasn't come home. He chews the rough skin of a knuckle until it cracks and stings. From a simple protest, a full blockade animates itself, goaded into place by the ill-considered raid. To Joe it looks like the loneliest place in the world.

Then a car speeds down Highway 3 and brakes to a whinnying stop before the fallen tower, the trailer, the junk that obstructs its passage. The driver doesn't get out. One of the protestors, a tall man with a broad chest, clambers atop the heap and stands with his legs apart, the morning sun high behind him as he waves a flag back and forth, a flag that's not for a country but for a people, for an understanding of place. Against the sun he is dark and powerful, a winged messenger.

CHAPTER 12

He bit her ear as he landed hard on top of her. His hot breath pressed against her cheek. *Who gives a fuck about a ten dollar Pocahontas?* Her nose twisted on the sand. *I will lie here forever,* she thought, *never open my eyes again, and when he is done with me, I will shrivel up in the sun like deer gut.*

Her cigarette had flown from her grip, its ember, its little fire bright as the eye of something small and scared. She watched its fire, watched its fire. Then she closed her eyes and slipped away from the heat, from the cigarette's hot eye, from the pain of what was happening to her. She closed her eyes and it didn't have to be summer. It wasn't summer. She went looking for ice. And found it in the memory of a cooler season, years ago, when an uncharacteristic plummet made the leaves surrender early, the light grow dismal. Daddy Joe bellowed in the afternoons. He kicked things because the trailer was damp and drafty and there was no relief from grey skies and worrying about money.

But she didn't care. She had the dog, a little furnace of white fur. It curled up inside a tent of blankets on Cherisse's bed, or it chased pieces of string. The games set the dog yipping and Joe yelling at them to stop, so they'd leave the trailer and wander for hours along the banks of the Smoke. The dog's legs were short but it had the heart and lungs of something bigger, and better, than both of them. Cherisse and the dog – which she dared not name – already knew all the trails by their balance beams of fallen trunks, beaver dams, and marshy inlets where wood ducks mated and where, in that first winter, the river narrowed and froze into acreages of ice.

The problem with ice is that its dangers are so obvious, so clear. Its beauty too. She was a girl who liked beauty, things that shone, their voodoo of desire and reprisals. Just like the dog, the ice was scoured of hue, of colours, so it held light like a fuse. And she couldn't resist; all that winter Cherisse went down to the frozen river bend and dared herself out farther and farther, even as the little dog stayed on shore, running and scolding her. Then one day she was standing in the middle of the river's bend, and in the distance she could see a scalloped edge where the ice gave way to dark, oily water that slunk into the horizon. The view was vast and dizzying. And she had the urge to do something beautiful, to pirouette and glide like the ice skaters in spangled bodysuits she'd seen on television. She stuck out one leg backwards, airplaned her arms for balance, and lifted her head to the sky. A cold February wind shook the brittle trees on the shore; the sound that reached her in the middle of the river was like a low gasp of wonder, followed by hurrahs from the little dog.

When she looked down, one leg still stretched out behind her, she saw how the ice bubbled, crude glass underneath which the river slid incorrigibly. She didn't know how long she had held her balance, her heart beating with the subterranean flow, but a sudden high inhale from downriver pulled her forward. Her fall was a hard *thump*, bringing her to hands and knees. She imagined that a satellite broke apart in the atmosphere the way that ice did – with loud sighs instead of explosions. Suddenly she was on a large puzzle piece cleaved from the rest. It moved ever so slightly. The little dog was a white blur, scuttling along the bank, its panicked yips insisting she return to safety. Cherisse crouched on hands and knees, pulled herself over the cracks. The ice was like a baby's skull – held together but not fused. She moved gingerly from one piece to the next, towards a long frozen tooth that still clung to the riverbank. But the instant her full weight was on that frozen peninsula, it shuddered wickedly, tore away from the edge.

The ice pieces crowded up against each other at the bend, split into ever-smaller chunks. Once the jostling mass turned the corner, the pieces scattered in the faster-moving width, chased by the dark serpent of water. Cherisse lay on her belly and inched towards the edge of her ice, waiting for the riverbank to be within jumping distance. She would have made it too, but her little dog, half-mad with panic at seeing her close and moving, leapt from the safety of earth to the moving ice. It fell just shy of the edge, scrabbling its little feet and nails against the frozen raft, trying to get purchase. *No, no!* Cherisse yelled. She stretched out her arm to the wet animal, her ears full of its frightened clawing. And this beautiful dog, unnamed because she knew it wasn't hers, was no longer beautiful, but all bone and sinew, bulging eyes and strange freckled skin, drenched and shaking. In the half-second when the scratching stopped, the ice slipped out from under the dog's paws, and the dark water sucked it under, she realized it had loved her more than its own survival.

She lay her cheek on the floe, which began to move faster, and she watched the water ahead, praying the dog would reappear. There was no going home without it.

———

"No!" Cherisse says again. And now the heat is back. She is lying in the dirt, smelling strawberries. The light behind her lids is tinted with the berries' bleeding juice. There's earth under her shoulders where she fell, running. Running away. Running home. The ground as giving as a mother's lap. How long has she been here? She remembers a darkness in which all the birds were awake, filling the night with strange cries. A rock landing at her side, close to her ribs.

She is hurting, her whole body mapped with soreness, and now she has a thirst greater than pain. She concentrates, and one eyelid opens to the rosy blur of morning and then its stripes of green, pale and porous. The green of life, of plants. She feels the back of her head leaning into a thick stalk. *Tobacco sprung from the grave of the Creator's mother*, she thinks. Dead would be good; dead would be cool as clay, cooler still.

CHAPTER 13

When Coulson was fourteen, his father said simply, *This is what we do.* For the next six weeks he was sentenced to picking tobacco in the day and sleeping in the barn at night. *You're not really part of a priming crew unless you eat and sleep like they do,* his father told him. At four-thirty a.m. on the first morning, Coulson quit his soft bed reluctantly. The farm kitchen was already distended with frying, baking, and percolating. Every burner was in use, the oven light glaring, trays of fresh baking stacked on the table, his mother already damp and beaded with exertion. Coulson tore open a warm biscuit, slathered it in butter and apricot preserves, and ate painstakingly, until his father grabbed his shoulder, pushed him out into the wet morning and away from his comforts.

Outside, men lined up on the picnic table benches under the laneway's pin oaks. In those days, primers were drifters from Quebec or Kentucky and seasonal migrants from Jamaica. The hardest workers were not necessarily muscled and were often sallow and thin. All of them wore rumpled clothes and greasy caps, wiped their coffee-wet lips along their sleeves or bare arms, ate their eggs and biscuits with their heads low to the table, as if condemned. Angel, a Mohawk woman who worked afternoons on the tying line, filled tin cups with coffee, wordlessly swatted away impatient hands as she moved down the tables. Beyond them the fields hung with a tight mesh of tiny droplets that slid off the tobacco leaves, dripped into the sandy loam. For the rest of the harvest, Coulson would work, eat, and rest with the hired men and his father wouldn't look sideways at him. He was orphaned, with his parents in full view. *Keeps the primers honest and my boy humble* – that was the way the old man explained it.

He wouldn't have stood a minute of it had it not been for Big Junior. His father had first hired the man the summer Coulson turned eight, after the government relaxed regulations so farmers could bring cheaper seasonal farm help from outside the country. Big Junior had returned every year since. For the nearly two months he spent at the Stercyx farm, the man laughed; he drank every drop of his evening beer as if it were a grace; he lampooned the other workers with a mix of affection and astute mimicry that would make Coulson's mother tear up in an anguish of giggling. The family began waiting for him, though none would admit it to the other; they waited through the long winters of quiet suppers, dim lights, and the parsimony of their affections. When he arrived late July, Big Junior would wrap Coulson in his arms and hug him in a way that was too demonstrative, too liberal for his father to ever consider. Then he would laugh, and Coulson would feel as if the man had lifted a heavy canvas off the top of the world to let the sun in.

I can't teach you how to pick with talk, Big Junior told him the summer he joined the crew. *Just follow me and do what I do. And do it the way I do it, or else you gonna be hurting bad.*

Within the first hour of priming, Coulson's shirt lay flat and wet along his back because of the dew-beaded leaves. His fingers were numb. He heard the staccato of other men's grunts as they bent to snap ripe young leaves at the base of the plant stalk. Coulson made a science of Big Junior, following him through the rows, copying his position, noting the angle of his knees, the precise way he folded his body at the waist so that his spine was almost perfectly parallel to the earth but for the slightest arch in the small of his back. He listened to the man's slow rhythm of breath, visually estimated the length of the gait that took him from one plant to the next. Big Junior bent at the hips and softened his knees to reach the sand leaves at the base of the tobacco stalk. Along the length of a row, 650 plants deep, he used one hand to pick and the other to hold the leaves. In the next row he switched hands. Big Junior didn't stand up until the arm farthest from the plant clutched so many leaves to his side that he risked dropping one. Then he used his picking hand to secure the leaf bundle, and in one smooth movement that left him bending again, scooped them into the tobacco boat that followed the primers.

Don't straighten too much, kid, Big Junior warned him. *Or you'll never get yourself back to bending.*

Before finishing his first row, Coulson felt the pull in his calves, in his buttocks, the armful of fresh-picked leaves making his right shoulder throb. The sun had burned off the fog by then, baking dry the back of his shirt. His socks were still damp, his cheeks flaming from heat and mounting despair. *Sips, honey*, Angel reminded each man as she handed out cups of water at the end of the row. *You sip for a drink out here, or you'll piss yourself dry and keel over.*

Near midday the steam was out of the soil, the sun bearing down on them hard, and Coulson, who was too proud to stop to pee, let urine slide down his leg and into his shoes. It didn't matter if he stained his pants; all of him was damp and reeking by then, numbly borne forward by the rhythm of the work – pick, step, pick, step, pick, step. With each plucked leaf, he felt the periphery of his vision wobble and his eyes sting from the saltwater streaming from underneath his cap. With every new row, he thought, *I'm not going to make it through the first day.* Coulson imagined the pressure of his father's work-swollen knuckles on his shoulders, the way it felt as if the older man were pushing him down into the earth in order to root him there.

That night he lay on his cot in the barn while men moved about him, smoking and talking, and he wondered how he'd got there. There was a dull complaint at the base of his back and his knees; the rest of him was sun-whacked, buckling with a tiredness that was gravitational, sucking him towards the centre of the earth. Being a tobacco grower's kid would have consumed him in a fever of resentment, if Big Junior hadn't come along, shaken his shoulder, and offered him a sweating beer as if he were just another tired man. *Nice priming, kid,* he said. Coulson groaned in response, pulled himself up to sitting.

The beer rinsed him clean; it was cooling and delicious. Big Junior leaned back and told him things: the tricks to picking sugar cane and bananas, how good rum can turn friend into foe, the fish he'd caught in water bluer than Coulson's eyes, until the boy fell asleep, the step, pick priming rhythm sloshing against his ears as if he were doing laps in the swimming pool.

There are five bikes leaning against the bunkhouse; three are brand new, the other two Coulson pulled from the barn and tuned up in the spring. Five bikes for five primers – the first rite of harvest. Leaving the farmhouse to join his crew already out in the fields, Coulson restrains himself from retesting the brake pads, adjusting the tire pressure, re-greasing the chains.

There's a bike for each of you this year – you won't have to share, Coulson said to his first three primers, the veterans, when they arrived on a direct flight from Mexico City to the small regional airport a week ago and walked the tarmac to his truck, a rucksack of clothes slung over each of their shoulders. *It means you can go into town together. Anytime I head out with the truck, you're welcome too. But driving into town is a bit complicated lately . . .*

Ramirez, whose English is strongest, is from a small village near Palenque, in Chiapas. James and Diego are also Mayan but from the cities. On the ride home from the airport, Coulson told them about the barricade. They nodded their heads. Ramirez's smile was wry, a bit weary. He looked out the window and muttered at the passing landscape like an old acquaintance.

They all have families waiting for them. Coulson never asks to see photos: he doesn't want the responsibility such intimacy demands. But this year Ramirez insisted. He had to look: a boy, maybe nine or ten years old, holding his younger sister's and brother's hands, all of them tentative and half-smiling. The image puts pressure on Coulson's temples.

He walks through his fields, stops, and tops a tobacco plant. The head of trumpeting pink flowers gives a shudder, falls as lightly as a child's hand into Coulson's palm. Ahead of him on the harvester, the three men have become a topping crew. The two younger ones have stripped to singlets in the mid-month heat. But Ramirez wears long sleeves and doesn't perspire. Coulson figures it will take a few days to finish removing the blossoms, which even now still impress him with their delicacy, a balance of wildflower and hothouse exotica. His mother counselled him against this kind of romance – she must have seen it in him. *Farming is a showdown between us and nature's spite,* she'd say. *So you best be spiteful in return.* When the tobacco shoots were newly planted, she'd sweeten huge tubs of bran with molasses, then mix in lead arsenate. *It tricks the cutworm grubs. They think someone's left them dessert.* His mother would laugh like Hecate as she spread her concoction over the fields on early spring evenings.

Still, Coulson can't resist the alchemy of sun and flowers. He selects the seed heads with the most open blooms to later plunk in a Mason jar of water on his kitchen table. Beyond the rows of shoulder-high tobacco, the grade of the land rises at the highway, where there's a blur of movement. Overnight the barricade has morphed from a small protest against the development into a carnival crowd spreading over a blocked highway, carrying banners for poverty action groups, trade unions, urban Métis. There are first-aid and food stations and a crazy quilt of tents. It looks like some apocalyptic ruins on the horizon; parked vehicles catch sunlight in short sparks as if the air around them is overly ionized, ready to combust. This morning he dug out his father's old binoculars, telling himself it was okay to be curious. He could not find Shayna in the crowds. By noon there were at least a thousand people milling around the blockade. He knew she'd be the one navigating the logistics of food, fuel, toilets, and trash. Her cellphone was busy every time he called, until he lost the heart to try again.

The last time they were together, he flipped her on her stomach, pulled her up on all fours, knelt behind her with one fist dug into the flesh of her hips, the front of his thighs slapping the back of hers, his free hand pushing into the small of her back, then twining her hair with his wrist. When he was done, he fell to the bed panting, and a confession of feeling burst from him. He can't remember his exact words, only that she stayed silent, her head on the pillow, eyes staring past and right through him. When he woke in the dark hours before sunrise, she was gone without a note or a brush of her lips against his cheek.

He wishes he were more like his parents. Such a singularity to a life centred on plants and earth and sky. It spoiled them for love. The old man never raised a hand to Coulson's mother, but neither did he place one tenderly on her neck or shoulder. She was, like his land, something inextricable, a constant: sorrows and joys mixed in her like the temperaments of sun and rain. To have made her special would have been to doubt her inevitability.

Coulson doesn't notice that the harvester has stopped ahead of him until shouts pull him from his thoughts. James and Diego have jumped off their seats, pulled out water bottles and cigarettes as Ramirez marches forward, investigates. He sees the three of them circle, hears nothing, and then Ramirez turns, his arms up in the air, his mouth flared. Coulson drops the topped flowers and runs.

It was the dog, mewling and scratching at the barn door, that led him to a patch of uncultivated field that harvest season when Coulson turned eighteen. He'd slept in his underwear, his waking belly empty and tight, the sun not yet fully risen. The other primers were still snoring as he snuck out into a half-lit dawn. He stopped after crossing the highway, followed the dog with his eyes. There was something about the way Big Junior's body was twisted, the clothes torn, the blood candied over his grey-lipped gape. Coulson knew. He ran towards him, lifted the man's head into his lap, touched his cool skin, pressed his fingers into the pulse-less neck; nothing of his friend was left inside that casing. Coulson tried to carry the body, but in death the powerful man had even more heft. So he grabbed the dented bike thrown to one side, because he had to carry something.

His parents paid for Big Junior's wife to come and take his body home. The woman sobbed with an ancient grief full of spit. She jammed the heels of her palms into her eyes. No, she didn't want to press the police for more answers. She pushed a dog-eared photo of her children, their faces small and afraid, across the table, and Coulson saw the wasted beauty of their trusting eyes.

For years after he woke up in a sweat at night, cradling the bloodied, swollen face of their father, the weight of heartbreak,

anger, stigma pinning him to his bed. He knew from the way
Big Junior had been thrown. He knew how it had happened.
And this knowledge added to the wreckage of that summer: a
skilled worker, a good man, a parent, had been tossed off the
road like jetsam. The whole town, even the farm, was tarnished
for him. He left eagerly for university that fall and stayed away
as long as he could.

Coulson's mouth dries. Before he arrives at Ramirez's side, he
can feel it already, something as light as a dented bike in his
arms and himself running, running towards the farmhouse,
Ramirez already yelling behind him, *The harvester! Take her back
on the harvester!* In his imagination, his feet serve a master outside him. He is moving; that's what matters. He won't know if
he is doing the right thing or if he is making things worse, but
certainly his truck will reach a hospital faster than waiting for
an ambulance.

He can picture the farmhouse getting closer, and when
Coulson makes out the shape of the kitchen door, he sees his
father there, waiting on the stoop with a morning cup of coffee
in his hand, his expression hardening into denial as Coulson
nears, carrying something queerly broken, the dog whining and
yipping behind him. And Coulson sees again how his father, for
whom action and thought were fused, in whom there was no
muscle for hesitation, freezes instead of running forward to help.

His mother bursts through the door, takes something from
his arms, and recognizing it, seeing the blood on his forearms,
yells at them both to fetch cloths, blankets, water while she calls
the police. It is she who charges into the fields: a woman fierce
about accepting the sorrows of a place along with its gifts. His
father remains still for seconds more, staring at his fields, his
face painted with disbelief.

———

There's a large oak in the middle of a southern field. Coulson never had the heart to cut it down; he's arranged the tobacco to frame the tree so none of the plants languish in its shade. Underneath it are a broken Scotch bottle, a fieldstone firepit, heaped ashes, and cigarette packages flattened into the earth. The workers murmur. They stand back from an abandoned heap of clothes tucked into a furrow of earth surrounded by trampled tobacco plants. Coulson's eyes catch the gloss of remarkable hair fanning across the dirt, reflecting sunlight. A girl. Swollen face, ripped shirt, jeans yanked down to the ankles, thighs striated in red, a stiletto heel torn from her boot, tossed liked a used wishbone. Ramirez is bent over her, his fingers on her neck.

"She's alive."

CHAPTER 14

Nate says, "Close your eyes," and he grabs Stephanie's hands, pulls her forward. "Take a step up."

She moves forward tentatively, letting each foot hover as if she could suspend this dependence on him for judgment, for safety. His hands are warm and firm around hers. His lips brush against the crook of her neck. "Not yet," he whispers. "Just stand still."

Stephanie is wearing new flats. The blockade is three days old. During the thirty-minute walk from their rendezvous south of it to a destination Nate won't name, the shoes dug painfully into the backs of her heels, squeezed her toes. Now she can't admit that her feet sting, she's thirsty, and the screw-top bottle of wine she swiped from her parents' rack is making her backpack purse sag, its thin straps abrading her shoulders. But she says nothing, just stands and keeps her eyes closed, because he asked. Love has turned her into someone she barely recognizes.

He moves away and she deflates a little at the loss of his proximal warmth. She hears rustling amplified in a large space, imagines field mice nesting in a tunnel. Then there's a strike, a hiss, the whiff of sulphur. He's lit a match. The idea of a fire starting somewhere nearby, while her eyes are shut, excites and unnerves her.

Her world is all combustible of late: Nate, the dairy bar, her family and home. The sharp way her parents talk to each other and to her. The tight suffocation of the house at night, in the morning. And worst of all, the family dinner table, when the few words spoken are dry sparks. Just this evening her brother reappeared at the evening meal after taking two days to sleep off an epic drunk. She watched his blond tendrils move as he ate, hiding, then revealing an angry sickle-shaped scratch, starting under his earlobe and curving along the side of his neck, stopping before the clavicle. The scratch had two parallel ridges: one raised, from something deep and sharp, and the other dragged alongside, breaking the skin in a ragged line. She couldn't stop looking at it, was surprised that her mother's eyes, which usually scanned the boy like a raptor's, had failed to notice. But lately her mother ate staring down or off into space.

She debated mentioning it aloud, just to fuck her brother up and watch her mother's eyes widen with alarm as she took in the breach of her son's July-brown skin before running off in search of Polysporin. But before she could decide, Las pushed away from the table with a grunt and a *Gotta go* and was out of the house within seconds. Her mother looked up helplessly in the direction of the slammed front door, as if newly resigned to her children's unexplained comings and goings. Before sneaking away herself, Stephanie noticed that her brother's bedroom door was ajar. She couldn't help herself. She slipped inside.

"Nate?"

"Soon," he says. "One more thing."

He comes back to her. She feels him gently lift the knapsack off her tender shoulders, pull the straps off one at a time, so that his fingers glide along her bare arms and her skin rises to his touch. Then one palm is in the small of her back, the other pressed gently against her eyes, and he guides her as if she were a blind dance partner, a few more steps. "Kneel," he says. "But keep your eyes closed."

She bends until her shins hit something thin and soft over a harder surface, and finally she topples onto her bum with a little yelp of surprise. His hands are there to steady her, to keep her from falling on her back, and when she is sitting up straight, his fingers encircle her ankle. He removes the left flat, then the right, and the cool night air is a salve to her flayed skin.

"Now," he says, and she opens her eyes, at first to a mottled darkness and then, as she adjusts to the light of the candles he has lit around them, she sees that they are inside a cathedral-sized building. Liquefied colours move across the walls, up to the ceiling, with the dim candescence of stained glass. She looks down. The softness underneath them is an opened sleeping bag.

Stephanie puts her hand to her mouth, tries to focus. "Are we in a church?" she says.

Nate smiles. She stands up barefoot and turns slowly to survey the space. The walls reveal themselves: they are covered in dark adumbrations of figures that are realistic but half-finished, as if the night has eaten them away. Trees that bleed like severed limbs. Huge winged birds. A hideous child emerging from a woman's armpit, another between her legs. A gallery of monstrous faces that are bug-eyed, their mouths twisting up grotesquely, framed with ropy hair – black or gold – that floats seaweed-like out from them. The colours are flat, saturated, comic-book bright. And connecting it all are words, a scrawling wild-style, up and over and under the images like some funhouse helix. She thinks it's graffiti, though it's unlike any graffiti she has ever seen. It hurts her eyes; it exhilarates her. How could this be here in small, fusty, unworldly Doreville?

"I don't understand. What is this? What is this place?" Stephanie asks finally.

Nate sits with his hands wrapped around his knees, surveying the work. "Studio, gallery, laboratory." He shrugs. "Secret society. The building's an old cheese factory, abandoned."

"So is this your work?" She wants his hands, so easy with kindnesses for her, to be the instruments of this wonder.

"Yes, but not all. There's a crew of us from the rez. We started coming here about eighteen months ago. And you know, everybody just found their thing – oil-based chalk, Krylon, Montana, acrylic. We worked out a manifesto. No stencils, no stickers, no copycat work. We look at the stuff from São Paulo, Berlin, L.A., New York. Find it on the net, in magazines. But then what we do is ours, all ours. We're working out something that's all our own, y'know."

He nods his head at the work as if meeting a group of friends. Stephanie imagines the hours he's spent here, laughing and collaborating with others, losing all sense of time. And what a space – how its bigness, its cold warehouse air, would quicken his lungs. She prickles with envy, the shame of her own evenings driven by boredom to television or the internet.

"Those are mine," he says. "The Sky Mother, the Twins, the false faces." He points to the largest depictions, disturbing and beautiful.

"They're amazing. Too good for here," she says, falling back to the ground beside him. "This fucking small-minded town."

He moves closer and draws a finger from behind her ear, down along the side of her neck, to where her clavicle meets the top of her shoulder. "Thank you for saying that," he says.

"Someone will find us soon enough. Tear it all down or paint over it. But for now, it exists."

"No!"

"It's the risk you take; makes the work better. This idea, you know, that it may be temporary." His hand slides down the side of her arm and then his fingers circle, ever so slightly, at her elbow, and she realizes how very quiet it is, how alone they are.

Stephanie reaches for her knapsack purse. She has to pull out her camera to free the bottle of wine and the two plastic cups she pilfered. The wine is lukewarm, slightly sour, but after tapping their glasses in a toast she is suddenly nervous, eager to feel a buzz. She gulps hers down. Her hand falls to the side with her empty cup and brushes along the camera, which makes her start.

"My camera," she says, and he looks down at it. "I can document all of this. Put together a portfolio. I'm good at that. I'm good with a camera."

He considers it for a moment and then says, "I believe you." His lips are travelling over her chin, down her sternum, towards the lowest ebb of her scoop neck. "I believe you're good. We'll help out each other a lot. We're a team now."

He snags the edge of her T-shirt with his teeth and pulls, pushing his lips in against the skin, nuzzling his face into her breasts, and with one arm bracing them both, he gently lowers her to the ground. Before she is completely under him, he stops and looks into her eyes. "This okay?" he asks. "I want this to be okay."

Stephanie nods. Her skin feels damp, her heart a yammering tattletale, her limbs as pliable as fresh clay. Was she ever going to resist? Already she can't remember.

∽

The activist is up on the dais of St. Cuthbert's basement auditorium telling those gathered in detail about the injustices they've suffered. Las feels disappointed. He abandoned a half-full dinner plate hoping for someone more imposing, heroic. This guy has a beakish face and a braying edge to his voice, not unlike a wheezy farm animal. Las looks around; there are about thirty others in the room, most of them middle-aged like his parents. There are posters on every telephone pole downtown. He expected a room full of hot-headed young men creating a swoon of adrenaline, imminent violence, not old-sters dressed for a mall walk or a Sunday picnic roast. But at least they seem impressed, willing to take the activist seriously, some of them nodding as the guy makes a point. That has to mean something. *He's from the big city,* the pub owner, Will Jacobs, told Las when he came in, slapping his shoulder. Las wanted to ask why the citizens' group wasn't being organized by an actual Doreville citizen. *He says God wants him here,* added Will. *Oh, Jesus effin' Christ,* Las thought to himself. He'd shot out of the house jonesing for anger, a desire for hard-fisted vengeance that mirrored and justified his own, not a candidate for the priesthood named Kenneth.

The basement is muggy and nobody has thought to put out chairs. Las recognizes Gordo's mom hovering off to his left. *Not here officially,* she says over and over to anyone who approaches her. *Just curious.* Las nods at her and she looks surprised to see him.

Kenneth likes to talk. As his speechifying drags on, Las finds it hard to concentrate on all the ideas Kenneth insists should be attached to their outrage as upstanding Doreville citizens. Las already knows what to be mad about: wishy-washy policing, bleeding-heart judges, politicians running scared with their tails between their legs, entitled natives. Some of the people in the room begin to shift from foot to foot as if they have to pee. Las detects the rank ammonia of body odour and

scrunches his nose. He leans his chin into his shoulder for a furtive sniff of his armpits. Not him.

Kenneth stops for a breath. "Now, folks, " he announces, "I
am going to outline my ten steps for a citizen counter-insurgency."

Las's ears prick up. He likes the sound of *insurgency*, even if
it's the *counter* kind, which he guesses waters down some of the
anarchy and fun. All is fair in love and war – isn't that what the
guy is saying in so many words? Kenneth rhymes off the steps
so fast that Las is still trying to sort through them ten minutes
later, trying to understand which of them actually means fighting back, throwing things, fucking things up a bit, when the
crowd organizes itself into sign-making stations.

"Kenneth thinks signs are a very important aspect of counter-
insurgency," Will Jacobs says as he hands Las a paintbrush, clean
bristol board. The mayor has already hightailed it out of there.

"Bullshit!" Las says. He doesn't care who hears.

Kenneth, who has alighted from the dais and is instructing
a wannabe counter-insurgent in Bermuda shorts and bright
white sneakers to print neatly, stay within the margins, bobs up
his head. "Is there a problem?" he asks. Off the stage, he looks
even pointier, his voice sounds even more adenoidal.

Las's thirst for bravado, for brawling, for something big,
becomes an overwhelming thirst for beer, catching him at the
throat. "Yeah, there's a fucking problem. It's over there, blocking Highway 3, while we're in here fingerpainting like four-
year-olds."

Kenneth twists around his head in alarm, raises his arms.
"Nobody should be doing their signs with their fingers. Use the
brushes, everyone."

Las throws up his hands in disgust and storms out of the
church basement, knocking over a row of paint pots so that a
chorus of cheeps from disgruntled sign-makers follows him into
the night. Outside, he unleashes himself on the parked sedans,

vans, and utility vehicles belonging to the sheep inside. He elbows car doors, twists hood ornaments and side-view mirrors. "This fuckin' useless place!" he yells at the empty lot as he wrenches one mirror free, tossing it so it bounces off the hood of a car parked four spots away. He waits for someone to come out of the church, to start yelling, but there is only quiet, but for a low chuckle.

Las turns to the dark wall of the church. A figure crouches there. He smells the joint before he sees its hot eye.

"Be careful there, rebel. Don't want a vandalism charge to stand in the way of that glorious future of yours."

Gordo. Las has avoided his friend since he left him moaning in the grass, the morning of the raid. He went home, fell onto his bed, and woke more than twenty-four hours later in a dark room, vaporous with the musk of his unshowered body, gasoline-soaked clothes, and a foggy despair about exactly what happened that night, how far he'd slipped into the murk of unredeemable acts. He has a vague memory of his mother's thin entreaty from outside his bedroom door calling him to dinner – or was it breakfast? Both? Certainly meals were missed before he finally dragged himself into the shower. But nothing could make him feel clean. He hasn't been in the pool for nearly a week.

Now Gordo will be pissed. Some line has been crossed that might trigger a new spree of unpredictability. A church, inside it or out, is an unlikely place for either of them to show up, much less both. Las wonders if the mayor ratted him out to her son. He wonders how long Gordo has been waiting for him.

"Wanna toke, fuckhole?" The joint is held out to him, a molten bead against the darkening air.

Las sees he won't be able to say no. There's no excuse not to tighten the distance between himself and Gordo, though instinct tells him space is his one advantage. He walks over, slides down the church wall, squats beside the other boy, and accepts the joint nub, its strong fragrance dizzying. He inhales deeply. "Thanks, man," he says, handing it back. "Good shit."

The tops of their fingers touch, and instead of taking the nub from him, Gordo lets the contact linger, like a dare or a challenge. Las pulls away, letting the joint fall to the ground in front of them.

"That was stupid," Gordo says calmly. His fingers move, mantis-like, to retrieve it.

Las unfolds himself to standing to ease the knot in his belly. He's just about to offer to buy his friend a beer, to get them somewhere with light and people, when he notices Gordo, still squatting, grab something brick-shaped at his side, turn it to vertical. It comes down hard on Las's bare toes, exposed in his flip-flops. He feels a crunch, a jarring disbelief, a flame of pain. A wildfire of sensation races up his calf. Las crouches over, holds his knees. He pukes.

Gordo laughs, straightens, takes a long final drag on the joint, and throws it at him. "You think I'd let you get away with being an asshole?" he says. "You went too far, pretty boy. And guess what – I'm an elephant. I never forget." He saunters away.

Las crouches. He counts to ten. The pain saws through the flesh and bones of his foot. He counts to sixty. When he hears Gordo's truck engine slip into gear, he stumbles over to the lit doorway of the church basement. Three toes of his left foot have a deep slash across them, their tanned skin split like fruit, revealing a red-bluish pulp, a whitish gristle. Already they are puffing up, raw as scored sausage. He tries deep breathing to slow his pulse. Will he need surgery? How will it throw his training? And his mother – God, his mother – won't she just be crazy mad in that way that chews up her face.

He empties his lungs too fast. The pain overwhelms everything, including the hot wick of shame that's been burning inside him for days. He feels dangerously alive.

A few hours before dawn, standing in the tobacco field, Nate watches Stephanie sneak into her house through the back entrance. She turns and waves just before jiggling the latch and ever so quietly sliding the patio door wide enough for her to squeeze through. He waves back, and when she disappears, he pulls his hand to his nose, where the smell of her lingers; he feels washed in her, brand new. "I love that girl," he says, and it sounds just as true aloud as it did in his head. He turns into the tobacco field and walks back to the blockade.

If there was other love in his life, it never seemed enough. His grandfather, for instance, loved him with a kind of respectful distance, even when he was a little boy. In place of hugs and words of praise, that old man, an ironworker, cradled his rough hands around the stories he told, braiding them like a rope to give to the boy.

Why do they hire Mohawks? Nate asked when he was a young kid convinced he'd be an ironworker too.

Because, even up there, we have the earth directly beneath our feet, his grandfather said, pounding his solar plexus. Reminding him how he'd stood atop the railway bridge spanning the St. Lawrence Seaway, between Montreal and the mainland Mohawk territory, to do the final welding. *It's always here, right here in us. All of us. It's our story; we're people made from clay.*

The creation story – a sky mother, twin gods born in different ways, and the whole of humanity made from a clump of wet dirt released from a muskrat's claw – was more complicated every time his grandfather told it, with its coexistence of poison and medicine, night and day, wolf and deer. He didn't realize until later, long after the old man died, that through all the craziness of Nate's messed-up parents, juvenile detention, isolation, and boredom, the rope of stories remained. He only had to grab hold of it, use it to pull himself out, to save himself from being submerged.

Stephanie is another kind of salvation. She touches every part of him – the weird graffiti, the high hoarseness of his laugh, the amateur tattoo on his chest, even the forearms scarred with self-inflicted despair – and seems to love it all. Her attentiveness emboldens the new purpose in his life. He sees ahead of him the smoke trail of the blockade, imagines his people waking up to another day of protest, hugging cups of coffee, burning a smudge of sweetgrass, nodding *Shé:kon*, and he feels his chest expand. Purpose and love, he says, together they're pretty potent.

The rows of tobacco are interrupted by a large oak tree that's within metres of the road. The rising sun wiggles through its canopy and lands like liquid silver on the small oasis of sandy soil underneath. Nate stops, dazzled. He squints, shakes his head, moves forward. Where the tobacco plants begin again at the outside edge of the oak's shade, he sees a final glint of silver on the ground that makes him stop, bend, and brush his fingers over the soil, like the young boy he once was, hoping for treasure where there was only the illusion of light.

Except that everything in his life is different now, so when his fingers catch on an object that's cool and metallic, he is only half surprised. Pressed between thumb and forefinger, he feels something intricate and delicately made. He waits until his eyes have adjusted to the new light and looks down at his palm to find a single silver earring in the shape of a dream catcher, a hoop with a web, hung with engraved feathers made of silver. Nate smiles and crosses the highway. These earrings are so common they are almost a joke, trinkets that tourists buy at powwows before hurrying off the reserve. Still, he thinks it is a good omen, this object that keeps bad spirits away, and slips it into his pocket like a charm.

CHAPTER 15

The hotel room is dappled with men wearing pressed white shirts, holding small black phones, poking the keys of their laptops with soft, clean hands. On the long table in front of them are name cards, glasses of water, microphones, coffee cups – little armies that advance and retreat on the linen desert as the morning progresses. Helen smooths the table-cloth in front of her, tries to steady her mind. It is a bright, busy room decorated for civility and industriousness. She wants to trust, but she can't help but think the shades of taupe and tawny are a blind for an ambush.

Years ago, when she returned from the residential school to find her mother enfeebled, she began to hunt for their food in a land mostly ransacked of game. Deer, rabbits, the occasional grouse or pheasant could still be found. *Hunting is not about pursuit but anticipation,* her mother would croak from her rocking chair on the porch when Helen left. *And waiting.*

Now the quarry is truth. Across from her is the federal negotiator, in a wide-shouldered jacket, a prim striped blouse, hair the colour of wet ironstone. Her name is Antonia Taylor, a former minister in a former government and now a consultant with a mouldering law degree. According to the local paper, she bills the government $3,000 a day. Helen wonders what experience she's had with blockades, with natives, with history. The negotiator keeps raising her eyebrows in exasperation, checking her phone, sighing audibly, and whispering to the white-shirts huddling around her. And she nibbles and nibbles, constantly reaching for the dry little cookies as if she can never be sated.

Linda Goodleaf, an elder and clan mother, is speaking, and six more wait to have their turn. But the negotiator doesn't understand this as necessity. She interrupts. "With all due respect, folks, this is an expensive process. And the first order of business is to establish who the federal government recognizes as a fellow negotiator."

The clan mother who is speaking stops, and with a wry smile she lets the negotiator demonstrate her lack of respect. A whole lifetime of interruptions has taught her to press her tongue hard against the back of her teeth, to wait.

Then Linda takes a deep breath and smiles as if she is talking to a younger brother, slowing everything down, making it simple. *"Skennen'kó:wa kenh*, Miss Taylor? With all due respect, I must remind you that your ancestors borrowed our version of democracy and then abandoned it for something less democratic. Then you told us we must practise your democracy. At the end of a gun. Your government sent police with sharp sticks, with black boots, with bayonets. Just as they did again a week ago. That's how they deposed our traditional chiefs, took away our traditions. Though my granddad, *rakshótha*, got in his licks."

Laughter teases the throats on Helen's side of the table. The clicking of the laptops stops. There is a chorus of crinkles:

wrappers being peeled off sticks of gum and cellophane being stripped from yet more cookies for the negotiator.

"An elected government must deal with an elected government," the negotiator says. Helen knows this tone, its confidence that a rule is as good as a truth. The negotiator clears her throat, wipes some crumbs from her chin, reads something an aide thrusts in front of her, adjusts her glasses, and waits.

Linda takes a sip of water. "You know, Miss Taylor, we're not a culture, as you government people like to say. We're a civilization. We have our own way of governing. We have our own civic codes, institutions. You just keep trying to take them away from us. After the first raid, my grandmother, *akshótha*, a powerful leader who helped choose the chief, became a woman with no power. Without even a vote."

Helen watches the negotiator, waiting to see understanding register on the woman's powdered implacability, waiting for her to recognize that the elder's talk, and her listening, is part of the process, part of how they earn each other's time and respect. The negotiator looks down at her phone and starts to text.

The clan mother's voice dips as she finishes her talk. "We kept resisting, returning to our true leaders. The next time, your government sent in the black boots. I was a young girl, mostly well behaved."

There is more laughter, followed by whispering across the room, like a wind through dry leaves. Linda removes the pins that keep a tight roll at the back of her head. Long grey hair falls to her shoulders. She reaches behind, grabs a fistful, and yanks it up from the back of her head so her face grimaces. The negotiator startles.

"This is how they dragged me out of our traditional council meeting when the raiders came again, Miss Taylor. Do you know how painful that is? My scalp bled. For six months I could not brush my hair. I had it cut off. These things you don't forget.

That and the feel of a black boot in your ribs from a man who thinks you are lower than a dog." She drops her hand; a warm, thick banner of grey rolls down between her shoulders. And for a moment Helen sees the elder shape-shift into that young woman – smooth-cheeked, straight-backed, with beautiful hair – who bled. Like Cherisse.

"This democracy of yours is a funny thing, no? You wanted us to rule ourselves with a government like yours, yet it took you long enough to let us vote in your democracy. Ha, good trick, that! But we were better off without it. We already had our own government, our own democracy. Still do. Nearly four hundred years ago, the Two Row Wampum treaty ensured we'd live side by side with Europeans, parallel lines that didn't interfere with each other. Then in 1763, your predecessors again proclaimed they'd respect our rights to the land we occupy, and thus, how we live. You have broken that promise. *Eh ne'e na'a wen'ne.*" The clan mother sits. And she is old again, defiant still.

Three days earlier, looking down at Cherisse in the hospital bed, Helen thought only, *She's alive.* Native women were tossed from cars like fast-food wrappers; their bones were plucked clean by coyotes and vultures; they disappeared with nothing left but poster pictures and the water-drip torture of hope. Before the drive to the hospital, she'd gone to Joe's trailer to gather some things and found the smoky atomizer in Cherisse's bedroom. It was a queer object, but Helen recognized its magic. She tucked it into her hand, and later under Cherisse's hospital pillow, hoping it was as powerful as a witching bone. As long as Cherisse was safe from further damage, Helen wanted her to stay in the hospital, so she, an old woman, could coax the demon of truth out of the darkness with a bowl of blood and a hunter's patience.

Shayna's head and heart are splintering. A baby on the way. A niece in the hospital. A blockade that's packed the negotiating room with too many men: government aides, Chief White and his cronies, Clarence in designer eyeglasses, the unreadable Elijah Barton sitting with two Warriors, thick-necked and bulging in their dress shirts. And among them a woman with sleek hair and manicured nails doing a man's bidding: Antonia Taylor.

The negotiator pushes her glasses up her nose, takes off her blazer to reveal a cap-sleeved blouse. Her arms look soft and pale. She forgets to thank the elder. She turns and whispers loudly for someone to fetch her a juice. A man returns empty-handed; the juice has run out. "What, no juice?" says the negotiator. She calls a recess to remedy her thirst.

Helen finds Shayna and presses a paper bag into her hands, another care package from Ruby: two tuna sandwiches, a carton of milk, fresh strawberries, and yogurt. Shayna has felt her aunt watching her these past few days, making a meditation of what she eats, counting the calories and nutrients to herself as if they were rosary beads. Another woman with a child in her belly would not let herself go hungry, would not sleep outside half the week under stars muddied with barrel-fire smoke. She folds the bag closed, her appetite vanquished by worry, stores it in her satchel, and squeezes the older woman's arm. "I have to catch someone first," she says, and she is up.

They can't talk about Cherisse, not yet. Shayna wants her niece to come home to the reserve. She has no trust in the medical system, in any institution. Shay will wrap her in old hunter's blankets. She will lie her in the sun by the window, sponge the young woman's wounds with witch hazel, and feed her bowls of broth. Together they will beat the walls, burn her clothes, cut her hair. One day Cherisse will be strong enough to cast out the spirit of her tormentor. She will sing again. Her hair will grow back.

———

Standing outside the hotel lobby with a cigarette drawn to his lips, Louis Greene, bronzed and vacant-eyed, straightens so his big chest stretches his dress shirt when Shayna approaches. She is not surprised by the trombone slide of his look, from her lips and down her neck to the first button of her fresh blouse. Her face feels tight from weeks in the sun. She offers a reluctant smile, clears her throat, tries to sound authoritative. "We need to talk," she says. "Two of your men got drunk last night. They rode their ATVs over the lawns of residents out on County Road 13."

He nods his head but offers nothing.

"The clan mothers forbade alcohol and drugs at the reclamation." She retrieves a folded newspaper from her satchel, shoves it, headline first, into his pitted face. "That little incident made the newspapers. It makes us look bad."

His smile is more like a wince of pain. He reaches into his pocket and pulls out a pack of cigarettes, holds it out to her.

Shayna looks at the skin of his forearms, strangely scratched, as if he's wrestled a frightened animal. She grabs his wrist, turns it over, and examines the marks. "You get into a fight with a wildcat?" she asks. "Or a girl?"

Louis tips his head back and laughs. "Something like that." He lets his hand be held like a hopeful boy, as if he were giving her a gift.

Shayna lets go of the large fist, the white package falling with it. She recognizes the label. "You on Barton's payroll?"

Louis lights up his cigarette, leaves the question unanswered, his smile arching upward.

"I need you to discipline your men. We already have an image problem," she says.

He laughs again, stretches his neck.

Another small story in the *Interlake Post* that morning quoted a Doreville citizen who claimed to have seen two natives, their ball caps and kerchiefs replete with Warrior insignia, sniffing gasoline and torching a police car in the early morning hours on the day of the raid. She wants to ask Louis about that. A police spokesperson said they have fingerprints and footprints. She wants to ask Louis what else travelled with them from the Seaway besides tents and sleeping bags, ill-fitting dress shirts. Shayna imagines milled steel, cold as chromium plate, the colour of a moonless night. She wants to ask Louis about her niece. Did he see her? What does he know? Those scratches. But now more people from the negotiating room are outside; she senses Elijah Barton circling closer to them, curious.

"This conflict will not be won with public relations," Louis says. "It will be won with history, the history everybody forgets." He reaches out to her and gently gathers a few strands of her hair in his large hand, rubs it between his thumb and forefinger, as if he has always done this, as if he needn't ask.

Her body springs to attention. She does not want to feel desire. She wills herself not to. "Guns," she says, finding the right words. It is almost a whisper. "You can't use them. You can't bring them out. We'll lose any goodwill we have." If he places his skin against hers, a slight brush of his roughness against her fretful dampness, she will make him bleed. So it will be anger he remembers her for, not pleasure. "Even the rumour that you are armed, and all these poverty groups and unions and environmentalists will hightail it outta here."

"Panama, Estonia, Ireland, Persia . . . You know, they recognized our sovereignty in the nineteen-twenties," Louis says. His eyes look beyond her. "We had our own passports."

"I need you to promise . . ." Shayna calculates. A swift kick to the nuts, a gouge to the eyes. She wants maximum pain with a minimum of time for him to react. She is surprisingly fleet under pressure. A jackrabbit. *Just try,* she thinks. *Give me the excuse.*

"Since they started to take our land, since they started to impose their elections, control our money, we've resisted," says

Louis. "This reserve resisted! Since when did public relations matter more than peace, power, righteousness?"

"But you don't need guns."

"An enemy's foot is in our country."

Shayna slams a heel into the ground, raising a small cloud of dust. Now heads have turned in their direction. She lowers her voice. "I know my fucking history. Guns aren't our history."

Louis drops her hair. He looks at her sadly. "There are no guns, sister. What kind of fool do you take me for?"

She feels her chest collapse. Her eyes fall to his forearms again. "You should have somebody look at those scratches."

The negotiations resume, but now the room is warmer, as if the government aides have cut the air conditioning in an attempt to hasten the proceedings. Jackets are abandoned, sleeves rolled up. The water jugs are passed around, depleted. No one comes offering refills.

When the next elder gets up to speak, Antonia Taylor raises her hand to stop him. She pulls herself close to the microphone. She reads a long section from the Indian Act, then another from the Constitution and a select passage from the U.N. Charter. "We are bound by these charters, conventions, and legislation to negotiate with democratically elected governments. The band council is the only legitimate leadership recognized by the federal government. And so I must ask, is there a member of the band council here?"

Disappointment, like a reprimand, makes the elders flatten their lips. Shayna turns. Chief White occupies one of the chairs designated for spectators, set up behind the half of the U-shaped table across from the negotiator and her team. He looks smug, expectant. She watches Clarence take off his glasses and wipe them, avoiding her glare. He is about to speak, to hijack the proceedings, to poach authority from the elders and her – this much is clear. Shayna stands up, walks to where he sits beside the chief, and blocks his view of those across the table. If he's going to betray them, he will have to do it looking right at her. She hears uncomfortable coughs, legs crossing and uncrossing, whispers on each side of them.

Clarence puts his glasses back on and she sees that his eyes are tired, his face puffy, his vigour paid out steeply to city living. He smiles at her, a smile that has remnants of love for her, a hint of the vulnerability he showed when they were at their best.

Antonia Taylor leans into the microphone again and repeats, "Okay, folks, one more time for good measure. Is there a member of a democratically elected band council here?" The federal negotiator looks squarely at Chief White. He turns to Clarence with an impatient gape.

"Shayna, you need to move," Clarence says, leaning forward. "You heard her; they won't negotiate with you. You can't just keep standing in the way of things."

Off to one side, Shayna sees that Elijah Barton has also left his seat. Now he is kneeling, whispering to the clan mothers as if he were one of them.

"Standing in front of things can be very effective, Clarence," she says, using the same half whisper he used with her. "You might try it sometime. Take a break from shuffling papers."

Behind her comes the sound of amplified throat clearing. Shayna turns to see Linda Goodleaf at the microphone again. Behind her is Barton, smiling, with his arms crossed. "I have a question for you, Miss Taylor," Linda says.

There is a moment when it appears that the negotiator will disallow this. An aide whispers in her ear; a reluctant nod follows.

"Are *you* an elected member of the government?"

The room becomes very quiet.

"I was with a previous government," the negotiator answers.

"But are you now?"

"No," she says, the salt of resentment in her voice. "But I am the hired representative of a democratically elected government."

The clan mother smiles with kindness. "We too are representatives, Miss Taylor, but we won't receive any payment for being here. We represent the peoples of the reclamation. And I suggest that we have arrived here very democratically. A vote was taken among all those involved, and they asked us to be their representatives. There is no one else in this room, or on the reserve, who can claim such support."

The negotiator forces a smile. Again she looks at Chief White, as if appalled by his truancy, his silence. Clarence whispers to him. The chief mutters, casts his eyes downward, and Shayna returns to her seat.

A sharp sound exits from the negotiator's pursed mouth – a tongue-flattened expletive. Then her hands are up and she calls for another recess, exiting to the lobby with a cellphone stuck to her ear, swatting papers at the aides who approach as if they were gnats. "Is there any juice in this godforsaken place or what?" she snaps at one.

Linda Goodleaf clasps Elijah's hands. He beams triumphantly. Shayna realizes she will have to congratulate him. It makes her nervous, his easy move into being their redeemer. She opens the paper bag from Ruby. Finally she's hungry, as she hasn't been in weeks. The tuna sandwiches are warm but the celery in them still crunches, and there is just enough mayonnaise, salt, and pepper. Shayna devours them greedily, one after the other, before anyone can approach her and she feels compelled to share.

The break stretches into an hour. Then it's announced that negotiations have ended for the day. The elders who did not get to speak put their names on tomorrow's list, despite the entreaties of the aides to wait for the official agenda.

Shayna finds Clarence sitting alone in the hotel courtyard, and she watches him for a moment. He's waiting for her, she sees that. He is waiting not to say anything in particular but to restore some ease between them.

During their marriage she had a talent for righteousness. Pete-Pete arrived on the fifth-floor maternity ward of the Pemcoe hospital, during a long summer night when her water wouldn't break and the doctors and nurses became irritated with her stillness, her refusal to shout or even pant. The quietness she demanded for her son's birth was stolen by the heart monitor, its tiny *boops* and infuriating *whoosh* like muffled waves. She was struck dumb by the epidural, the cold intrusion of forceps, the yank and the long tear, the blood that flowed and flowed, the bruised, dented head of her baby covered in the alien green of meconium. Her righteousness ripened, as red as the bedsheets became with her blood. Sick from the Demerol, she was barely able to hold up her head as the nurses brought in her swaddled son, pink-brown and already too strong for her, eager to suckle. How their lips curled with scolding at the sight of the blood-soiled bed, when the child they pressed to her veined breast was so soft and clean. The coldness of such a place: the way they eyed her skin and asked her where the baby's father was – Clarence was in court, winning his first case – and cooed over the woman in the next bed, whose name was Kayla and whose side of the room was crowded with flowers, fruit baskets, stuffed bears holding Mylar balloons, and relatives who blocked the shared bathroom.

After Pete-Pete died, she made a backyard heap out of the photo albums, his little overalls and T-shirts, books, stuffed toys and plastic trucks. She poured kerosene over all of it, thinking that what wouldn't burn would melt beyond recognition. When Clarence came running out the back door, yelling at her to stop, she let the lit match fall from her hands. He grabbed her wrist too late: every photo of the little boy was pulled into the tarry cone of smoke, sent to the spirits scented with tobacco and sweetgrass. This was what their mothers and fathers had done with grief, and so this is what they would do. When Clarence was out of the house again, Joe Montagne came by to take away Pete-Pete's dresser and grown-up bed, the one she had found Clarence curled up in, the mornings after the fire. The room was repainted a depthless shade before dinnertime.

She didn't say her child's name for six months; she didn't tell stories about him. But Clarence clung hard to his memories, and so forced her to remember too. And what she remembered most was how it had been her, not him, who'd turned her head – really, it couldn't have been longer than a few seconds – on a spring evening made hopeful with early heat, the scent of chokecherry blossoms. A moment of inattention. It was the thing he wouldn't say aloud: she'd looked away and their little boy had died. Clarence never weakened, never laid the blame she felt. Instead she took their dirty dishes outside and smashed every one on the patio stones. Clarence went silent, and silence became its own accusation between them. When she finally stopped trying to make him say something, it was too late. He didn't come home.

Shayna startles Clarence by kneeling at his feet in the empty courtyard. She tells him about Cherisse. She tells him that their pretty niece, their wild runaway, their fledgling pop star, was found in a tobacco field, hurt in ways that make her lower her voice. She doesn't say that the tobacco farmer who found Cherisse is her lover. Or that she carries that man's child, a child that may turn out queerly fair, blue-eyed, with hair the shade of indecision. Or that she can't imagine such a creature toddling behind her on the reserve – not like Pete-Pete, who had her hair, Clarence's eyes, their skin. Instead she wonders aloud if the protest made her less watchful over Cherisse. It is a relief to say, finally, how she wishes she'd paid more attention. "I'm sorry," she says and wipes her nose on her sleeve, and she says it again and again. Then she lays her head on Clarence's lap and he bends over, holds her close.

CHAPTER 16

Her laptop balancing on her knees, Stephanie is in her bedroom in the early morning, writing vertical lists to get a grip on all the things that need remembering. And forgetting. Last semester, her Careers teacher, Ms. Ellwood, emphasized the usefulness of a vertical list, with proper parallel construction, to convey a series of ideas in a job presentation or even a longish cover letter.

The positive things in my life right now can best be described as follows:

- I am love in with Nate Bastine
- I am helping Nate with something meaningful
- I can blow off all of Brittany's shit-tastic remarks and attitude at the dairy bar because with Nate in my life, none of it matters

- I am losing weight without even trying
- I have never known my parents to care so little about meals and housekeeping and where their kids are; the blockade is working!

Stephanie pushes back in her chair, reads her list and smiles. She thinks of Nate's hand snaking under her top, his fingers sandwiched by her waistband, his palm resting in the small of her back. The gentle pressure of a claim on her.

But she has another list to tackle. The scratch on her brother's neck is now faded and insubstantial, but it made her curious; she couldn't stop looking for it whenever he sat down to eat or passed her in the hallway. A week earlier, when Las had stormed off from the dinner table, she wandered into his room and lifted up the clothing on his floor a piece at a time, all of it off-gassing beer and sweat, a microbial guy-compost. Secure in her top desk drawer are a camouflage kerchief and a black baseball cap with an insignia: a sun framing the face of an Iroquois Warrior. Filaments of blond hair are stuck to the cap's Velcro strap. The cap and kerchief were shoved under his bed, and both reeked of gasoline. A sharper boy might have burned or buried them. Or noticed them missing.

The negative things in my life right now can best be described as follows:

- I think Las has done something, maybe even a few things, that could put him in jail
- I can't tell Nate until I am sure, but I don't know how to be sure
- I think my parents will hate me if they find out about Nate
- I think they will hate me even more if I am right about Las
- I can't talk to anyone about it
- I think I will go insane if I don't talk to someone

She opens a new file, creates two columns, and labels them MOM and DAD. Then she divides each of these columns into PROS and CONS. Under her Mom's cons column, she writes WON'T BELIEVE ME. She thinks about it for a while and then writes the same under her dad's cons column. There is no splurge of type, as when she does a free association exercise or a mind map. After twenty minutes, all she has been able to add is WILL BE EVEN COLDER TO ME under her mom's cons column and COULD HURT HIS BUSINESS under her dad's. There really are no pros.

Stephanie goes to the kitchen, wrestles a new filter into the coffee maker, and dumps two big handfuls of dark roast coffee into the filter. It looks like the amount her father uses. She pulls two mugs from the cupboard. Into one she pours two heaping spoonfuls of sugar and a splash of cream, just the way her father prepares his. Waiting for the coffee to drip through, Stephanie wonders if this is her turning point, her moment of courage. She takes the second mug, fills it with black coffee for her mother. There is enough left for her, so she grabs a third mug and finds a tray. She envisions how things will go down. She will sit on the edge of her parents' bed. All three of them will drink coffee and they will talk in the calm, logical way adults do.

Maybe there should be something to eat too. The refined carbohydrates of toast might distress her mother. She will bring fresh fruit. In the refrigerator there is a honeydew melon. She shouldn't have poured the coffee; with the time it takes to prepare the melon, it will be too cool to drink. Which of her parents needs it piping hot? Stephanie starts to perspire, worries she will lose her nerve if one of them complains about the coffee or, worse, leaves to make a better batch. She is cradling the honeydew in her palms, propping the fridge door open with her shoulder, when her mother comes into the kitchen in her sweats and no makeup, her hair pulled back into a messy ponytail.

"Stephanie! What are you doing with that melon?" Her mother's voice breaks with agitation.

Stephanie cringes. She is more tired than she realizes.

"No, no, no, sweetheart."

With two strides and one bend, her mother advances, grabs the fruit, places it gently back in the crisper as if it were a baby's lost head. She knocks the refrigerator door shut with her hip. "You can't eat that. I have plans for it."

Her mother looks at the three mugs, wrinkles her brow. "Did you have friends sleep over? And when did you start drinking coffee?"

Stephanie's gut gets heavy. She wants to do the right thing. She grabs the mug closest to her, takes a swallow. It scalds her throat.

"Mom," she says, sounding hoarse, rushed. "I have to tell you something about Las. Something's wrong." A pearl of water rolls from the side of Stephanie's nose to the crook of her mouth. Is she crying?

"Where is he?"

Please don't cry, she tells herself.

"Where is he, Stephanie?"

"I don't know, Mom. That's not the point. What I'm—"

Her mother moves, shoves past Stephanie and the cups of wasted coffee to the stairs, which she takes in twos. There is a single knock on the door of Las's bedroom at the very top. Stephanie hears it yank open and climbs the staircase with dread.

The sight of her brother is as terrible as it is beautiful. Las lies across his bed sprawled out on his back, as if his body has been tossed there. The bedsheets are thrown. One arm is flung over his head, his nose nestles in the crook of his elbow, all of him is naked but for a pair of cotton shorts. Stephanie can't help but be struck dumb by him in such moments – the toasted mallow of his skin, the firm swells of his thighs and pectorals, the slender ridge of his jaw.

Her mother rushes to the window, pulls up the blind, and leans into his face to confirm that he is breathing. Stephanie follows her mother's gaze as it trails along the length of him, until she sees his feet dangling over the edge of the bed, caked with mud along the arches, his flip-flops abandoned on the floor below. Something about the top of one foot looks strange – as if he has stuck his toes into the carcass of an animal.

Stephanie moves closer and sees it is Las's flesh that has curled and darkened like a fatty brisket, burnt on the outside and with a pulpy centre of blood and gristle.

Her mother looks up at her. What comes out is a weak rasp. "Get your father."

⟨⟨⟩⟩

Mitch can't hear his family when he's in the office, an advantage he wouldn't do without. It is the one room in the house where he feels that all the disparate litter of his life is gathered and sorted, made tidy and manageable. Despite Ella's preference for barely perceptible colours, the walls are painted golden brown, the medium dark shade of an Arturo Fuente cigar's broadleaf wrapper. Mitch still has a dozen left from his most recent purchase – there is one smoke shack that specializes in cigars – and it is a continuing source of antagonism between himself and his wife that he smokes in the privacy of the study, which he's gone to the expense of having separately ventilated to appease her prickliness. There's a long wall of windows with wooden blinds, another wall of bookshelves – he isn't a great reader, but Mitch is comforted by the smell and heft of leather-bound sets – and in the centre is the ponderous oak desk, solid as a favourite uncle. He stashes his humidor in the bottom left of its six capacious drawers. He would keep his Scotch there too, were he able to lock the drawers against his plundering son.

Mitch rubs his forehead. His eyebrows feel rammed into his hairline, as if paralyzed in a state of perpetual alarm. He is withered and underslept. He reaches into the humidor, plucks out a Cañones Natural, slides the cigar under his nose, breathes in hints of the Spanish cedar it was aged in, and wills all the day's tasks already over so he can pull its peppery heat right into his lungs. He will have a good-sized Scotch with it. But that is hours and hours away. First there are more calls to be made to lawyers, mid-level bureaucrats, creditors, builders, clients. Nervous or evasive – ten days after the blockade stoppered the highway in front of the development, these were the only two responses he could count on.

When he hears a short knock, he half hopes it's his wife, arriving at his office door with a piping hot cup of coffee, her face free of accusation, knowing that he needs the relief of a small kindness, unspoken recognition of his doggedness in fighting for the development and their future. He feels a slight twitch in his mouth, a swell of love pushing against the acid reflux in his chest.

But there is no wife. There is no cup of hot coffee, though its aroma sneaks into his office. There is only Stephanie.

"Dad?" she says. It's a voice that melts him every time.

"Yes, sweetheart?"

"Mom needs you because something's wrong with Las."

"What's up with your brother?"

"It's serious. You better go now. They're in his room."

A sneeze has been twitching in Mitch's nose; it bursts out of him loudly. The papers on his desk dot with moisture. He looks up to see his daughter recoil. She could be a little more understanding, that one.

"Steph, honey," he says. "I desperately need a cup of coffee. Will you make me one?"

She doesn't move.

"Pronto?"

Mitch puts the cigar back in the humidor and stares at it for a second with the longing of a man who knows what he deserves, and then he closes his bottom desk drawer.

∾

Las is laughing, laughing. And fuck, fuck, fuck, if this wasn't the worst day ever, getting all this backwash of noise in his head from nights and days before. Pants and whimpers and the sensation of his fist against a small face, knuckling plump lips, the slick of blood against a cheek and a delicate hand. Release. So wild, so disturbing – the sensation kept cutting through the fog of booze and gasoline. The smash of a brick on his exposed foot, slicing open the buzz from Gordo's strong weed. And now there is the soft, light touch of hands on his legs and his ankles, the tickle of something cold against the throb that has gone dead in his foot. He is laughing because it is his mom and dad lifting him off his bed as if he is a little boy, slinging his arms around their shoulders, talking in whispers. He is laughing because this too is fun, unexpected. They are going on a car ride again, and he hopes they go fast. He never wants to stop laughing. He never wants to slow down.

∾

Stephanie puts the cup of coffee she made earlier for her father in the microwave. *Pronto*, she hears. Fucking pronto. Both her parents are in the bedroom with Las. She hears their hushed voices. She has taken out two travel mugs. She saw the foot – they'll have to take him to the emergency room. Such a guy move to ignore an injury, let it fester until it becomes a drama. She wonders how long he has been walking around like that, and she can't help a tinge of admiration for his pain tolerance. The microwave dings and she throws the other cup of coffee in to heat. It's sacrilege to microwave coffee, according to her father. But this is a pronto situation. Stephanie is all about pronto right now.

Her parents emerge from the bedroom, her brother draped between them. *Las Pietà*, she thinks. Stephanie follows, with travel mugs in place of palm fronds. Her mother stays in the back seat with Las. Stephanie hands her dad his coffee as he gets into the driver's seat. She knocks on the window to alert her mother to the coffee she's offering, but her mother doesn't acknowledge it.

"Mitch, let's go! He's in pain."

It's a thin, high bark. Her father backs out of the driveway, and Steph is left holding the travel mug as they pull away.

CHAPTER 17

This one won't give him any trouble, Joe Montagne thinks as he watches Coulson Stercyx approach him through the tobacco field. Yup, Coulson may be a tough-looking dude, but his eyes are the colour of water, not flint, and the skin around them puckers with good humour. So even though the crosshatch of Joe's tire tracks has flattened two dozen of the man's mature tobacco plants closest to the highway, and Joe has added insult to injury by erecting a small structure of unsteady joints and peeling paint atop the desecrated plants, the farmer is sure to let him be.

Joe stops chewing up a plank counter with bad nails and cackles hello. Before Coulson says a word, Joe drops his hammer, reaches into the back of the truck, and hands him a still-hot takeout coffee. He then produces one for himself and raises it in a salute of friendship and peace. For the moment there is nothing to do but sip and size each other up: two men for whom worn denim and wariness are like a second skin. *You don't take a man's peace offering before swinging a fist or calling the cops*, Joe thinks.

He needs cash flow. Cherisse has been in the hospital for two weeks, and he wants her to stay there. The sight of her makes him cry, reminds him of all the things he has not properly fixed: the trailer's toilet tank that never refills after flushing, the crack crawling across the kitchen window like a stick insect, the bum leg on the pullout couch. He wants the doctors to mend her, believes they have the magic to return her to exactly who she was before. He will give them time. If she comes home to the trailer now, she will be the most broken thing there, the one he can't ignore or put back together.

Still, a big wad of cash will help him make some things right. The barricade has stopped white folks from coming to his smoke shack, so he will bring it to them, at the elbow of Stercyx's field that juts out before the blocked part of the highway. It's a quick drive from the suburbs, and after they've made their purchases, a one-eighty on the deserted road will take them home in minutes.

"Funny, eh?"

"What's that?" says Coulson.

Joe lifts his paper cup. "The white man brought this habit to my people." Then he nods towards the expanse of green and yellowing tobacco. "But we taught your ancestors how to grow tobacco, didn't we?"

Coulson looks over the bent-up tab on his drink. "You did."

They both take sips and stare into the fields, and a moment of quiet hangs between them.

"Lot more money to be made growing tobacco than drinking coffee, huh?"

Coulson smiles. "I suppose you're right about that."

Joe lets that sink in.

"Nobody's coming to my smoke shack with the blockade. And it's just a corner of your field. I need the business."

Coulson doesn't answer, and Joe watches him take another sip as if he's weighing the pleasure of the drink against the insult to his property.

"My girl is hurt."

The mess of Cherisse's face makes him crazy, makes him want to flatten something, someone. His back molar is throbbing and his saliva tastes faintly of rot. He's been thinking a lot about whisky, and that won't help. He has to keep his head screwed on. Having a place to go, customers to serve, will help.

"I know," says Coulson. "I was the one who found her."

Joe's heard as much. They both look down, go quiet.

"She's not talking yet. Barely awake at all. Surgeries. They've got her on a bunch of drugs. Hallucinating."

"I called the cops about the tire marks under my oak. Took their sweet time to collect evidence. Good thing it hasn't rained until this morning."

Joe turns abruptly, starts to poke around in the back of his truck. He's not ready for too much more of this kind of conversation. The who, the how, the why, what next. He pulls out a lawn chair, unfolds it, and plunks down in it.

Coulson stands in front of him. "You gonna offer me a seat too?"

Joe gets up, pulls out a second lawn chair, and unfolds it for Coulson. Why not? There was a bonfire of midday sun. *Something 'bout this guy might be as sorry as me,* Joe thinks. He watches Coulson sit down, a coffee in one hand and in the other a thumb-smeared cellphone.

∽

Peg Redhill moves through the blockade from Doreville's emptied downtown. She left early for her scheduled rendezvous with Constable Holland and drives at a relaxed pace. Lately she wakes up with her head spinning, as if she's in a helicopter on a cloudless day, looking down upon the interlake basin, a green-brown bridge between the dancing blue of two great lakes. Through it runs the silver band of the Smoke River. It would be a beautiful, peaceful image but for the traffic. Nose-to-back vehicles wend their way down the highway that connects one lake to the next. But just before the two-lane bridge spanning the Smoke, the blockade forces the cars off the road. The line of vehicles beetles horizontally towards the west and the east, crawls over smaller bridges that span the river in other towns before moving back towards the highway again, joining it farther south. In her dream state, from her sky-high vantage, their movement is viscous and painfully slow, making a ragged box bisected by a stripe of empty highway. And that empty ribbon of asphalt runs the length of Doreville's downtown. The caravan of little specks in Peg's imagination includes compact cars with kayaks strapped on top and GO VEG bumper stickers; RVs; trailers; SUVs with tidy Yakima roof racks; long-haul semis transporting tanks of flammable chemical, fresh off a boat from Pennsylvania, or stacked with new cars, treated lumber, or frozen food products. All of them mobile crucibles of economic vitality, moving away from and around Doreville, isolating it, blaming it, holding it responsible. It leaves her head vibrating like a grasshopper wing just as the day begins.

Now Peg looks out the window at the passing downtown and considers the limestone buildings with their quaint Victorian flourishes. Without the leaf-blower hum and spew of highway traffic, Doreville looks and sounds lovelier than ever. Through her car window she smells the richness of rain-wet tree bark. She hears birdsong. She tastes the air – it's light, mineral-fresh, sediment-free. Still, it infuriates her. Such an idyllic town deserves prosperity. She hits the gas.

Twenty minutes later she pulls in behind several cars

parked on the side of Highway 3, in time to see a sign-wielding horde of citizens advancing towards the blockade, chanting. Facing them is an assortment of natives and day-tripping liberals, unemployed students, and harem-panted poverty activists have lined up in front of the overturned hydro tower and its foothills of detritus. Peg notes that the police have taken up a position on the highway thirty metres from the piles of gravel, the hulk of the tower and trailer in a kind of imposed neutral zone between the town and the stalled development and the reserve. Cops with helmets and shields assemble and link arms to face the placard-wavers, dividing them from the people in front of the blockade.

A television van churns up dust as it passes Peg. It stops ten metres from the line of police and a man with a camera hops out, starts to follow the skinny activist named Kenneth who leads the sign-wavers.

As if on cue, Kenneth yells through a bullhorn hanging from his neck. "This is a march of emancipation! Who wants to be free from land terrorism?"

Behind him are about fifty townspeople. Peg recognizes the pub owner, the auto mechanic, the florist and his wife. All of them have signs with awkward grade-school printing. More than one sign protests TWO-TIRE JUSTICE. Peg would giggle if it weren't her town, her constituents with the poor spelling being recorded by the TV crews. They answer Kenneth in a tentative call and response. It's watery outrage, trailing off in its end notes. Not quite the bristling threat to inequality Kenneth promised with his *citizen counter-insurgency*. Still, Peg is concerned. She hops out of her truck.

As their leader, the imported Kenneth looks even more like a jerry-build of awkward angles than he did at the church: pointy knees and elbows, the swallowed egg of his Adam's apple, a thin, sharp nose. When he marches up to the police line, not stopping until he is toe-to-toe with a hulking officer, a few of the cops openly chuckle.

"Non-natives have rights too!" he yells, his voice high and thin. Kenneth rolls his arms, signalling his supporters to create a shadow line in front of the police. The townspeople scuttle forward as if learning the steps to a dance. The sign-wavers' voices gradually grow louder and shriller as they repeat Kenneth's chant. Behind them, two more cars drive up with photographers. One man jumps out, instantly rolls to the ground, and points his camera upwards. The other clambers onto his car rooftop, snapping his shots looking down and across the parallel lines of police and citizens, their chafing solitudes. The sign-wielders, energized by the cameras, yell even louder, thrusting their bodies aggressively around the upright police. The chanting becomes more frantic and uncoordinated. The townspeople are so close that their spit dots the visors of the police helmets.

And then a plane goes by pulling a banner: DOREVILLE FALL FAIR FUNFEST! AUG. 30–SEPT. 2. The twin-engine whine cuts through the chorus of yelling. Somebody points, and half the crowd crane their necks skyward. For a few long seconds there is silence, followed by a collective *what next?* A radio crackle breaks the impasse. The police move forward in lockstep, a coordinated march that shoves the parade back down the highway towards the town. Cheers and whoops sound from the blockade.

Kenneth's voice screeches indignantly through the bullhorn. "Freedom from land terrorism! Freedom from government appeasement! Where's the justice? Police protect the terrorists!"

Signs rattle as they hit the ground. Peg watches as Will Jacobs, the pub owner, shoves an officer and starts to flail with his hands. He is pushed to the ground, a knee in his back to subdue him. Next the junk-shop owner – a slip of a woman with a large frizz of hair – takes a swing at a broad-shouldered officer with her TWO-TIRE JUSTICE sign. It makes a sharp crack against his helmet.

Shit, Peg thinks. *It's a full dust-up, a melee.* The old Peg would get right in there, instill some order, allow the citizens to protest and the police to do their job, and herself to look like a beacon of practicality. But this new Peg – sanctioned by her own council, humiliated in the press – is hobbled, second-guessing, jettisoning confidence. She is not sure anymore about what to do with her energy, her need to problem-solve. She scrambles back to her suv.

What? You did what? Reid Wellings shouted at her just that morning. His tone suggested she'd become a liability for his own political ambitions. She'd let it slip that she'd gone to visit the native girl in the hospital.

When they were alone, the mayor had brushed her large hand over the girl's forehead, a familiar gesture that belonged to a mother or an aunt. And this is what she is known for, being a leader with a soft touch. She shows up at important birthday parties and anniversaries, takes casseroles to the family when someone has died or got injured at work, clasps their hands and looks them in the eyes and says, "I'm sorry" in a way that people believe, in a way that takes on some of their sorrow. *I'm so sorry*, said the mayor, leaning near Cherisse's face. *This is a terrible thing that has happened to you in a good place. A good place, I promise.*

How could you explain such a thing to that Chicken Little Reid Wellings?

She defended herself. *Think about it. It will show I'm neutral, that I maintain my care for everyone in need, regardless of which side of the blockade they're on.*

The man actually harrumphed at her on the phone. Harrumphed! *You need to lie low, Peg, if you want to ride this out, save your career*, he said. *I mean, what if the assailant is white, a guy from this side of the blockade? Did you consider that? Do you realize what a tinderbox this place will be?*

She went silent, made an excuse to get off the phone. When he hung up, she regretted not thanking him. Later on she might need that pinch-faced little weasel in her corner.

Now, watching her constituents – almost all of them avowed Redhill supporters – duke it out with the police while behind the blockade the protesters clap and egg them on, she feels punctured with doubts. She had assumed it was a native man who hurt the girl, left her face misshapen with bruises and a coffee-coloured crust on those pretty lips. Her ex-husband's right hook could do that if his thumbnail was uncut; he'd catch the soft of her mouth so the gush would make an iron moat around her teeth. She never whimpered, lest it wake Gordon.

They all had trials to bear. At the hospital's information desk, she made a point of asking about the university-bound son of the clerk. She squeezed the shoulder of the ward nurse. Enough to be taken notice of, while still being the model of discretion.

Peg puts her key in the ignition and is just about to reverse and pull away from the blockade, but she catches sight of something interesting in her rear-view mirror. The door of a black Buick Regal opens and a woman steps out. She would be mannish and hopeless, thinks Peg, were it not for the impeccable oxblood-coloured hair, the pricy-looking box-shouldered skirt suit, the owlish glasses. The woman lifts a pair of binoculars and sweeps them over the blockade and back again, taking in the horseshoe of police straddling or handcuffing ordinary citizens while those at the blockade whoop and cheer. She drops the binoculars, her chin pulled in like a surprised emu, and returns to the car's back seat. A second later, Elijah Barton climbs out the other side and reaches back as if to shake someone's hand. *Barton,* Peg thinks. *What has he got to do with any of this? That man is always gaming trouble for his own profit.*

She is still watching the Buick through her mirror when Reggie Holland pulls up in front of it in his burgundy Crown

Victoria, obscuring her view. *A quick chat,* he said earlier. *Can we meet at the blockade? I've things to see to there.* He hops out, gives her a little wave of recognition, and jogs in her direction. Peg makes a quick check of her lipstick, rubbing her finger along her teeth, opens the car window, and studies his approach from the rear and side-view mirrors. She wonders about that eyebrow tic of his, considers all the ways she might work that into the conversation.

Constable Holland comes to the passenger side, dips his head, and gestures at the empty seat. "Do you mind?"

She removes her purse and pats the passenger seat with an inviting smile. He slumps onto the umber-coloured leather, smelling of drugstore aftershave and spicy lunchmeat. He stares at his shoes for a moment; he's worried. She has an impulse to run a finger along his temple. Instead she rests her hand on his shoulder in a way that shows concern but is above reproach. "Everything okay, constable?"

He doesn't answer. She is about to risk a hand on the back of his bent neck when he straightens and looks at her with his adorably tired eyes. "Peg, did you visit an assault victim in the hospital recently?"

"The native girl?" she asks, shifting to face him. "Yes, I did. It's something I make a habit of doing – community outreach. Terrible thing. Beautiful girl."

He nods his head and looks down again. "Did you know I'm investigating the assault? Just me. There's no one else they can spare."

"Oh, I don't envy you that, what with this blockade business. Will the reserve police at least let you into their jurisdiction to question suspects?"

Constable Holland looks up at her. Then he squints his eyes in a way that makes her scalp prickle with warning. He takes a deep breath. "Peg, I need to talk to that kid of yours. Get a fix on his whereabouts. Pretty standard stuff."

Her next breath feels too big for her lungs. "Pardon me?"

"Peg, there's an eyewitness tip about a red truck seen in the vicinity of the assault the night it occurred."

"Oh, now, seriously?" A little rush of relief tickles the bottoms of her feet and she claps her hands. "Well, constable, you have your work cut out for you. There are at least four dozen red trucks in this town. And the reserve is lousy with them."

Constable Holland clears his throat, examines the backs of his hands. "Peg, we've got tire impressions. Still good. I'm not an expert per se, but I know a thing or two, and these tires have deep voids, large lugs cut for flex. They're specialty tires, Peg. Expensive, and barely street legal."

His voice has morphed from friendly to phlegmy. She can see a grimy ring on his collar, a rogue nose hair tickling his septum. Up close, the man is unkempt, slightly repulsive. She straightens her spine to its full mayoral length.

"Well, you don't need my permission to contact him. He's an adult. I'm pretty sure he has some run-of-the-mill tires on that ride of his, but of course it's important that you clear him."

They both know it's a lie. Peg bought the boy the truck as a gift, an extravagance. Gordo tricked it up like a Christmas tree, drove its special-order everything slow as a parade float through town, his arm hanging out the window. It took three months for his tires to arrive.

"All right, then." Constable Holland slaps his thighs. "Just wanted you to know."

"Sure thing." She works to sound relaxed, as if the whole idea is too routine.

But as she watches Constable Holland lumber away from her suv in his ill-fitting pants, a slightly hunched quality to his posture, she is marooned by doubt. Her boy – the child who ran to her, trembling, every time his father raged – was he capable of such a thing? She thinks of the comfort she's taken in Gord's vagueness, their habit of merely orbiting around each other, indifferent and cold as night stars. If his father's violence is surfacing in him, she's spared herself the opportunity of seeing it. She pounds the steering wheel with a balled fist. It's a godless universe that would put a woman through that twice. Already she feels adrift in the vast, lonely ink of scandal.

CHAPTER 18

Mitch stands with his arms crossed in the corner of a curtained room, watching the tears in his wife's eyes. They won't spill; it's not Ella's style. The liquid will just wait on the reddened rims, brightening the grey irises, making her eyes look wider, flushing her skin pink, increasing her beauty. It has been so long since he has seen her like this.

She has climbed onto the hospital bed where their son sleeps. The boy leans against his mother's side with his legs pulled up, knees bent like a small child. One foot is wrapped in fresh gauze, already stained with yellow ointment and brownish ooze. Under the wrapping, he is missing three toes. An IV snakes from a pole to the wrist he rests on his mother's forearm. The sepsis means he will be in hospital for a few more days.

Mitch doesn't know how three missing toes will affect a promising swimmer. He imagines some lost thrust, speed leaking through the peephole at the top of the boy's left foot. Ella's brimming eyes must mean that she comprehends the loss better than he. She rubs the boy's shoulder as if lulling an infant to sleep, stealing looks at her husband with her glassy stare. *Too much, Ella,* he thinks. She is overripe with that boy.

His wife whispers reassurances to their dozing son, and Mitch feels himself constrict with the need for such comforts himself. They can go home. Las will enjoy a long, drugged sleep. He wants his wife in his own bed, those eyes resting on his face, her long, slim hands strumming along his forehead, his temples, the way she did when they were first married and the troubles of establishing himself outside his father's grocery trade robbed him of sleep. Now the stress of the blockade has spent any gentleness left between them.

Mitch moves over to the hospital bed, grasps the boy's legs to straighten them and allow Ella to disentangle herself.

She leans forward, twisting her head, hissing. "Mitch! Careful. Careful!"

He reaches to take his son's arm, move it to his hip. The boy's jaw points towards the ceiling, his lips slightly parted.

Ella shoos off her husband. "Just leave him be. Poor kid, he's been through so much."

Mitch stands back. Would he like Las more, feel more for him now, if he'd been more active in the shaping of him? He's been content to think of him as Ella's son – her boy, her project, her problem.

"We'll come back first thing in the morning, Ella."

She screws up her mouth. "I don't think I can move without waking him."

"He'll just fall back to sleep anyway."

Mitch waits by the end of the bed, massaging the cool metal of his keys as if he does not quite comprehend. And he doesn't.

∾

Ella looks down on her son. Her eyes trace a faded scratch, like a ligature burn, on his neck. She is seized by a panic of doubt. Something is wrong with this boy, something more than this mark on his neck, the unexplained butcher-shop offal of his toes. It's as if he has run very far from her and left behind a decoy. She no longer moors him, and she feels unmoored herself, spinning, vertiginous.

Her husband slips his hand under her elbow but she resists. The idea of Las alone for hours in this room, under the accusatory red eye of the iv pump, makes her frantic. She imagines a riptide of infection pulling him away from her. "Let me stay with him tonight, make sure he's okay."

She has failures to make amends for. Recently she has given up on the family meals. Their eating has become unstructured, loosely cobbled together. She makes salads, cold pasta dishes, grilled meats, and leaves them out like a self-serve buffet. Her children come and go like comets unbound to her gravitational pull. For the first time as a mother, she has not been able to say with any certainty where they are at different hours of the day. When did she last see Las, exchange a word with him? A day ago? A week?

"No, Ella. You can leave him here. You could use a good sleep. Staying is totally unnecessary when we can come back first thing."

Ella brings her finger to her lips and shushes him, then waves away her husband and his unspoken reproaches. Her son is a rudderless boat. She stopped trying to fix his direction and now he is veering, listing. *There's always a point in any season when I get the feeling Las will pack it in, that he resents his talent,* his swimming coach said once. That haunts her – it rang a little bell that won't stop resonating.

Mitch is angry with her. He kicks the empty bed beside the one Las occupies, so hard that it makes a metallic screech as the braked wheels scrape across the tiles.

Ella gasps. Footsteps sound from down the hallway. Mitch winces, looks down at his foot, and she's tempted to show concern. Instead she says, "Don't forget to find Stephanie. Take her home with you."

He grunts and limps a little too dramatically out the door without looking back. She senses that the prospect of Scotch and a cigar is a siren song to him, pulling him away. He will have a nice little session of it. She imagines him keeping his office door open so the fragrance of the Fuentes will linger for hours afterwards in the halls and the curtains of the entire house, to infuriate her, to assert his command of their space.

∾

"You can hear me," Elijah Barton says to the girl in the bed. "You've dug in pretty deep inside yourself, but you're still there."

There is a shameful lack of security at the hospital. He just walked in. He had to see for himself before believing the wild, high buzz of rumour. She looks neither better nor worse than he imagined. Her bruises have yellowed. The imprint of recently removed stitches has left a treacly crescent under her cheek. The quirky, pretty girl from behind the smoke-shack counter is re-emerging in that battered face. Still, he feels light-headed. There's failure here, and it surprises him to realize he may have a part in it.

He pulls up a chair. "The whole Indian princess thing, you know, is a load of crap," he says to the unmoving face. "All the tobacco that's up here today, making us all so much money, is because a starving John Rolfe saw a pretty Algonquian girl whose people knew how to grow food and tobacco. That marriage made the colonizers rich. But there was nothing in it for her. She died of tuberculosis in a cold, rainy city that was foreign to her."

The girl does not move. Her closed eyes do not twitch. But he sees the delicate flare of her nostrils and knows she is conserving her energy, surviving in her own way, in the old way. He wants to give her something, a way to get through this. But his emotions cloud him. There are two kinds of anger, and the kind that wells ups, crawls into a man's belly and temples, is no good to him – it lacks cunning. Yet this is the feeling crackling behind his jaw, turning his fists into mallets. He waits for it to pass. He watches her breathe.

Seven years earlier he plucked her from the river, from a piece of ice. The strangest thing – a girl on a piece of ice floating down the Smoke, drifting farther away from the edge, moaning for a certain, quiet death like some legendary Sioux princess. Had he been looking a different way, facing the direction of the current instead of against it, there would be no story to tell. He'd blinked, looked again, and then there was no time to think. He backed his truck down the riverbank until it hit water; he jumped into the truck bed, hooked up the rope, wrapped it around his waist, and waded into the river, his toes cramping painfully in the icy water, his legs instantly leaden and senseless, his fingers and forehead a palsy of chills. When he reached out and grabbed her by the ankle and yanked her towards him, pulling her off the ice into the river with him, the frigid water brought her to life, flicking some butane behind those green eyes. She flailed; the dark icicles of her frozen hair scratched his face. *My dog! My dog!* she cried.

But he saw no dog. All he felt, with the weight of her resisting him, was that he knew this girl, that he'd known her forever, that Rita had used some kind of witching to put her in his path, an almost-baby floating through the frozen bulrushes. A rebuke. *You are always choosing not to belong, Elijah,* she'd said on the banks of this very river. And when he had wrapped that shaking, sobbing, wretched daughter of Rita in the hunter's blankets from his truck cab, poured her tea from his Thermos, waved his own red knuckles over the vents blasting heat from his running engine, it didn't matter that the girl was Joe Montagne's. It didn't matter that he himself had no wife, no offspring. Saving the girl made her a different kind of progeny – one with whom he had no legal, familial, or blood tie, yet a child of his no less.

"Don't be a martyr to anyone else's system," Elijah whispers into Cherisse's ear. He pulls a wad of bills from his pocket, gives it a quick count, and slips it under her pillow. His hand brushes her forearm and he feels that it is warm. She is in there, listening.

He leaves the hospital smiling. Now that he is calm, he will find a way to do something for her that matters. He feels no loyalty to anyone but her.

∾

One summer, for three happy months, Cherisse woke to hear her mother singing along to the radio in the trailer kitchen, with a voice as big and high-ceilinged as church. All her June days that year began with burnt sweetgrass and ended in long hikes. Sometimes her mother remembered to make them peanut butter sandwiches ahead of time, and other days they just set off walking through meadows for hours, counting the number of butterflies, picking handfuls of tickweed, patting the paddocked nags they encountered, flushing out crayfish from stream beds until they were dizzy with heat or hunger, and her mother would say, *Don't tell your dad,* before sticking out her thumb to hitch a ride home. There were days when her mother talked and days when her mother did not speak at all. And one special day when her mother opened her mouth only to sing, nudging Cherisse's shoulder so she would sing back to her.

And then it was July. Heat settled over them like heavy cream, making their skin slip against the trailer's Naugahyde sofa, their breath thicken in their throats. Too hot for long walks. Her mother took her down to the banks of the Smoke River instead, and they swung into its warm, olive-coloured waters from scaly tree vines that chafed their elbows and thighs. Her mother showed her how to lie completely still floating on the Smoke, so that the part of her above the river's surface was heated by the midday sun and the part below cooled by its shadowy waters. They floated side by side, her mother telling tales of princesses and witches while the river slouched forward, slow and relentless, cradling them in a soft otherworld between dreams and wakefulness. It always stopped abruptly – her mother's grasp on her forearm, the quick, sharp command, *Up* – and then they were both wading out of the river within yards of where it dipped into rocky shallows or the current quickened. Her mother laughed like a young girl at this trick of hers for knowing. In the afternoon when they had returned to the trailer, the heat pinned them into stillness and they fell asleep side by side.

The temperature broke with the arrival of August. The cooler air woke her mother's craving for freshness, for food. They pulled beans off the runners in front of the snack shack, shelled peas by the bushel for freezing, and squeezed their neighbour's corn husks, testing them for fatness. Her mother stopped men on their riding lawnmowers, pointed to their fruit trees and offered to pick them for a cut. They ate sweet cherries by the handful and salted the green apples they'd taken too soon. But her mother seemed most pleased by the peaches: three six-quart baskets for two days of picking. Cherisse shimmied into the higher branches and lowered them with her weight so her mother could reach.

Pie, her mother announced. *I am going to make Joe a couple of fresh peach pies for his birthday.* This was an exciting development: there had never been any baking in the trailer. Cherisse sat quietly at the Formica counter while her mother spread open a book on the table, pushing her palm down on the crease so it would stay flat and tracing her finger under the black type, squeezing her eyebrows, pushing out her lower lip. The studying of the book went on for a long time, and Cherisse began to wonder if baking was like schoolwork. Her mother picked things out of the cupboard, slowly at first, reading the label of each, then reading the book. She chose spoons from the drawer, and a bowl and a cup.

Everything was lined up but nothing seemed to be happening. *Run over to Mrs. Porter's and tell her we need these things to make pie.* Cherisse was handed a scribbled list and released from the dull tension of the trailer kitchen to sprint through a ditch of Queen Anne's lace. When she returned, her mother seemed to be frozen over the same arrangement of ingredients and utensils, worrying them with her eyes. Cherisse started to unpack the bag from Mrs. Porter, careful to put each item in the right category.

Her mother's eyes flitted down. *No, no, not there,* she said, hands batting at her as if she were a tiresome housefly. Cherisse backed away into a corner, and for the next hour her mother mixed and sifted and rolled. When she lifted the pastry, it stretched and tore like damp newspaper. Her mother tried to patch and plug it enough to cover the pie plate, until finally she cried out in anger, balled up the pastry, and threw it at the sink. She looked at Cherisse and said, *Go find something else to do. I need some time.*

Cherisse sat outside the trailer, played hangman in the dirt with an old stick. She sang to herself to misplace her hunger – her mother had forgotten about lunch again. She snuck back into the trailer, into the cubby with her mattress and treasures, and flipped through her comic books and counted the change in her piggy bank. Finally she lay her cheek on the little mound of quarters to cool her face and promptly fell asleep.

Hey, little one, her mother whispered when she woke up and wandered into the trailer's quiet and dark main room. The kitchen was clean but for a pie with a braided edge and a golden crust that smelled the way Cherisse imagined newborns smelt: buttery and floral. *Only took me three tries and eight hours,* her mother said with a tired laugh.

Okay, little wolf, back to bed for you. And her mother returned her to the mattress in the corner. *I'm hungry,* said Cherisse. Her mother kissed her again. *No mind. I'll make you a big breakfast tomorrow. Now you must sleep.*

Outside the trailer, Cherisse heard a man clear his throat and she knew it was Joe returning late from work, impatient to go visiting. As she lay in her bed, her eyes filled with tears at being alone all day, cast out of the kitchen and the pie making, only to be left behind again. Her stomach cramped from hunger and her mouth was gummy with a terrible urge – the very worst kind. She flung all her quarters at the trailer's walls so they made a loud noise, flickered, and fell like dying stars. It was over too soon.

In the morning, her mother was singing, the same as always. The taps were on. Cherisse woke up smelling coffee. Her tongue found sweetness in the crook of her mouth, glazing her lips. She looked down at her fingers; they were stuck together with crumbs and glue like dried honey. Her first impulse was to bolt from the trailer, yet her mother continued to sing. Cherisse washed her hands and face in the small washroom at the foot of her parents' bed and entered the kitchen, afraid and curious.

Good morning, Cherry, her mother said and kissed the girl on her forehead. *G'morning,* Cherisse said staring at the table. Her mother put a plate of eggs in front of her, poured a small glass of juice. *Hungry?* Cherisse nodded. Her mother topped up her own coffee, turned her back to the girl, and started washing the frying pan, letting her voice glide lazily over the surface of a song. Cherisse looked at the eggs, made her favourite way. She wondered if eating them would be like a confession.

Funny thing, her mother said, interrupting her song. *Some animal got into the trailer last night and ate Joe's birthday pie.* Cherisse held her fork in the air. *Had quite a party of it too. The counter was a mess.* Her mother remained at the sink, looking out the small kitchen window, her voice light as cotton. *What kind of animal do you think it was, Cherry?*

Cherisse thought about it for a moment; she knew what her teacher would say, and wondered if this was what her mother wanted to hear. *A very bad animal?*

Her mother laughed. *Oh no, I think probably a hungry animal, in a bit of a temper too. Maybe one of the Rim-Dweller's owls whispered in its ear, put the thought in its head. Ya think?*

Cherisse wasn't sure what to do with her mother's interpretation. She nodded.

Still, Joe doesn't get his birthday pie, and that's too bad, because it's not his fault. Any idea what can be done to make it up to Joe? Her mother took her plate and washed it. She never once looked at her daughter but began to sing again until Cherisse answered.

Another pie?

Her mother picked up the remaining six-quart basket. *Well, maybe. Some of these peaches have turned but there's enough for at least one pie. Only one problem – we're out of sugar and butter.*

Mrs. Porter? Cherisse asked.

Her mother shook her head. *Mmm, we leaned pretty hard on her yesterday.*

Cherisse hesitated, then left the kitchen and went back to her cubby, which was still scattered with her piggy-bank change. She'd been saving to buy something pretty, the kind of things the other girls at school had. Now she picked up the coins where they'd fallen, delivered them in fistfuls to the kitchen table. Her mother stayed at the counter, scrubbing the coffee maker and fiddling with the radio dial. When every coin from her piggy bank was on the table, Cherisse cleared her throat. *Is this enough to buy what we need?*

Her mother turned and barely looked at the change before answering. *Yes, it is, Cherry. That is the perfect amount.*

In the dreams that shepherd the knitting together of her bones and tissues, Cherisse calls out for her mother, this mother. When she is alone, she awakens briefly to the hospital room with a phantom sweetness still on her tongue. The people who love her have come many times; she knows by their smells of the outdoors, tobacco smoke, a familiar warmth so different than this place's odours of plastics, stale air, and human seepage. Then it's their voices that give them away, hanging over her low and sad as November clouds. She smells their good smells, feels their love, but also their desire to see her eyes open, hear her speak – and the force of their wills, the old tug-of-war, as if she is contested territory. For now that makes them too like the other, more recent strangers, hovering near and around her with their less welcome smells.

She pulls away from them all to burrow back into the dream sleep where the sweetest smell of all is peach pie, one that her mother and she make together in silence, using ingredients purchased with all her change, a pie that spreads a smile over the width of her father's face. If she sleeps, her mother will never leave, never slip unexplained from the trailer on a crisp evening in early September, only tucking a shiny quarter under her sleeping daughter's ear. If she sleeps, her father will not sob himself into unconsciousness or burn dried tobacco leaves, blowing smoke in the direction her mother went, relying on the old ways to bring her back to them. If she sleeps, the failure of his magic will be forgotten, but not the pleasure of warm fruit.

∽

Stephanie steps into the hospital elevator. Her parents think she has gone to find the cafeteria, buy them coffee. The sharp corners of her digital camera stick into her ribs through the book bag's thin canvas. *Hide it,* Nate told her. She left the professional case, with its pockets for zoom and wide-angle lenses, filters, batteries, USB cords, at home. *As many pictures as you can,* he insisted. *The more she heals, the more evidence we lose.*

But the police must have taken photos. The hospital . . . I mean, they do tests, keep notes. Collect samples. He kissed her then. On the cheeks and then behind her ears and then along her neck, her shoulders. *Optimist,* he called her first, *Bambi* next.

It made her spin. She'd pictured being in love so many times, but she hadn't the imagination for this. She does not sleep. She forgets to eat. Her life too suddenly wonderful, wrenching, and purposeful.

Nate repeated rumours he's overheard about the girl, the niece of a woman he calls his leader. He asked her point-blank, *Stephanie, are you interested in justice?*

Getting to the ward takes longer than she expected; it's in an entirely different building than the one where her brother dozes in their mother's arms. When Stephanie steps off the elevator, the sound of her heart is in her ears.

Act like you know exactly where you are headed. Take something, a plant maybe. It would be easier if he could remember the room number. *Three doors past the nursing station, right side.* This was as much as he could give her. *Oh, and she'll have a room to herself.* That was unusual.

Won't there be security, a cop posted at the door?

He shook his head. *You watch too much television.* He stroked her forearm. She wondered if he would kiss her some more. Being wrong had become so pleasurable.

Stephanie pulls out a large teddy bear she bought in the lobby gift shop. It has a yellow sateen bow and a small red heart embroidered on its chest. There were smaller stuffed animals, Mylar balloons, stems of gerbera daisies, all of them cheaper. But this gift suggests a deeper tie to the patient. It emboldens her.

There are several people behind the nursing station, moving in and out. She marches ahead with her eyes fixed on the doors beyond them, and nobody even notices her. At the fourth door she sees a single bed in dim lighting. Stephanie sees the outline of a petite body under sheets, a small head, a bonnet of smoky hair tucked behind small shoulders. Cherisse is sleeping.

What if she wakes up and I'm taking pictures? It might scare her. She'll start screaming. They were lying on the ground then, among the tobacco plants across from the fires and sounds of the blockade, her head cradled in the crook of Nate's arm, her cheek against his chest. Through the plants, the porch lights of her neighbourhood twinkled like tiny pieces of broken glass.

Nah. The talk is that it's pretty brutal. She's already had surgery for internal stuff. There might be others. She's pretty drugged up right now, according to her aunt. Doubt she'll come to while you're there.

Stephanie pulls a chair close to the bed so she is facing the door. The bag at her feet exposes the camera. She's still deciding where to put the teddy bear when a nurse comes through the door. Stephanie startles.

"Oh," says the nurse. "She's sleeping."

"Yes. I'm her half-sister. I'll just sit with her a bit." She uses a breathy voice, doesn't make eye contact, clutches the stuffed animal. Nate says that Stephanie's hair and eyes are dark enough to pass for part native. *Indian pale ale,* he calls her. *It's worth trying,* he said. *White people think we're all hybrids. A friend would be easier to turf.*

The nurse checks the iv, makes a note on the chart, gives Stephanie a scrutinizing look, then pulls a curtain across three-quarters of the room's width. She leaves with a tepid smile – sympathy, pity. Stephanie reaches down, grabs her camera, adjusts its settings on her lap, and risks flicking on the bedside light.

Nate showed her an earring. *I found it under the oak tree.*

It was small and cool in Stephanie's hand. *Shouldn't we give it to the police?* she said.

He laughed. *Are you kidding? They're useless. Took them almost a week to collect evidence.*

Stephanie looked down at the earring, tried to imagine wearing such a thing herself.

When I found it, Nate said, *I thought it was a sign of good luck. But I was being greedy – everything's already great in my life. I mean, you're in it. So now I kinda think it's a sign, like the Creator is asking me to do more than just walk around the blockade acting defiant.*

She kissed him then, convinced that there was nothing he could ask that she wouldn't do.

Click, check. *Click*, check. She brushes back the girl's hair, photographs each side of her puffy face, the misshapen profile. Her ears are pierced, no earrings. *Click.* Check.

With her old camera, Stephanie recorded thousands of images: Japanese maples on groomed front lawns, suvs with vanity plates, golden retrievers, yoga pants on women who didn't know sivananda from bikram, Australian gumboots on men who ironed pleats into their khakis, jogging strollers, and mp3 players. But her art teacher, Mr. Ward, who was usually supportive, complained that there didn't seem to be an entry point to any of them, a place to begin their deconstruction. The *punctum*, he called it. *Did you ever consider allowing a face – an actual person – into the frame?* he asked.

What the fuck? Stephanie had thought. *But my pictures are about what's missing – uniqueness, originality,* she argued back.

Yes, but as far as photographs go, they're not telling a story. Sorry, he said. And Stephanie, who made it a practice to adore her art teachers, adored him less.

Now she wants to ask Mr. Ward if photos can find the story. Can they discover a truth the photographer can't see? Stephanie takes a deep breath and grabs a corner of the hospital sheet. Nate has said, *Yes, if you can. That's important.* This will take nerve she doesn't know if she has. She closes her eyes and imagines the earring, and she wonders if she can borrow some of its meaning for herself.

She peels back the sheet without waking the girl The bunched-up hospital gown reveals fading bruises along her legs; they gather like thunderclouds on her upper thighs. *Click. Click. Click.* The gown is untied, and Stephanie lifts it. The girl is bound up around her ribs. Her pelvis, the skin a patchwork of welts and abrasions. Beneath the injuries' distortion, Stephanie can tell that the girl is beautiful, perfect. She feels a prickle of jealousy, then shame. *Click. Click.* She does not check these shots. Stephanie pulls the sheet back up, turns off the bedside light, sits down. She's out of breath, fighting tears. The girl's head moves slightly.

Nate said, *No, we cannot count on anyone – your police, our police, your government, our government – to protect us. The pictures are insurance.* She combed through a week's worth of newspapers and there was no report about what happened to the girl. Nate said the reserve papers hadn't touched the story either. Why? It didn't make sense to her, not when every stolen bicycle, new graffiti, or lacrosse game dust-up got headlines. *She's native,* said Nate. *A native woman getting assaulted is not news. Even in a town as small as this one.*

Cherisse moves again, and Stephanie delicately takes one of her hands, rubs circles against her palm. Her fingers are long and delicate, curled with tension. A wonder they didn't snap. Stephanie pulls to straighten them. A single beautifully manicured nail is intact on the ring finger of the girl's left hand. The index fingernail has been torn down to a sharp nub. Stephanie gently pushes the two digits together and compares them. She stands up out of the chair and moves closer. Her throat is dry and an ugly heat constricts her chest. Without thinking, she presses the two fingernails into the soft flesh of her own fore-arm and drags. The girl's eyes startle open. Stephanie drops the hand and jumps back.

A nurse appears from behind the curtain. The girl has closed her eyes again but is forcing sound through her swollen lips. The words are impossible to distinguish.

"You'll need to go," says the nurse. She carries a tray with a packaged syringe and a vial.

Stephanie grabs her bag. At the end of the bed, the teddy bear has toppled over. She rushes out of the room, off the ward, out of the hospital like a thief. All the time she is aware of a subtle stinging on her forearm. But she's not ready to look at this thing she has taken with her.

Outside the hospital, in the wee hours of the morning, Ella lights a cigarette she found in the pocket of her son's shorts. She is slipping, she can feel it, under the ether of small things: the extra glass of wine at dinner, the one she takes with her to bed, the lack of exercise. She has not jogged for three weeks, the longest she's gone without a run since she was pregnant with Stephanie. The oversleeping. This cigarette. Her failure to remain positive when everything is going to hell.

What story is there to explain Las's troubles? He does not speak – he is too stunned, too confused. The possibility that some-body might have deliberately hurt him fills her gut with such a bubbling molasses that she takes a long suck on her cigarette to calm down. She has set her son up to be the hero of his own life, like a prince unaware of his pedigree. And he is screwing it up on purpose. She can feel it. Ella drops the cigarette to the pavement, squishes it with her foot, and instantly misses its comfort.

CHAPTER 19

Cherisse waits until the risk of visitors, of interruptions, passes. In the dark of her hospital room, she lifts the blade and presses it into her bottom lip. It takes a second to draw blood and there isn't much, but it tells her the scissors are sharp. The nurses and doctors here have no quiet movements. That is why she has the scissors from the lunchroom and they don't. These men and woman move against their own bodies – she hears them coming from a distance, skin chafing against skin, rubber soles giving back-talk to each linoleum tile, rings and watches and phones clinking. Her mother told stories about how the best hunters let go of their bodies, give themselves over to something. *Lift your feet like a springtime fox. Spread your arms like a cormorant drying its wings. Quiet, quiet. Don't scare your prey. This is how you eat, how you live, how you rest. Quiet, watching,* her mother said.

Cherisse was a little girl when she mimicked the storyteller's pantomime of a soft-footed animal, stayed silent as a rabbit crouched low in the meadow for hours against her mother's sleeping body, so they'd never be parted. That is how she got the scissors from the lunchroom with all its windows overlooking the nurses' station, where two women in pastel uniforms tapped at computer terminals and chatted about what they would do if their lotto numbers came in.

The lights are turned off in the rooms. Cherisse moves the scissors, cool against her palm, under the sheets and positions herself so it appears she is asleep, facing away from the door. She smells the yeasty warmth of the night nurse who looks in on her, hears her shoes squish, the rustle of the woman's polyester against polyester. The point of the scissors is against her thighs; Cherisse presses harder, without flinching. Her skin punctures and stings, but she does not blink.

The nurse leaves and the scissors come back up to her mouth. Cherisse opens them and licks the edge of each blade. She tastes metal and blood. Lying on her side, she cuts her hair in tidy handfuls, as close to the scalp as she can. She flips over and repeats the hair cutting on the other side of her head. When it is done and she hears no movement from the hall, she is up and out of the bed.

For a week now she has pretended to drift in and out of lucidity and sleep, getting herself ready to leave. Her thefts have been stowed under the mattress, in the pillowcase, the single drawer of the nightstand. She stuffs pilfered pillows under sheets, creates the silhouette of a small figure sleeping in the fetal position. Off comes her hospital gown, and the night air pimples her slight nakedness. She balls the gown and covers it with the cut hair so that it spills over the top of the sheet, across another pillow; in the night shadows it appears to be a face obscured by a long, beautiful mane. All her clothes have been taken as evidence, but Cherisse has stolen a pair of plastic clogs from the lunchroom, clean scrubs and a lab coat from a passing laundry cart, a headscarf from another patient. She puts them on quickly and smears her cheeks with the cover-up foundation she lifted from a purse hanging from a hook at the back of the staff washroom. She's ready to leave.

At the last moment she yanks the clipboard from the end of her bed and carries it with authority out of the room. Then she walks out of the ward, off the floor, into an elevator, and through the lobby, still moving quietly, but boldly too. *Some animals aren't afraid to be seen*, her mother would tell her, *because how they are seen is their advantage. Like the wolf,* she said just before she left for the last time. *Remember, it is good to be a wolf sometimes.* And so Cherisse walks with her head held up, her gaze fierce and direct, the clipboard grasped in one hand banging against her hip. Inside one pocket of her lab coat is a wad of cash, more money than she has held at once in her whole life; the atomizer makes the other pocket sag. A woman smoking outside the hospital doors doesn't give Cherisse a second look. She continues walking, right into the street, and disappears into the bustle and shadows of late afternoon.

The time she ran barefoot over a rusty nail and it sank deep into her heel, it took Joe forty-five minutes to speed to the hospital's emergency room. He would have been travelling at top speed – 120 klicks at least – since her father couldn't bear the sound of a woman's whimpers. Cherisse walks and works out the calculation with her smoke-shack math. She puts the distance between the hospital and the reserve in the ninety-kilometre range, a big walk at the best of times. And she is not at her best. Her head is high, but already unsteadiness is working its way into her gait. *Fifteen hours more of this*, she thinks, *at least.* For a moment she is fearful.

But she's also free. And it feels good to be moving, to look back and see the hospital become a shoebox on the horizon, and then just a line. She walks at the bottom of steep ditches that hug the road, where she can't be seen. After three or four hours, the early evening's warmth disappears. Cooler air gets past the thin hospital cotton, her own thin flesh, inside of her. She climbs up the embankment to check the road signs. Soon she will reach the edge of territory she recognizes. By then the light will be gone, but she won't need it; she can abandon the asphalt tributary she follows now. The fields – canola, corn, tobacco, potatoes, ginseng – will be her way-finders to the river, and the river will take her home.

There are two cigarettes in the pocket of her lab coat and a pack of matches, last-minute thefts. She did not think to bring water or food. Her growing dizziness tells her this was a mistake. But Cherisse breathes low and even and matches the pace of her breath with her steps. Her mother told her that hunters smoke to numb their hunger and fatigue and enter the minds of their quarry. When she turns a corner, she sees a field of canola on the horizon, fluorescent yellow against the darkness, and beyond it the moonlit waters of the Smoke blinking. She pulls out a cigarette, lights it, and takes a long suck without breaking stride.

Into the deepest hours of morning she clings to the eastern banks of the river, holding branches to keep herself steady, stubbing her plastic shoes on fallen logs, scratching her forearms on brambles, avoiding boys hooting from truck windows and parked cars steamed with hushed conversations, dodging late-night dog walkers and the watchful back-porch lights of elegant old riverfront homes that will lead her to the bridge and the highway.

By the time the sun flares in a smoky sky and makes her face flush with new heat, Cherisse's lips are crackling dry and she can feel her heart beating against her sternum like a boxed swallow. She wants to lie down. But she is close now. She cuts through the *o'tá:ra* at its periphery, out of view of the sleeping

blockade, and reaches the meadow that will take her somewhere safe. She takes the wad of money out of her pocket and
holds it so loosely in one hand that the bills slip out, fluttering
away from her like milkweed silks. Wildflowers and grama
grass rub gently against her shins. It is a comfort to be touched
when that touch can never be other than warm and soft.

Helen thinks she might never go back into the snack shack to
help Ruby. Her patch of sun is too good – warm but not hot. She
is tired from shuttling between the shack and the blockade, and
now to Coulson Stercyx's farm to cook breakfast and dinner for
his small crew. As a little girl, she would curl up on the kitchen
floor in the horn bell of mid-morning sun. Her mother's steps
around her smacked – the tiles were tacky with spills. Helen
would pretend she was a child at the beginning of the world,
when the dark and the light were twins who fought and then
compromised. Her dead grandmothers ground quartz into sparkling dust, threw it into the light to keep her happy. Eventually
her mother would lift her up, cradle and nuzzle her as if she really
were a newborn, then set her on the back stoop, where the sun
had moved. There was nothing more whole than warmth.

Ruby has no such memories. She is only two years younger,
but it's if they grew up in different families. The demons got to
their mother even before her daughters were taken away, one
by one. The quicksand of memory pulled Lena in, pulled her
down. The horror of her schooling: priests with rough hands,
nuns with leather belts, food that was sour and pushed her near
the edge of starvation. Helen reminded Ruby that there were
moments of sunshine, that their mother was good in those
moments, full of tenderness and indulgence for a child luxuriat-
ing in a patch of warm light.

In the snack shack there has been no talk of the blockade. Ruby refuses and Helen is happy to avoid the conversation. A sense of responsibility and failure makes her eye twitch. On the back stoop in the sun, she has an unfamiliar yearning for a cigarette, if only to work her mouth around something, to extend the comfort of the sun with another warming sensation.

The doctors said it was cigarettes that killed her mother in the end, but Helen knows better. The cigarettes were what kept her mother alive: the comforting rush, a thing to occupy her shaking hands, the small cylinder that made it easier to talk. Smoking was a long inhalation of hope, of the desire to keep moving, keep breathing, keep aiming for something better, even when all the evidence suggested it wasn't coming.

Sure, Helen wants a cigarette, if only to remind herself of the ashy kisses her mother once pressed onto the top of her head. She stretches around, sees Ruby through the shack's back door, cleaning the windows with a towel soaked in white vinegar. Funny, that. Helen is a wiry slip of a thing, but Ruby is her mother remade, round and billowing, with an unexpected lightness and vigour in her movements.

The blockade has changed business at the snack shack. There are two or three mad rushes of customers buying trayloads of tacos and french fries, followed by long hours of quiet. Ruby wants her to come only for the lunchtime rush. During that busy time she and Ruby brush up against each other by the small kitchen's grill and fry baskets, reaching over and under and around the sister flesh, smelling each other's damp heat, hearing the grunts of effort, exasperation. They anticipate each other, too familiar to require words. But in the long periods of quiet that follow, Ruby attacks every grease splatter with a spray bottle of diluted vinegar, renews herself by renewing order. And Helen feels her sister's hostility, how her mere presence obstructs this renewal. She is happy to quit the shack, to feel the tug of sun, to shut her eyes and open the spigot of the past, to wait for the sound of trucks wheeling onto the gravel and booted feet landing hard on the soft pine plank in front of the order counter.

An inconsequential shadow makes her open her eyes. There is no sound, really, only a presence, delicate as a lit match. Helen cannot take it in at first, this visitor from the spirit world, this two-legged coyote-woman with its hungry, mottled face, its dead green eyes. The shadow does not move and Helen pulls herself up, shakes the blurring brightness from her old vision. Then she focuses. It is a girl with sallow skin and pale, dry lips. Helen notices the hospital stamp on the hip of a pair of baggy cotton pants. She stares hard at the face, the shorn scrub of hair. Finally, with her hand over her mouth, she lets out a wail.

"Ayeeee. Cherisse! Ayeeee!"

Helen lunges at the girl, and the body she wraps in her arms is frail, catgut and balsa.

Ruby hurries out onto the back porch, making the old door squeal with alarm, and then she too has a hand to her mouth. "Cherry, your hair! What's happened to your hair?"

Helen waves an arm to shush her sister. "Get her some water, quick."

Helen pulls the girl to the step, cradles her in her old, sun-brown arms and starts to rock. "You're okay. We're gonna take care of you. We're gonna take care of you now."

And the girl, she is like an eyeless pup, the way she curls up against Helen, the way she surrenders to the dream of safety.

CHAPTER 20

The mayor has been sitting on the Bains's patio for the past twenty minutes. Stephanie watches her from the kitchen. *Jesus, this is weird*, she thinks.

The mayor won't leave. Stephanie offers tea. The mayor says, "No, thank you. I could use something stronger."

Stephanie stays silent. The mayor wants to know if there is an open bottle of wine in the house. "Y'know, your mother and I were friends. Good friends. From the time just before you were born right up until you were five or six," she says.

Stephanie nods. She finds a screw-top Grenache-Shiraz and pours a generous glass to take out to the patio. The mayor receives it with barely a nod and reaches for Stephanie's hand.

"How long did you say your mother would be?" she asks.

"She's at the hospital again. Las has some appointments."

"I'll wait," says the mayor, and she looks at Stephanie, whose captive hand feels spongy in the sandwich of mayoral flesh. "You must be a blessing to your parents. So smart, so nice."

Stephanie can barely grunt. What could be more depressing than being a blessing to your parents? She wiggles her hand free. If only the mayor knew how she wakes up with her hair smelling like smoke, her body burning up.

"Is your brother okay?"

Stephanie starts. "His foot's messed up," she says.

The mayor nods. "Serious?"

Stephanie shakes her head. She doesn't want to talk about it. Her mother has rules about family business, about discretion. She'd chalk it up to more of her mother's control-freakishness, had she not once been a snoopy, bored thirteen-year-old who found an old tin tucked into the garage roof rafters filled with white-bordered photos, date-stamped like quaint artifacts. In one picture there were two squat, dark, kohl-eyed people, barely distinguishable from one another with their thick wrists, large hands, and wary stare into the camera. And between them this willowy girl with red-gold hair in a pale summer dress, reflecting light like fresh paint, as if for whimsy or prank she'd been Photoshopped into a *National Geographic* spread of rough, remote mountain peoples. Kneeling on the garage floor staring at the photo, Stephanie realized she was looking at an image of her grandparents, dead before she was born, with the unlikely child they produced. She felt an unaccustomed flicker of empathy for her mother.

"Do you have a good friend, a female friend?" asks the mayor. "One who matters to you?"

Stephanie considers the question. She shakes her head. The mayor waves at her to sit down. And because Stephanie is not sure whether protocol allows her the option of not sitting down with the mayor, or with her mother's former friend, she slumps into the closest plastic chair.

"That's a certain kind of loneliness for a woman, wouldn't you agree, dear? Not having a decent friend. Women need their female friends, almost as much as they need men. Maybe even more."

Mayor Redhill drains her glass and holds it out. Stephanie is tempted to tell the mayor that the way she framed the question is heterosexist, or androcentric – whichever one is worse. She's tempted to say, *You just gave me a queenly wave to sit down.* But she can't see that going very well. So Stephanie gets up and refills Peg Redhill's glass.

In the kitchen, she plunks the two-thirds-empty Grenache-Shiraz plus a full bottle of Pinotage on a tray and fills a bowl with pretzels, another one with cashews. If she's learned anything from the torture of health classes, it's how food helps metabolize alcohol. And the mayor arrived in her suv – the keys are on the patio table. At the last moment she adds a glass for herself and brings the whole shebang out to the patio. If the mayor is settling in, there are ways to make it bearable.

The night before, Nate told her about a bad feeling. Something in his gut told him he'd find the man who hurt Cherisse on the reserve, or even among the Warriors. *They're friends of mine. I guess I've kinda infiltrated them. They've talked about her. Said some not-cool shit.*

Stephanie hesitated. She didn't want to do any more investigative work, and she couldn't tell him why. Nate's eyes clouded. *You gotta understand something,* he said. *If she were white, and from the suburbs like you, do you think we'd have to do this? C'mon, your parents would raise fuckin' Cain. There'd be an official investigation. There might even be news coverage.*

Stephanie imagined her parents hovering over Las as if he were a colt with untried legs. What would they do if she told them about Gordo lying on top of her in the basement, his palm pressing hard against her chin so it felt as if her neck would snap? She pictured her mother's mouth made thin and bloodless by doubt and the inconvenience of justice seeking.

But this girl – Jeezus, she's Joe Montagne's kid. She works at a smoke shack, Steph. She's not on anyone's radar. She can't cause political fallout 'cuz she's native. And that makes it so much easier to ignore what's happened to her, or shove it under the carpet, forget about it.

Stephanie wondered if this was true. Weren't there people who'd benefit from making a stink about what had happened? And why was so much of their time together focused on this other girl? She kissed Nate to push away this ugly, resentful part of herself, to make it untrue. She led her tongue over the changeable topography of his lips, chin, neck, sternum, belly. His body rose in response. But the redemption she chased across his skin couldn't be caught; there was too much to worry about. To tell him would invite a withering heat upon these tender new feelings. Leaving it unsaid was easier. And worse too.

The mayor shifts in her chair, holding her refilled glass in one hand and a bitten pretzel in the other. She is a big woman. Her hair is teased and eggplant-coloured. The skin it frames looks bloated and windburned. Stephanie takes a long sip of her wine. *Please don't let me become that*, she thinks. *Please.*

"The thing about women and their friendships is that they usually end with a whimper and not a bang," says the mayor. "A bang would be better." She takes a long inhale.

Stephanie wonders if this is one of the privileges of holding public office: you take your time saying things because you expect to be listened to.

"Your mother, for instance. She was so great when we first met. I mean, two babies! And she was stylish, fit. And fun. Migod, that woman made me laugh."

Stephanie rolls her eyes. Her mother being hilarious – since when? She's seen only the barest glimpse. Her mother's face flushed with wine, her twitchy frame uncharacteristically slumped on the basement sofa, and out of nowhere a story about her inexplicable parents and their storybook old European ways. How Stephanie's grandmother stuffed bread in her pockets if she walked in the woods, to protect herself from the *mullo* – ill-intentioned ghosts and little people. Or how at ten, Ella, febrile and nauseated, was led out into the bush to shake a young tree. *Shake, shake!* Stephanie's grandfather instructed his wilting child. *Fevers like movement. It will go to the tree.* But the quivering sapling did not get hot and sweaty, nor she any cooler. Still, when she vomited on its roots, Stephanie's grandfather clapped his hands. *There, it is done. It is good.* Caught up in the reminiscence, her mother took another gulp of wine, giggled. *I did feel better. I hated him for that.* When her grandfather died, her grandmother packed his nostrils with wax so bad spirits couldn't enter his body. She tucked screwdrivers and hairbrushes, warm socks and sugar cubes into his casket, despite the funeral director's alarm and her mother's adolescent humiliation. As she told these rare stories, Stephanie's mother's laugh became wet-eyed and was followed by a stretch of quiet.

Now the mayor's eyes are similarly wet-rimmed. Stephanie squints and can see that those eyes were pretty once, likely her best feature.

"You know – and this is embarrassing to admit – I always thought your mother would turf me as a friend, because I was such a loser when we met. Fat. Struggling with being a mom. Married to an angry man." The mayor turns in her seat. The red wine has made crumbs of her lipstick; they cling to her lower lip, the corners of her mouth. "As it turns out, your mother turfed me when I became more of a winner. I didn't see that coming."

The idea of her mother coming home to find them both warm-cheeked and talking loudly begins to both alarm and amuse Stephanie.

"And it's not like she ever said, 'I'm done with our friend-ship,'" the mayor continues. "She just sort of phased me out. Gradually. The way grocery stores get rid of an underperform-ing brand you rely on. Less shelf space every week. And then – whammo! It just disappears. As if it was never there."

Stephanie reaches for more wine and tops up the mayor's glass after her own. *If I am totally fucked up,* she decides, *I can't be accused of betraying my mom.*

"You know, I racked my brain for months. What had I done? I went over entire conversations, how much I'd spent on birthday gifts, how quickly I responded to answering machine messages, whether I'd been too friendly with your dad. I left her messages apologizing for whatever it was. Nothing." The mayor's voice cracks. She pulls back into her chair.

My mom broke the mayor's heart, Stephanie realizes, sur-prised. "It's getting hot out here. Let's wait inside," she says aloud. Late afternoon sun has chased shade from the patio.

The mayor gets up, holding her wineglass, opens the patio doors, and heads to the kitchen's breakfast nook. She slides into a banquette seat and perches there awkwardly. The seats are unforgiving – Stephanie hates the way they make her even more conscious of her curves – and she wants to tell the mayor how her mother insisted on building the painful seats into the tight space so they are practical only for an ectomorph who wears size three jeans and has a tight coil of muscle for a bum. Like her mother. This would make the mayor laugh, possibly lighten the mood. But the thought of acting like besties with a woman her mother's age feels pathetic to Stephanie. Even in her increasing tipsiness, she doesn't want to feel pathetic. She takes the tray to the kitchen counter.

Peg sips and clock-watches, sips and clock-watches. It's only a few minutes later that her glass is empty again. "That's one long appointment," she says.

The second bottle has only an eighth of its liquid remaining. Stephanie empties the last of it down the drain and then slips both bottles into the recycling bin under the sink so they won't be the first thing her mother sees on their return. "We're all out of wine," she announces. "Can I make you some coffee?"

Her nod to sobriety has come too late. The mayor is suddenly holding up her head with the heels of her palms and sobbing. Her shoulders graze the ends of her near-purple hair, sending little tremors up to its roots. And Stephanie is very, very sure she is up shit creek for aiding and abetting this outburst of emotion. She fetches a box of Kleenex and slides back into the banquette across from the mayor, reaching across the table and rubbing the mayor's arm and nudging the tissues towards her at the same time. She feels dangerously grown up in this act of comfort.

"Can I ask you something? If you're not still friends with my mother, if she hasn't been good to you, then why are you here?"

The mayor tries to gain control of her breathing and raises her head. Her eyes look wasp-bitten, as if they could disappear into the wet, swollen skin. Stephanie pulls a tissue from the box and offers it directly, hovering within an inch of the mayor's nose. After an unembarrassed honk that makes the Kleenex sag, the mayor clears her throat.

"It's my son," she says with a waver. "I'm pretty sure the ass-clown has got himself into trouble. Serious trouble . . . it's complicated. Your brother may know something. Maybe he even said something to your parents."

The mayor starts to cry again, but this time in little whimpers. Stephanie drops her hands to her lap. It's as if relief has cut the strings holding up her shoulders; all her weight collapses inwards. She wants to cry too. That scratch on Las's neck – she's only entertained one possibility. Now she sees what she has missed: Gordo, the verging-on-psychotic creeper, had been there. And if this was true, Las likely intervened, pulling Gordo away from the girl who'd meant her nails for him. Las's foot another casualty of that struggle. Stephanie feels seismic with gratitude. She lets out a laugh.

The mayor looks startled, girding for insult.

"I was worried my brother did it," says Stephanie.

She will see in retrospect that this is when the wine and relief from the weeks of strain get ahead of her. She tells the mayor about gathering evidence: the pictures of the girl's injuries, the girl's broken fingernails, the scratch on her brother's neck, the black baseball cap and camouflage kerchief that reeked of gas, the inexplicable foot injury. And how she convinced herself it was him. Because added together, the facts and artifacts sorted themselves into a story that was hard to ignore. More so if you're a little sister, always in the shadow of your brother's triple threat of good looks, athletic talent, and uncanny luck. Wouldn't you be more likely to let your imagination go there, ignoring that facts and reason point to Gordo, who everybody knows is sketchy? "No disrespect," Stephanie says to the mayor a few times.

Suddenly the mayor is up, pouring the freshly made coffee, bringing milk and sugar to the table, and rubbing Stephanie's forearm, encouraging her to slow down and continue. Stephanie trusts that the disclosures of the preceding two hours – the mayor's vulnerability, the revelations about Stephanie's mother, the shared wine – have put them on the same team. And Stephanie has a hunger for disclosure. What is it about wine that makes the background story seem so important, urgent even? So much of your life, your actions, your privacy becomes that necessary context. She tells the mayor everything, starting with Nate in biology class and then Nate in the dairy bar, and finally the weeks of meeting Nate in the tobacco fields, coming home with sand in her bra and panties, still rosy from the prickle of his cheek stubble. Because it's as awful being alone with doubt as it is with happiness, isn't it? Having to swallow everything you know into a tight bloat inside you.

The mayor's tears dry as Stephanie speaks. Her eyes reassert themselves in the swell of skin, she withdraws her elbows from the table, sinks her back into the thin banquette pillows, and folds her arms across her waist. Stephanie's head is furry from the wine, and by the time she has revealed everything to the mayor, she is the one who is crying, and it feels good. It feels as if she could spend the rest of her life crying.

The sound of a car whooshing into the vacuum seal of the garage, followed by a slamming door, interrupts them. The mayor speaks to her in a soothing, motherly tone. "Perhaps it's better if they don't come in to this scene."

Stephanie pats under her eyes with a tissue; it comes away stained with mascara and foundation. She takes her coffee into her bedroom.

∞

Peg rinses her coffee mug and straightens her clothes. Two hours earlier she arrived with a vague design of unloading her woes, asking for sympathy, crying in her friend's arms about her failures as a mother and a mayor. She was almost looking forward to it, throwing up the white flag to Ella Bain, grovelling even. *Yup, still a loser after all these years, Ella. Rescue me. Please.* Now she has another, more satisfying option.

Ella looks wan, uncharacteristically unkempt as she enters her kitchen and throws down her car keys. She starts at the sight of her old friend leaning against the counter.

"Peg, what are you doing here?" Her tone is cold.

Peg matches it with mayoral officiousness. "I've come to talk to Mitch. It's important business. I was hoping he'd come back with you." There's something spacey and distracted about Ella that almost makes her feel bad.

"No. No. I don't know where he is, quite frankly."

Peg's head throbs from too much wine in the afternoon. She wishes middle-aged memory were less like a purse with a torn bottom seam. She needs to hurry home, write down what she remembers from the conversation with Stephanie, details that insure her against future inference that Ella's son is less culpable, less rotten than hers. "Well, I'm sorry to bother you, then. Please tell him it is urgent."

Peg takes a step as if to leave and Ella stiffens. "Is there something I can do? Can I tell Mitch the nature of your business with him?"

She wants to know, Peg thinks. *And it's going to nettle her, keep her up at night, that she couldn't wring the information from me.* "I think I will need to talk with him first. It's up to Mitch what he shares with you." She smiles at Ella. An almost cruelly professional smile.

Her former friend moves towards the door. "Well, I'd offer you a drink—"

Peg puts up her hand. "No need. I'm driving," she says. "I hope Las gets better soon."

Ella squints, nods her head.

Peg crosses the threshold and then stops and turns just as the door starts to close on her. "Ella?" The door freezes.

"Yes, Peg?"

"Well, I don't know how to finesse this, so I'm just going to come out and say it. There's a bit of talk around town – not spare on the details, if you know what I mean – that Stephanie has been seeing a native boy. One of those wild kids from the blockade."

Ella's face blanches. She does not open her mouth.

"Just thought you should know."

❧

Stephanie feels lighter. She feels as airy as she ever has. She hasn't eaten all day and she can barely remember those days when food was the analgesic that made it all bearable.

Right now her parents and the mayor will be in her father's study; they are dealing with the news together. The mayor will report what she knows to Constable Holland. Maybe voices will be raised and then subdued – she has no template for such things. All she hears is quiet.

Stephanie thinks she might become religious. Not a shrewish Christian – too judgey – but something light-filled and near ecstatic, like a Zen Buddhist or a Zoroastrian. She sits down at her computer, does a search of Zoroastrianism, and bookmarks a few sites for when she has the head for reading. On the computer she sees the folder where she has stored the pictures of the girl from the hospital, and she wonders what she should do. A queer mix of shame and sadness about taking them in the first place weighs on her. She grabs an old memory stick from her drawer, drags the photo file onto it, and places the stick back in the drawer among paper clips, thumbtacks, Post-it Notes, and a crocodile-shaped stapler. Then she permanently deletes the photos from her computer. Her buoyancy returns. Eventually they will want her to join the discussion, but she can wait; she is filled with a largeness of spirit that gives her patience. She looks up the Bahá'í Faith and bookmarks a few websites before going over to her dressing table and considering her reflection in the large oval mirror. The reddened pouchiness from wine and crying distracts from the prettiness of her eyes and hair.

Beautiful, her mother said just a week ago. Stephanie was passing her in the upstairs hallway between bedrooms, where sun laddered through a skylight, when her mother turned and looked at her in such a way that it made her freeze. *You look beautiful, Steph. Absolutely radiant,* her mother repeated before disappearing behind a door. That was all. Steph stood there, flushed and incredulous, a whole lifetime of believing her mother found her ugly thrown into question. She ran to the bathroom mirror to be sure. And it was true. Love had brightened her, made her luminous. Her mother had noted it as if unsurprised, as if Stephanie was destined to it all along.

She pulls open the top drawer and gets to work with concealer, then searches for the right lipstick. Something too glam or too dramatic would be inappropriate, even though it is evening, so she works with her daytime palette, adding the palest pink to her lips. She finishes with a kittenish stroke of eyeliner and leans back to survey the effects in the mirror.

Her reflection includes a figure standing in the doorway behind her. Stephanie turns to find her mother, arms against her sides, face slick and tight, watching her. She divines the remorse in her mother's pain and is ready to offer comfort. Stephanie stands, smiles shyly, and opens her arms, moving forward. A good daughter, finally. She hopes she looks as beautiful to her mother as she did a week earlier.

Her mother windmills a hand from her hips. The slap meets Stephanie's modestly applied peach blush with a powerful and exacting sting.

CHAPTER 21

Mitch suggested a doughnut shop but Peg said, "No. You might need a drink." He wanted to be somewhere where few would know him. "Then come by the house. I have a nice Scotch." Peg said no again. "I don't think I'm welcome there." Now Mitch sits in the Squeaky Vicar alone. The mid-afternoon light is unkind to the pub's stained velveteen seats, the beer embalmed carpet. He takes a gulp of subpar bar Scotch for which he has overpaid. Peg is late. His hand shakes. Twice this week he's grabbed Ella's wrists to keep her from flailing at him. "What's it about, Mitch? What's it about? Don't you dare go without me!"

He doesn't know. Is he a good man? He has always thought so, mostly. He worked hard for his dad. He has few vices. He loves his wife. He's cobbled together some material comforts for his family. The worst thing he's done, as far as he can figure, is take a risk on a development – with his wife's money, a second and third mortgage on their house, and investments from a dozen friends whose calls are increasingly prickly. On paper it was a sure thing. Everything was right about it: timing, demographics, the exurban shift, land prices. There are so few things in life that happen in ways better than expected.

He didn't anticipate how much worse it could become. The blockade. His wife newly shrill and unpredictable. Las with his meat-grinder foot. And now this news about Stephanie, once his little cherub with a doll's face and a lightness about her that was nearly confectionary. Even when adolescence freighted her with sadness, he became used to that, found it navigable. This new Stephanie – fiercely pretty and betraying them all – makes a rubble of his certainty. For an hour last night he paced outside her closed bedroom door, waiting for her to stop crying so he could ask why. Of all the available boys, why choose one so intimately attached to the family's despair? When she finally went quiet, he gave her a few more minutes before he turned the knob. The room was empty. The window was open. She was gone, this daughter who suddenly needed to run away from the burden of having everything. Mitch didn't tell Ella; her cold fury was being vented on cleaning the refrigerator. But he stayed awake most of the night waiting for the sound of Stephanie sneaking through the patio doors.

"Thank you for coming." Peg stands by the booth, waits for an invitation to sit. When she was his wife's friend, there was a jokey ease between them. *How'd Ella end up with someone almost as fat as me?* she'd ask, poking her elbow into the give of his waist. There's no room for levity now; too much has happened since.

Peg slides into the booth, waves to Will Jacobs to send another round. Mitch has always liked that she's a Scotch drinker. She puts her hands on the table. Her posture is upright.

"Why are we here, Peg?"

She exhales, a long leak of air that is sharp and mouldy. *Drinker's breath*, thinks Mitch. The Scotch arrives. She lifts her glass, nods for a toast, and takes a large swallow. Then she speaks.

Mitch listens, and as Peg is bluntly describing the assault of a native girl, he's unzipped by thirst. He lifts two fingers to the barman. "Have you got anything better than this Scotch? Give me your best. Doubles."

For the first time in years, an image pops into his head of his son as a small child, a toddler with a beatific face – the first of his angels, all golden curls and roundness. His eyes were the colour of a cloudless June. He was the most kinetic child, a boy who redeemed Mitch's disappointing genetic contribution to physique and motor skills.

"I've got good reason to believe that Gord and Las were behind the stolen and burned cop car, Mitch. But I'm not touching it. Right now they're looking for two native kids. I'm not going to implicate my boy or yours."

She's all business. Mitch feels at a disadvantage. Peg has more information and has had time to think, to work things out. His head is reeling and she's already grabbed control. He's beginning to despise her.

"What they may or may not have done to the girl is another matter."

When a boy realizes he is stronger than his father, a delicate negotiation defines their adult relationship. Mitch grew more fearful of his son as he morphed from a rambunctious kid who adored his dad to an athlete whose physical prowess was encouraged by his mother. At age thirteen, Las could have handily pinned Mitch to the floor. He knew it; so did Mitch. Better men would have weathered the moment with an internal grace, a trump of wisdom. But Mitch's imagination produced only one response. With every new shoe size, every bicep inch that Las grew into, Mitch treated the boy as if he were less intelligent, less responsible, less competent. Ella protected her son from anything outright hurtful, so Mitch took to diminishing Las in ways his wife couldn't intercept.

"I'm not going to ask Gord outright," says Peg. "It's one thing to have my own suspicions, but if he confesses directly to me, I have a legal duty. What you do about Las is your own business."

Mitch drains his third Scotch. It is hard to keep his thoughts hinged. As he lifts his glass, he feels a tickle in his throat, a small spear of pain. It makes him cough loudly. He puts his hand to his neck and massages under his jaw as he swallows. There's a hard lump under his left ear that's sore to touch. Now that he thinks of it, his throat has felt raw all week. It could be red and aggravated by infection, or worse. He imagines barnacle-like growths occluding the passage of saliva, food, Scotch. He has an urge to interrupt Peg and ask her to look into his mouth. Would she see swelling or angry redness? Should he drive to the urgent-care centre in Pemcoe?

"How do you know Las was even there?" he asks after another wet cough. His tonsils throb. He wishes he'd had Ella come along; she carries oil of oregano in her purse. He notices Peg pull a piece of paper out of her hip pocket and glance at it.

"Those boys are always together. Can you account for your kid's whereabouts lately? Ask your daughter about the scratch on Las's neck, the things she found under his bed. What she knows."

"Stephanie talked to you about this?"

Peg waves away his concern. "Doesn't matter. If rumours break that they are being investigated for the assault of a native girl, that alone will be the ruin of you and me. Even if they are innocent, it will take a long time to establish that. In the meantime, who knows what will end up in the paper, the town tittle-tattle."

The bar bobs like a blurry carousel, up and down. Mitch stumbles from the booth. He ploughs through the bathroom door mid-retch. His vomit sprays the urinal with a rough pointillism of orange and pink. He rinses his face, his mouth, and gargles tap water. His shoes are flecked with vomit but he doesn't care. Back at the booth, he orders another Scotch.

Peg has a plan. Its logic cuts through his inebriation and the throbbing.

"We're going to get out in front of this, Mitch. Solve the blockade and our own little troubles with one big offensive."

"I'm not clear what you're saying."

"Well," says Peg, "it's pretty simple. We offer the girl and her family a chunk of change to not talk, even to go away. At the same time we convince the government that now's the time to step in, buy the land from you, shut down the whole carnival. Let them deal with the natives in civil court."

"The development's dead, then? Just like that?"

Peg doesn't answer. Mitch drops his head into his hands. The exhaustion he has been fighting for weeks presses him into the table. He wiggles his Scotch-soaked tongue in his mouth, imagines the alcohol's antiseptic staunching the contagion in his throat.

"Where's the money for the girl coming from?"

"Don't worry, I've got someone who is willing to help us out. Let's just say he has an interest in the outcome."

She is in control, and Mitch wants to be in control. He loathes Peg now, more than his wife does. He avoids her eyes.

Peg gets up to leave and Mitch doesn't stand. "My ride's out back. I'll be in touch. Just do what I say, okay?"

He nods his head.

"And Mitch, your cough – get that checked out." She slips out the rear exit like some sort of B-movie operative.

Mitch looks around. There has been no one to witness this sorry moment in his life, not even Will Jacobs, whose business has so declined because of the blockade that he's taken to drinking in the afternoons and napping in a booth. Mitch takes out his cellphone and calls his wife.

"You home?" he asks when Ella answers sharply. "I have news. Wait for me in my office. Lots to discuss."

Mitch lets his head slide right onto the table's surface, his eyes slick with tears. Peg noticed he's unwell – that's something. He feels grateful for it.

The first time Mitch saw Ella Nagy, he was sixteen, the tobacco harvest had just begun, and Doreville's downtown was electrified by the dark-skinned novelty of seasonal workers.

After a day in the fields, the primers would lean smoking against the walls of the Legion or sip sodas outside his father's grocery store, eyes bleary, heads bowed with fatigue, skin glistening under white singlets. Ella would walk past them, her cotton sundress sliding deliciously along her legs, a small kick of wind reaching up to her thighs. Mitch could tell she wanted men, and especially these strangers, to stare. There was some sport in it for her. It may never have occurred to her that the very things that secured her vanity – shiny whorls of red-blonde hair, buttery skin, dainty chest, small buttocks – might be repulsive or simply curious to them. Instead she breezed by these hot, tired men staring forward, her chin held a little too high, as if to say, *You can't have me.*

She gave the same look to the tobacco growers' sons who scarred the summer asphalt with their muscle-car tires, screeching to a halt at the traffic lights or in the Legion parking lot just in time to see Ella pass, spot the flame in her cheeks, watch the hired men swallow her up with their stares, the incomprehensible words they snickered to each other under their breath. And those quick-to-anger progeny of hard-working immigrants, who took their daddies' money to fuel their dreams of not being farmers, felt heat against their temples and in their bellies. The brown strangers assured their father's livelihoods and their own privileges, but did that give them a right to desire their women? Every evening Mitch cocked his ear to hear his father mutter about which farmer's boy had drained one beer too many at the Legion, made a remark, thrown a punch, or brandished a broken bottle, only to find himself tumbling out into the street under the weight of a man who was a parent, who didn't have health insurance or an education, and thus had much more to lose than a tooth or a patch of blood vessels if he couldn't go to work in the morning. Mitch gave Ella credit for every fight that came after one of her strolls through town.

Watching unseen from his father's store, he studied her beauty so he could see past it, to the uneasy mixture of egotism and insecurity underneath the good skin, behind the big eyes. It was Mitch who divined she'd likely never summon the nerve to leave Doreville, and so would need to be distracted from regret. Casting off the shame of her poverty-line childhood, resisting the town's rough agricultural pedigree – that would be enough. Knowing this, he won her. Kept her, too.

But what had *he* really wanted? Ella's admiration, not just her mild gratitude, her civil appreciation of the comforts, the safety and compromises he offered. He wanted to be a rogue wave, the thing that brought her to her knees with desire, if possible. Or, failing that, respect.

"We have something to discuss," Shayna says on the phone. "Can we meet?"

Coulson assumes it's about the girl; they haven't had any contact since he found her. Even then it was perfunctory. Shayna left a message to say thanks. He wanted to hear more – how she missed him, for instance – even if the context was wrong. He's called her back several times since, hoping to hear her voice if only for a minute. Her line is always busy. Once it rang three times and then went dead. Her voicemail is full.

"Where?" he asks. Already anticipations tickles the back of his neck, his gut.

"That pub," says Shayna. "The squeaky thingamajig. Wouldn't mind seeing the inside of it this time."

Coulson chuckles. It's a test – or a friendly *fuck you*. He'll find out which soon enough. "Sure. I could use a drink."

He walks through the Squeaky Vicar's doors twenty minutes later, wearing his new shirt for the second time. He wonders if she'll notice, understand that it's for her. Inside there's a fug of frying oil, spilled beer, and ineffectual air conditioning. So many places of beauty and breezes where they can talk and hold hands freely, but she chooses here. The pub is deserted, other than Will Jacobs snoring wetly on a bar stool. Coulson is relieved at the lack of judgmental eyes but knows his relief is problematic. He's been waiting for her through the better part of every day, long into the night, for the past two months. He can't afford to care about what other people think.

He pops his head through the kitchen's swinging doors in search of a barmaid. A blousy girl lifts her head from a newspaper spread over the ice machine and grins so that her eyes send high beams of delight in his direction. "Long time, no see." She winks.

Coulson hesitates. On some dreary winter night she must have appealed to him. He doesn't remember. "Could I bother you for a couple of pints?"

She hustles towards him, and Coulson moves briskly to the edge of the bar. He pays for his beers, grunting responses to her small talk and pretending not to notice her indignant pout when he carries the pints away to the farthest booth. He sits with his back to the barmaid. Why did he so readily agree to meet here? What did it prove?

Shayna's small shadow lengthens across the pub's front window, followed by her form. He watches the wind pull wisps of hair from around her face, revealing her jaw, her lips, her nose. That's all it takes – he's split wide open by the sight of her. She enters the bar, plunks down across from him, and shoves a small heaped quart box towards his resting forearm without a word of hello.

He smiles. "Black raspberries." He wants to wrap her in his arms, run his lips against her skin.

She shakes her head. "Wrong season. Blackberries."

He looks down and sees his mistake. Each fruit is the size of a thumbprint, their colour as unyielding as her eyes.

"Try one," she says. "I found a few canes at the edge of the *o'tá:ra*. The bulldozers got the rest of the patch. They're ripe."

He pops a berry in his mouth and pushes the untouched pint of beer towards her.

She waves it away, hangs her head, takes a deep breath, and pops up her chin to look straight at him. "I'm pregnant," she says.

Coulson sinks back in his seat. He takes a large gulp of beer, pushes his shoulder into his mouth to wipe it on his new shirt. Suddenly his head fills with an electric din: the hum of the ice machine, the crackle of the bar's old stereo speakers, the whine of the neon signs, a fan in the kitchen. It builds like tinnitus inside his ears. He fights the urge to leave, to escape her and those two words that tether him wholly and completely to this place, when he's nurtured a private conceit that he can leave at anytime, do something else, wear an H. Huntsman suit again, take trips to Prague and Buenos Aires, train for a triathlon, or learn to sail. Read all those big fucking books he never got through in university.

He looks at Shayna and sees that she is speaking. Her eyebrows are raised in a question and her forehead bunches, but through the din he can neither hear nor clearly see her for the vision of Marie rolling over on top of him in bed nearly a decade earlier. She was so pretty after lovemaking when she was without makeup, her face flushed and damp, her hair a wild and full misbehaviour. He was about to start kissing her all over again when she said it: *Baby. Let's have a baby.* He took a long breath and widened his eyes at the loud bass of panic working its way from his gut to his throat, filling his ears. After a few seconds Marie leapt from the bed in a storm of tears. His silence, the strange look on his face were the confession he wouldn't voice: he didn't want to be tied to her in that way.

"I don't think I want it," Shayna is saying. "Just thought I should tell you."

She is speaking more loudly, and it is her loudness that pulls Coulson back into the present. He takes another long swig of his beer and looks around as it slides down his throat. The light is waning and the pub has begun to populate with townies returning home from work. Coulson can hear Will Jacobs, awake now and voluble, behind the bar, offering drinks to every arrival.

"Sorry?" he says.

"I don't *want* it." Both her body and voice are rigid.

A few people meander past their booth towards the back room, strain their necks with expressions both curious and hostile. Coulson wishes he could think strategically. But now he can think only about the long nights he has stayed awake listening, aching for the sound of Shayna's soft feet landing on the back step, her small hands working open the screen door, rattling the aluminum like bracelet charms.

"Hold on there," he says. "I'm just taking this all in."

"You're freaking out. I can see that much."

He musters the energy for a fledgling smile and lets out a long sigh. His mother once admitted she never wanted to have kids. Her ambition had been to teach in Africa. He remembers feeling stymied at first, even betrayed by this confession, as if she was suddenly unknown to him. *You changed everything,* she added, with an uncharacteristic touch to his face. *Once you have one, you want more. You miss the small burdens of a baby.* The women of her kin felt motherhood in their knees, the small of their backs, she told him. *It makes our teeth soft.* She squeezed his hand for a long time. *Couldn't have more than one, as it turned out. Some don't ever get the experience. Can't tell you how thankful I am.* It was the most tender feeling his mother had ever expressed to his face.

Coulson reaches past the nearly empty pint, the quart of blackberries, and wraps his hands around Shayna's smaller, lighter ones so his thumbs rest in the delicate clefts of her wrists. They stay like this for a few minutes, each staring off into space, smiling weakly, with a small acreage of their skin fused.

The barmaid appears suddenly at their booth, a greyish cloth scrunched in her hands. She grabs the unused paper coaster behind Shayna's elbow and reaches for Coulson's pint glass. He encircles it with one hand.

"Whoa, there's a good half swallow left in that."

She pulls back, rests her hands on her hips. "Well, you folks ready to settle up?"

"I'll just pay at the bar when I'm through, like always, thanks." He tries to hide his irritation. The barmaid leans back towards the table, unfolds the cloth on its surface, and pushes its sour smell close to where Coulson's fingers are again entwined with Shayna's. Shayna loosens her grip as if to pull her hands away from his, but Coulson hangs on and shakes his head slowly. The barmaid leaves with a scowl.

"I think we should go," says Shayna, her glance wheeling around the filling tables.

"I want you to hold off," he says. "About the baby. You can't be far along."

"Three months. Four, tops," she says.

"Let's talk some more."

Will Jacobs appears at their booth wearing a stained, faded T-shirt stretched like a leotard over his belly. He looks bilious and flushed. His hands move in front of him, play-fighting nervously, and his eyes are trained on where Shayna's fingers intertwine with Coulson's. "You'll have to leave. You're upsetting my patrons."

Coulson laughs heartily. Over Will's shoulders he can see a half-dozen sets of eyes fixed on their booth. Shayna wiggles her hands free, slides them across the table, and hides them along her thighs.

"Do you always throw out your quietest customers?" Shayna is already getting up, moving out of the booth.

"I don't know what your game is, Stercyx, you being a land-owner and all. But I don't appreciate it. Your point's made. Now go home."

Coulson stands up quickly. He towers over Will. Shayna puts a light hand on his arm but he resists. He wants to test her, see if her mettle is a match for his. Once a hailstorm laid waste to his entire tobacco crop in twenty minutes and he didn't turn away, just watched the green plants tremble and rip under a drum corps of ice pellets. Cruelty, even the kind delivered with glee, can be endured. Love is harder to take.

She nods in the direction of the bar. Among the slump-shouldered regulars there's a small knot of bald-headed young men he doesn't recognize, their eyes trained on him like underfed dogs. She instinctively places a hand on her abdomen, and he looks down, sees something there, the subtlest swelling. He grabs her wrist, pulls her close, wraps his other arm around her shoulders, and leads her to the door, sheltered by as much of his body as he can muster.

As he is about to step out, a beer bottle grazes his calf and shatters on the tile beside his boot. Coulson jumps; a shard flies up and bounces from his knee. He jerks around, and Shayna slides away from him out the door. The pub has gone quiet, become a horseshoe of watchful figures, including the barmaid, with her crossed arms and bitter smile, and others he could greet by first name, many he's known for years. Reflexively he flips his middle finger to them before stepping outside, calling out for Shayna. He hears jeering laughter, sharp, then muffled as the door closes.

He stops. Ahead of him in the fading light, Shayna is a small moving shadow pulling him towards a future he's unsure of. For a moment he feels a terrible thirst and wishes he could turn around, go back into the pub, and order another steadying pint.

⁓

Ella bends at the waist as if she is in pain. Mitch watches her pick at the kitchen floor with the focus of a hungry pigeon. When she straightens, her face is pulled into a point. "So, let me get this straight. You believe Las is guilty based on a scratch that Stephanie saw, a stupid baseball cap, and Gordo's truck tires? You've got to be kidding."

Mitch shifts nervously. Las lies in his bed only a floor above them. He doesn't know if Stephanie is home. Ella's voice is about to crescendo. A *quiet down* gesture – that one with his hands – will only set her off. She's the kind of woman a man dare not shush.

"It can't be true," she says, shaking her head, becoming more shrill. "It can't be true. Stephanie hates her brother. She's jealous of him. And Peg is getting back at me."

"Stephanie does not hate her brother," Mitch says quietly. "And what's true or not true doesn't really matter, Ella. We have to act or lose everything." Mitch feels his throat, still tender, and wonders if there will be an opportunity to mention it to Ella.

"It *does* matter what's true, Mitch. It's the *only* thing that matters."

He looks at her angrily, his right arm extended. "Out," he says, pointing, pushing her towards the patio door with his left hand. "I won't have this conversation here."

When she steps under the pergola, he keeps pointing, past the backyard gate, beyond the earshot of neighbours at their barbecues or weeding around delphinium borders. Ella marches away from their property into the rows of tobacco. The dusk-lit sky is worthy of a Flemish painter, Mitch thinks. And he yearns for a moment of repose, a quiet walk with his wife under its mauve and smoke. When she turns, he sees that she belongs in the painting: a flame-cheeked fishwife with a cudgel-like tongue. Beautiful and ferocious in the same moment.

"You, this is your fault! You spoiled Stephanie. You let her feel victimized by Las's achievements. She took up with that native boy to spite us. And now these unseemly accusations, this fantasy!"

Mitch grabs his wife's shoulders so they are eyeball to eyeball. He has never understood how a mother could not adore her own daughter. It's the single thing about Ella he finds repulsive. "Do you have any idea how insane you sound? Stop talking about her like that or I will shut you out, Ella. I will deal with Peg and her silent partner myself. And I will keep you a hundred miles from the action. Do you hear?"

Ella slumps into the tobacco, her face in her hands.

"This is about Las," Mitch says.

"You've never been kind to him," she says in a biting whisper.

"Whether he has done something or nothing at all, we can't let people talk, Ella. We won't have a future in this town. Those boys are always together. The fucking tires on that cretin's truck—"

She starts to sob. The tobacco plants beside her shiver. Mitch searches his mind for a soothing blandishment, something that will make this day end sooner. "I'm going to make everything okay," he says.

A cricket lands on her shoulder, and when he reaches to brush it off, Ella wraps her arms around his knees so tightly that the wetness on her face soaks through his cotton pants. "I don't know anymore. I don't know my own kids." She reaches her hands up to his thighs, grabbing handfuls of his pants' thin, inelastic fabric, yanking the waistband to his hips. "Have I been a good mother, Mitch? Tell me I've been good."

She is pleading, and Mitch's eyes well up with his own doubts and regrets. "Yes, Ella, you're a good mother. You're too good. Nobody could have done better, could have given more."

She pulls him down to the ground and he is dizzy, feeling anew the rawness of his throat, the hugeness of what lies ahead. What he didn't expect was desire, but here it is, an untimely gift. His wife helpless in his arms, her body ransacked by emotion, the violet sky and the balm of loamy smells rinsing him of sweat and soured Scotch, his own long hours of desperation. His hands slide up the outside of her thighs. He kisses her hurriedly, fumbles sloppily with her buttons, as if the smallest hesitation will make him stop. Her skin is clammy and pimpled in the evening air.

"You are the best part of my life," Mitch says. He holds his breath, and then Ella holds on to him, with her pelvis, her mouth, her hands. Mitch makes her pant and cry out for him, for the idea of themselves that neither can give up.

CHAPTER 22

Joe Montagne thinks the guy walking towards his smoke shop looks like a federal spook, or one of those plainclothes RCMP officers who think that a shiny suit is going to make you blend in, look like a regular freakin' Joe. Nice car, that's for sure. Snub-nosed and silver, convertible top; Joe thinks maybe it's an Audi. But shit, he can never get those city cars right. The guy, though, he's got him figured. Something about his face that's already working overtime. Man's gotta be five metres away and already his smile is blazing like a casino entrance. *Wants something*, Joe thinks, *and I don't suspect it's smokes.*

"Hey, there," the man says. A large palm, bright as the inside of a seashell, slices through the air towards him.

Joe stays put in his lawn chair. He doesn't reach for the extended hand but lifts his coffee cup in greeting. "How's things?" he says.

The man gestures towards the lawn chair that Coulson has been sitting on for a week of sunsets, now folded and leaning against the back of the Ford.

Joe shrugs. "I'm guessing you're not here for rollies."

The man in the shiny suit unfolds the chair and laughs a bit nervously, then sits and leans forward. "You're a smart man," he says.

Joe doesn't even lift his eyes. "No. No, I'm not," he says. "What can I do for you?"

"My name is Saj Vinay," he says. "I'm with a law firm called Krantz, Russell, Simpson."

"I didn't do nothing," Joe says, raising the pitch of his voice in mock defence.

"Are you able to talk privately, Mr. Montagne?"

"You see anybody else here but us?"

The lawyer wears a gold chain bracelet on one wrist, an expensive watch on the other. Light bounces off the man. It makes Joe's eyes smart.

"I was so sorry to hear about your daughter," he says.

Joe stands abruptly. The lawn chair falls back hard, makes the sound of a crunched pop can. He drops his coffee and it splashes the lawyer's shiny shoes. "What the fuck do you know about my daughter?"

He looms. His shadow dulls the lawyer's sheen. But the shiny man is not rattled. He stands too, picks up the fallen chair, and places it so that it's facing his.

"Sit down, Mr. Montagne. I have something to say that might be very profitable for you."

Joe does not like this perfectly groomed person. Still, the word *profitable* has a sound he cares for and that makes him curious. The man is too calm, too certain he has something Joe wants. It can't hurt to find out whether he's right.

Ten minutes later he's holding Mr. Vinay's business card so

tightly it's already damp and creased. *That's some kind of Indian,* he thinks. *And that's one shitload of money he's wanting to give away.* The amount makes Joe jumpy. He repeats it over and over his head. Even as he folds up the lawn chair the lawyer helped himself to, he's dividing the money, quartering it like a freshly felled buck, a season's worth of meat. One piece to pay off his loan from that asshole Barton. One piece to Helen Fallingbrook, because she's bailed him out more times than he can remember. A trip to the dentist – he'd get a whole mouth of new teeth. A big chunk for Cherisse. He could send her away to an aunt across the border, maybe even put her through school – she'd make a good nurse. Pays well. Or she could record an album; that would make her smile. They could take a trip to the Dakotas, have a house that's not a trailer, a big-ass four-by-four . . . hell, he could lease a Hummer for that coin. Never have to sell another rollie again, and he'd still have money for Rita when she called, her voice ever huskier and more remote. He'd do right by his women, for sure.

But some of it is meant for him, the lawyer made that clear. If he gets an agreement. If he gets on it fast. Oh man, he wishes he hadn't spilled that coffee. He feels like he should just take a second, a moment to get it all sorted out.

We'll need to hear from you no later than the end of this week, after you've talked to your daughter, the lawyer said. *I'll deliver the money order myself. But it's time-sensitive, you understand. And we'll need papers signed by both of you.*

Joe nodded his head, his thoughts shooting in a hundred directions like a video game.

I could drive you to the hospital right now, Mr. Montagne, even wait in the lobby while you discuss matters with your daughter, bring up the papers and the money straightaway. Git 'er done, as they say.

Joe didn't like that. Who the hell says *git*?

I've got my smoke shack open, mister. I'd have to close up for the day or get somebody to take over for a few hours. Not likely. Plus I got my own ride right here. Joe patted his truck as if it were the flank of a strong horse.

The lawyer squinted, surveyed the vehicle in a manner the older man didn't appreciate. And then, with a bounce of his head, a point at his cellphone, Mr. Vinay turned and left so fast the gravel dust curtsied behind his shiny silver car.

Now Joe watches it become a silver termite nibbling away at the horizon and he thinks, *I should have asked for more money. Fuck! I could have asked for way more money.* There was something too smug about the way the coffee-coloured man turned on his heel, jabbed at his phone, made his wheels fishtail on the embankment as he sped away. Yeah, the bugger was probably having a big old laugh at Joe's expense right now.

His tooth starts hurting again. Joe kicks the tires of his truck. There's something he hasn't put together. According to the lawyer, there are things his daughter can never talk about. Such as who messed her up. He looked hard into Joe's eyes as he said it, as if he were simple, couldn't understand. Joe just nodded. *Of course, of course*, he said. But now he sees the lawyer's advantage: that little man from the big city knows who attacked his daughter, while he doesn't. And *who* is certainly important, *who* has to be someone with connections and money for a lawyer sleek as this dude. *Who* is the price setter.

Joe isn't a bad man. The image of his daughter's face, dented and split like thrown fruit, is all he can see when he closes his eyes at night. It makes him sad. It fills him with rage, makes him want to kill someone. Yet her beauty has been both bounty and burden to him. Certainly it's sold more cigarettes than he could alone, but every time he looks at her, he feels anxious. She is almost too much for this place, her quicksilver spirit too hard to contain. The two beautiful runaways of his life – his wife, his daughter – have unmade him, turned him into a man with no dreams other than keeping them at home. A little broken, a little frightened, even perhaps a little less pretty, Cherisse might at least stick around for a while, need him close. He feels bad for thinking it, even if its truth is plain.

And now there could be money. Joe starts to load his cigarette inventory from the stand into the back of the truck. The thing he hasn't told the lawyer is a niggling detail: Cherisse is no longer in the hospital. She is sequestered with strong women, and that's a harder set of doors to get through than what the hospital can throw between them. She won't want to see him. He'll have to find the words to unlock Ruby's bolted heart.

Something good waits for you, he'll yell out to Cherisse. *Just give me five minutes.* She and him aren't given to talking personal, but he'll find a way to get it out of her. *Who did this to you?* He practises asking it straight like that in his head. Part of him doesn't want to know. But that information means freedom. They'll come up with a figure together. They'll create a different life for themselves.

Joe hums to himself, pats the pockets of his jean jacket, and looks over to the tobacco fields. He sees the backs of men leaning off the harvester, the sweat on their bare shoulders catching in the sun. The harvester moves like a hungry slug through the east fields, which means it will be another few days before they'll be working up the rows to where his shack stands. He'll be long gone by then.

As he surveys the green tremble of the plants, the beginning splashes of harvest sepia on their lower leaves, the sun feels good against his neck. The money might change everything, he thinks. That has to be a possibility. He packs away the smokes in the back of his truck and drives off, leaving behind two empty lawn chairs turned towards each other.

Federal negotiator Antonia Taylor's Buick Regal is parked beyond the sightline of the blockade, where the highway gently curves. Shayna looks over her shoulder, feeling traitorous as she walks towards it. It felt odd to get the message from the negotiator, and more so when she called back and Ms. Taylor herself picked up on the first ring.

Private tête-à-tête. Friendly and unofficial. Can you give me twenty minutes? Keep it under wraps?

Shayna hasn't told anyone about the meeting, especially Helen, who wouldn't approve of its terms. *A negotiator who hand-picks whom she negotiates with is a colonialist,* she'd say. *Or a terrorist. You choose.* Shayna passes Joe's temporary smoke shack at the edge of the tobacco fields, smiles at this evidence of Coulson's good nature, and notes that it's deserted, Joe's truck gone. She's relieved there will be no one to witness her slipping into the back seat of the negotiator's car.

I looked you up, Ms. Fallingbrook. Impressive start to your law career, the negotiator said at the end of their phone call. Shayna could tell the comment was bait, an appeal to her vanity, which made it no less satisfying. Earlier that morning she slipped home for a quick shower. She painted her fingernails, a habit she'd abandoned after Pete-Pete was born, because it seemed impractical and fussy. In the very back of her closet hung what remained of her lawyer clothes. She fished out a scoop-necked white cotton blouse that was shirred along the placket and button edges. Paired with her new jeans and ankle cowboy boots, the blouse made her feel uncharacteristically pretty when she saw her reflection. There was a half-second in which she hesitated. Then she rummaged in a drawer and pulled out Rick's old watch, wrapped it around her wrist, using the last hole to fasten it, before she drove back to the barricade. The watch hasn't worked for years, but it doesn't matter.

Ms. Taylor's driver hops out and opens the back door for

her, and Shayna ducks her head inside. The negotiator's expensive perfume, the sodium glow of her titanium-coloured laptop command the space. Shayna regrets her girlish blouse.

"Thank you for agreeing to meet," Antonia Taylor begins. She snaps shut her laptop and slips it into a bag at her feet. Her tone is warm but authoritative. "I know you are a woman in a position of leadership, so I won't waste your time."

She draws in a long breath, and Shayna sees that, up close, she is more feminine than her boxy jackets and long face suggest from a distance. Her fingers are exquisitely thin, breakable even; one is encircled by a showy cluster of diamonds. The crinkles around her eyes, the deep commas at the corners of her lips hold some kindness, the tension of private sufferings. Shayna wonders how many compromises she's made to survive in a world governed by rules that are broadly interpreted and wildly manipulated, and always in flux.

"The blockade has to come down," Antonia says with a loud exhale. "It's as simple as that. The negotiations won't restart unless that blockade is dismantled. My bosses are digging in their heels on this one."

Shayna smiles. "So this tête-à-tête is not so friendly after all, eh?"

The negotiator twists in her seat; her body turns, makes soft little ripples in her cream silk blouse. She looks powdery up close, as if she could easily disintegrate.

"Can we talk frankly? Woman to woman?" Antonia says. Shayna wonders if there is more than one way to answer that question. She stares back wordlessly.

"You strike me as someone who's taken a bit of a detour from a promising career. Love, loss . . . doesn't matter. You're still young. And you clearly have a lot of respect in your community. My guess is that you can leverage this bit of celebrity to do something important, to really make a difference on these land claims issues. And in the process relaunch yourself, your own dreams."

She takes in another breath and looks directly at Shayna. "If you want to make a difference, Ms. Fallingbrook, as you know, good intentions are no substitute for results. Whatever you do next will be easier, more productive, vastly more meaningful if you walk away from this protest with a victory."

She looks down, and then smiles as if sharing a joke with herself. Her eyes soften. "If I'm being perfectly honest, I too need a success. My bosses are a little less than pleased with the headway I'm making here, especially now that the opposition are having a field day in the press about my fees." Antonia Taylor reaches out one of her delicate hands to Shayna and lays it on her forearm. "But, unlike you, I cannot relaunch myself after this. This is the wind-down of my career. I wouldn't mind making a difference myself, getting some results. And if you can trust me, I can use my experience to ensure that we do achieve something important here."

Antonia lifts her fingers and Shayna pulls her forearm away.

"And that starts with me telling my people to go home?"

"Not home. Off the highway. Get them off the highway, keep your protest within the boundaries of the development for now, and negotiations can start again. In return we will drop the requirement about negotiating with elected officials, deal directly with your group – I have secured Chief White's support for you – and dive right into the issues of treaty disputes, broken covenants, and so on. No waiting. No delays."

The car goes silent.

Antonia Taylor sinks back into her seat, pulls a bottle of water from a polished leather valise. "Would you like some? My driver has a cooler in the front seat."

Shayna shakes her head.

"We have the potential to set a precedent here – for the kind of negotiating we do, the agreements we make," Antonia continues between sips. "I'm excited by that. As women, there's so little turf left to call our own, and yet the things we get done are extraordinary."

Women. Shayna feels collected on the term's mantel, like some prize from a fall fair. They are both women for sure, but she feels no *us* with Antonia. Shayna wonders if the negotiator has any children. *Pregnancy has a way of interrupting extraordinary, precedent-setting acts,* Shayna thinks. She considers her own ringless fingers, the inexpertly applied nail polish. At the pub she was aching to have Coulson relieve her loneliness. Yet the minute he wrapped her protectively in his arms, she wanted that loneliness back for just a little bit longer – an unclaimed universe that was all her, the planet of her body, whatever grew inside.

"How much time have I got?" she asks.

"They will pull me from this role by the end of the week if I don't have an announcement to make about the blockade."

"That's four days."

"Three days," says Antonia. "We'll need one day to get people on the phone, write the communiqués—"

"Three days," Shayna repeats, and she reaches for the door handle.

"The talk is that my replacement will be a business-as-usual type," Antonia says, offering a cool, dry hand to shake. "More interested in placating than setting precedents. He will push for the kind of compromise that will shut things down, make people forget, stall the process."

Shayna gets out of the car. She cradles her belly with her palms, turns towards the blockade, and a familiar loneliness bears down on her again.

At twilight, when he comes upon Joe Montagne's empty smoke shack in his south field, Coulson wonders if he has offended the man. He's taken to moseying out here at the end of the day with two mugs of fresh coffee brewed up in the farm kitchen. They talk about nothing in particular or don't talk at all, just watch the twilight clouds jostle like spawning trout, a wet shimmer of colour.

Without Montagne there, Coulson hesitates, then resigns himself to honouring the ritual alone. He sits on a rickety lawn chair, watches a grasshopper bend and unbend its legs on the toe of his boot, and sips one of the coffees he brought.

His father spent a life making fretful assessments of the sky's cast and the wind off the lake, divining which trick of climate would steal the promise of abundance from the loose, light loam. Would his father trust the season his son is enjoying? The sand leaves he and his crew harvested a week ago were the colour of pale lemons, flat as sheets of paper. They loaded into the racks beautifully. The cutters look just as fine – big, broad leaves with few buckles. He should be buoyed. It is a rare season that works out better than anticipated.

But two mornings ago he awoke to a large, angry scrawl of graffiti on the side of his barn. FUCKS NATIVES it read in a pugnacious red, the letters as tall as any one of his primers, who were asleep in the barn while it happened. Then last night the phone started ringing minutes before midnight, greeting him with a click every time he picked up. At one a.m. he unplugged the kitchen phone, the one in the upstairs hallway too. Shortly after two his cellphone started ringing. Since the barricade began, he's kept it on at night in case Shayna needs him. It felt like a shameful capitulation when, around three, he powered it down so he could grab a few hours of sleep before sunrise.

He awoke rattled, with fear not for himself but for everyone he might not be able to protect. He insisted on driving the primers to town after their shift, rather than letting them ride their bicycles, then sat in his truck and waited for them as they did their errands.

"You're like a lady chicken today, boss," Ramirez said, his eyes twinkling.

How to keep Shayna safe? He phoned her twice before noon. "I'm okay, Coulson," she said each time, and begged off to attend to something else. He's brought binoculars out to the field with him, a flask of Scotch in his back pocket to keep him steady. Now Joe Montagne's absence makes him clench his jaw. He tells himself to get a grip.

He pours Scotch into the remaining coffee, lifts his mug to sky, toasts the worry of tobacco growing and all its charms too. Funny what you can love – and whom – with a bit of living under your belt. "This will be a good one, Ma, Pa."

While he drains his drink, a breeze spreads rumours among the tobacco plants and a gull makes a high, hoarse plaint overhead. The sounds obscure others approaching from behind, the slamming of car doors, the contrapuntal chatter of men excited by purpose, the crunch of gravel.

"Dismantle it!"

Coulson jumps from his chair just as a half-dozen men in pastel golf shirts, creased shorts, and unfaded jeans reach for the splitting planks of Montagne's hastily constructed smoke shack. He raises his arms, yells. "Hey! Hold up there, folks. This is my land you're on."

The men stop, open-mouthed. One of them is a smiling, red-cheeked fellow, a mortgage broker named Ted who advertises himself as "Dr. Dream Home." He steps forward. "Hey, Coulson, didn't expect you here. You got a problem if we get rid of an illegal smoke shop and squatter? Thought perhaps you hadn't noticed it, 'cause one call to the police would have taken care of this."

Coulson laughs. He takes a look at the faces in front of him, their pleasant outrage withering in the twilight's drying heat, and tries to remember which of them was at the Squeaky

Vicar the other night. He looks wistfully at his aluminum lawn chair, the undrunk second cup of coffee with its jigger of Scotch, and he wants them gone; he wants them all to disappear. "Joe's not here, " he says finally. "See, there's nobody here. Nobody to arrest."

"You don't need him on site to take definitive action," Ted continues. He adopts an avuncular voice, and it grates Coulson to be addressed like a boy who can't understand a civics lesson. "We'll dismantle the smoke shop – you're fully within your rights to have it removed from your land – and the police can put out a warrant for Montagne. "

Coulson stares at the laundered men in front of him, their faces unweathered by the elements, and he wonders if this is the cut of man he'd be now if he'd stayed with Marie. He tries to imagine Ted wielding a can of vermilion spray paint or staying up late to make hang-up phone calls. He'd almost like him better if it were plausible.

"Tell me," Coulson says. "How's this helping matters at all?"

Ted's brow creases. "The town's bleeding lots of money, Coulson. Damn blockade. Nobody's doing anything – not the police, the government. Do you have any idea how many people are at risk of losing their businesses entirely? What this could do to real estate values? Aren't you concerned about the value of your land?"

"I'm not selling this land anytime soon," Coulson says. "The price will recover."

The mortgage broker drops his hands to his sides. There is a murmur of disapproval from the waiting men. "Well, that's all well and good for you Mr. Stercyx. But what about Doreville's other hard-working folks, who don't have a valuable crop in the field?"

Another man moves forward. He is younger than Ted and wears hiking pants and a tight nylon T-shirt that shows off a weightlifter's definition. "Mr. Stercyx," this new spokesman begins politely, "I think your property shelters you from the effects of the blockade. You don't hear the noise at night."

The man turns and gestures towards a row of brand-new homes sitting slightly west of the Bains, closer to the highway where the blockade is situated. "That's my neighbourhood over there. We bought a few years ago. Since the blockade started, nobody sleeps anymore. All night, trucks race up and down our streets, native men standing in the back, holding flags, hollering."

He stops for a moment, looks down. "My oldest girl – her name is Maya – she's an anxious thing. And, um, this sound of the flags at night? She thinks we're being attacked by large birds. Every night I try to put her to bed, she refuses. 'The birds are coming, the birds are coming,' she says. She won't sleep for fear of the sound. We shut the windows, put a fan on. She can still hear the screeching of the tires. There are dark circles under her eyes – a little girl. I hate being helpless. We all do. We have to do something, take action where we can. Send a message to these people that they can't get away with whatever they want."

They have gathered around him now. Ted pats the younger man's shoulder. Coulson wants to feel kindred to his suffering the way the other men clearly do. But the young father has pointed to a new development, part of the sod-and-asphalt tsunami laying waste to the country of Coulson's memory, its tobacco-stained dirt. And he can see that this guy has a wife, perhaps not unlike Marie, with whom he must have lived happily in a cramped semi-detached in the big city, until one of them fell for the dream of small-town living accessorized with a brick-veneer turret, a robber baron's square footage. Coulson thinks of Cherisse, of carrying her broken, violated body through the tobacco plants, and wonders if these men know how they might square her suffering with that of a sleepless child in a home whose bathroom taps cost as much as a mortgage payment.

"You're right," he tells the man. "I am sheltered from what's going on in your neighbourhood. But here's the thing. See this chair? It's for Joe Montagne. He's not 'these people.' He's a person. See this coffee mug, and that one too? Montagne and I, we're talking. We're working things out. And while we're working things out, he is a guest on this land. That's my decision. That's *my* right."

Coulson wonders if he'll regret declaring his allegiance to Joe Montagne. But all he feels is impatience and a reckless buzz in his fists. "Okay, folks, you need to vamoose, get off my land."

There is a moment of disbelief and immobility. Coulson raises his arm, shepherds them towards the road like wayward ewes. The eyes that turn to his are humiliated and hurt. Soft pink rings the younger man's neck. They shuffle out of the field, over the highway, back to their shiny cars. For a moment Ted stands in the middle of road, turns again to him with a scolding stare.

They will forget, thinks Coulson. They will have a good jaw about it, sure, but their forgetting will begin the moment they uncork their bottles of Shiraz or settle into the oblivion of an air-conditioned snooze. Coulson readjusts his lawn chair to sit alone in his cathedral of evening light.

More than once, as a young boy, he'd come into the farmhouse kitchen at the end of the school day to find a clean-shaven man in a dark suit sitting at the table, a polished valise placed beside the fresh cup of coffee and plate of warm biscuits his mother had set out. His father would return from the fields or the barn, slam through the screen door, and barely give the stranger a nod before he'd grunt, *Not interested*, and start scrubbing his hands at the sink with his back to the guest. *Let the man speak, André,* his mother would say, and the man would hurriedly rhyme off the particulars of the offer – who wanted to buy their land and at what price, the number of new homes they would build here. It never occurred to Coulson that his mother was being anything other than hospitable, that she might pine for a life different from one of assured toil and worry. To the boy it was all a kind of entertainment. If the man pushed too hard, threatened to delay his father's dinner, there was sure to be an eruption, a sudden growl – *Out!* Then his father would hold open the kitchen door and follow the man so closely to his car that his gritty farm boots would catch the heels of the visitor's polished brogues. From the front step, Coulson would watch the retreating car churn up a dust storm on the farm laneway. Before he took his place at the dinner table, he'd imagine all the ways to spend the impossible-sounding amount of money that was leaving them behind.

CHAPTER 23

Helen washes the dishes while Cherisse sits at her kitchen table, drinking tea and staring at the door.

"I liked him," she says to Helen's back.

"Liked who?"

"The boy."

Helen does not turn.

"He came to the shack just once before, with his ugly friend. Didn't even smoke. I liked him right away. He had the kind of face that's never seen trouble. You know how some of those rich white kids can look, Auntie. As if they've only ever slept in beds with clean sheets. As if they've never had a cavity. He didn't say much or stay long that first time. But I wanted to know what it would be like to be close to someone like him. As if his luck could rub off on me. I imagined being his girlfriend, having dinner with his mom and dad, getting a puppy with him. Then he shows up out of the blue one night when I'm packing up the shack. It was late. Still, I was relieved to see him. If it had been just his ugly friend, I would have been creeped out. And we got rid of the greaseball pretty fast. The ugly one was so drunk, and he went behind the shack to pee. The keys were in the ignition and the cute one winked at me, slid behind the wheel. 'Let's play a joke on that asshole,' he said."

Helen wraps the dishtowel around her wrist, picks up a rinsed mug gingerly, afraid a sudden noise or sharp movement will make Cherisse retreat into silence again.

"Oowee, you should have seen that ugly boy curse and run, his fly still open. We laughed and laughed, me and the cute one, and just took off. Left him there. I was glad. He was so crude, so sketchy."

The dish Helen places in the rack makes a distracting *clang*. But Cherisse looks forward, addressing the kitchen's middle distance.

"I thought I finally had some luck. Driving down the highway in a big-ass truck with the prettiest boy I've ever seen. So pretty, Auntie. He was such a beauty."

Helen hears Ruby wrestle the front door. The border collie howls to be fed. *Shit,* Helen mouths. There's a wasp caught between the screen and the pane of glass above the kitchen sink. It bumps its body along the glass, buzzing its wings. She nudges it gently. *Hang on,* she whispers and resumes drying dishes, telling herself not to expect too much. The story has started and stopped so many times – the phone's unexpected trill, a honking car corking the words back into Cherisse's throat.

"Ooh, Auntie, I drank too much. He wouldn't tell me his name. I kept asking. I tickled him. He said, 'Let's go for a walk.' He stopped the truck by the tobacco fields. We both jumped out. I wanted him to kiss me."

Ruby rumbles into the kitchen, the dog nipping at her heels, a metal leash slipping from her grip to the floor. Helen raises her palm to her sister, holds her breath. *Shhh*, she signals. She forms a prayer with her hands. The wasp offers its own buzzing invocation.

Cherisse stares trance-like, unmoved by the commotion. Ruby grabs the dog's scruff, wheels it back outside, then slips back into the kitchen and leans into the door to muffle its closing.

"He did. He took me in his arms and kissed me. It tasted of liquor and was a bit rough, I thought, but not horrible. I reached behind, slipped my fingers into his back pocket, and pulled out his wallet. Daddy Joe always said I'd make a good pickpocket. I just wanted to know his name, Auntie. I did it for fun."

She stops, tears at a broken fingernail until it peels away. "I was afraid he'd never tell me. One night and he'd be gone. He went for a pee and I opened the wallet, flipped through, looking for ID. Used my lighter so I could see. Don't remember much after that. Except the blows. *Thieving cunt*, he called me. *Stealing native cunt.*" Cherisse starts to cry a little.

"*No, no, I just want to know your name. Honest!* Him swinging at me. Pulling my hair. I tried to fight back. I tried to run away. Stupid boots. He went apeshit on me, Auntie. I never knew a guy to go so apeshit. Wanted to grind me into dust. Like dirt."

Ruby moves forward but Helen shakes her head. *Wait.*

Cherisse smears snot and tears along her forearm. "The way he hurt me, I wanted to die."

Ruby draws in a breath. The wasp exhausts itself, falls silent.

"Cherry, do you remember his name?"

Helen is surprised that Ruby asks just like that. But it is better coming from her – soft and direct.

"It was a funny name." She pronounces it.

Ruby straightens, turns towards Helen with eyes wide. Her chin begins to tremble.

"Come again?" says Helen.

Cherisse repeats the name, and her face, framed in shorn

hair, is ageless, is a child's face, but for the gemstone eyes and their anguish. She lays her head on the table.

Helen holds her stomach, tries to calm her racing pulse. The dog clamours indignantly at the kitchen door. Ruby walks over to Cherisse, crouches beside her, and rubs circles on her back. Helen lets the dog in and feeds her. She's not sure what to do next, how to act with this new information, so she fusses at the sink, stares out the window.

There's no time to consider: Joe Montagne's truck comes bullying down the drive to the house. "Oh, Jeezus, not now," she says under her breath, and nods to her sister.

Ruby hears the choking engine, wraps her arms around her niece, and says, "I think your dad's here, hon. Do you want to see him?"

Cherisse shakes violently. "No! Not today. I can't."

"It's okay, you don't have to. Helen will visit with him."

Ruby pulls her niece up from the chair and leads her out of the kitchen to the back hall with its small bedrooms, just as Joe begins pounding at the door of the small clapboard home.

"I need to see her. Let me just talk to her."

Every day for the past three, Joe has charged up to their little house with the same percussive urgency. *Money like we've never had. Opportunity. Just let me talk to her.*

"Joe, stop it!" Helen hisses through an open crack of the window. "You can't talk to a girl in her state about money, Joe. She needs to get better. She needs quiet."

"Five friggin' minutes is all I need. You have no right to keep me from her!"

There's a tense silence; Helen hopes he has left. But what comes next is a sharp sound. She sits down and watches a split cleave the entrance's dry wood. Suddenly, sunlight spears through wrenched hinges. Her door falls with a clatter, coughing dust onto the kitchen's pretty black-and-white tiles.

That man, she thinks, *has come unhinged himself*. "She's not ready, Joe."

He drops his crowbar, pulls up a chair, cups his sore jaw with his hand, and asks for a beer.

"You're going to have to fix that," Helen says, getting up and reaching into her refrigerator. She slides a bottle across to him and Joe tells her about the lawyer's offer, about all the relief the money will bring, about his desperation as time ticks away.

"You don't think that's a bit off? Selling your kid's right to speak for a wad of cash. Nothing about this situation strikes you as fishy?"

He drains his beer. For a second, Helen doesn't blame him for wanting some relief from trouble, for wanting the pot of gold for his daughter, for wanting a chance to escape.

"Promise me you'll tell Cherisse. I only got so much time." He wipes his mouth on his sleeve, just like his kid, gets up, props the fallen door against the outside wall. "I'll be back tomorrow with some new wood for the frame." Before stepping off the small porch, he turns again to her. "Promise?"

Helen looks at him with a blank face. He's a kind man who married a woman ill-equipped for happiness or motherhood. There is little she can guarantee him. Helen stands, watches through the kitchen window as Joe leaves, then picks out the wasp from between its panes, grabbing it delicately by its leg. She places it on her palm, where it lies on its back, kicking. "I can't decide for you," she says. But she blows ever so gently so it can get back on its feet again.

∽

Las is not sure where he is at first. It is dark. There is pounding. His temples. His foot. The sheets and pillowcases seem fresh, perfumed with fabric softener, still crisp from drying in the sun.

But the air closes in around him, stuffy with the odours of anti-
biotic ointment and perspiration. The throb of his head, the
throb of his foot, the familiar must of his room, the whispering
coolness of the sheets make him want to cry. He feels a flutter
under his palms, a frightened heartbeat that's not his. Crying
would only make the throbbing worse, would make it tighten
around him like a chokehold.

With the big toe of his undamaged foot, he explores the
bandaged surface of the wrecked one. There is little feeling but
he can tell that it is newly misshapen. There is a gap, and the
gap is really an ending. He senses that the swelling has retreated
to just below his knee, where it is hot and tender. He thinks he
should feel sicker, but he doesn't. Nothing can crawl all the way
through to his insides.

But there is something else that keeps him still, that makes
him lie heavy on the bed. The shadow in his room. If he opens
his eyes just a slit he can see it, smell it – faintly soapy, floral, and
electric. His mother.

"Las."

She has seen the small opening of his eyes. That acute
vision so attuned to the smallest movement; even when he was
a little boy, her awareness, her perceptiveness frightened the shit
out of him.

"Las."

He hates that she sounds so harmless, so trustworthy.
Because he wants to believe that it's that simple, giving himself
over to the comfort of her protection.

"Las, we need to talk." Her voice wavers slightly.

He is throbbing and numb, so he makes her into the
mother he dreamed about as a boy, a double agent or the Queen
of Darkness, a bird with a terrible wingspan. He puts her in line
behind the numbness, the pain, the fading sensation of queasi-
ness. She is just another shadow in a room crowded with them.

Ella feels sick. She stands in her son's room watching his prone body, and she sees a damaged work of art, something once beautiful that she had a hand in. *There's just no way,* she thinks. *There's no way this boy did anything wrong.* It's circumstantial. A noose of inferences, weak associations, overactive imaginations. He got a little drunk with Gordo. The girl found her own trouble.

"Las."

Her stomach is hot and acidic. A long shower has left her feeling dehydrated and she just wants to lie down. She wants to lie down beside her beautiful boy and forget what she has heard. Beside his bed, she leans towards him. Her eyes catch a small glint on the carpet.

"Las."

Less than a week has passed since they brought him home from the hospital, Las half awake, his arms slung around their shoulders. Her husband could not look at her; she could not speak to him. They laid their son on his bed. She pulled off his top and shorts and brought in a bowl of warm, soapy water, washed the hospital's chlorhexidine and iodine smells from his face, his limbs, while Mitch watched from the doorway. When she came to the boy's injured foot, she started to cry softly, her tears dropping into the towel she was dabbing on his skin. She leaned and kissed her son's foot at the ankle, above the gauze swaddling. Then Mitch was at her shoulder, yanking. *That's enough! He's not fuckin' Jesus.* But he *was* innocent. He *was* misunderstood.

"Las."

First impressions, the short brunette public relations professional said at a meeting with her and Mitch days earlier. *You have two main issues and we're going to get out in front of both of them right away – one publicly, one privately.* She drew a rough flowchart, ripped it from a clean yellow pad, and handed it to Mitch. *He didn't do it,* Ella interrupted. *Just for the record.* She wanted this woman in her prim summer shift and sling-back pumps to know she'd raised an exemplary young man, a good son. Mitch's eyes blazed. The woman didn't blink.

What can a mother do but attend and hope? She's done more. Too much, perhaps. But a woman such as she loves through action, through movement, through tossed car keys and extra bacon strips and credit cards, reassuring touches, and overindulgence. She doesn't know what it means to withhold, to mete out praise or buy birthday gifts with parsimony. Still, what has her way wrought?

"Las, we need to talk."

There is only silence. *What has he done? Really, what?* asked Mitch. They've stopped and started the conversation so many times under their breath, Mitch talking as if their son's guilt is both assured and inconsequential. *He had a few beers. He and a friend took a girl to a field. A native girl with a reputation bigger than the reserve she lives on. You don't ruin a boy's future over that. You don't ruin ours.*

Ella bends beside the bed, kneads her fingers in the weave of carpet, where an object blinks at her. She pulls out something small and metallic and presses it into her palm. The pinch doesn't register.

∽

Stephanie sprawls on her bed, wide awake, listening to murmurs down the hall. She touches the cheek that met her mother's hand a week earlier. The morning after the slap, she'd gone back and forth to the mirror, waiting for the colour of crushed violets to seep under her skin, hoping for a lifted welt below her eye. But there was nothing, not even a redness that compared to rubbing her cheek hard with a hot washcloth. Her mother had a talent for getting away with bad behaviour.

I see it, baby, Nate said that night. He smiled, traced his fingers under her eye. *How dare she? How dare she touch my beauty's face?* They were naked on the soil between the tobacco stalks. The sand scratched her shoulders, the flesh of her hips. Night dew dripped from the tobacco leaves. Their bodies brushed up against the gummy stalks. Panting, Nate laid his head across her belly. Stephanie stroked his damp, matted hair, his skin the colour of earth against her paleness.

You're glowing again, he whispered in her ear. And she told him. The words crawled out of her like a parasite, something that didn't belong inside her. Gordo in the basement. The scratch on Las's neck. The girl's broken nails. The kerchief and cap. Gordo's custom tires. And the mayor gathering up her confessions like tinsel for a nest, ferrying them away before Stephanie came to her senses. That is why her mother slapped her, she told him. That is all of why.

Nate's skin cooled underneath her touch. His body went still. There was a cricket near her head, bleating like an alarm clock. Then Nate was on his feet, diving through the pockets of his pants, searching for a cigarette, leaving Stephanie's skin damp where his warmth had been. She pulled herself up slowly, found her bra necklacing a tobacco plant, her panties underneath. He smoked and stared towards the blockade, then into the sky. And sometimes he pulled his hands to his head, as if he could keep it from breaking apart by squeezing and squeezing.

You should have told me sooner. Fuck, you should have told me.

She started to cry, and her tears bewildered her. Why had she told him at all? *It's not proof. It's just suspicion and a few little details,* she said.

It's worse than that, Stephanie, and you know it.

He fell to the ground in a sprawl, then pulled up into a squat with his face right by her knees. Like a wrestler. She moved away from him.

It's okay, he said. *I'm pissed, baby. Oh, I'm pissed. And I'm not going to lie – I want to kill those boys. I could fuckin' run over there right now and strangle that bleached blond varsity champ asshole brother of yours. And enjoy watching him go blue.*

She crawled farther from him, still crying, and grabbed her T-shirt, her leggings, and yanked them on, the fabric dragging sand against the flesh of her underarms, her thighs. She got up.

Steph, Steph, Nate said. He had his arms around her, tightening. *Don't go. Please don't.*

The embrace loosened. He stepped away to finish his cigarette. Then he laughed. His head fell to his knees and he laughed. The tobacco leaves shook in the breeze with him, his mirth falling on them like hailstones. *What are you doing?* she said.

He straightened again and she could see that he too was crying, or sweating, something shining his face like vegetable oil. *It's awful, but it's better. You gotta see that. It is so much better. For my people. For the reclamation. For everything. It's so much better that a white guy did this.* His arms widened. He gestured her to come to them, to be enclosed, but Stephanie was frozen. He dropped his cigarette in the sand. *It's not better,* Stephanie said.

Now her hand is on the once-slapped cheek, kneading the skin for something lost. Her stomach fills with a clawing hunger. She's been eating like an opossum, at night, whenever the chance to forage announces itself. Stephanie stands up, pulls at the waist of her pyjama bottoms, shakes them out, feels for extra roominess. There is that swoon again, that slightly blurry feeling that makes her lean on her desk for balance. She can't think straight.

Heading towards the stairway that leads to the kitchen, she hears a voice, small and plaintive, coming from her brother's room.

"Las."

Stephanie stops. The door is ajar. In the darkness, her brother's misshapen foot dangles off the end of his bed. She sees the silhouette of her mother: her bent elbow, a hip jutting into the shadows.

"Las."

Her mother's voice sounds wobbly. Stephanie feels a pang of pity. That boy is breaking the poor woman's heart. It makes her mad. It makes her spitting mad at all of them.

"Las."

He is sleeping, or pretending to. In the house of the emotionally undead, her brother is the oblivious lamb. What a fucker. What a complete ass.

"Las, we need to talk."

She hates the beaten sound of her mother's voice. *Don't*, she wants to counsel her. *Don't always prostrate before him.* She opens the door farther just as her mother launches at her brother's prone body. It is so demented that Stephanie freezes.

"Talk to me! Did you do it? Did you do it? You owe me an answer!" Her mother is astride Las, shrieking and yanking his head by his hair, up and down. He moans but doesn't fight back. She starts to slap his face. She starts to bawl. "You'll wreck everything. Answer me! Did you do it?" His protests are indecipherable, gargled. Her mother pummels his chest with her fists.

I should do something, Stephanie thinks. Her palms sweat. Her lips tremble. *Where the fuck is Dad?* She considers running to the stairs.

Her mother jumps off the bed, but she is still a fury of movement, using her heel to thump Las's side. "Tell me you didn't do it. Tell me! Tell me, you coward! You self-sabotaging prick!"

Then it happens. Her mother gives a hard, swift kick to Las's injured foot where it hangs over the edge of the bed. His scream is high and girlish.

Stephanie launches into the room, grabs for the waistline of her mother's pants, and pulls. All those years of running have made the woman's body lean and wired for fury. Her mother swings around, shadowboxing, one fist unfurling into slaps. Stephanie ducks, wraps her arms around her mother's small hips, and pulls her into the hallway by falling backwards. Her mother's other clenched fist opens and releases something, a metallic twinkle. It bounces off Stephanie's cheek.

They both sit there saying nothing, inhaling shakily. Las's moans go quiet. Stephanie can see dust in the shaft of light the bathroom sends into the hallway. It moves upwards, defying gravity. She stares at it, trying to understand. There's a suck of air, the sound of a door opening on the main floor. The dust races towards it.

"Ella, where are you?" Her father, moving quickly up the stairs to them. The sound of his winded breathing gets louder. Her mother drops her hands, slouches. They both stare at the object on the carpet beside Stephanie's hip. It is an earring, sterling and delicate. A dream catcher with dangling silver feathers, belonging to neither of them.

"Ella, there you are. Didn't you hear me? We got it, baby. We got it!"

Her mother is slumped on the floor of the hallway, curling away from the light. Her father grabs Ella's shoulders, pulls her to standing, looks into her eyes. His face is waxy with mania and he's panting.

"Ella, the government is making an offer. A big one – all of our money back. Enough to pay off the debts, plus our expected return. And more. Are you listening?"

He pulls her into an embrace. She does not lift her arms. Her father is oblivious. He speaks into his wife's coppery hair, kisses it wildly, whole mouthfuls of it sticking to his lips, and fails to register the woman's inertness.

"It's over, baby," he says. His voice cracks. "This nightmare is over. There is some justice in this fucked-up place after all."

The movement was like a flutter of wings, too fast to say for sure what it was – bat or bird, startled into flight. It was a happy surprise to be grabbed, to feel his hair pulling from the roots, the sharp anguish of his scalp, the uncomfortable crack in his neck as she pulled his head. The sheer physical strength of his mother has always been a wonder to him. Her slaps cut hard across his face; she had an athlete's instinct for the physics of it, the tight weave of her fingers, the torque of her hips and shoulders, the way her hand connected with his flesh where she could deliver the greatest force. It would have been a relief if she'd just killed him. What a ride that would be – his mom beating him to death!

Las had heard his mother cry out, but he turned off her words. He was glad she was pissed off, that she'd finally seen through him. He was glad there was no going back. Where could they go, now that she'd pummelled him hard, now that he'd felt her sharp knuckles break skin under his clavicle?

It took him a half-second to realize that her weight was gone from his middle and the thumps along his side were from her foot. A thrill shot up to his throat – she really wanted to hurt him. She was going for it, that crazy bitch. When her foot connected with his injured one, he ceased to exist but for the pain. It broke him up. It shredded him. He deserved it, that much was true. He deserved every bit of it.

Then *splash*, he was back in the pool. There was the cool, enveloping embrace of water. His arms in front, opening, pulling him through. His feet like motor blades, scything, scything. How whole he was there, all power and beauty. And the silence. The way the silence relieved him of being anything other than movement.

CHAPTER 24

Cherisse walks to the banks of the Smoke in a thin cotton nightie, the atomizer cool against her palms. Her feet are bare, and the soil, swollen with rain, squishes up between her toes, stains the edges of her soles. She hears murmurs all the time now. Now that Shayna comes to the house, the low throb of talking crowds out the sounds of midnight and late afternoon's drowsy heat. It's a small house. Discontent makes its thin walls hum. She hears words, fearful words, the held breath of Ruby's sobs, the plosives of Shayna's frustration, Helen's quiet protest. Their murmurs fill her ears and she can't shake them out. Money or justice. Money or justice. She won't face the choice they would have her face, the one they can't agree on themselves.

The way you float, her mother said, *you lie on your back, spread yourself wide, and you trust. Let the river do the work.* The August she turned six, the last they spent together, her mother told her the story of a beautiful Mohawk princess captured by an enemy and held in their camp. In her captivity, the girl collected glass and shells to bead an intricate belt.

Cherisse unties a headscarf from her wrist and lays it across a flat-faced boulder, places her atomizer on top, and searches the shore until her hands finds a rock with a beakish angle. Both her hands bring the rock smashing against the atomizer, again and again until the glass falls away from the gold-plated neck and puffer in small, ragged jewels with a fine, shiny dust underneath.

In the story, the best of the enemy's warriors were about to portage across the river to ambush her people's encampment, when the princess slipped into the great river, wearing her belt, and floated on her back. The sun reflected from the beads. Their dance of colour and blinding rays bewitched the warriors. Instead of crossing the river, they put their canoes in the water and followed the beautiful lights, the witching lights. The princess understood the river's tempers, but the enemies of her people did not. She floated into faster-moving water, her belt glinting, and the canoes followed. The current pulled her to the edge of a waterfall and carried her over. Branches tore her belt and scattered the beads, while her body fell to the rocks. It was too late for the warriors to change course. They too were dragged over the waterfall. Her people were saved.

See the glint in the water, the way the sun makes diamonds in the river that are too bright for the eyes? her mother said. *That is where the princess went to live; that is the princess's unravelled belt.* Her mother would reach a hand into the river and sprinkle water over Cherisse's neck as she floated. *Look at your pretty beads,* she'd say. *My princess.*

She pulls out the atomizer's metal bits and tosses them into the forest, then wraps the broken glass in the headscarf, balls it in her hand, and wades into the water. The river in August is a warm brownish slumber that barely moves at the edges, so Cherisse sidestrokes out to the middle depths, where there's a weak current.

Did she have to die? Cherisse asked her mother. *Couldn't she have grabbed a tree branch hanging over the river just before the drop-off?* Her mother thought about it, but then she shook her head. *In order to become the diamonds in the water, to be part of the river forever, she had to do something pretty special, to give something up, don't you think?*

The cotton of her nightie sags and billows in the water, clings to her limbs. She stretches back her head, kicks up her feet, pulls her trunk straight. And before she spreads out her arms like wings, she empties the kerchief of glass across her neck and chest. She is floating. For a moment she reflects light. She is extraordinary.

⁓

For Elijah it's a good day to be out in the sun and on the river, to be swinging around his rod like a sonofabitch whose lotto numbers have come in. He is feeling fine. It's not every man who gets to be the hero of his own life, and it's certainly not Mitch Bain. *Got his balls in a vise,* Elijah thinks. *He will get his money back, but not his pride, not his name, not a chance to start over in this town. And he'll have to turn around and hand most of that money to Joe Montagne.* The cigar hanging from his mouth wags with his laughter. *Better, I saved that girl from the evils of the white man's justice. I saved her, Rita!* He raises his arm in an arcing salute to a beautiful woman he's never outgrown. *I saved her. I own him. And that surfer-boy shit of a kid of his . . . well, there are other kinds of justice.*

He is certain that today is the day he'll get that bastard largemouth. It's not even seven a.m. and he's sipping a coffee and staring at the still kettle of water by the McKelvey Street bridge where he stalked the fish in June. The town is quiet. Another man might feel urgency, figuring the fish is more likely to feed before the sun chokes oxygen from the water's surface.

But Elijah knows that the obvious is not always the most strategic, or the most fishlike. And it's thinking like his enemies, sinking into their own murky depths, that makes him the man he is today. Everyone takes the bait – if it's the right kind, arriving at just the right moment. Elijah smiles.

He starts to pay attention. There is a dusting of pollen on the river, a chartreuse dandruff over dark, sluggish water. A black-winged damselfly darns itself among tall plants at the water's edge. Elijah watches the jewelweed's orange blossoms tremble and lean; it tells him that cooler air is slipping by him unnoticed, because it's lower than the banks. He begins to see thin streams eddying around the feeding spot, his clue that a soft current is mixing it up below, just enough to piss off a cranky, small-brained fish that likes its water unmoving, warm, nearly stagnant. The early morning sun is already making him sticky, and in two hours it will be stinking hot. Even such an animal with its uncomplicated circuitry would have figured as much and retreated upstream before light broke. A half-mile west along the river, three old willows hang over the riverbanks, cooling and slowing the edge water so the mayflies cling to their drooping branches and the frogs come into their shade, panting on the warm, wet earth beneath them. Elijah doesn't imagine it; he *sees* the hungry largemouth there, its blunt olive snout obscured in the murk below the willows, its movements practised and imperceptible. Except to him.

Five minutes later his truck is parked at the new spot, on the outer edge of the reserve. He puts on his waders and ploughs into the middle of the river and its stronger current, so he is almost hip-deep before he turns towards the willows; there is a peephole there between the branches, which requires a deft cast. A small tremor of nausea shudders his body. He has forgotten his breakfast, and now the coffee has his heart pumping too fast. Elijah closes his eyes. He listens to the current and tries to match his breathing to its lapping intervals. After a few minutes it seems to work; his hands feel steady again.

When he opens his eyes, a bright flash from the periphery makes them smart. About twenty metres downriver, a strange flotilla is riding the current away from him. He wonders if he's hallucinating. Something – a branch? an arm? – reaches up, and light jumps from it like salt crystals on hot oil. Were it not for the fish, Elijah would investigate. And now that it's farther away from him, he no longer sees anything extending skyward. All the things it could be: a log entwined with discarded drapery, some tinfoil or plastic cradled within, a pyre of misfit refuse. He hates how the townsfolk mistreat the river.

He turns back to the fish he cannot see but knows is there. The nine-foot rod bows over the river, and for a moment he thinks how precarious it all is, using such tools of finesse and deception when a short, harsh blow to the fish's skull would be more direct and honest. His bait is an ugly deer-hair popper, a newly sharp hook extending from it. He's added a halo of wire to guard it from weeds. The plunge pool under the willow stirs with a quick movement. Elijah casts too far under the willows on purpose, then pulls at the slack line so the fly bounces back towards him, breaking the surface with satisfying burps before sitting low in the water. As he expected, there's minimal drift. He flicks the line subtly so there's the slightest mend in his cast that will allow the popper and fly to meander longer, look natural.

The first tug he feels is half-hearted, and for an instant he's worried that the hook has snagged some weeds or a ragged filament of willow. But then there's a pulse of tension, and another. It's all surprisingly lethargic and sloppy for such an athletic creature. Elijah dips the rod's tip into the water to smarten up the fish, show him he's serious. The next pull is so sharp the line nearly snaps. The largemouth's tactics are guerrilla-like, a bit dirty. Still, it's the fight Elijah's been waiting for. On a hunch, he takes three large steps into the river, pulling up his rod so it arches like a Gothic window, freighted by the fish's determination at the other end. Then he gives a final tug, and the large-mouth comes flying out of the water. Smaller and more darkly pigmented than Elijah expected, it falls into the rocky shallows.

When he finds it, the fish barely beats its tail against the rocks. Disappointment sours Elijah's belly. The largemouth's protruding lower lip is slicked with blood. The deer-hair popper and hook have been swallowed. He picks it up – it feels slimy and underweight – and flips the fish over. Elijah lets his rod drop into the water. An oval of ulcerated flesh, grey and putrescent, radiates from the fish's upper lip towards its mid-body on the underside. Elijah palpates the rotting flesh, and his fingertip hits the barbed ridge of a hook. *Shit!* He pulls it away, and his skin blisters with a single drop of blood. Embedded and rusting inside the largemouth's necrotic cheek are the hook and fly from their encounter several weeks earlier.

Elijah studies his finger and worries about what will fester there later. He has an urge to toss the fish. He won't eat such a creature, so much of its flesh already spoiled. He can't mount it as a trophy – there's no titanic struggle between him and the fish to retell. If he abandons it, within an hour it will lie dead and bloated on the river's surface, the sun raising a stink from its flesh. Elijah looks around. There is no one here to witness what he does. He wishes he could see the strange floating lights again. Were they a sign he misunderstood? Then, with his shoulders slumping, he carries the fish – the prize he no longer wants – up the banks of the Smoke to his truck.

∽

The river's rhythmic nudge forward, the water's upward lift relax Cherisse. Slowly the murmurs trapped in her head free themselves to become something beautiful: a humming river-song. The sun paints her cheeks, her torso, her necklace of glass with heat. The water cools what's underneath. Finally there is nothing but comfort and the gentle, sure pull of the current. Perhaps the rest of it will also wriggle free: the weight of her heart, her history. She's exhausted from carrying it. A dragonfly hovers by her face. The river smells sweet and rich as maple creams. Somewhere in the distance a dog barks, insistent, playful yaps. She thinks she might be happy. If she floats and floats and never stops, she can relieve her pain and, in doing so, relieve others of the trouble she has caused.

When the current quickens and the river slopes, Cherisse wills her eyes shut and ovals her mouth as if she has only a hollow reed to breathe through. She is ready. The glass jiggles on her skin, and some pieces slide into the water. She feels the first nettles of discomfort in the tensing of her jaw, the soreness of her hip when it grazes a rock. But if she slides off the edge of the world, the sensations will end. So it must be a trickster's arm, the tree branch that, half submerged, reaches out from the shore and snags the floating hem of her nightie. Cherisse pivots in the water, one foot brushing the fulcrum of wet branch. Suddenly she's head first, suspended in a part of the river that spills and tumbles over a sloped outcropping of oiled rocks. With her neck yanked back by the current, water lapping into her nostrils, Cherisse sucks in a breath, holds it, and pulls her head underwater. She thinks she might die, will die, can die. She imagines being pinned beneath a piece of moving ice, a small animal for whom submission feels better than struggle. She'd expect her mother to come to her in such a moment: the gingery smell, the way her whispers fizzed against Cherisse's neck, the indulgence of her smile. Or the white dog with its giving heat, the wonder of its dark eyes and pink tongue.

But it's Shayna's face, twisting around a mouthful of disappointment, that parts her memory. Shayna, leaning into the bedroom door when Cherisse was twelve and both of them knew it wouldn't be long before she ran away again. Swaddled in the Little Mermaid sheets Shayna had bought her with some misgivings, she'd pulled herself up on her haunches, the bright sheets flowing like raiment from her shoulders, and with great flourishes she retold the legend of the princess, the beaded belt, and the beautiful death on the river.

Her auntie stayed silent in the doorway. *That's not a Mohawk story*, Shayna said finally. Cherisse was stung. *Sure it is. My mom said so. It's famous.*

Shayna shook her head. *I don't know where your mom got that story. She took it from somewhere else, or made it up. It's not a Mohawk story.* She spoke coldly, plainly, like a school principal or someone on the news.

Cherisse used her auntie's words to build a terrible kind of smoke inside her, the burning kind. *Shut up! I hate you!* she screamed. She flung off the sheets, jumped from the bed, and slammed the door on Shayna, pushing her out of the way, out of her life. All the while, her auntie's voice came from behind the barrier, a steady intonation: *It's not one of our stories. It's not your story.*

Every part of her is in pain now. The current drums the back of her neck against a flat river rock; her heart's a panicked animal in her chest. It occurs to Cherisse that death hurts as much as life. She grabs hold of the rocks with her hands, levers her torso up against the slope and the current, coughs and sputters the water out of her nostrils, out of her lungs. The nightie's cotton tears like used tissue and the branch lets her go. She tumbles backwards down the little slope of rocks, into quieter, pooling water below. And for a second she is floating again, a little stunned. The water smells fetid here. She sweeps fingers across her neck, where the glass was lying and now is gone. An embroidery of scratches tickle her fingertips.

There's nothing left to do. She stands up. There's pressure above her eye, hot needles of sting. Cherisse touches her forehead; it comes away covered in blood that is brighter, redder than the berries of summer, redder than petals or lipstick. She's never liked red much. But this is a pretty colour. She sucks at her fingertips. It's a sharp taste, neither sweet nor entirely unpleasant. She imagines that truth tastes much the same, and it surprises her to realize that she has an appetite for it.

CHAPTER 25

Stephanie lets the front door thud behind her. Now that she's leaving the house forever, she notices what an overbearing *clunk* their front door makes. Seventeen, she tells herself, is not so young. In an earlier century she'd be married, popping out the babies, tilling the fields. There must be nations of adolescents out there right now, making do on their own in places where parents don't ferry their children everywhere in cars or text them to ask what they'd like for dinner.

She'll find a job, take her senior year at one of the city high schools, put her first and last month's rent down on a little apartment, using the savings she'd earmarked for a more powerful computer. Maybe get a cat – she'll need a cat. And a tattoo, finally.

An hour earlier, while packing up her bedroom, she pulled out the USB stick with the photos of the girl, the cap and kerchief, and the earring that fell out of her mother's hand when she'd pulled her away from Las. She will not carry them into her new beginning, so there's the matter of who to leave them with – the police, Nate, the mayor? She rummaged and all she could find was a small gift bag, printed with balloons and candles, and a piece of plain tissue, with which she wrapped the cap and kerchief. The earring and USB went into a fresh envelope that she sealed. Stephanie thought about the evidence, how it was like words that couldn't be taken back, and how unfair it was to be left with responsibility for it. After a few minutes she checked the time and scrawled *Make yourself whole* on the envelope, slipped it into the bag, and wandered downstairs, hesitating at the door of her father's office. She re-climbed the steps to stand by her parents' shut bedroom door. The door to Las's bedroom was partly open, but inside it was dark. She took this as a sign, walked the length of the upstairs hall, and snaked her hand around and hooked the bag on the inside doorknob, where it couldn't be missed.

Out on the street, she struggles with the weight of her knapsack, the camera bag around her neck, a purse over one shoulder that bumps against her arm, and the duffle bag that is pulling her other shoulder from its socket. There is a lot of Doreville sidewalk between her and the bus station. She feels a small wave of panic. It's a current she must swim against, that and the heartbreak of items left behind – a favourite red wool scarf; the photography manual her father slipped under her door when she was only twelve, because he knew she was different; the vintage dress she wore to prom, the one her mom conceded was "pretty glamorous."

The street curves. Stephanie stops to readjust her load. She hears the *ding* of her cellphone and pulls it out of her pocket to find a text from Nate. WHERE ARE YOU? I LOVE YOU. I'M SORRY, it reads. Her heart lifts momentarily. She starts to thumb in a response but reconsiders. *Later,* she thinks. On the bus she'll be less at risk of running backwards or standing still. She puts her phone away and turns one last time to look at her house, to see if her parents are on the front stoop. They're not. "I'm sorry," she whispers, and she repeats it over and over, matching it to the rhythm of her steps, as if it were a Sufi chant, a prayer of expiation.

⁂

Ella stays in her bedroom, where it's dark and she can think. Her hands fold over her belly and she locates for a fleeting moment the things that have gone missing, the happiest times of her life. She remembers Las when he was unnamed, just a bubble in her tummy and yet already special in ways nothing else has come close to. Pregnancy hung on her lithe frame like a pretty frock. It made her so stupendously confident, as if walking around with this child inside her was an athletic achievement, a personal best, a win switch she'd finally located. She and Mitch had moved into this four-bedroom house with the automatic garage doors, the largest in the new subdivision and perched imperiously at the end of a cul-de-sac, its steep front lawn dotted with mature butternuts. She'd wake up at night in a sweat of self-satisfaction – arranging the living room furniture in her head, painting the nursery in a comely, fashionable shade. And all the time her hand would circle over her belly, left to right, right to left, a carousel of contentment.

Her mother was admitted to hospital with congestive heart failure just as Ella began her second trimester. With the right clothes, the slight swelling was easily hidden. She held her mother's papery hand and wiped her resinous brow. She didn't tell her about the pregnancy lest this new joy tax the woman's faintly pulsing heart, the slowly flooding lungs, embitter her last days with regret. Ella denied the thrum in the recesses of her conscience: a growing impatience for her mother's death as a week stretched into four and she had to wear dresses with looser waists and dirndl skirts to hide a more perceptible belly.

One day she heard loud cackles come from her mother's room as she alighted from the elevator. From the doorway she could see three women sitting on chairs around her mother's bed. They'd cranked it so her mother was sitting up, tubes coming out of her like some strange sea creature. It shocked Ella to see her mom's eyes rheumy with laughter. The women around her – one on each side clutching her mom's swollen, needle-punctured wrists – had opened little buckets of food on the bed, tucked them into the folds of the bedsheets, turned the Javex-scented room into a picnic party. She would have stepped forward, protested, but a flash of recognition stopped her. She knew these women – Angel, Linda, Delisle. All were Mohawk. All had worked the tying line with her mother for twenty tobacco-picking seasons, and then sorting and grading in drafty barns during the fall and winter. They were her mother's friends. It was something the teenaged Ella, bursting through the front door after a day of school to find them draining cups of tea at her parents' kitchen table, had never accepted. There was enough social stigma in how her parents earned their living, their thick accents, the tilting verandah. She'd brush past these women on the way to her bedroom as if she could not see them, or how her rudeness was reflected in her mother's hurt expression. They remained invisible to her even after her father died and they filled the refrigerator with venison stew and dumplings, Mason jars of strawberry lemonade and corn chowder, food that sustained Ella when her mother did not rise from the shrouded bedroom for weeks.

Now Ella is the one who lies in a darkened bedroom, conjuring the faces of the women who brightened her mother's smile for the last time before she suffocated from her own lung fluids a few days later. She hadn't wanted to notice them, hadn't acknowledged them, had rarely even thought of them until now. And it occurs to Ella that what you choose to notice, and what you don't, shapes your understanding, and so your life. She turns her face into the pillow, closes her eyes.

∽

Las is sitting on the front step. He is sitting on the step and looking at things as if for the first time, as if he hasn't lived on this property for his whole life.

For instance, on the step a planter spills with mutinous growth. Las hears his mother reciting her springtime mantra – *thrills, fills, and spills!* – and telling him, as if he cared, that she's planted canna, petunias, and sweet potato vine for their blend of colours. *It is too much*, he thinks, *too much of everything*.

He stares down at his feet, a flip-flop on one and on the other a bulk of bandages, covered with a sock. And he thinks, *Holy shit, I love flip flops*. They've been a constant, a comfort, for most of his life. At age six his toes and arches were already strengthening around the flip-flop gait. There must be dozens of them he's outgrown or broken, still degrading in the municipal dump. When the thong ripped clean out of the cheap foam Spider Man flip-flops he had at age ten, he burst into sobs in the hallway of his elementary school and had to be taken home. It's a story his father still brings up during family dinners.

He shudders. He is never going to wear a pair of flip-flops again. Ever. He wonders why it has taken him until now to realize this. A toe beside the big one is absolutely necessary, and he's missing all three in the middle of his foot. He'd trade both his baby toes for any one of them, but he can't. And it's hard to believe, hard to accept, because there isn't much else left to look forward to. His throat gets tight and tears stream down his face, and of course the police car pulls into his driveway now – *Oh Jesus, there are two of them* – and this is not how he imagined it going when he called, insisting they come and get him, not how he wants to be taken in, crying, holding a girly gift bag, and with a whole life before him where not just the obvious things will change, but the things he has always counted on – such as wearing flip-flops – will be gone forever too.

∽

Ella hears the departing cars but she doesn't run to the window. She walks to the basement, silently passes her husband asleep on the couch, finds a stack of empty cardboard boxes, and carries them up to Mitch's office. She starts in the east corner, the one farthest from the windows, and begins to pack away his things. She feels differently about the room right away. She wonders if it's too bold to call out to Stephanie, ask her to brew up a fresh pot of coffee, come and help. *Not yet*, she tells herself. First she'll make such a change here that there'll be no turning back.

CHAPTER 26

'd like a pie, Ruby. Can you make me a peach pie? Cherisse asked, standing in the hole of the kitchen doorway, soaking wet in a ripped nightie, blood streaming from her forehead. Ruby wrapped her in blankets, dressed the wound, put her to bed. And now Helen is picking peaches, the memory of her grandniece's face making a lump in her throat. Enough peaches for Cherisse's pie and dessert for Coulson's primers, and enough to can or freeze so the taste of summer can soften a mean January night.

She stands under a tree, cups a hanging fruit, tests it for the slightest give in its skin, then twists it from its stem, places it in the basket. Ruby says she has the touch for picking. A peach can disappoint if it is taken too early or if it has ripened too quickly. And Helen loves the feel and smell of peach trees, the vulnerability of young fruit, the heft of a full basket as she places it on the earth, the hopeful weightlessness of the empty basket she carries up the stepladder. She tires more easily, aches sooner than a few years earlier, but still the repetition, the stretch of her limbs, and the fragrance under a tree's canopy allow reverie to creep in.

There's a snapping turtle that lives in the reedy pond behind the snack shack. Every spring that turtle moves up into the sandy drive to lay her eggs. Helen protects the nest from cars and people with chicken wire and scrap dowel rods. But every year, in the jet of spring nights, a mother raccoon plunders the turtle's nest to feed her own young. The turtle keeps trying again, spring after spring, waiting for the universe to make amends. Helen prays for a goshawk or a coyote to deliver the justice – take to the air or the woods with the soft neck of a raccoon pup snapped in its jaw. She has to believe the universe is so ordered. Even if she waits another season for justice.

Shayna called, Ruby said this morning. *Can you fetch her after you're done picking? She wants to make a run to the grocery store.* It wasn't even six a.m. Ruby lowered her voice. *She was up all night, finalizing an agreement to dismantle the blockade. I guess she needs to feed them, make a party of it.*

They were quiet. *I wasn't there,* thought Helen. *She did this without me.*

You're staring into space again, Ruby said. *You need to get out of here.* She handed Helen a list.

After three hours of picking, Helen stops at the blockade with ten six-quart baskets in the truck bed. She's overheated, her skin tacky with fuzz and punctured fruit. Shayna piles into the front seat.

"I had to do it," she says immediately, as if Helen's silence is judgment. "Otherwise they wouldn't negotiate. Today's the deadline."

Biting her lip, Helen looks in her rear-view mirror, sees the peaches lined up in the back of the truck. Every struggle for justice has its compromises. That is why she has been left out.

One of the Warriors, a large man with an open face, is ambling towards the truck.

"He argued with me last night. Kept at me for hours – didn't want the blockade to come down," Shayna says, watching him. "Now he insists on helping pay for the food."

Louis Greene opens the back door, folds his big body into the small seat, and nods to Helen, who starts the truck. Shayna says nothing to him, just slumps against the passenger-side door. The route to the grocery store takes them back through the reserve to its far western boundary, where a new bridge spans the Smoke and connects the reserve to Doreville's outskirts and a gleaming big-box store anchoring a massive parking lot. To relieve her own unease, Helen turns on the radio and hums along to the local station's tinny pop music.

A few blocks from the grocery store, the music stops for an hourly news report. Suddenly Shayna's fingers wheel frantically across the dials and she loses the station. The truck hiccups. "What? What the fuck? Turn it up!"

Helen slows the truck, slaps Shayna's hands away from the radio, adjusts the tuning dial and volume.

"A spokesman for the minister responsible could not be reached, but developer Mitch Bain confirmed by phone that he's accepted an offer from the federal government for his land. Asked if this means the development is cancelled, Mr. Bain said, 'Yes, until the government sells the land, nobody can develop it.' Anyone who bought a lot in the development will be fully compensated, he said. Meanwhile, federal negotiator Antonia Taylor has issued a statement saying the blockade will come down today."

"My job is done here," a chipper-sounding Antonia tells the radio reporter. "Now that the blockade is coming down and development of the land is a non-issue, the need for formal negotiations, their urgency, is moot. The protestors can deal exclusively with government lawyers and the whole process will move to the courts."

"Stop the truck! Stop it!" Shayna shouts. She jumps out and bends her small body over the gravel shoulder. Helen watches the shuddering figure. Among the women of her family, morning sickness was rare; Bertie shone like a polished apple when carrying her two daughters. Helen hears sobs. She opens the truck's glove compartment, searches for a tissue, and turns to Louis, who looks uncomfortable and sweaty compressed in the back seat. The expression on his face tells her she has missed something. "What's going on?" she says.

He looks at her as if she, of all people, should know. "They did an end-run on us."

Shayna gets back into the truck, slams the door. Her face is ashen, grimy with tears. Helen reaches with a tissue, but Shayna swats her hand away. "Food. We still need food," she says. Her voice is a croak.

Helen puts the truck in gear. She turns towards the bridge that leads to the grocery store entrance and comes to a full stop. Other cars have stopped and pulled off to the side of the road. A small, wiry man stands in front of about twenty townspeople who have lined up lawn chairs to block the bridge. A straggle of bystanders and gawkers gathers behind. Helen recognizes the pub owner, Will, in a lawn chair sandwiched next to the nervous woman who runs the junk shop. It's such a perfect August day. Why aren't they on their back decks or walking by the river?

The activist is yelling orders through his bullhorn, his face a rictus of outrage. "Turn your cars around and go home. This is a blockade, folks. Natives keep us off the highway, so we are keeping you out of our grocery store."

There is a cheer from the assembled group that sounds tentative. With a show of effort, the townspeople hoist their signs and begin to circle their lawn chairs, chanting their slogan: "Rule of law is the rule for all." Cars with non-native drivers approach the bridge from beyond the reserve's western edge and are waved through with high fives and applause. A van – Helen catches Bobby Horse's unmistakable profile behind the wheel – tries to barrel through, but the crowd cinches up, beats it back with their signs and sticks. This energizes them and they chant louder. Helen notices a dozen shaved heads bobbing like peeled potatoes among the townspeople, their pale arms raised. She gets out of the truck. Shayna and Louis follow.

Others who've come from the reserve empty out from their vehicles and stand watching. A few men, some teenagers. All clutching handwritten lists, eager for items they've been doing without: light bulbs and plastic wrap, a can of coffee, bacon and hot dog buns. And for Helen, sugar, pastry flour, freezer bags. The grocery store has been their Switzerland, a place the politics of the blockade couldn't spoil. Everyone understands the need to feed a family, especially the big-box store's managers, who rely on the reserve for business.

Two cyclists arrive in front of the bridge. Helen recognizes Coulson's primers, James and Diego. There is some conversation she cannot hear.

"Natives on bikes are still natives!" a young man from the bridge yells at them. There's a cheer from the crowd. James and Diego look confused. They remain standing before the chain of townsfolk blocking their way until somebody yells, "Go back to where you came from! You're not getting through." James shrugs his shoulders and whispers into Diego's ear; then they both walk their bikes towards the others who have been kept from entering.

Louis Greene marches up to the activist, so they are face to chest. A truck screeches in behind the scene and a TV cameraman jumps out. *Not again*, thinks Helen.

"It's over. Don't you listen to the news?" Louis tells them. "You should let people through. Children going hungry doesn't dignify this protest."

The activist, his face flushed carmine, pulls up his bullhorn, turns to the crowd, and addresses them. "It's not over," he screams. "They take land that isn't theirs. Block roads that aren't theirs. Terrorize our neighbourhoods. Then they saunter in for bread and cheese as if we're on the same team." His righteousness sprays out of the bullhorn, casts a driftnet of spit over the crowd. There is a chorus of hurrahs in response.

Louis says nothing. He doesn't move. The bullhorn swings around, and now the activist is yelling directly into Louis's unflinching face. "Police won't enforce all the laws you break. So I'm making one, buddy. You don't get to come here anymore. Got it?"

His words hang in the air for half a minute. The cameraman moves in closer. There's a twitch in Louis's jaw. He simply takes a step forward, a big man using up all the activist's space, forcing him to stumble backwards with a yelp. Louis stretches his legs wide, folds his bare, tattooed arms so that their muscles clench. The crowd goes quiet.

And then a rock comes sailing out from behind the townspeople on the bridge. Helen lifts her eyes to see the shadowy path, curved as a swift's flight. All the attention is on the two men facing off in front of them. And that is where the rock strikes, missing its intended target, hitting another.

Helen thinks how summer squash cracks under a sharp knife. The thin man's head splits open at the top. His blood is thin and fast, and red drips from his chin like berry juice. He drops to his knees and Louis bends to help him, but the cameraman is there, moving in. He has stumbled onto great footage. Helen sees how awful it will look, how the picture will tell the wrong story.

Louis grabs the camera and levers it with his weight. The expensive piece of equipment falls to the ground, the cameraman stumbles after it, and then the Warrior has his foot on the cameraman's back. He stomps.

"No! No!" Helen shouts.

A group of young men rush forward from the bridge and pile on Louis as if it's a down in a football game. And Helen, who is tired of injustices, of waiting for the truth to alight from the sky like a bird with sharp talons, surprises herself by plucking a peach from one of the baskets in the back of her truck. She throws it. A soft orb of fruit, the colour of an Interlake sunset, hits one of the young men square on his shaven head. Orange-yellow viscera stream down his face and stick to his T-shirt collar. Helen rolls up her sleeve, picks up another. Shayna joins her. The families behind her are clapping and whistling now, and then James and Diego are at the back of her truck, and she nods her head in permission. The morning sky fills with rosy trajectories. The peaches fall and split against the townspeople's signs, slime their faces in a baptismal of flung fruit. A few land in the river. The sirens get louder.

By the time the police cars arrive at both ends of the bridge, the peaches have been answered with rocks and eggs, pop bottles, a Thermos, dismembered lawn chairs. Two lines of officers form quickly. One pushes the townspeople off the bridge, the other compresses them in one quadrant of the parking lot. The air grows tight with angry jeers. Louis and the activist are handcuffed, taken away in separate squad cars.

When it's over and the crowd begins to fall away, they remain sitting in the front seat of Helen's truck, Shayna's head hanging. Helen surveys the peach-dotted pavement and remembers her mother's hair curling in the steam of jam-making. In the back of her truck, one basket of fruit remains, every one of its peaches singularly perfect and untouched amid the waste.

The way is clear to enter the grocery store, but neither woman has the heart. There are enough peaches to make a pie, perhaps two. She'll borrow the rest of the ingredients and pay back her benefactors with a tithe of sweet pastry.

∽

News of the government's purchase of the *o'tá:ra* spreads around the blockade like rumours of an audacious theft, the dignity of disassembling it voluntarily, being the ones to announce it, stolen from them. Food tables are cleaned; plates, cups, utensils are thrown into plastic hampers. Some of the protestors drift off, and the remaining Warriors roll their sleeping bags and tie them, toss their tents and duffle bags into the backs of vans. They are gone within an hour, the white vehicles like sun flares on the asphalt horizon.

By late afternoon the police cars arrive. The officers are friendly but firm. It is time for the blockade to come down. "It's your land now," they're told.

They all know that's neither true nor untrue – impossible to decipher which.

"Give us a few hours," Shayna tells the police. "It will be down before dark."

The elders confer and organize a thanksgiving ceremony for those who have stayed, a sacred address normally used as an opening ritual. "There's a beginning here too," Linda Goodleaf says to Shayna.

Al Miller makes the address in the old language. Shayna has a stitch in her side that clangs with pain, but she holds herself still. *"Etho niyohtonhak ne onkwa'nikonra* – so now let our minds be as one on this matter," the old man intones.

When it is finished, she slips away across the street to

Coulson's fields. The day hangs with heat, the air as heavy-sweet as newly picked mint. A deerfly bobs around her head, and Shayna waves her hand, ducks. The fly intensifies its interest. It dives, swoops up, and dives again. She escapes deeper into the tobacco, unsettled by the biting insect, determined to outlast it, using both hands to flap at the space above her head. And because of the deerfly she does not notice right away the gathering of cars at the galvanized steel and wooden post barrier between the dead end of the asphalt and the beginning of a south field row.

She deciphers the motion of a swing, an arcing sledgehammer that knocks the posts out of their concrete casings as if they were teeth, leaving a ragged gap. Metal clatters as it hits the asphalt, sounds that crack open the quiet suburban twilight with a gleeful violence. There's a hurrah and she sees a half-dozen figures run back to their trucks parked on the side of the road, and hears the engines turn on. The trucks plough right into the tobacco plants.

It seems to Shayna, as she runs through the east field, her arms waving, her screams of "Stop!" unheeded, that the tobacco puts up a fight. The plants cling to truck grilles, tangle themselves in rusted axles, rebound from the first flattening blow of rubber tires with their limbs snapped or crooked. For a moment they are shabby scarecrows. Then they are no more. The trucks are followed by a few cars and suvs.

"Wait! Wait! The blockade's coming down! You don't need to. It's coming down!"

The cars don't follow each other in single file. Instead they spray like rifle shot, dirty and damaging. The south field, the largest acreage, which Shayna remembers from earlier that week as a low tent of summer yellow, is a holocaust of leaves and stalks. The vehicles career wildly into part of the east field, its nicotine-rich mid-leaves and tips still unpicked, plundering half of it as well, as quickly.

Three months of sunshine, rainfall, cool nights, morning heat. Ninety days of out-thinking weeds and birds and fungus, worrying about late frosts, rogue hail, dry spells. The bank loans secured by a future crop. The pleasures deferred.

She looks back to see Coulson running from the barn, carrying a hoe. Ramirez is behind him, wielding a shovel. Coulson swings at the cars, the metal clanging against windows, dragging along the paint of side doors. When one car veers too closely to Ramirez, Coulson grabs him, pulls him out of the fray. They are sidelined by the strength of combustion engines, arms limp at their sides, the garden implements fallen to the ground.

In twenty-five minutes it is over. The plants, a phalanx of good soldiers, are down. Shayna falls to the soil, bewildered. A man shouts at her through a rolled-down window. "We're taking back our rights! Our highway!"

She stares at him. "Why hurt one of your own?" she says in a voice he won't hear.

A few townies have finally found their way around the blockade. And the half-dozen who press their faces against the windows of their vehicles look bright with revenge, drunk on righteousness. A few are young but the rest are middle-aged, senior members of their community. It is already too late when the sirens reach them. Shayna watches Coulson from a distance and worries over the crimp in his stature; he looks like a standing heartbreak. It would be better to yell, she thinks, to pull out a shotgun and wave it around. What is it about land, about taking one's living from it, that can crush a man? The one natural disaster he won't have counted on is the impatience of his fellow citizens to get to work or the cottage or the shopping mall on a weekday evening.

She reaches up to her neck, touches the new bite there, swollen with itch, and turns around to finish her work across the road.

After the cars leave, Coulson runs into the farmhouse, up the stairs to his old bedroom to survey the damage. If he had a gash or a burn as a boy, he would lift the bandage to stare at it, if only to be awed by the queer sight of his own flesh rudely split, red-purple, gelatinous. Something alien, like an octopus or jellyfish.

There's nothing pretty 'bout our kind of farming, his father warned him early on. The summer before Coulson was born, his old man had been driving a highboy through the fields, spraying heptachlor to control budworm, when his horse got a scare, bucked, and sent his father keeling over backwards, bouncing off the chemical drums and dragging his face along a broken metal rib before he hit the ground. He got up with the white of his cheekbone peeking out from a flap of flesh, his smile ripped open at one side. He climbed back on the highboy to finish his work before he drove himself to the hospital. The scar that resulted – an ugly purple line that cut across his cheek and sank deep as a fishhook into the side of his lip – made others recoil. But to Coulson that scar was as intrinsic to his father as the old man's strong nose, his heavy brow. He barely noticed it.

Now he can't stop staring through his bedroom window at this new defacement, so many of his plants suppurating, the rot setting in. The south field took the worst of it. Half of the east field remains. The west field is untouched. But even with what he has already kilned, it won't be enough to fulfill his contract, pay his bills. He feels a loss of will. He might just sell it all to Elijah Barton, even though its quality is too high for his discount cigarettes.

It's been a cruelly perfect day for tobacco harvesting. The morning sun poked through a cheesecloth of cumulostratus, the kind of cloud that slows the heat but keeps the plants ripening apace, makes the air temperate and still burns off the dew – an ideal morning. They spent it priming the south field's cutters and moved to the east field after lunch. Now it's dusk and Helen has laid out dinner on the picnic tables. No one is eating. Ramirez walks through the spoiled rows, holding his head.

Coulson rolls his hand along the chalky walls of his bedroom. He can still sense the young boy in this room, the long seasons alone with work-wearied parents, the resentments that sent him away, the loyalties that would draw him back. It was a test, in a way, living with such continuity of place without feeling stuck. He feels he has passed the test. He has nothing more to prove. He grabs the keys on his bureau and runs down the stairs.

∞

The way the blockade came apart was as practised as a theatre set being struck. A backhoe scooped away the gravel. Debris got thrown in a large waste bin delivered by dusk. A group of men hooked up the trailer home and pulled it from the highway, abandoning it on the edge of the development. What was created with such joyful defiance was dismantled sombrely.

Shayna wondered if a feeling of triumph, so absent from this grimy labour, would build gradually. That rested, cleaned up, and properly fed, all of them would feel altered by what they had achieved. The prizes were small: a moment or two of visibility, the brief drawing of attention to an injustice, a piece of land neither reclaimed nor lost entirely. With the blockade gone, tensions would lighten. Should lighten. Must lighten. Their voices, still hoarse from this recent thrill of being angry all the time, would recover, and somehow they would all slide back into a polite, if wary, coexistence. Still, things could never be quite the same. She looked over again at the destruction in Coulson's fields.

When the work was completed, the garbage cleared, the two dozen who remained stood off to the side of the highway.

Soon enough the first car whizzed past. And then the next one, the driver's face turned away from them. Shayna had put her faith in action and then negotiation, and now the blockade was gone. And she understood that shrewder, more political people than she had thrown their hands into the clay of what would come next, given it a shape that was already hardening.

They hugged each other. There were some tears. *Good work*, they told her. She was offered rides home, but she told them she preferred to leave the way she came – on foot. Then it was just her picking up empty coffee cups, watching the crows alight to bargain-hunt the litter.

Now she crosses the asphalt once more. Her shoes come off. She steps from fallen leaf to fallen leaf. Juice seeps from crushed tobacco plants. It makes a sticky poultice under her weary feet. She feels level with this ruin. When Pete-Pete was born, she asked the nurses to save her placenta so she could bury it in the backyard just as her mother and sister had, to ensure their children would always return to them. The nurses said it was against policy.

The instant the car struck her young son, she felt a terrible calm. It was over quickly. Long enough. His little body sailed seven metres through the air. She saw his hands open. It wasn't a trick of physiology. With whatever consciousness her boy had left, he understood something of what was to be. He let her go. She couldn't forget that. She would wail and weep and wreck her body with grief, yet he'd begun for her the thing she wouldn't do on her own. When she ran to where his body had landed, he was still. His eyes were closed, his small pink mouth curled into a smile, his hands open in a shaman's benediction. *Sonkwehonwe*, she said as she laid her head on his small chest.

She kneels down now and gathers up a handful of unbruised tobacco leaves. They are supple and perfect. She fans them out on the soil so they look like opened hands. "Goodbye," she says, and she straightens, a hand resting on the pulse of her belly.

Coulson's truck rushes past in the farm laneway. Shayna watches him escape but understands that it's momentary. He will go to the river. He will yell and throw things. Then he'll come back, because he can. *There is no leaving everything you love*, Shayna thinks, and she turns towards home.

EPILOGUE

One June it was strafed, turned into a moonscape of mud, something injured. Now in this, another June, there's a winding tangle of milk vetch tickling the hardpack. Patches of low wood sorrel and clusters of fleabane reclaim long berms with delicate blossoms of yellow, white, mauve leaning into every breeze. Like all land, it is finding its own way back.

Elijah Barton sits in his Mercedes at the edge of the former Jarvis Ridge development and smokes. The billboard is long gone; only its posts remain. The hydro tower lies at one edge of the field, a toppled giant. The trailer – set ablaze one dark night in the fall – is a shredded carcass. The wildflowers and weeds weave around, tumble over, nestle inside the structures like trusting children.

He likes to come here and think. Who owns the *o'tá:ra*, how it will be used, what is to become of it – all that has become a pile of papers, a small file in the large portfolio of an uninterested deputy minister. But wildflowers don't wait for bureaucrats. Neither do people. Elijah sees a picnic table near the border with the reserve. A square has been cleared and planted with vegetables. Small walking trails wind through the scrub of weeds to the highway.

She has come before on this path, and today she does not disappoint. Shayna walks with a straight back. Her hair grows long down it. Swaddled against her chest in a bright cloth is the infant with extraordinary eyes. She held the child up to him one day, when they bumped into each other at the snack shack. The child was big. Hair the colour of flint. And blue eyes, deeply blue. A big, blue-eyed, laughing girl.

He knows where she is going. She will cross the highway, walk up to the farm, enter through the kitchen door without knocking. All spring he has been watching, making a game of guessing the arrangements, the negotiation that goes on between these two people with such a glorious child between them.

There are rumours Stercyx will sell his farm. He has not put in crops this year. Speculation is rampant, potential buyers falling over themselves. All those acres without a treaty claim registered against them. Elijah chuckles. He knows something they don't. The land is a bridge between these two people, an isthmus. If the woman cannot carry their child unimpeded from the land she fought for to the land he husbands, she will not come. It's a simple metric, one Stercyx would understand. *Next year there will be crops,* thinks Elijah. *Maybe even tobacco.* He'd put money on it. In fact, he'd line up as a customer.

He turns on the radio, finds the reserve station. A song is playing, some simple tune about home and how you're always coming back. Elijah cranks the volume. This singer has something, he thinks, a gutsy delivery saved from being ordinary by a hitch of heartbreak. It redeems the somewhat obvious lyrics, the unaccomplished guitar playing. Elijah doesn't need the announcer to tell him who she is. He knows that anguish. *You think you'll leave and never look back*, she sings with a big voice that slides into a ragged vibrato.

This is the very thing that Elijah gets about land: What's on it may change, even what's underneath, who controls it. But in the lifetime of a people, even that of a single man, the fact of land remains constant. Individuals, nations, ways of life may have to wait without justice, displaced from their own soil. But the land itself has its own kind of justice, its own understanding. It can outwait them all. There is something comforting about that, he thinks. Elijah blows a puff of smoke skyward, watches it curl away from him like a river, and laughs.

ACKNOWLEDGEMENTS

Kanyen'kehá:ka speakers will recognize I have taken liber-
ties with the word *o'tá:ra* – which means "clay" or "clan,"
and thus "family." Thank you for your indulgence.

Editor Lara Hinchberger is a marvel of instinct, intelligence, and artistry. I'm truly grateful for the potential she saw
in this book, and for her grace and hard work in shaping it. I've
become a better writer because of her.

My smart-as-a-whip and charming agent Samantha
Haywood has been another champion. So many thanks to her
and to Stephanie Sinclair for their insightful readings.

Without the generosity of friends and fellow writers, the
manuscript would never have been finished. As my thesis
adviser in UBC's MFA in Creative Writing program, Lisa Moore
managed to see something worthy in a rough early manuscript
and gave me the courage to stick with it. Trevor Cole was an
influential role model for his focus and craft as a novelist. Jeffrey

Griffiths, John Roberts, Miranda Hill, John Martin, Rick Montour, Sally Cooper, and Ania Szado provided expert reads and thoughtful feedback. Both my sister, Katrine Foss, and Mary Vincenzetti read the manuscript twice and offered insights, encouragement, and much-needed laughter. Conversations with Amos Key Jr. and Brian Maracle (not to mention Brian's language lessons) provided critical perspectives. *Nya:wen.*

Many books and journalistic media were invaluable resources to me, notably the reportage of *Turtle Island News, Tekawennake,* and the *Hamilton Spectator; Back on the Rez: Finding the Way Home,* by Brian Maracle; *People of the Pines: The Warriors and the Legacy of Oka,* by Geoffrey York and Loreen Pindera; *Entering the War Zone: A Mohawk Perspective on Resisting Invasions,* by Donna Goodleaf; *Conflict in Caledonia; Aboriginal Land Rights and the Rule of Law,* by Laura DeVries; *Helpless: Caledonia's Nightmare of Fear and Anarchy and How the Law Failed All of Us,* by Christie Blatchford; *Dancing with a Ghost: Exploring Aboriginal Reality,* by Rupert Ross; and *A Fair Country: Telling Truths about Canada,* by John Ralston Saul. A memorable afternoon in the Delhi Tobacco Museum and Heritage Centre, along with *Tobacco in Canada,* by Lyal Tait; *Smoke and Mirrors: The Canadian Tobacco War,* by Rob Cunningham; and *Tobacco Use by Native North Americans: Sacred Smoke and Silent Killer,* edited by Joseph C. Winter, aided my understanding of the history and agriculture of this important crop. My former student Megan Weatherbee was a wealth of information about growing up on a tobacco farm, and Alex Podetz shared his experiences priming tobacco.

Many thanks to my mother for inspiring wonder and respect for the natural world and providing four wonderful siblings with whom to enjoy it. My daughter, Fehn, has filled my life, and thus my writing, with meaning, and I am grateful to her for her abiding interest in this book, not to mention her talents as a photographer. Finally, thank you, John, for starting a conversation about a book I was reading.